Praise for *Castle of Shadows*

An elaborate and far-reaching tale that makes for compelling reading. A family saga that boasts ambitious, sophisticated, and controlled storytelling.

—*Kirkus Reviews*

This novel has a strong visual impact. The narrator, inspired by her family album, brings to life through vivid images the shadows that still linger in their country castle. Captivating characters spanning three generations act out their lives against the background of historical turning points.
A fascinating reading that reminds me of *Downton Abbey!*

—*Willee Lewis, Vice President, PEN/Faulkner Foundation.*

This novel is a large narrative fresco with visual impact, historical scope and sustained pace, which makes us think of Bertolucci's cinematic epic *1900*. It can also be regarded as a kind of Piedmontese counterpart to *The Leopard.*

—*Roberto Severino, Professor Emeritus, Georgetown University, Washington DC*

Anna Lawton has written a beautiful book of place, time, and character. Lawton includes powerful description at no expense to plotting.

—*NetGalley Review*

A well written and engrossing novel. I liked the style of writing, the fleshed out cast of characters and the setting. I look forward to reading other books by this author. Highly recommended!

—*NetGalley Review*

A castle in the Italian countryside, captivating characters, class/gender/generation conflicts, private lives on the background of historical turning points (Unification of Italy, workers unrest, WWI, Fascism, WWII, partisan struggle). All this in a polished language, not devoid of irony. A contemporary take on the classical family saga, historically accurate and absolutely enjoyable.

—*Finlay Lewis, Contributing writer, CQ-Roll Call*

This book brought back sensations that had partly disappeared, and made me forget the particular in favor of a universal world into which everyone can project himself. . . The reference to *The Leopard* is the first thing that comes to mind because of the analogous situation of an old prominent family experiencing its gradual decline, but also *Buddenbrooks* by Thomas Mann and *The Family Moskat* by Isaac Singer.

— *Riccardo Riccardi, composer, artist and author. Rome, Italy*

I liked the book immensely, from beginning to end. I found it enticing, evocative, at times heart rendering, at times even comic… The narrative carries you from page to page relentlessly. And now that I'm finished, I want to start again. . .

— *Paul Buckmaster, movie music composer. Hollywood*

It's a beautiful story. The language is impeccable, not overly literary (unnatural), and not overly conversational (sloppy) either. It's the perfect language for this story, a saga with its truth filtered through the fabric of narration. It's the work of a novelist, not of a memoirist.

— *Camilla Baresani, author of four novels, including* Himalayan Pink Salt. *Milan, Italy*

I'm sure certain scenes from this novel will forever be etched in my mind—scenes that in a few words gave me a picture of fascism more complete that the many volumes written by historians and scholars. Moreover, this book gave me a better knowledge of contemporary Italy than all of the books I have read so far.

—*Magda Zalan, Journalist. Budapest*

This novel, which has its beginning in family photos, reminds me of the monumental work of Amos Oz, *A Story of Love and Darkness*. It traces a family saga over three generations, weaving the stories of the many characters with the facts of Italian history. The mythical castle, which provides the visual frame to the novel, serves as the backdrop for the family album which the author used as the literary expedient to begin the narrative.

—*Ugo Cardinale, Professor of Italian Literature, University of Trieste, Italy*

Castle of Shadows

Castle of Shadows

A Family Saga

by Anna Lawton

Translated from the Italian
by Antony Shugaar

Washington, DC

Library of Congress Control Number: 2019941846
ISBN 978-1-7330408-1-5 paperback (alk. paper)
ISBN 978-1-7330408-2-2 hardcover (alk. paper)
ISBN 978-1-7330408-3-9 ebook

THESPRING is an imprint of New Academia Publishing

New Academia Publishing
4401-A Connecticut Ave. NW #236, Washington DC 20008
info@newacademia.com - www.newacademia.com

For the characters of this novel,
who chose me as the author

A Note to the Reader

The places and the characters in this story are fictitious, as is the voice of the narrator. Only the historical figures referred to in the narrative are real people.

The reader who chances to venture through the valleys of Piedmont on a hot summer afternoon may be tempted to identify the main setting in one of the many castles that over-look the countryside from high atop the green hills. However, this novel is entirely the product of the author's imagination.

Table of Contents

Cast of Characters

Principal Characters

Pietro Ducati: businessman and industrialist, owner of the Castle of Cortalba.

Leo (Leopoldo) Ducati: his brother and business partner.

Olga: Pietro's wife.

Ada: their daughter.

Elisa, Lidia, Giulia: their other daughters.

Luca: their only son, weakminded.

André: Leo's son, a film producer and director.

Ernesto Bonardi: Ada's husband, an art photographer.

Mina (Alma) and Gio (Giovanni): Ada and Ernesto's children.

Dardo (Edoardo) Celti: Alma's husband, an actor and stage director.

Nina (Antigone) and Lina (Angelina): daughters of Alma and Dardo.

Other Characters, in order of appearance

Miss Langfield: governess of the Ducati girls.

Saturnino Montanari: a worker at the Ducati Plant.

Romoletto: his son, a socialist agitator.

Giusto: a coachman in Cortalba.

Giustino: a stable boy, son of Giusto.

Viola: Olga's sister, a horsewoman and poetess.

Magda D'Ambrose: Olga's other sister, married to a Parisian banker.

Francesco and Luigi: her sons.

Letizia: Olga's mother.

Count Riccardo Ralli d'Ostellata: Letizia's second husband.
Erminia: a housekeeper in Cortalba.
Cecilia: Pietro and Leo's niece, daughter of their sister Nelli.
Domenico: a servant in the Ducati house in Turin.
Rosina: a Turinese milliner who's crazy about the movies.
Mario Mariani: a screenwriter for Itala Film.
Ambra Sylvestry: an actress at Itala Film.
Monsieur Lesavoir: Luca's tutor.
Maggiorina: wife of Cescu, a gardener in Cortalba.
Tunìn: their son, later a gardener.
Almetta Bonardi: Ernesto's mother.
Don Gerolamo: the parish priest in Colisso.
Veglia: a cook in the Bonardi house in Turin.
Major Spencer: an American officer during the Great War.
Billy: an American soldier, attendant to André Ducati.
Uncle Candy: Olga's brother.
Cathy: André's wife, and the daughter of a Hollywood producer.
Jane, Jimmy, Leo: their children.
Aurelio Costa: the Podestà of Cortalba, husband of Giulia Ducati.
Piero and Marilù: their children.
Marta and Chiara: Elisa's daughters.
Lucilla and Marcello: Lidia's children.
Lillì: Luca's dog, a Volpino Italiano.
Vittorio Cortese: a functionary of the National Fascist Party.
Romano, Codliver, Intrepid: *Squadristi* (members of the Fascist Action Squads)
Cussót: a thirteen-year old orphan and a victim of the fascists.
Matteo: an anti-fascist intellectual, Giulia's lover.
Vigìn: an elderly inhabitant of Cortalba, source of memories.
Gino Barone: a con artist.
Kili: a domesticated leopard.
Madame Irene: the owner of a brothel.
Catarì: an honest prostitute.

Davide Della Rocca: a friend of Gio and a victim of the "race laws."

Miriam Lehrmann Della Rocca: his mother.

Uncle Bastiàn: a baker in Cortalba.

Aunt Delina: his wife.

Dino: a manual laborer in Cortalba, later a partisan.

General Camilletti: Magda D'Ambrose's personal squire.

Don Giordano: the parish priest of Cortalba.

Mother Palmyra: a nun.

Dimitri Lvovsky: Russian prince.

Giacomo Celti: Dardo's father.

Manon, Norma, and Lucia: Dardo's sisters.

Giggino: Dardo's brother.

Zi' Guglielmo and Zi' Zazà: Dardo's uncle and aunt.

Eduardo, "the Maltese": Dardo's grandfather.

Lothar: a German officer.

Celestina and Mariuccia: housekeepers in Cortalba.

Nardina: a seamstress in Cortalba.

Carletta: her daughter.

Redstar: partisan commander.

Blast, Cartridge, Gram, Octobrine, Brutus: partisans.

Ercole Battaglia: a captain in the Republican National Guard (RNG).

Amilcare Aquiletti and Serafino Scopola: militia members of the RNG.

Signora Maria: Don Giordano's mother.

Franz: a German soldier.

Leo Ducati: André's son.

Part I

In the Shade of the Linden Tree

1

Group Portrait
1908

I

They're sitting beneath the linden tree in the Hello Garden, at the top of the slope that runs up from the ancient feudal village to the castle. Someone's just snapped the picture. It's the turn of the twentieth century. Ada has turned toward the camera and is caught in three-quarter profile, gazing into the lens, a young woman with large, serious, intelligent eyes. She's holding a sketch on her knees, with a box of pastels and paints on the chair next to her. She's eighteen. In my recollections, Ada is my grandmother, an aged person who was afflicted by creeping paralysis. But on this quiet summer afternoon, her destiny and her story were only just starting to take shape.

The others are looking into the camera, too, momentarily distracted from their usual pursuits, no doubt at the photographer's command, "Ready... Hold still... Done!" Giulia is standing, six or seven years younger than Ada; she's come to a stop with the ball in her hands, between one bounce and the next, ready to resume her leaping progress around the water well that stands at the center of the garden. On the right, sitting on a bench, Olga has her back almost entirely turned to the camera, her head bowed over her pillow lace. Unlike her daughters, she ignores the camera, remaining willfully absorbed in her handiwork. At her side, little Luca stands erect on the bench, one hand gripping the seatback, face and shoulders emerging, head-on to the camera. He's wearing a white sailor suit and a broad-brimmed straw hat, and he's observing the photographer in awe. Miss Langfield has been frozen in place by the shutter just as she was entering the frame; in one hand she holds a book, in the other her eyeglasses, attached to a fine string dangling from her neck. The governess seems slightly hesitant in her pose; aware that she is not a member of this family group, she lingers almost in seclusion to the left side. Pietro, in contrast, is right at the center. A handsome man in his early fifties with fine features, emphasized by a Chekhovian beard and mustache. He's clearly relaxed in his oversized wicker chair. He's lowered the newspaper he was reading for a moment and has raised his eyes toward the camera with unaffected indifference.

The two eldest daughters, Elisa and Lidia, weren't there that day. They'd gone down to the village, to the nuns' kindergarten to help organize the charity festival that was held every year at the castle. Or else—and this is something impossible to ascertain—it might have been they who took the picture, and simply went to help the nuns the following day.

The fact is that cameras have always played an important role in the lives of the Ducati family. Ever since the girls were small, the camera recorded their life stories in pictures. Perhaps at first it was Pietro who delighted in dabbling in this relatively novel technology. His daughters then followed in his footsteps, both for fun and out of a sense of duty.

Only Ada possessed a genuine love of the visual arts. Miss Langfield encouraged her, giving her supplementary painting lessons alongside the regular lessons with her sisters. Miss Langfield had sent off to London for reproductions of the work of her favorite painters, Dante Gabriele Rossetti and the other Pre-Raphaelites that she had so doted upon in her youth. This predilection for a school of art that was considered anti-academic in Victorian society had caused her considerable difficulties at the Girls' Institute of Secondary Education, an exclusive private school, where she had been taken in on a scholarship bestowed by some anonymous benefactor; people said that it was Miss Langfield's natural father, married and highly placed, who had always chosen to remain in the shadows.

The girls knew only a few snippets of Miss Langfield's personal history, vague hints picked up from their parents' conversations. They knew that, after finishing school, she had been a governess for an aristocratic London family, but whatever the events that had then brought her to Italy, they remained shrouded in mystery. To fill that gap, the girls had assembled *The Aventures of Miss Langfield*, an open-ended narrative that they enriched on a daily basis with new episodes, including a young Italian gentleman visiting London as a guest in the home of her aristocratic employer, a passionate love affair between the young Italian and the governess, especially scandalous because the young Italian was engaged to be married to one of the master's daughters, the two lovers eloping to Italy and narrowly escaping shipwreck in a raging tempest on the English Channel, the young Italian's death in a duel before the couple could be married, followed by long years of mistreatment as a lady's companion to a wicked and cruel octogenarian dowager. At last, however, salvation: a trusted person had recommended her to Mother and it was Miss Langfield's good fortune to be taken on as governess in the Ducati home.

"Ada, darling, I'd put a bit more yellow in the foliage. Bring out those highlights. Remember, it's the lighting that makes the picture," said Miss Langfield in English, as she studied Ada's work.

Ada set down the sketch and turned to look at the governess, "Alright, I will. But not now. I feel like taking a stroll." And she hastened to point out, "Alone."

* * *

How that day went, and the days that followed it, I can only imagine. But knowing those characters—directly, or from portraits, documents, and oral accounts—as well as the setting and the basic details, it's not hard for me to trace the progress of their stories, filling in the narrative spaces with action and dialogue recreated, perhaps, from the recondite suggestions of my subconscious.

The richest source of information and inspiration was doubtless Alma, my mother, who loved to hark back to the happy days of Cortalba to escape a present that struck her as gray and, at times, desperate. Her stories, then, were filtered through a nostalgic lens that gave them the quality of fairytales, to my eyes. But Alma wasn't my sole source. Other accounts from family members, or townsfolk, offered differing points of view, discordant interpretations, new facts, which taken together produced a more complete picture, though not necessarily a more accurate and realistic one.

And then, there's the album, or really, many albums and numerous bundles and stacks of loose photographs. There's also the collection of my grandfather Ernesto Bonardi, a distinguished practitioner of the photographic art—a collection whose subjects were frequently members of the family entourage. Photographs, too, tell a story all their own, just as the verbal accounts do. They too present moments of life that are more or less truthful, fleeting luminous impressions created for the eye of those who observe them.

II

The typical sweltering heat of July afternoons in Monferrato failed to reach the top of the hill where the castle of Cortalba loomed. The heat remained further down, at the level of the gates, because the dense woods, and then the series of hanging gardens dotting the slopes, were natural air conditioning elements. At the summit, the broad umbrella of the centuries-old linden tree, which reared up over the tower's crenellations, created a zone of coolness for the hours of afternoon idleness in the Hello Garden—so-called because in the atrium of the front entrance there was a fresco with the welcoming phrase, "Salve!", Italian for Hello! The building's wall, on that side, was covered with a dense blanket of wisteria that created a lilac-mauve backdrop to all the figures sitting in the garden. The plant's perfume was intoxicating. Buzzing swarms of bees moved busily around, tending to the delicate bunches of flowers and generating a relaxing, monotonous soundscape.

Ada started down the lane that led to the Tower Garden, past boxwood hedges and flowerbeds full of passionflower. When she came to the turnoff for the drawbridge, she continued straight, skirting the base of the tower. She arrived at the grounds of the ancient bastion to the west of the castle, situated between the greenhouse and the so-called "observation wall." Dwarf palms imported from Africa and other botanical rarities made this garden an exotic spot, filled with charm and allure. But since it was also the only garden exposed to direct sunlight, unsheltered by the protection of branches thick with foliage, it was generally unfrequented. People went there only "to observe." And that is precisely what Ada had come there to do. Leaning her elbows upon the stout wall, she let her gaze range out beyond the roofs of the village and the fields leveled by the harvest, a symmetrical pattern tumbling away downhill, made up of red and yellow rectangles. She was observing the provincial road, the narrow white ribbon that twisted along down in the valley, running around the village. To the left, it continued toward Asti; on the right, toward Turin. In that direction, on clear days it was possible to see the entire Alpine range that encircled the city, from the lower heights up to the peaks of Mont Blanc and Monte Rosa glittering with ice.

Ada looked off in the direction of Asti. She was expecting a visit. Uncle Leopoldo and cousin André were coming up from Rome, on their way to Turin. Ada greatly loved Uncle Leo who so resembled Papà, though he was much jollier. When she and her sisters were younger, Uncle Leo had always been ready to play with them. In those days, his pockets had been a bottomless mine of surprises: whistles, tin trumpets, colorful glass marbles, papier-mâché animals, ragdolls. André would join in the games, and the company wandered off into extraordinary worlds of adventure. André was his only child, and for that reason Uncle Leo had always taken great care of him, personally seeing to his education and participating in his amusements. Aunt Luisa had died giving birth to him, and for Leo that had been a profound trauma. He had never remarried because, he said, he didn't want to endanger another woman's life.

Ada hadn't seen them for two months now, since her family had left Rome, as it did every year, to come north and vacation at the castle. From time to time, Ada would receive a postcard: André was in Paris, André was in Vienna, André was on Capri. André was twenty years old, and his father encouraged him to travel so he could stockpile experiences of the world. The most recent postcard, which Ada had lovingly placed with the others in a box lined with lilac silk, came from Ostia, where Uncle Leo spent the hottest months in his villa in the pines. He couldn't venture far from Rome because he had to tend to the family business. For some time now, Pietro hadn't been feeling well and the doctor had ordered him to get plenty of rest. Responsibility for the plant had thus fallen almost entirely upon Leo's shoulders.

2

Building the New Italy
1870-1885

I

The two brothers had founded the company in Rome at the turn of the 1870s, just after the Italian troops entered the Papal State. Young enterprising citizens of Piedmont, they had traveled to the new Italian capital to take advantage of the business opportunities offered by the change in government. They'd recently come home from Paris with degrees from the Sorbonne—Pietro, in architecture, and Leo, in economics—and had been encouraged by their spirit of patriotism and Romantic ideals to contribute to the construction of the New Italy. Their enthusiasm was also based on pragmatic financial considerations. For generations, the Ducati family had owned spinning and weaving manufactories in the Biella area. But Pietro and Leo—having been raised in Turin with their mother and their sister Nelli in the elegant house on the boulevard overlooking the Valentino Park, a road that later came to be called Corso Massimo D'Azeglio—felt a certain detachment from the family business, which fell under their father's complete control. Working with their father meant spending most of their time in Cirié, in a provincial setting that they found blinkered and suffocating. Especially after their experiences in Paris. Their father, for his part, was a broadminded man who favored industrial progress and wanted to see the family business expand in various new directions. He therefore not only encouraged his sons' initatives, but even procured the necessary seed money.

Ada had learned from her history textbook that the Pope hadn't been a good ruler, nothing like Victor Emmanuel, who transformed Italy into a united and prosperous kingdom. In the book, there were color illustrations, and she especially liked the one that showed the Bersaglieri Corps breaking through the Breach of Porta Pia, their helmet plumes fluttering in the wind, their trumpets blaring a fanfare, and the Italian tricolor waving proudly. She admired the features on those strong and daring faces; that must have been what Papà and Uncle Leo looked like when they were twenty.

When the brothers ventured down to Rome, following in the Bersaglieri's footsteps, there were only a few stretches of railway. Where the railway ended, they took horse-drawn coaches, facing the challenges of a journey filled with hardships and danger. By some miracle, they survived the attack of the brigands on the Bracco Pass; truth be told, Leo recounted, they never actually saw the brigands, but they knew they were certainly there, lying in ambush among the trees, with a blunderbuss slung over their shoulder and a feather in their hat.

Pietro and Leo adapted easily to their new setting. Thanks to the letters of introduction to the various government functionaries and men of finance who had been friends of their father's and who, like them, had recently ventured south from their native Piedmont, the two young men soon found the necessary support to deploy their talent and their energy. The first step had been a construction company. It was clear that Rome had a great and pressing need for housing. It seemed that the city had nothing but aristocratic palazzi, ancient ruins, and churches. And on the city's outskirts, huts and hovels. Soon, thanks to the initiatives of the government, which built roads and drained swamps, there were new residential zones surrounding the city center—at first, within the walls and then, gradually, further and further without them. Pietro designed modern and efficient apartment complexes that offered comfort and practical living for the new Roman bourgeoisie and, under Leo's management, the company soon prospered and ventured into other lines of business.

In the center of Rome, everything was majestic but slightly ramshackle, or *délabré*, as Pietro liked to say, having preserved his love of the French language. He therefore devoted himself to restoration projects, both with government funding and for private clients. In the pursuit of this work, he was offered the opportunity to purchase the entire main floor of Palazzo Castellani on Trevi Fountain Piazza. The vast residence, with various drawing rooms and a dozen or so bedrooms, overlooked the gushing cascades of the ornate fountain, which splashed the brawny limbs of seahorses and tritons. This mansion became Pietro's home. Leo chose to build himself a house, with a garden full of hydrangea bushes, not far from the Pincian Hill. Business continued to thrive; after construction, they ventured into the milling business.

While conducting an inspection of a construction site in the Pantanella zone where work was due to begin, an unexpected meeting blazed the way for a new entrepreneurial venture. Leo was examining the site, accompanied by the surveyor Musso, whom he had brought south from Turin. Not far away, Pietro was collecting technical data from an old mill scheduled for demolition to make way for the new housing. Leo wanted to be sure that the marshy ground had been adequately drained, as he had been assured by the agency with jurisdiction, and the surveyor told him that, even though it was still winter, he could safely state that the ground had in fact been properly drained. Then, all of a sudden, he changed the subject and asked whether Signor Ducati would be so kind as to hear the entreaties of a group of laborers who had formerly worked at the mill, because they were good people, now out of work.

"All right, Musso. I'm willing to listen to them," said Leo. "Bring them over."

Musso waved his hand, and a small knot of twenty or so people who were idling on the side of the road made their way down the slope and drew near. There were many women among them, wrapped in multicolored wool shawls; the men wore sheepskin vests and floppy felt hats. The group's spokesman, a young man who looked about twenty-five, took a step forward, doffing his hat so that dense locks of unruly curls tumbled over his face.

"You can speak now," said Musso. The man was standing a few feet away from Leo, crumpling his hat in his hands, but he stood erect and his gaze was frank and open.

"Your Excellency, we hope you'll excuse us. We are all poor folk and we shouldn't have made so bold. But we hear that the Piedmontese are more understanding when it comes to the working folk, people say that they have more pro... progressivistic beliefs. Well, we all don't much understand this sort of thing. But, Your Excellency, we're here to tell you: please don't take away our mill. We're asking for our children, and don't they have a right to eat too? Those children over there, you see them?" With a wave of his hand he indicated the young women in the group behind him, next to their men, with their youngest child in their arms and various other little ones hiding behind their skirts. "Hey, Romolé, come here," he said, taking his son from Mama's arms. "Why don't you tell His Excellency yourself about this bad habit you have of wanting to eat every day?" Little Romoletto was smiling with a finger in his mouth as he looked at "His Excellency" out of the corner of his sly eyes. His curly black hair was identical to his father's.

"What's your name?" asked Leo, addressing the man.

"Saturnino Montanari, Excellency."

"That's fine, Saturnino. I'm glad to have met you. Tell your comrades that we will consider their request. You can go home now."

That night, sitting in front of the fireplace in two ample leather armchairs that reflected the gleam of the flames on the shiny armrests, Pietro and Leo discussed the day's events. Leo was in favor of hiring the collective from the mill as construction laborers. But Pietro had a different, brilliant idea.

"Let's say we try something new," he said, pouring himself a glass of the Moscato di Canelli that their wine cellars boasted in great abundance. "Why not renovate the mill, installing all the latest machinery, all the most up-to-date technology? So far, we've built housing, the next thing we should think about is the food supply. That sector of the economy is struggling to keep up. With the recent explosion of the urban population in this part of Italy, and the resulting spike in flour consumption, old-fashioned methods of production are no longer sufficient. In fact, I not only want to rebuild the old mill, I want to build two brand new ones. And then..." Pietro reached his hand out toward a tray of biscotti on the nearby table, grabbed one, and bit into it, "... and then, a biscotti factory."

"I prefer Luigina's biscotti," said Leo, taking one for himself. The old cook who had plied them in their childhood with exquisite home-baked desserts and treats in their home in Turin hadn't forgotten her little boys, her *ninìn*. Every three months, as reliably as the change of seasons, a package would arrive from Luigina—a large tin box, full to the lid with fragrant biscotti. They were simple biscotti, made of flour, eggs, milk, and sugar, rectangular in shape, with rounded edges, but the flavor was something much greater than the sum of the ingredients. What made them so unique and so superior, in both Pietro's and Leo's opinions, was some intangible element that must have had something to do with the quantities and the mixing, or with the temperature of the oven, or the baking times, or else with Luigina's sheer culinary genius.

"Leo, we'll produce Luigina's biscotti. We'll find the best baker in Rome. We'll send him to Turin to learn how to make biscotti, and then we'll employ him as the head of the production department. We'll call them 'Biscotti Torinesi'."

The biscotti were a smash hit. The sky-blue tins with the trademark of the rearing bull against a background of wheat fields sold like hotcakes. In practically no time, they were being distributed throughout all the regions of Italy, and even north of the Alps. The mills not only supplied flour for the biscotti plant, they also supplied the leading flour wholesalers. Saturnino had taken a technical course and now he was the supervisor of the new grinding machinery. Toward the end of the decade, the plant consisted of three grinding mills and three industrial sheds for the production of the "Biscotti Torinesi," along with other specialties. All around the plant stood employee housing that Pietro had built for his workers.

II

The first one to marry was Leo. The day of his thirtieth birthday he announced his engagement to Luisa. For some time now, he'd been an assiduous visitor to the young woman's home, a setting that took him back to the years of his childhood. Luisa's father, now a senatorof the new Kingdom of Italy, had been a member of the Piedmontese parliament going back to 1848. In that period, the family lived in Turin in the house next to the Ducati home. Leo and Luisa became great friends, but then as adults they fell out of touch. When they saw each other again in Rome, it was a bolt from the blue. Before the year was out, they were celebrating their wedding.

Pietro married soon after. He met Olga during a summer stay in the mountain resort of St. Vincent, through acquaintances of his mother's, who was vacationing with him. They hit it off, but the period of their engagement was challenging because Olga, the daughter of a Genoese shipowner, lived in Genoa. Their engagement by and large was epistolary in na-

ture, and lasted little more than three months, since the young
fiancés were eager to eliminate the distance separating them.
During those months, Pietro went to Genoa to see his intended not once, not twice, but three times, taking advantage of
the fact that the railway had now been completed and was
operating quite efficiently.

Pietro's letters were frequent and fond—and I can state
that without fear of contradiction because the entire packet
of correspondence, tied up with a pink ribbon, is in my pos-
session. I found it in one of Olga's old trunks, many years
after the castle was sold off and her personal effects had been
removed and taken to Ada's home. Concerning Olga's replies
I can say nothing, because they were not included in the packet. It is possible that Pietro preserved them in a drawer in his
desk and that, over time, they were lost. The packet is quite
substantial because the lovebirds wrote each other daily. The
envelopes are small in format—barely 3.5 x 5 inches—and the
stationery within, with elegant monograms in relief, is carefully folded in four. The color of the paper varies, one day it's
light green, another it's mauve, or light gray, or off white.

In one envelope, Pietro also included a photograph of
himself.

*"Beloved bride, here I am! I don't know if I'm utter perfection,
but from what I'm told I'm better than the original. At last I've kept
my promise and here is my photograph as I am today. The other
one had the advantage as far as I'm concerned of making me look
about six years younger, but I'm glad that it didn't meet with your
approval and you are welcome to destroy it."*

To judge from the photo, I have to say that Pietro was being too modest. This is the picture of a handsome young man,
with a broad forehead and longilinear features, at once delicate and decisive. Even though the photo is sepia in tone, it's
possible to guess that the hair is a golden chestnut, slightly
wavy, as is the beard and mustache. That natural waviness
gives him a relaxed appearance, which is emphasized by

the floppy shirt collar over the jacket lapel, completed by a soft ribbon bowtie. His light-colored eyes stare into the camera without revealing any emotions, as the pose demanded. Those emotions, however, are revealed in the letter.

"I'm not as lucky, and will have to wait another long month before I have a portrait of my Olga, so that I can fool myself into thinking from time to time that I'm in her company. Fortunately, I bear so deeply graven in my soul that serene, profound gaze of hers, and those two enchanting stars from which that gaze emanates, that I feel as if I always have her before me, and even with the greatly desired photograph, she couldn't seem any more present to me."

Olga's eyes must really have made an impression on him because he mentions them frequently.

"How I miss my Olga, who so enchanted the loveliness of that stroll near the Source and that scanty, sun-scorched patch of grass, where as I sat by her side I could take her dainty hand and admire those large dark eyes of hers, so exquisite that from the first moment I glimpsed them, they engraved themselves so deeply into my thoughts that I could no longer eject them from my mind's eye. It's true though that I never even tried, nor will I, as I'm just too lucky to have them always present in my thoughts."

In the album is a portrait of Olga, a picture that was probably taken in that period. Maybe it's the very same photograph that Pietro was awaiting with such eager anticipation. The image is set in an oval medallion that includes the person's torso and shoulders, from the waist up. Olga's elbows are propped atop the backrest of an armchair, as if she were leaning on a windowsill; in one hand, which is resting gently on the quilt-stitched velvet, she's holding a small bouquet of lilies of the valley; the other hand, beneath her chin, is delicately supporting her head, tilted ever so slightly toward her shoulder. The dark-colored dress is brightened by cuffs and collar in white lace, emphasizing the dazzling white hue of hands and face. The photographer must have had a good instinct for composition, because the visual rhythm of the lilies of the valley, the hands, and the face create a luminous line, with a sinuous movement from below to above, that stands out against the dark background, highlighting the young woman's delicate femininity. And the eyes—Pietro had been right—are large and deep, though veiled by a screen of reserve, as demanded by the conventions of portraiture.

Aside from these romantic thoughts, the letters also contain various practical observations, because Pietro was eagerly redoing the interior decoration and furnishing of their future home, in keeping with Olga's tastes.

"Since I have no relatives to advise me, I'll certainly be uneasy in my arrangements for housing; I'll do the best I know how and I hope you'll be kind enough to show pity for my missteps. Couldn't you help me with your advice? Already you told me that for the bedroom, you'd like the color yellow. Your wish is my command. Tell me now how you'd like the dining room and if, together with your mother, you can offer me any suggestions at all, you'll be doing me a great favor."

His eagerness to please, at once moving and comical, reveals a certain agitation over the important role that he was about to assume. In a subsequent letter, he returns to the topic.

"In another letter of mine, I asked you for advice about the choice of colors for the fabrics in our future nest. I expect that your reply won't reach me in time and in fact I have to confess that I was so anxious that this morning I went ahead and selected the necessary fabrics, though even for the bedroom I was unable to obey you completely. Having failed to find a yellow fabric that met with my satisfaction, I was forced to make do with a fabric that was a mix of yellow and other colors."

In the midst of all these tribulations, and because of Leo's wedding, Pietro felt lonely and occasionally gave in to melancholy.

"How kind you are not to let a day go by without sending me your dear and informative letters. It's true that you had promised me as much, and I couldn't expect any less of your amiable nature,

and yet let me assure you that I'm only too grateful and that I thank you sincerely. You still have relatives who keep you company, but I'm all alone and so it is needful to me to have some written note from she who is now a part of me, she with whom I will soon have the sweet consolation of being indissolubly united with the most lovable of chains; she with whom I will have to share all and every-thing: pleasures, sorrows, affections, esteem, relatives, parents ... and others (we hope)."

As we'll see later, his wish for "others" was fully granted, because the couple had six children.

Olga too had her moments of melancholy, and especially of apprehension for the radical transformation that was about to sweep through her life. Pietro reassured her, fully investing himself in his role as a husband.

"From your beloved letter I see that you have moments of mel-ancholy at the thought that you will soon have to leave your dear parents and family, and in fact I can't blame you in the slightest; they are such good people that having to leave them must be a very painful thing indeed, and in fact I sometimes fear that I will never be quite able to adequately take their place. I hope you'll never doubt my good will though, which as I've already promised you, will never fail me, and I hope and trust I'll have all the necessary strength to support it. Still, all prospects smile upon us, we love one another, we share a similarity of character, financial resources superior even to our wishes, relatives who love us and are, they too, convinced that we will never fail to live in the most perfect harmony and complete happiness. And so, let melancholy begone and face cheerfully up to all the consequences of the dear answer you gave me last June on the road that runs from the chestnut groves of St. Vincent to the Source."

They married in 1880. The letter that Pietro wrote a few days before going to Genoa for the wedding bears the date of September 20th.

"Today in Rome great festivities for the tenth anniversary of the entry of the Italian troops into this city. Our plant is closed, we've

given the workers the day off, and Leo and I are standing guard. But I'm afraid that the celebrations will be spoiled by the rain that appears to be imminent. Nothing however could possibly spoil my good mood at the thought that soon I'll be able to embrace my Olga.

Forgive me if I can't go on any further, but there are certain matters I can't put off. Please accept two big kisses from your enamored spouse. Yours forever. Pietro."

After their honeymoon through all the European capitals, Olga found serenity and contentment in the elegant residence prepared for her by Pietro, lulled by the murmuring splashes of the Trevi Fountain beneath the windows of her "mixed-yellow" bedroom.

But there's rarely a case of domestic bliss that isn't marred by sorrows and misfortunes, and the same was true of Olga and Pietro. Their first son, Biagio, was born a hydrocephalic and he died when he was just three. Two years after his birth came Elisa, and then Lidia, followed after a certain interval by Ada; several more years went by before Giulia came into the world. Olga had sworn to herself that she wouldn't rest until the Good Lord sent her another son. And, at last, Luca was born. The baby boy was beautiful and healthy. Olga thanked the Good Lord, and stopped. It emerged, though, as the years went by, that Luca wasn't entirely normal. In the family, what they said was that the boy was "innocent," but outside of the house more malicious tongues uttered the word "retarded." And, in effect, his mental development was arrested at the age of seven and went no further; Luca remained until the age of forty under his mother's loving and protective wing. Then, when Olga died, he moved to Ada's house, and Ada's husband was named his legal guardian. When I was a little girl, that middle-aged gentleman, with a receding hairline and a bit of a gut—Uncle Ducati—was my most assiduous playmate.

After the birth of Elisa, when Olga became pregnant again, Pietro decided that it was time to find a summer residence for the family as it grew at a constant clip. His father mentioned to him that he might look at the castle of Cortalba in Monferrato, in hopes that the grandchildren might have been close by them at least a few months a year. The marquis who had been owners of the feudal landholding for more than two centuries, overwhelmed by their burden of debt, had declared bankruptcy and taken refuge in France to escape the reach of the creditors. The castle was sold at auction, and Pietro bought it.

III

Here is how it is described in the township records:

"Cortalba was already a populated settlement in the Middle Ages, and the first documentation we have of its existence dates back to the tenth century. The original configuration of the castle, which we can reconstruct conjecturally, was a typical instance of lesser military architecture of the late Middle Ages [apocryphal legends would have it that this was a residence of Frederick Barbarossa during one of his campaigns in the Monferrato area]. ... *The floor plan of the complex appears to have been trapezoidal in shape* [here and there I'll skip over certain paragraphs that are too detailed and off-topic]. ... *The residential wing, which lies to the south, was built as a simple structure with three floors, overlooking a courtyard embellished with a central well* [the Hello Garden, as it was known during the time in which our story is set]. *The English basement level, which still preserves its original structure, consisted of a single room with a vaulted roof, five cross-vaults with an ogival arch, lowered and outlined by ribbing in terracotta tile, equipped with decorated keystones in sandstone* [this was originally an armory, housing armor and halberds, and was later used as a greenhouse by the Ducati family for the cultivation and conservation of exotic plants; the main room was inundated by the afternoon light that poured in through

large arched windows]. ... *The south cylindrical tower, which served as a flanking structure, rose four floors, and was crowned by a jutting frieze, similar to that of the hanging turrets that still exist* [this imposing crenelated tower keep with swallowtail battlements is the only one to survive of the two original towers; Pietro had the lower room of the tower adapted for use as a chapel, on the same level as the greenhouse, with stucco decorations in the Neo-Gothic style, and there his daughters' weddings were held; higher up, on the floor with the drawing rooms, he installed his office in the large circular room adjoining the library; the highest floor, which still housed the old medieval prison, underwent no restoration at all]. ... *The connecting wing and the north wing were the subject of numerous renovation projects which radically altered the castle's original appearance, starting as early as the eighteenth century. ... At the time, nearly all the castles in the kingdom underwent a Baroque reshaping, in emulation of the example set by the most prestigious Savoy palaces. ... The new style affected every room in the castle, the floor plan became more intricate, the outlines softer and more sinuous and the furnishings and interior decorations more spectacular. In the master wing, the procession of rooms of the main floor, built at the same level as the interior courtyard, was enlivened with five intercommunicating drawing rooms adjoined by service rooms obtained through the addition of a structure on the courtyard* [when the Ducati family lived there, the suite consisted of the grand hall of honor, the iris drawing room, the green parlor, the piano parlor, and the dining room]. ... *The grand hall of honor was roofed with a fake vaulted ceiling. The drawing rooms were also frescoed with floral motifs in geometric stringcourses and embellished with imposing marble fireplaces. ... The eighteenth-century interventions left indelible marks on the appearance of the castle, restoring it to that appearance of an "ennobled" grand medieval manor that still distinguishes it. Over the course of the nineteenth century and in the first quarter of the twentieth century maintenance and consolidation work was done on the perimeter escarpment."* This work was done at Pietro's behest. Pietro also devoted himself to the reconfiguration of the gardens and the restructuring of the woods with the addition of various species of trees and lanes and boulevards; he was responsible for the elegant and orderly design of the descending terraces: at the first level down, the Chestnut Lane, and, further down, the meadow and the tennis courts; on the second level, the Lane of Roses, which led to the third level; this was divided into two sections, the Lemon Garden and the Tower Garden, connected by the Avenue of the Palms; and at the top, the Hello Garden; the surrounding territory was not farmland. These were vast territories given over to woods and meadow, though there were some farmhouses with vineyards to supply the castle's needs.

The township records also speak of a constant churn of changes in ownership over the course of the centuries. But in that connection I'll limit myself to mentioning the fact that there was a long succession of seigniories subjugated through vassalage to the bishop of Asti, and that succession lasted until the seventeenth century, when an illustrious aristocratic line of marquis took over the exclusive title to the feudal landholding. Two centuries later, through a reversal of fortune that began with the suppression of feudal rights at the end of the eighteenth century, the marquis were forced to hand over their property to their creditors. The nobility was giving way to the bourgeoisie, the emerging class with a firm grip on the tiller of the New Italy.

3

Illusions
1908

I

The sun had already set behind the facing hill and the landscape, immersed in a rosy light, had taken on sharper outlines. The bell tower by the church, which rose from the piazza beneath all the way to the elevation of the "observation wall," chimed six o'clock. Ada was expecting to see the gig round the curve in the road at any instant. The train from Rome had pulled in that morning, and Pietro had sent the coachman to Asti to meet Leo and André. Leo took advantage of that day to take care of some business in the neighborhood and André willingly accompanied him on his rounds.

Ada was now sitting on the wall, her arms clutching her knees, pressing them against her chest. "An indecent pose," Mother had told her more than once — and, in this case, also a dangerous one, because she could easily fall off into the void, though the wall was in fact about two yards across.

And there was the gig now, rounding the curve and appearing on the sun-baked, clayey road, kicking up a white cloud of dust behind it. Ada stood there a few minutes longer to watch the carriage as it approached, and once it veered right and started up the series of switchbacks that led to Cortalba, she sprang down lightly off the wall and strode briskly toward the path that ran under the drawbridge and down to the Lemon Garden. There, she opened the wooden fence that gave onto the boundary between the inhabited area and the woods, and started down the Lane of Roses that led to the main entrance.

She reached the bottom of the slope just as the gig was pulling up before the front gate. Giusto pulled back on the reins and handed them to his son Giustino, who had run up to tend to the horse. Giusto helped Leo down from the carriage and then got busy unloading the luggage. André, standing in the gig, was waving his hat, having seen Ada coming toward him; he jumped to the ground and in two long bounds he reached her and gathered her to his chest in an affectionate embrace. Then it was Leo's turn and he planted two vigorous kisses on her cheeks, rosy from her brisk walk. Walking arm in arm, with Ada between the two men, conversing animatedly all the while, the trio climbed back up the front drive.

II

There are relatively few photographs of interiors in the album, due to poor lighting. The only photograph of the dining room was taken in daylight, with the large windows thrown open and the drapes drawn to let the sunshine in. There is no one in the dining room, but I can easily place the characters of this story around the vast table, surrounded by the massive carved walnut buffets surmounted by two large paintings, still lifes with game. The dinner table would be covered with Flanders linen tablecloths, each of them depicting a different theme in the damasked weft: the hunt, the grape harvest, the wheat harvest... I still have those tablecloths today; Olga left them to Ada, Ada left them to Alma, and Alma left them to me and to my sister Lina. But we've never owned tables large enough to be able to use them.

At dinner that evening, Ada maintained her position between Leo and André. There were other guests as well, all family members. There were more people around the table than was usual.

Viola, Olga's younger sister, was sitting across from Ada. She used to spend her summers at the castle because, given her love of horses, she loved to gallop freely over meadows and hillocks, far from the restrictions of the riding stable. Aside from being a fearless horsewoman, Viola wrote poetry and was an elegant and refined society lady; eccentric, people said, because she remained unmarried all her life. In town, whenever anyone mentioned Viola's name, they did so with a knowing smile, as if to say: Eh, we know a thing or two about that one. Rumors circulated. It was whispered that Giustino would saddle her horse and then go to wait for her in the hunting lodge which had long stood abandoned. A certain Pino swore that he had seen them go into the lodge, and that Giustino had been carrying a little bouquet of violets that he had picked in the meadow while awaiting her. Pino, spying from the window, had seen them kiss, but then they'd vanished behind a stack of bundled branches, and after that he'd seen nothing more.

Olga's other sister, Magda D'Ambrose, married to a Parisian banker, had come to stay for a week with her sons Francesco and Luigi. Magda preferred spending her summers on the beach at Santa Margherita to "soak up the rejuvenating energy of the Italian sun after the gray winters of Paris," but she never failed to make a stopover at the castle.

Miss Langfield, sitting between Elisa and Lidia, never wavered from her mission as an educator; with her left hand she gave discreet little taps to Lidia's shoulder blades—"Sit up straight, dear. Don't slump," she'd admonish her in an undertone; with her right hand, she'd squeeze Elisa's wrist sharply every time she laughed with too much gusto—Elisa, in particular, needed to maintain the demeanor of an adult because she was engaged to a young diplomat and was expected to marry him before the year was out. Giulia eluded her direct control, sitting as she was on the other side of the table, but Miss Langfield's darting glares were supposed to dissuade her from pursuing the war of breadballs that she was waging against her cousins.

In this effort, Miss Langfield was backed up by Magda who, though deep in conversation with Pietro, kept shooting intermittent and very stern looks of admonishment at her children sitting beside her.

"Pietro, I really must thank you for your suggestion that we take the Simplon Tunnel. It's an itinerary we hadn't taken with the boys before now... *Louis! Ça suffit...* We hadn't taken that route yet, as I was saying, and the boys were so excited to go through that railroad tunnel which boasts the distinction of being the world's longest... *François! Arrête...* The Wagons-Lits service is first rate and the restaurant car... *Allez, les enfants. J'en ai assez. Montez dans vôtre chambre, tout à l'heure!"*

Giulia intervened on her cousins' behalf, "Aunt Magda, don't send them away, I implore you. We'll stop playing with the bread balls, I promise." Francesco and Luigi stared down into their plates—"*Excuse moi, maman,*" they said in unison— and only raised their eyes after they'd been forgiven.

Their eyes met Riccardo's gaze, filled with solidarity, "Cheer up, boys. Tomorrow we'll hold a tennis tournament, and that way by the time evening comes, you'll no longer feel like batting bread balls back and forth."

"I want to play, too," Giulia put in.

"Of course," Riccardo reassured her, "you, your sisters, André, Aunt Viola, and anyone else who wants to try."

Count Riccardo Ralli d'Ostellata had only recently become a member of the family, having married Olga's widowed mother. They made an odd couple, because Riccardo was a strapping forty-year-old man, Romagna-born, exuberant, a captain in the army though not on active duty, while Letizia, a woman of remarkable beauty, was already well over sixty. In the circles of their acquaintances, it was whispered that Riccardo had made a marriage of convenience after squandering the Ralli family fortune at the casino of Monte Carlo. But those who knew him well said that he actually had simply fallen in love with that still-captivating woman.

Letizia placed her delicate hand on her husband's large and powerful. "You can count on Riccardo. He's a master at all forms of sport." She smiled at him admiringly. Then, addressing the housekeeper, "Erminia, another helping of veal roast for the count."

"Mister Count, would you also like a portion of roast potatoes?" asked Erminia.

"Why yes, how could I say no! You, my dear Letizia, you are bound to spoil me. Erminia, here we need another glass of Barolo."

Ada had remained extraneous to the general conversation, engaged as she was in an intense tête-à-tête with André. Her eyes were glowing, and her face, a sweet oval in shape, was suffused with a very particular light. They were speaking in an undertone, so that no one else was able to hear what they said to each other.

There were so many stories to tell, about things that had happened in those two long months apart. André was surely telling her all about his travels and the things that postcards couldn't communicate. Not even Leo, who was sitting right next to Ada, was able to overhear a single word. In fact, he made sure not to listen, instead dedicating himself to Olga, who was sitting on his other side. They too talked about André's travels. Then Olga addressed her nephew directly, jarring him out of his conversation with Ada.

"André, when are you going to go to Paris? Your father is telling me that after visiting the Lumières establishment, when you were just a boy, you swore that you were going to devote your life to the cinema."

"It's true, Aunt Olga. But I'm not going to go to Paris. Instead, I want to stay in Turin for a while. It's been such a long time since I've seen Grandma, but the main reason is the cinema. Already in the past few years they've brought the Cinématographe Lumières to Turin to screen films. But now a Turin-based company is getting involved in the production of *movies*—that's what they call them in America."

"And just how do you know all this?" asked Pietro from the far end of the table.

"Giovanni wrote me about it," said André.

"Giovanni who?"

"Pastrone, from Montechiaro. Don't you remember that we were taking violin lessons together?"

"Ah, right. How's his father?"

"That I couldn't say. But Giovanni is doing very well indeed. Now he lives in Turin. For a while he worked as second violin at the Royal Opera Theatre, then he gave up music for business."

"But wasn't he studying to be an accountant so he could help his father in the company?"

"Yes, in fact, he is an accountant. And he worked as a bookkeeper for a production house. But now he's out on his own and he's opened his own film studio. In his opinion, the cinema is going to become a major industry."

Now Ada was listening in silence, eyes lowered, concealing a sudden agitation. Clearly, André's plans to move to Turin had upset her.

At that moment, a great commotion was heard in the hallway. Then the door flew open and Luca came running in, pursued by the nanny. His little feet were bare and he was wearing a long nightshirt with lace at the wrists. Weeping, he threw himself into Olga's arms. She welcomed him lovingly and tried to comfort the child with caresses and cuddles. The nanny had come to a halt at a respectful distance, awaiting her orders. She seemed incongruous in that setting in her traditional Ciociaria costume. A red kerchief knotted around the back of the head as a sort of bonnet covered her hair; a black felt bodice over her white blouse, tight around her narrow waist, emphasized her prosperous bosom; an ample skirt with colorful flounces hung down to her ankles, revealing the white cotton socks and the black slippers. On the front she wore a white apron with a frill at the bottom. She wasn't wearing the black velvet jacket that normally completed her uniform, meaning that the nanny had probably taken it off in preparation for bed—that is how she is dressed in the photographs that depict her; and that is exactly how my nanny was still dressed thirty years later. Then, after the Second World War, that costume vanished, along with so many other things that are now gone with the wind.

All eyes followed the scene.

"Nanny, what's happened?" asked Olga, in a tone of reproof.

"Signò, it was just the blink of an eye, then I turned around, and Signorino Luca jumped down off the bed and told me, I'm going to see Mamma; and he was already galloping down the stairs and I just wasn't fast enough to snag him."

"Nanny is bad. I want to stay with you," Luca said through his sobs.

"Yes, certainly, my love, you'll stay with your mamma," said Olga, drying his eyes with her napkin.

Pietro shook his head. "Olga, please, you're indulging his whims. Let the nanny take him upstairs."

But Olga ignored him. "Nanny, wait out in the hallway. We'll call you when we need you. We'll talk about this incident again tomorrow."

Dinner was drawing to a close. Erminia had already served the dessert. Luca fell asleep in Olga's arms. The men withdrew into the smoking parlor; the ladies, into the piano parlor, where there were bridge tables. The evening concluded like all the other evenings, in a slow fade: the images of the day dissolved into the reality of the following day, marking the ongoing course of time.

III

The belvedere overlooking Chestnut Lane offered a panoramic overview of the tennis courts. The lane marked the lower end of the woods to the south; beneath it stretched a steep meadow. Through it, wooden steps zigzagged downhill from the belvedere and led to the tennis courts. But the young people preferred cutting straight across the meadow, running through the tall grass, and the littlest ones enjoyed rolling and tumbling from hillock to hump, staining their dazzling white suits with nasty patches of green.

Ada was sitting on a stone bench, watching from a distance the players, involved in their interminable sets. Two centuries-old cedars of Lebanon at the entrance to the belvedere covered the entire natural terrace with their branches, forming a sort of bowery grotto from which it was possible to observe unobserved. André was leaning against the railing that bounded the belvedere from the meadow side. He was turned at a three-quarters angle with respect to Ada, dividing his attention between her and the tennis match going on below.

"Riccardo isn't an impartial referee. He should have given that point to Giulia, not to Aunt Viola," André commented.

"You can't say from this distance," Ada retorted. "Giulia's ball might have been out of bounds. You're always ready to criticize Uncle Riccardo. I know you don't like him."

"Fair enough, I don't like him. And after all, he isn't our 'uncle.' If anything, we could call him 'grandpa,' which would be more appropriate. But the last time I tried it, he practically challenged me to a duel."

"You enjoy getting under his skin."

"And you defend him because today you've got it in for me. Do you mind if I ask why?"

"Since you're asking, I'll tell you. I didn't know that you'd decided to stay in Turin. That was a nasty surprise for me last night."

"Ada, you've never seen a movie so you can't understand. It's pure magic. Images in motion. The spatial dimension moving over time. No other medium of expression offers you such freedom. The artistic possibilities that it offers are immense."

"Surely you're not going to try to tell me that the cinema is an art? They have it in Rome, too, but I've never gone myself because, from what I've heard and from what I read in the newspapers, it's really little more than a sideshow attraction. And after all, we had other plans. Do you intend to abandon the New Painters' Club? If you leave, who will organize the exhibition? You had accepted the responsibility for overseeing the administrative aspects."

"You're certain to be able to find someone else. And I'll come to the opening to admire your paintings." André sat down next to Ada and took her hands in his. "Aduccia, you have always been my favorite cousin, and that will never change. Do you remember when we were little and we used to play Sleeping Beauty? You'd lie there with your eyes closed between the hydrangea bushes and I'd awaken you with a kiss on the forehead. Every time I'd say to myself: When I grow up I'll give her a real kiss. I'd love to give you that kiss now. If we were filming a scene for a movie, I'd take your face in my hands... like this... and I'd place my lips on yours..." André pressed his lips against Ada's mouth, then he slipped his hand around the back of her neck, wrapping his other arm around her waist. Ada felt the imperious summons of that gesture, which to her wasn't a game but absolute reality, and surrendered to it.

"Oh, oh! Ada, darling, where are you? It's your turn to play doubles with Lidia." Miss Langfield was struggling up the steep stairs, sheltering herself from the sun with a parasol made of St. Gallen lace.

Ada leaned over the railing, clipping a lock of hair that had escaped the hairpins, "I'm here, Miss Langfield. I'll be right down." She rapidly perched her "boater" on the top of her head, fastening it in place with a hatpin, grabbed her racket, and headed toward the stairs. In her athletic outfit, with a skirt that hung just below her calf, she looked like a carefree boarding school student. But her soul was heavy and her eyes puffy from the tears she'd choked back.

André looked at her with a smile of amusement, "This interruption wasn't in the script. We'll have to do a second take."

Perhaps Ada didn't hear him; in any case, she didn't answer and she hastened to catch up with Miss Langfield.

But there was no "second take," because André left for Turin the following day with Leo. As they said farewell, Ada held out her hand without embracing him.

"I'll write you, sweet cousin," said André with his most dazzling *charmeur*'s smile, "and I'll convince Aunt Olga that it would do Grandmother a world of good if you came to Turin and spend some time there with her."

"André, I'm happy to live in Rome. And you were happy to live there, too. Reconsider your decision."

André doffed his hat and kissed the tips of her fingers. Then, with a brash gesture, he put his hat back on and darted off down the lane behind the small group that was accompanying Leo.

4

Tango of the Roses
1908-1909

I

The grandparents' house felt empty and sad. Grandpa Ducati had died many years ago, and Aunt Nelli had moved to Cirié with her husband who was now running the family company. Grandmother almost never left her bedroom anymore. Cecilia, Nelli's eldest daughter, was in charge of her care. Cecilia was a pale, silent person, a year older than André. She glided through the rooms, sliding along on felt footpads, without moving her shoulders or her head, noiselessly except for the jangling of the keys that she carried in a large bunch hooked to her belt. She saw to every aspect of operations—she supervised the kitchen staff, the housekeepers, the gardener, and entertained the doctor who came to care for Grandmother and the priest who brought her communion on Sundays.

Leo left almost immediately, summoned by the demands of business. André took up residence in the ground-floor study, which offered greater independence than the bedrooms on the upper floors. The study boasted a French door that allowed him to come in and go out through the garden, thus avoiding the front entrance. Inside, the walls were lined with books that had belonged to Pietro and Leo. There were books of all kinds, from the illustrated books of early childhood to history and philosophy textbooks from high school, from the the Latin and Greek classics to modern Italian and foreign literature—though the last forty years were missing; if André had wished to read, say, *Anna Karenina*, he'd have been forced to look elsewhere. A screen in front of the fireplace depicted a scene of the eruption of Mt. Vesuvius at Pompeii. Between the two windows a large desk enjoyed pride of place, inviting one to study and reflection. Facing the desk was a comfortable sofabed upholstered in green corduroy. A capacious armoire completed the furnishings.

André spent very little time at home, and when he was there, he almost never came out of his study. He tried to avoid the company of Cecilia, whom he found depressing. She considered the presence of André to be just one of her many duties: every night she made sure that the housekeeper had made his bed and every morning she personally brought him his breakfast tray, set it down on the desk, drew the curtains, letting the sweet-smelling air pour in from the garden, and said, "Wake up, André, it's a beautiful day. Let us thank the Lord." Or, if it was raining, "Wake up, André, it's raining today. Let us thank the Lord." If André wasn't there, because he'd spent the whole night out, Cecilia shot a quick glance at the untouched bed, crossed herself, and then, leaving the study, she'd tell the housekeeper to remove the tray. "Ginetta, you can take the tray. Signorino André won't be eating breakfast this morning."

Ginetta was young and good looking and had been forbidden to enter the study when André was present. In any case, she was only permitted to set foot across that threshold under Cecilia's watchful eye. If she met André in the hallway, she was under strict orders to lower her eyes, curtsy briefly, and hurry away as quickly as she could.

In effect, though, Cecilia had no reason to worry because Ginetta wasn't to André's tastes. She had only recently arrived from the village and she still bore the marks of a peasant roughness on her otherwise handsome face. André preferred

a finer type. Shortly after his arrival, he'd met Rosina and fall-
en head over heels for her. Rosina was slender and fair-haired,
with an angelic little face, made even more delightful by cunning little hats trimmed with ribbons or flowers. In fact, hats
were her specialty because Rosina worked as a milliner at the
atelier of the Gerbino Sisters. For years, Grandmother had pa-
tronized that fashion house, ordering three hats every season,
and even now that she never left the house, she still carried on
that tradition. Rosina came to the house periodically to try on
and deliver the hats.

André chanced to see her one day as they crossed paths
in the front hall. Domenico had come running when he heard
the doorbell and had opened the door:

"*Ceréa, tóta Rusín.* Hurry, hurry! The lady has already
asked three times if you've arrived," Domenico urged her in
dialect.

"*Ceréa, munsù* Domenico. I'm sorry I'm late. I apologize,"
Rosina replied, slightly out of breath.

Then they both stood aside to let André by as he was leaving the house.

"Good day, Signorino André," said Domenico. Rosina
bobbed her head in greeting, blushing at the gaze of frank
admiration that André had given her as he walked by.

The following morning, André went looking for Domenico and found him, as usual, in the garden, watering the roses.
The garden, with the large magnolia, the rose bushes, and the
jasmine hedges were now his chief occupation. Once Domenico had also been the coachman, but ever since the horse died,
the carriage had lain forgotten in the garage. In the house, he
performed a few light duties, but by now he was too elderly for any heavy work. He had spent fifty years as a part of
the Ducati household along with his wife, and he'd had the
satisfaction of seeing his children become factory workers for
the Fiat automobile plant and emancipate themselves from
domestic service. Now he was getting ready to go back to the
village to spend his old age in the places of his childhood.

In response to André's questions, he replied that yes, he knew where Signorina Rosina worked, at the atelier in the porticoes along the Via Cernaia.

That very same evening, when the staff was let out, André was leaning against a pillar out front of the fashion house. In one hand he was holding a large bundle of roses that Domenico had gathered for the occasion, sacrificing some of his rarest specimens. The working girls came out in small groups, arm in arm and chirping like so many birds "in that strange Gallic language of theirs," André thought to himself, because he didn't understand much Piedmontese.

Rosina stepped out of the shop, and she saw him immediately. She stopped, baffled. And as André was walking up to her, her girlfriends moved away with high-pitched giggles and mischievous glances.

"Signorina Rosina, please forgive my behavior which, I'll certainly admit, is rather bold," André began, with a bow. "Please believe me, I'm speaking to you with only the greatest respect, and I certainly hope that you'll be willing to listen to what I have to say. I had no other way to get in touch with you. After our meeting yesterday, I knew that I had to see you again… immediately. The image of your face had been etched into my mind like a photograph. From that moment, I have thought about nothing but you. I'm ailing, Rosina, and only your presence can cure me. I hope you'll show me the extreme kindness of accepting these roses which will set a seal upon the beginning of our friendship." With these words, he dropped the bundle of roses in the arms of Rosina, who had listened agog to that diatribe.

"Signor Ducati…" she said at last, recovering her wits.

"Please, André… Rosina, I hope you'll call me André. I want you to think of me as a friend."

"André, I hardly know what to say. These roses are lovely. But I feel *gena* when … "

"*Gena*?" How funny is this dialect.

"Yes, that is, I mean to say that your attentions put me in an awkward situation. I'm not accustomed to these things. And after all, we don't really know each other, though it has been my great honor to serve your lady grandmother."

"But that's just why I'm here. Because I want to get to know you better, Rosina. I want to know all about you, about your family, about your life. Please, be so good as to allow me to walk with you." With a gallant gesture he offered his arm, and Rosina took it.

They strolled through the gardens of Piazza Solferino, heading toward Porta Nuova. They walked in the shade of the plane trees, in the still bright light of the summer sunset. Along the way, André learned that Rosina lived with her mother and was an only child. Her father had been killed at the battle of Adwa, when she was still a little girl. Her father had worked on the railroad before being drafted in the years of the Italian campaign in Ethiopia, and he'd never returned home. Her mother had a photograph on her nightstand and a bronze medal that had come in the mail. Her mother had worked as an ironer in a laundry to make ends meet and send her daughter to school. When she finished elementary school, at the age of eleven, Rosina had gone to work at the atelier to learn the trade as a *piccinina*, a child apprentice. Now she was responsible for bringing home a salary, because her mother had fallen ill and could no longer work. Just now, her mother had gone back to the village to stay with her sister, because the doctor had ordered her to get some fresh country air.

"Your mamma is lucky to have a daughter like you, Rosina. You're not only lovely to look at, you're also good-hearted, generous, and kind. But soon you'll need to think about making a match, marrying and starting a family. Do you have a fiancé?"

Rosina blushed. "Those aren't matters I choose to discuss. For now, I'm giving the matter no thought," she replied with modesty.

"Rosina, do you still not trust me? I told you that you can rely on my friendship. Confide in me openly."

"There is a fine young man who has made his intentions clear. But I'm not ready, I'd prefer to wait."

"Ah, you mean that you don't love him… Oh, please forgive me, Rosina, I shouldn't have made so bold. It's just that when you love someone, you want to have that person close to you, every minute of every day… and physical contact…" André squeezed Rosina's hand, which lay lightly on his arm. Rosina pulled her hand away and came to a halt.

They had arrived at the street portal of the building where she lived, a tall apartment house blackened by the locomotive smoke that came from the nearby train station. The apartments with windows on the ornate front of the building were occupied by lower middle-class families, for the most part railroad employees. But Rosina lived in a much poorer apartment, which looked out on a long external balcony overlooking the courtyard.

At every floor, on those long balconies, women were hanging out laundry to dry, children ran the length of the walkways shouting and laughing, threatening to knock over the laundry baskets or trip over half-sleeping cats stretched out by the potted basil, or else to run straight into the black-clad little old ladies who were out watering plants and who would adroitly spank the little terrors whenever they could catch them on the fly.

"I really must go," said Rosina. "Thank you again for the lovely roses."

"Rosina, it is I who should thank you for allowing me to enjoy your company. May I dare to hope that you'll allow me to see you again? If you happened to be free this coming Sunday, I'd like to take you to the moving pictures. I could tell you many interesting things, because cinema is my profession. I work for a moving pictures studio."

"The moving pictures? I adore them!" Rosina exclaimed,

with a burst of excitement. "I sometimes go with my girl-friends. I'm a great admirer of Lydia Quaranta and I've seen all her pictures."

"That's wonderful! I'd be delighted to introduce you to Lydia Quaranta herself if you'd like to come to the Ristorante Paradiso after the show. That's where all the artists socialize at night."

Rosina hesitated for a moment. The Ristorante Paradiso and the company of movie artists intimidated her. But the allure of the movies was irresistible and Rosina accepted the invitation.

II

Just as André had hoped, his friend Giovanni had been delighted to give him a berth at Itala Film, the newly founded film studio that he had just put together. Giovanni had purchased the Carlo Rossi company where he had served his apprenticeship in the new industry, and that was the core of the new studio. André began working as an actor because, as the casting director had told him, he had the facial features of a seductive ladykiller. In fact, André was quite photogenic, as we can see from the photographs in our album. If I were to describe him to an audience of my own time, I'd have to say he resembles Alain Delon, especially in *The Leopard*. But his true dream was to be a director and, after his first two films, which didn't do particularly well and which have since been lost, he became Pastrone's assistant director.

He worked at Itala Film for three years. At first he walked to the studio every morning, because it wasn't far from where he lived and it was a pleasant stroll. He'd cross the bridge over the Po, then turn left down Corso Casale and walk along the river bank until he reached the complex of motion picture stages. But it wasn't long before Itala Film began to grow, and the studio moved to its new facilities on Corso Quintino Sella, a bit further up in the hills. The studio lot covered a vast surface of many acres. Turin became one of the capitals of the world's motion picture industry. Between 1908 and 1915, twenty-one movie studios sprang up there, rivaling the Rome studios.

The new film stages of Itala Film had been designed to take the greatest possible advantage of the sunlight, because Pastrone was a great innovator. He experimented with lighting effects, both diffuse light and reflected light, and he even experimented with a rudimentary system to equip film with sound and color. But the invention that marked a genuine turning point in filmmaking technique, and made Pastrone world-famous, was the *carrello*, the first camera dolly. This technique estabilished the principle whereby the camera was no longer a stationary eye before which the scene unfolded. Instead, the camera could now be a dynamic agent in the midst of the action. The camera could now "tell" the story, adding points of view and emotions.

Pastrone found stories suited to his new techniques, which allowed him to exploit vast spaces, grandiose settings, and mass scenes. He was the inventor of the epic film, with hundreds of extras and complicated battle and disaster scenes. But along with the element of contrivance, Pastrone also preserved the quality of realism that made the images believable. For instance, for his first historical drama, *The Fall of Troy*, he had an enormous wooden horse constructed, because he was unwilling to settle for scale models. And in his masterpiece, *Cabiria*, he brought real elephants up into the Alps to shoot the scene of Hannibal leading his army down into Italy.

Cabiria had enormous repercussions on both sides of the Atlantic—it's a well known fact that D. W. Griffith took inspiration from this film. But already, even before *Cabiria*, Hollywood was following Pastrone's work with great interest, both because of his shooting and editing techniques and his industrial organization. Pastrone, in fact, considered the movies to be an industry first and foremost, and he ran Itala Film like a factory; alongside film production, he'd added a distribution network and a chain of movie theaters. We cannot rule out the idea that the "vertically integrated structure" of the Hollywood studios had first been suggested by the Italian model. A number of employees of Itala Film received tempting offers from America, inviting them to bring their Italian know-how to the California film studios. One of these employees was André, as we shall later see.

III

The evening that André took Rosina to the Ristorante Paradiso, the production studio was just getting started on its first location by the Po. A troupe of ten or so people were sitting around a long table, and a couple of waiters were buzzing busily around them. Pastrone wasn't there, though, and neither was the famous diva whom Rosina so fervently admired.

Everyone shoved over to make room. The men complimented André on his lovely lady, while the women eyed her critically, sizing up the damage this new rival might wreak. Ambra Sylvestry, who had worked in one movie with André and was currently involved with him, felt a stab of betrayal and jealousy.

"Is the young lady an actress?" Ambra Sylvestry asked.

Rosina began to laugh, shaking her head, and André explained that she was only an enthusiastic movie fan.

"But she ought to give acting a try," said Mario Mariani, the author of many screenplays. "I already feel inspired to write a treatment for her."

The cameraman who was sitting across the table studied her face as if through the eyepiece of the movie camera, making a tiny frame with four fingers, intersecting at perpendicular angles. "You have the ideal features for the female lead in *Lost Innocence*," he said admiringly.

Rosina looked from one to the other, wide-eyed, at a loss for words.

"That's enough, gentlemen. You're embarrassing her." André didn't appreciate all that attention. "We'll think it over, we'll discuss it in good time. Rosina, come, let's toast to this cheerful company." As he spoke, he filled her glass.

Many glasses of wine and many cheerful toasts later, Rosina felt giddy and infinitely grateful to André for having introduced her to that magical world whose lovely, happy, talented inhabitants made her feel like the belle of the ball. The intermittent snide observations of the women, however bitter and ill-tempered, were lost in the chorus of male adulation. Rosina's cheeks were bright red and she laughed and laughed.

But now André decided that it was time to go, even though they had only just finished the appetizers and were still waiting for their bowls of ravioli-like *agnolotti*. Amidst a storm of objections, he helped Rosina to her feet; she turned to her admirers with a dazzling smile and, lifting her fingertips to her lips, she blew them a kiss just as she'd seen a diva do in a moving picture. Then she headed for the door, leaning lightly on André's arm.

"André, they were saying that I could become an actress. Were they being serious?" Rosina asked, once they were outside.

"Why not?"

"I can't believe it. It would be simply too wonderful."

Just then, a carriage went past. André hailed it and gave the driver Rosina's address. During the ride, the swaying of the carriage and the soft light of the gas lamps lulled Rosina into a pleasurable trance. André put his arm around her and she rested her head on his shoulder, happy to feel she was being protected and guided.

Their arms still wrapped around each other, side by side, they climbed the narrow stairs to the top floor and walked down the long, deserted balcony. They came to a stop outside Rosina's door.

"Good night." A dreamy look danced in her eyes.

"The key. Rosina, give me the key." His tone was unceremonious.

Rosina didn't react. Continuing to smile, she leaned against him. André reached down and took her little silk handbag, loosened the strings, and extracted the key. He opened the door.

As he walked through the door, Rosina weakly objected, "André, you can't come in. Mother's not here."

André shut the door behind him and lit a kerosene lamp. The dim light revealed a poorly furnished room. It was a kitchen with a square table in the center, covered with an oil-skin tablecloth dotted with a pattern of small blue flowers; drawn up around it were four straw-bottomed chairs. A cupboard stood against the wall and, along with a kitchen sink and a wood-burning stove, constituted all the furnishings in the room. There were cooking pots and pans hanging on the wall and a rosemary plant on the window sill.

André took the lamp in one hand and pushed Rosina toward the door leading into the only other room. Here, there were two beds with wrought-iron bedsteads and cotton piqué bedcovers. There was also a small wardrobe, a nightstand, a washstand with a basin and a pitcher, a wooden chair, and an icon of the Virgin Mary on the wall. In this practically monastic setting, the only coquettish note was a shelf lined with multicolored hats that Rosina displayed, just as an artist might show her works.

Perhaps André didn't notice every detail while he was in the midst of that experience, but he did remember them later, after it had all ended with Rosina. In fact, he told the story in its entirety in a short novel that he titled, *Let's Kill the Roses! An Autobiographical Account of a Brilliant Scoundrel.* More than two years had passed since that evening. By now, it was the period when Futurism was fashionable, and book titles guaranteed to *épater la bourgeoisie*, like that one, were *de rigueur*. So far, I've freely summarized the text, but at this point I'll allow André himself to describe the scene that ensued:

> *I was unaccustomed to finding myself in such circumstances with respectable young ladies and I wasn't certain about what to do next. Usually, the women I frequented took the initiative. But Rosina seemed to be in a hypnotic trance, she gazed up at me with a fixed expression, terrified and fascinated at the same time.*
>
> *I was starting to feel uneasy, and even to experience a certain irritation. I set the lamp down on the chair and grabbed Rosina, clutching her in my arms. She put up no resistance. I kissed her violently because at that very moment my passion had overpowered me. I felt her slender body tremble as it pressed against mine. The lamp was projecting our shadows against the wall; my silhouette took the shape of a giant eagle. I freed Rosina of her clothing with impatient gestures, uncovering her white, delicate forms. Then I placed her in the bed and we lay together.*
>
> *Rosina's innocence unleashed my most primitive instincts and filled me with a surge of intense pleasure, a wave of possession and destruction. She said nothing, and she kept her eyes closed, tender and consenting. Her yielding compliance only fanned my thirst for conquest and my conquering ecstasy. When the river of my passion flowed to the delta and burst impetuously into the vast sea of life, Rosina jerked convulsively, like the earth blasted by a lightning bolt, or like an automobile quivering under the whip of the electric spark. My intoxication became cosmic and attained the splendor of the sun. Then, it went out like a lightbulb.*

As I drifted off into a deep sleep, I heard Rosina saying, "I love you, André." But I had neither the strength nor the desire to respond.

This liaison went on for several months. At first, André went to Rosina's apartment almost every night; then, only once a week; and when her mother came back from the village, André no longer showed his face. During those months, André took care not to take Rosina back to the Ristorante Paradiso, but he continued to nourish her dreams of becoming an actress with promises and flattery.

"André, when are we going to start working on the picture? Have you found a role for me?" asked Rosina one of the many evenings they spent in her bare little bedroom. She was wrapped in a sheet, with her shoulders uncovered, and she was reclining in the bed, propped up on an elbow.

"Of course I've found it." As he was getting dressed, André noticed Rosina's graceful pose. "You'll play the part of a Roman maiden who's in love with a gladiator, but who's forced to submit to the whims of the emperor."

"Oh, what a pity," Rosina retorted with a hint of disappointment. "I would have preferred a more modern part, say a countess who falls in love and abandons her husband and young son, and her luxurious mansion, only to follow an impostor who is eventually arrested, but she loves him still and remains by his side even though he is in prison."

"Why, no," said André dismissively, "these are Russian plot elements, they're dripping with sentimentalism. The Italian public likes characters and settings that are rooted in our national history and which serve as pretexts to stage spectacular epics."

"All right, all right. I'll play the Roman maiden." Rosina was apprehensive, anxious to go along. "But when are we going to get started?"

"Just as soon as Mariani gives me the script. It shouldn't

take long, you'll see. Now give me a kiss because I've got to run; tomorrow morning I've to be at the studio at five to catch the special light of dawn."

She clutched at his arm. "But André, do you love me? You never say so."

"And why wouldn't I love you? Of course I do, I love you. And I prove it to you every night. But now I have to run. Come, now, be a good girl and go to sleep. And dream of your upcoming movie."

At last, when André had stopped coming for her outside the atelier, and no longer knocked at her door at night, Rosina desperately sought some way of getting in touch with him. Domenico no longer worked in the Ducati home, he had gone back to the village, and the new season for hats wouldn't begin until springtime. It was still the middle of winter. A Turin winter, chilly and dry, with the wind galloping down into the city from high alpine meadows and a thick blanket of snow covering the roofs, the streets, and the gardens.

Rosina decided to go to the studio. As she approached the front gate she could feel the strength draining out of her. The road still hadn't been cleared of the snow from the night before and her light ankle boots sank into the soft white blanket. Her feet were chilled to numbness. Though her coat was woolen, it wasn't enough to protect her from the freezing cold. She'd put on one of her most adorable little hats… but, alas, what she really needed in that weather was a Russian fur cap.

At the gate, the usher informed her that Signor Ducati wasn't there that day. Rosina braced herself against a pillar to keep from falling. She gazed in behind the gate, into that enchanted world that seemed so near, yet so unattainable.

On the plaza in front of the sound stages an Eskimo went by on a dog-drawn sled. He was looking over his shoulder with a terrified expression: he was being pursued by a ferocious polar bear. Suddenly the bear came to a halt and a human head emerged from the gaping jaws:

"Easy, easy. Damn it to hell, how am I supposed to keep up with you? You make my lungs explode. I'm not a real bear, you know."

The Eskimo stopped the dog sled.

The director, who was standing next to the movie camera started waving his hands and shouting at the bear, "What are you doing, you imbecile! You've ruined the whole scene!"

The bear was sitting in the snow panting and muttering to himself, "Absolutely crazy."

Rosina started to cough and her vision grew blurry. Just then, Mariani was arriving at the studio, saw her, and came over.

"Signorina Rosina, what a pleasure to see you again. I've asked André about you many times, but he told me that he'd lost touch with you... But, Signorina, you don't seem to feel well. Come in, let me offer you a cup of coffee."

Rosina declined the invitation and walked away. Mariani stood there for a minute, watching her with a sense of sadness, tracking the multicolored ribbons on her little hat, a dot of color in the white expanse that gradually vanished into the distance.

The next day, he told André about his encounter. "She was visibly unwell, she was coughing, she seemed to have a fever. She didn't tell me why she'd come. I wanted to invite her in so she could get warmed up, but all she murmured was, 'Please don't go to any trouble,' and she walked off down the road, weaving slightly, unsteady on her feet."

André said nothing, but he was troubled by what he'd heard. He resolved to go pay a call on Rosina as soon as was conveniently possible, in order to learn more. Still, what with the demands of work, friends, and women, he never seemed to find the time to put his good intentions into action. Spring arrived, and a new representative from the millinery atelier of the Gerbino Sisters came to take grandmother's order for hats. André learned of this development from Cecilia, who was accustomed to bringing him the latest bulletin of house-hold gossip along with the breakfast tray.

"Poor girl," Cecilia commented, "she was so pretty. But she had weak lungs and they had to take her to the hospital."

After that, nothing was ever heard of Rosina again.

5

The Ships Set Sail
1911-1914

I

This photograph from 1914 depicts a carefree moment prior to the tragic events that caused Leo's death. The picture was meant to be a snapshot, a slice of life caught unawares, but it's clear that, given the technical limitations of the time, it had required a certain amount of staging and lengthy exposure.

They are in the Lemon Garden; several couples are dancing on the gravel clearing surrounded by the large terracotta vases containing the graceful trees with their golden fruit. Beyond the lemon trees, the eye ranges over the rolling hills that cascade like the waves of the sea, all the way to the horizon. It's a long shot that takes in the whole scene, choreographed in such a way that the couples are in clear view. Everyone looks into the camera, as if to confirm to those observing them that they are enjoying themselves; but they don't openly smile, still bound by the painterly tradition that demands restraint, even in festive situations.

Elisa, married for several years now, is dancing with her husband. Lidia and Ada, by now young women in their early twenties, are dancing together. Giulia, too, has grown and her skirts have lengthened; Riccardo is pirouetting her around, and she is raising a hand to her mouth to stifle a laugh. Luca, ever since his nanny has been replaced by the tutor, has begun to learn new things, for instance, how to dance; still, he's tied to his mother's apron strings and here he's dancing with her.

The tutor, Monsieur Lesavoir, is standing off to one side, clapping his hands in time to the music. At the edge of the clearing is a new nanny with two new little girls, Elisa's twin daughters. Miss Langfield has taken on a comic role and is dancing with Lillì, Luca's pet Volpino Italiano, erect on his hind legs. Letizia is sitting on a wicker settee padded with cushions and watching the proceedings through her lorgnette. Pietro is sitting next to her, turning the handle of the gramophone. Pietro's health continued to deteriorate and the doctors didn't give him much longer to live. They diagnosed his desease as leukemia, still incurable at the time.

After the photograph was taken, the company scattered. Elisa and her husband busied themselves playing with their daughters; Giulia and Miss Langfield withdrew to the library for the daily lesson; Pietro went to his bedroom to rest; Olga and Luca headed down to the lower terrace for a game of croquet, followed by Lillì; Riccardo sat down next to Letizia to read to her for a while—Letizia's eyes were quite weak and she struggled to read; Lidia sat down for a game of chess with Monsieur Lesavoir—I doubt that that was his actual name, French for "knowledge," but it certainly suited him to a tee, because he always had an answer for everything, just like a living encyclopedia.

Ada had a specific plan in mind. She wanted to finish her portrait of the gardener's little boy, a portrait she had begun several weeks earlier and which still required a last posing session. She therefore headed off to Cescu's house with canvas, easel, and paints. Cescu had recently gotten married and had conveyed his wife to his father's house, the father who had been the gardener before him. The young couple had a little boy a few months old.

Ada entered the barnyard of the farmhouse adjacent to the castle's north wall. Perpendicular to the wall was the farmhouse itself, a rectangular two-story building with a long balcony overlooking the courtyard and an outside staircase; at a right angle to the farmhouse, a portico served as a granary on the upper story and contained the rabbit hutches on the ground floor. At the far end, the barnyard opened out onto a landscape of vineyards cultivated in regular, orderly rows, as if every furrow had been riven by a large-toothed comb. In the shade of a mulberry tree, against the vineyard's background, Maggiorina was sitting on a low stool with the child in her arms, tossing handfuls of corn to the chickens that were ranging free across the courtyard. She saw Ada and started to get up, but Ada stopped her.

"Don't get up, Maggiorina, after all I'd only make you sit back down again in the exact pose you were in. That's perfect for me to finish the portrait of Tunìn."

Once she had gotten herself situated on the folding chair in front of the easel, Ada observed the unfinished portrait. She didn't like it. It struck her that she'd been unable to capture the little boy's personality, the intangibility of the being that can become matter only in art. There was a lack of inspiration, the creative spirit that had driven all her finest work was not there.

Tunìn was clucking, "*kew, kew*," like the chickens that were pecking in the yard, and his little bare legs were kicking out of his sky-blue cotton blouse. In one hand he held a corn cob; he was shaking it like a toy and every so often he'd lift it to his mouth to nibble at it with his still toothless gums. His small blue eyes, lively and curious, frequently came to rest on Ada who, in her white dress with collar and tie, and her "boater"perched atop her softly puffy hairdo, must have appeared to him as an attractive and unfamiliar form, extraneous to the domestic images that made up his cognitive sphere.

"Signorina Ada, I'm sorry that the child won't stay still," said Maggiorina. The sun behind her ignited a brilliant flame of light in the curly wreath of blond hair that escaped from under the kerchief knotted at the back of her head. She too had blue eyes just like Tunìn and a sprinkling of freckles on her button nose and chubby cheeks. Ada thought that she ought to have painted a portrait of Maggiorina, because her female portraits always seemed to turn out better. But for the moment she set to work on the canvas she'd already begun.

"It doesn't matter if the child moves. In fact, it gives me a chance to better capture his expressions," said Ada. Maggiorina smiled and wiped away a little drool from Tunìn's chin.

Ada was painting automatically, without concentration. Her thoughts were elsewhere. She hadn't heard from André in quite some time. She'd received only a few infrequent letters since the day she'd last seen him wave his hat from the deck of the liner that was sailing for America. She went back to the day, exactly three years previous, when they had accompanied him to Genoa—she and Leo.

II

On the eve of the departure, the whole family had gathered at Cortalba for the farewell dinner. Aunt Magda came too, with her boys, as did Aunt Viola, Aunt Nelli and her husband, and even Cecilia who had grown fond of André after bringing him breakfast for three years. For good measure, they also invited the parish priest, Don Barbisio, so that with his presence he could invoke an "unofficial" benediction of André's trip—an actual religious ritual was absolutely out of the question because André was laic, and would not have been best pleased.

As usual, they took the aperitifs under the linden tree. Two waitresses handed round traysful of salt puff pastries and canapés and Erminia poured out the *Punt e Mes* vermouth in the crystal glasses. The conversation was full of forced cheer, but there was an unmistakable undertone of sadness for the coming departure and a sense of apprehension over the unknown fate toward which André was now heading.

Only Riccardo seemed genuinely pleased. He stood up and, lifting his glass, proposed a toast.

"My dear family, I want to congratulate our André who is preparing to take the Italian genius across the great ocean. In this year, 1911, in which Italy will win great conquests on the Mediterranean shores, a member of our family will venture even further, beyond the Pillars of Hercules, following in the wake of our daring navigators, and will plant the Italian tricolor on the coasts of the New World. André, we're proud of you."

"God's will be done," Don Barbisio concluded.

"Uncle Riccardo, I'm going to make movies, not war," said André, with a hint of annoyance.

"Well, it's just a turn of phrase," Riccardo retorted. "In any case, we *are* going to have a war here. At this point, with the Giolitti government, it's a sure thing that our infanty is soon going to be marching on the soil of Tripolitania, and the Turks are going to get soundly kicked by the Italian boot, right in the seat of their pants."

"Riccardo! That's barracks language. You're forgetting that you're in the presence of ladies," Letizia said indignantly.

"Forgive me, my dear. I allowed myself to be swept away by my patriotic ardor."

"And it's not necessarily such a sure thing that this war is going to be fought, after all," said Pietro. "I know that Giolitti is one of the proponents of military action, but that surprises me; it's not in his nature. All the same, if war really does come, are you planning to go back into active service?"

"Certainly. They've offered me a post in Rome, at the Ministry. It will be an honor to be able to fulfil my duties."

"I'm happy that your duties won't force you onto the battlefield, where so many poor boys are going to lose their lives," said Leo provocatively.

Riccardo didn't have the time to react because at this point Olga weighed in.

"Gentlemen, if you'll allow me, I'd like to change the subject. André, why don't you tell us a little something about your plans? What do you expect you'll do once you get there?"

"Yes, yes, André. Do tell," Giulia urged him. America fascinated her as an exotic land of adventure.

"Will you go where there are Indians?" asked Luca, apprehensively, thinking of the fearsome savages depicted in the *Children's Encyclopedia*.

They all urged him to speak, including Luigi and Francesco who greatly envied their cousin's life, since they were subjected to the rigid conformist views of the banker D'Ambrose—to them, *l'Italie* and the summer holidays with their mother were already synonymous with liberty, and America was an unattainable dream. But Ada and Leo, who sat side by side, said nothing; Ada took her uncle's hand and held it in her own.

"What can I tell you? I'll certainly have more to say when I come back, in a few years," said André. "All I know is that American Biograph, the studio who sent me my contract, has recently moved to California. From what I've heard, it's a challenging land, but extremely intriguing. I'll live in the village of Hollywood, which is becoming a major center for film production, set among hills covered with eucalyptus and golden beaches, under an eternally blue sky. What attracts so many producers is chiefly the climate and the light, which make it possible to shoot all year round."

"And just how did you find this position?" Magda inquired.

"They found me. Pastrone received a request for a filmmaker interested in working at Biograph for a few years. People say that our spectacular epics have made quite an impression on their best director, Griffith, and apparently the request comes directly from him. Giovanni didn't want me to go, now that we're in the planning stages for *Cabiria*, a super-epic so extraordinary that it will blot out everything that's been made so far. But I insisted, because not only will I be able to bring our experience to America, I'll also be able to learn a great many new things and apply them here when I return."

"Then, let's drink to your return," Leo suggested.

From the day André moved to Turin, Leo had gradually, and regretfully, accepted the fact that his son had given up on the idea of attending university and coming to work in the company as his legitimate successor. What had seemed like a youthful infatuation with the movies had been transformed into a career. Now Leo sensed that André's destiny lay elsewhere, and that he couldn't count on him ever coming back. Still, he pretended to believe otherwise.

III

In those years when André was in Turin, Ada had continued to think that soon that period would come to an end, that André would return to Rome, and that their friendship would resume at the exact point where it had been interrupted. Her thoughts were confused at best. She didn't know how to define her relationship with André. She understood that it was more than a friendship, that there was a romantic element to it, but she couldn't seem to formulate a precise thought of what that was supposed to mean, or of how the situation was supposed to develop. Especially after that kiss on the belvedere.

One day she talked about it with Elisa, who was married and must therefore understand more about these matters, and having explained the way she felt about André, received confirmation for her doubts. "You're in love with him," said Elisa with the demeanor of a doctor making a diagnosis. But this "being in love" was a vague concept for Ada, a state of mind rather than a real situation that demanded practical actions and solutions. She availed herself of the novels she had read in order to determine what became of people who had fallen in love, and she realized that literature presented two possible outcomes: either they got married at the end of the story and "lived happily ever after," or else they died—suicides, murder victims, or of some disease. She didn't care for the second solution and she discarded it. The first one didn't seem applicable to her case.

Though the novels never explained just how the newly-weds went on to "live happily ever after," Ada could make some deductions from her observations of the married couples that she knew in real life—her parents, for instance—where the husband was the support and guide, guarantor of the family's material welfare, solicitous of his wife's comfort, affectionate but strict with the children, fair and firm in his decisions. In other words, a pillar upon which the rest of the family could depend with the utmost reliance. Well then, if this was the model, it was impossible to think of André as a "husband." Her cousin inspired no domestic feelings in her, only dreams of romantic adventures, fantasies, and flights of fancy. Ever since they were small children, André had been a companion in their escapes from everyday routine, first by inventing original games, and later by helping her to develop her artistic talent as the mastermind behind the New Painters' Club, where Ada discovered avant-garde aesthetics and found fodder for her formal experimentation. André was also an athletic partner, and not only in tennis, which remained their favorite sport, but also in far more daring and unusual endeavors—as was documented by an edelweiss pressed between the pages of a book, which André had picked for her at the very brink of a precipice, at the risk of his own life.

This happened one summer when the family was vacationing at Courmayeur. Olga decided that, in order to strengthen their bodies and souls, her daughters were to climb, roped together in a line, the Dent du Géant, a rocky peak on the summit of Mont Blanc. She hired the finest alpine guide in the valley and entrusted to his care her three eldest daughters—Ada, at the time, was about fifteen. Since Miss Langfield refused to go with them, Olga designated André as chaperon. They set out at dawn on mules, which carried them halfway up the mountain. Then, where the mountain turned steep, they proceeded on foot; the guide first in line, followed by Elisa, Lidia, Ada, and André bringing up the rear.

That this story is true is unquestionable. I heard it with my own ears from Ada's own lips when I was five years old. Just how high they climbed isn't clear, perhaps up to the glacier, perhaps all the way to the base of the Dent du Géant. It's hard to believe that they actually scaled the rock face. Still, when I heard the story from Ada, I saw that line of individuals one atop the other, hanging on the rope and precariously dangling from spikes and rock spurs on a perfectly vertical mountain wall—the young women dressed in skirts that made their movements all the more challenging. That situation, so dangerous, gave me the shiver of the sublime; but at the same time, a funny thought occurred to me.

"Grandma, but if Uncle André was underneath you, then he could see your undies."

"Of course not, silly thing. We were wearing mountain britches under our skirts; corduroy breeches that button at the knee, with heavy wool stockings and hobnail mountain boots."

"Ah, well that's good." Still, I thought to myself that it would have been more fun if Uncle André had seen her undies.

Instead, he gave her an edelweiss.

And so André was a romantic figure for Ada. Still, sex wasn't part of the picture because Ada knew nothing about it, either directly or indirectly. In her family and in the social circles she frequented, sex was even discussed at all only rarely and in the form of euphemisms—"... and she was lost"; or, "the call of the flesh was stronger than the strictures of virtue"; or else, "he took advantage of her innocence." Sex resided in a remote and mysterious sphere that had nothing to do with everyday life. And so Ada had no idea that "being in love" equated with sexual desire. And her unsatisfied desire made her anxious and depressed.

André, for his part, never overstepped the bounds of cousinly flirtation. To him, the relationship with Ada was an extension of their childish games, but with an erotic component that added an exciting element of tension. He used Ada for his own amusement, indifferent to the emotions he might be stirring inside her. He did it without cynicism, perhaps without even being aware of it, having been accustomed since childhood to a state of naturally assumed privilege, as a male, and what's more, a male of high birth. Indubitably, he felt great fondness for Ada and appreciated her talent. Moreover, there was another factor that solidified their relationship. Ada, in some way, stood in for the person of the mother he'd never known, a void that had been left in his life. She was a stabilizing element that often served as a counterweight to his lightness of spirit. Just as Ada allowed herself to be transported by André's imagination, likewise André anchored himself to Ada's emotional balance, her commonsense instincts, and her center of gravity.

During those years they kept up a regular correspondence, even though it was Ada who wrote most often, and the longest letters; they also saw each other on various occasions. There were brief summer visits to Cortalba, where André arrived like a cyclone, bringing disarray and upset, only to part again the next day.

One time he came with his camera crew to get some footage from the tower. He was shooting a film set in the Middle

Ages; that day's scene involved the chatelaine who, from the top of the tower, sights Frederick Barbarossa's army marching on Asti to lay siege to the city. More than five hundred extras with helmets and halberds, recruited from the local peasantry, snaked slowly in a long procession like a massive python. Ambra Sylvestry, with a blond braid adorned with pearls, leaned out between two merlons to observe the enemy's advance; then, turning toward the camera, she opened wide her bulging eyes, heavily marked with dark eyeliner, and lifted both hands to her mouth as if to stifle a scream of horror.

Pietro had given permission to shoot the scene, because both he and Olga loved the arts and were open to new media and techniques. At the end of the day, they'd even offered the camera crew a glass of Moscato with a helping of Biscotti Torinesi. In that period, Ada had changed her mind about the movies. Having seen several of Pastrone's productions, she'd been forced to acknowledge that, in effect, the medium possessed considerable aesthetic potential. That day, André had been particularly gallant, holding hands with her and discussing the staging of the scene; he told her that she was the finest set designer he'd ever found and insisted on drinking with her from the same glass of Moscato. So unabashed was he that Ambra Sylvestry became jealous, and on the way back to town asked him whether Ada was his fiancée. "I only wish it were all so simple," André replied, "but the truth is much more complicated." Sylvestry couldn't figure out whether that meant "yes" or "no," but she consoled herself with the thought that that night André would be sleeping in her bed.

Her cousin's attentions continued to stir Ada's tenderest sentiments. She filled the interval between one meeting and the next with long letters, and fancifully anticipated the pleasure of seeing him again. Or else, for months at a time she'd relive the details of the last visit—like the last Christmas they spent together.

André had returned to Rome to spend the holidays with the family, as he did every year. On Christmas Eve they all went together to Piazza Navona to see the manger scene and the stalls selling nougat and dried figs. Hundreds of colorful hanging lanterns and the sounds of the bagpipes created a surreal and magical atmosphere. The cheerful throngs that filled the piazza pressed in from all sides and soon Ada and André found themselves cut off the rest of the group, all alone, clinging to each other in that sea of people. They continued along that way, from one stall to another; from time to time, Ada would rest her head on her cousin's shoulder, and he would turn his head to press a delicate kiss on her lips. After a while, they managed to rejoin the group. Elisa and her husband had been searching for them and were quite concerned; likewise, Lidia and Aunt Viola. Giulia and Luca, on the other hand, were intently gazing at the manger scene and peppering Monsieur Lesavoir with questions. He replied, doing his best to slip a little logic into the inscrutable mystery of the Nativity. Miss Langfield had momentarily forgotten the girls, while she was distracted by a couple of bagpipe players—*zampognari*; she wanted to convey to them, in her fairly rickety Italian, that they ought to use proper Scottish bagpipes instead of the local *zampogne*, because their sound was far superior.

"Hey, what the hell is the Stranger on about?" asked one of the two in thick mountain dialect. The other one shrugged his shoulders, "Who cares..."and they both went back to blowing into their pipes.

The magical atmosphere continued the following day. Especially in the evening, when the guests arrived and the great ballroom of the Ducati home filled with sounds and colors. The lights of the massive chandeliers were reflected in the multifaceted crystal pendants, multiplying a thousand-fold, and dancing with the couples on the shiny inlaid marble floor below.

Ada was wearing an off-white satin dress with an embroidery in tiny beads of colored glass; they depicted clusters of wisteria that descended from her shoulders and joined at the waist, and then cascaded down the drapery in the front of the skirt. In the back, the skirt clung to her buttocks and hips, and revealed the sinuous curves of her athletic yet feminine physique. The same wisteria branches made of beads adorned her hairdo and, on one side, hung down to caress her face. A modestly plunging neckline left her throat uncovered, and the short sleeves left her shapely forearms in plain view.

I'm describing a photograph, of course—and it's not entirely certain that it was taken on the occasion of that very ball. But it is certain that it dates from that period. Alma assured me as much, when I was a little girl leafing through the album with her. She told me, "Here Grandma was about twenty. Look at the refinement, such class." And she concluded with a disconsolate sigh, "And to think that she's been reduced to such a pitiful state... Poor woman!"

André put his arm around her waist and swept her into the whirl of a waltz. He seemed even more agile and elegant in the impeccable tailcoat that highlighted his broad shoulders and narrow waist. As they were spinning down the length of the ballroom, their image was reflected in the large mirrors with their gilt frames, situated between each window and the next. When they reached the last window, they slipped behind a velvet curtain.

The tourists crowded around the Trevi Fountain on the piazza below. Any of them who chanced to look up at the windows on the main floor would have seen, as if in some magic lantern show, dancing shadows going by behind the glass against an illuminated background; and in the panel of the last window, sheltered behind a heavy piece of drapery, a couple tenderly embracing.

In the months that followed, Ada entered a phase of high tension; the symptoms of "being in love" grew worse, her unease increased. She even made up her mind to take a trip to Turin, even though André had stopped insisting on that point. She begged Miss Langfield to talk Mamma into it. But Olga suspected the true reason and dismissed the request as unadvisable. Ada was forced to resign herself to wait for summer, when an opportunity to meet would certainly present itself. But what the summer had brought was the news of André's departure for America.

IV

After raising a toast to André's return, Leo felt a certain sense of relief. Now he could focus on a point in time, let's say, three years down the road, and then compress the time gap—exactly the way they do in the movies, where, in a case like this one, three years only last a few seconds: his son walks out the front door, there's a moment's darkness, then the same son comes back in through the same door, though maybe wearing a different suit, or now with a beard, to indicate the passage of time.

For the rest of the company as well, the wishes for a safe and happy return set a seal upon the farewell speeches. Over dinner, they talked of other things: domestic events, politics, high society. There was no talk of business because that was thought to be a vulgar topic in a social setting; Olga refused to budge on this point. If Pietro and Leo wished to talk about matters connected with the company, well then they'd just have to withdraw to the office.

Ada remained taciturn for the whole of the evening. She didn't want to think about André's return. She preferred to consider that break as the terminus, the end of their story. But she sensed that the story ought to have a real conclusion that might give it a significance in retrospect, when she thought back to it one day, and perhaps relived it, and even told others about it. These rationalizations had deep down an irrational cause, which could be summed up in her physical attraction to her cousin. And so Ada had made up her mind to spend that last night with André, even though the details of what that entailed still remained somewhat unclear in her mind.

Once everyone had retired for the night, Ada made sure that Lidia and Giulia were sound asleep; then she took a candle and, cautiously, left the bedroom that she shared with her sisters. She descended the stairs and walked down the dark hallways toward the suite of drawing rooms. André was staying in the study that was located on the ground floor of the tower.

Ada saw her own shadow follow her on the wall. When she reached the first drawing room, she put out the candle because it was a moonlit night. Her shadow vanished in the silvery light that poured in through the large windows. It was a night of ghosts, and Ada thought of the poor little marchioness, the Marchesina, who, according to legend, had been wandering the castle by moonlight for more than three hundred years now, having committed suicide for love. There were many versions of that story, some of them romantic, others tragic, and others still, salacious, featuring the parish curate as her lover. But they all ended with the violent death of the unhappy maiden.

Now Ada was standing outside the study door. Light was filtering out the cracks, a sign that André was still awake. Without knocking, she opened the door and walked in. André was lying on the sofa, in pajamas, reading a book; the jacket of the pajamas lay open on his chest, revealing his firm and well defined musculature.

The appearance of Ada made him leap suddenly to his feet. Buttoning his jacket, he took a step toward her.

"Ada, what's going on? What are you doing here at this time of the night?" He was gazing at her aghast.

Ada said nothing and didn't move, but just stood there

staring at him with an intense expression that said more than any words could.

André pretended not to understand and went on, "Aduccia, it's late. If you're planning to come with me to Genoa tomorrow, you need to get to sleep."

"I want to sleep with you."

André was forced to take her seriously now. He went over and gently took her by the hands. "My dear, you don't know what you're saying."

"Maybe I don't know what I'm saying. But I know what I want. And I want to be with you." Her tone was firm.

"That's not possible, Ada. There's no future for us. This might be the last time we ever see each other."

"But that's exactly why… at least once. . ."

André sensed Ada's misery and felt awful about being the cause of it. He led her to the stone bench built into the tower wall, beneath the Gothic arch window that allowed a slender shaft of moonlight to enter the room. They sat down.

"Ada, you have every right to your happiness, and one day you'll have it. You'll enjoy a happy life, but it won't be with me. I'm good at creating illusions, magical visions, colorful mirages, but in the everyday practical world, I'm a failure. You see, there was that fairytale of the girl who kisses the frog and he is transformed into a handsome prince and then they get married. With me, it would work the other way around; if I married you, I'd be transformed into a frog and you'd kick me out of the house. What I want, instead, is for you to always remember me as your handsome prince."

Now Ada was entirely calm and composed again. "He doesn't love me," she thought. That revelation hit her hard. She felt hollowed out but clearheaded. She stood up and said in a firm voice:

"You're right. I've never thought of you as a husband. I just wanted you for one night." Then she turned and left the room with a decisive step.

André stayed there for a long time, sitting in the shaft of moonlight, while his thoughts flew along the silvery wake toward the seductive adventure that awaited him across the ocean. But the Unknown, no matter how attractive it might be, still gave him a sense of anxiety. A heartbreaking nostalgia wormed its way into his soul: nostalgia for the good old familiar things; for the beloved people he was leaving behind; for Ada, so profoundly anchored to the soil, like the roots of the linden tree; for the scent of the linden tree blossoming; for the sounds and tastes of home; for the colors of the woods and the fields; and for the acrid odor of the stubble burnt on the bonfires of the nurturing earth.

Early the next morning, Giusto was waiting for the travelers outside the front gate. He'd harnessed the horse and loaded the baggage. When the passengers had gotten comfortable in the gig, he snapped the whip, yanked the reins, and shouted, "Giddyap!" The horse set off at a brisk trot.

When he returned from the train station, Giusto went to Pietro's study to deliver an account of the trip. He stuck his head in the door, "May I?" Pietro was sitting at his desk making notes on some papers. He looked up, "Come in, come in, Giusto. Well, has he left?"

"Yes, he left."

"And what kind of mood were they in?"

"The whole way there, they didn't say a thing. Signor Leo had a face on him… he looked like someone driving his son to the boneyard. Signorino André, too, wasn't himself; he wasn't moving, just gazing straight ahead with a fixed stare… like a man on the moon. Only Signorina Ada was normal, calm, like always. I'm glad she was there to tell me which way to go when we got to the station, otherwise the train would have left and—forget about it—they'd have missed it."

Pietro listened in silence and made a resolution to spend more time with Leo now that he was alone.

When they arrived in Genoa, Ada helped Leo to take care of the various bureaucratic procedures involved in boarding the ship, while André saw to the porters and the baggage. There was a huge crowd on the wharf around the ocean liner: many emigrant families with their bundles and their children, well-dressed couples embarking on a cruise, and corpulent businessmen. The line of emigrants snaked along a gangplank that led to the lowest deck, and from there they waved handkerchiefs and stuck their heads out the portholes to get one last look at the sorrowful faces of their families, before vanishing down a hatch and into the hull. The others climbed a larger gangplank that took them to the upper deck, and from there they were escorted to their comfortable cabins.

The time had come to say farewell. When André hugged them, both Ada and Leo were barely able to choke back their tears. André's eyes were glistening too, and he had to turn away quickly to conceal his emotion. He leapt lightly onto the gangplank and reappeared a few minutes later at the railing on deck, his silhouette standing out against the red sunset sky. The combo was playing a cheerful little tune, the flags were fluttering, as were the passengers' handkerchiefs, the boat horn blew and the ocean liner began to move.

Ada and Leo stood there on the wharf until the steamship was nothing more than a tiny black dot on the fiery western horizon. On the jetty, Christopher Columbus atop his monument was pointing his forefinger at André's ship. Locking arms, Ada and Leo turned and went home.

V

The portrait of Tunìn was almost done. Even though it was late afternoon, it was still very hot and Ada envied Maggiorina who was barefoot and bare-armed.

"Maggiorina, go get me a glass of water. I'm so thirsty," Ada said, fanning herself.

"Right away, Signorina." And Maggiorina was already on her feet, still clutching Tunìn close to her breast.

Ada abandoned herself to her thoughts. Letters had been few and far between ever since André had left, some of them addressed to her, others to Leo. She tried to understand what his life might be like in the godforsaken outpost—I had the opportunity to see the Taviani Brothers' *Good Morning, Babilonia!*, so I can at least visualize the situation, but Ada never had that aid. By putting together various snippets of information, she had assembled a rough picture of the life André was leading. His talent was valued, he had plenty of work, the resources to work with were as vast as the spaces of the California landscape; he lived in a white, Spanish/Mediterranean style villa, with orange trees that carried him back to his homeland, and exotic fruits called *avocados* that reminded him he was a stranger in a strange land. He was contented with his new world. Even though Ada missed him, she was getting used to life without him. But she felt no interest in her other suitors, however plentiful they might be, and Olga was starting to be concerned that at the age of twenty-four, Ada "was about to cross the threshold of spinsterhood." Ada spent lots of time with Leo. André's distance had brought her still closer to her uncle, who found comfort in her company.

"Signorina Ada!" Giusto called her as he came running, red in the face and out of breath. "Signorina Ada, Signor Pietro told me to tell you to hurry home because he wants to talk to you, to us, to everyone... Ah, filthy world of a world! What a disaster... what a disaster. They just brought a telegram from Rome..."

Ada didn't hear another word; she was already running out of the barnyard and up the lane. She was panting when she got at the top, hatless, because the hat had flown off her head as she ran. The others were all straggling in, one by one. They gathered in Pietro's study. They sat down.

Only Pietro remained standing, with his fists crammed against the desk as if to hold himself up. He looked at them all with a pale, grave face; then, with some effort, he began to speak.

"I've brought you all here because I have some very bad news. There was a strike at the plant. Violence broke out. Leo…" and here his voice broke and he was forced to pause, "Leo… is dead."

6

Red Carnations and Orange Blossoms
1914-1915

I

Reconstructing events through eyewitness accounts, police reports, and news articles, it turned out that Leo had been hit by a cop's stray bullet.

For some time now there had been civil disorders in Rome and other cities. On account of the war in Tripolitania, there had been a tax hike that had spread great discontent among the populace. In the most recent elections, the Socialist Party had doubled its seats in the Italian parliament—thanks in part to the fact that the male population had just won universal suffrage, including the working class, factory workers and manual laborers, so that the number of voters had risen from three million to more than eight million. The Socialist Party had become a formidable adversary in the political struggle, especially due to its opposition to the nationalistic tendencies of the conservative administration. Encouraged by the party, the workers often went out into the streets, especially now on the eve of the Great War, with Italy's neutrality in play.

In that hot summer, the party had ordered a strike. The Socialist cells at the Ducati plant had gone along out of solidarity with their comrades, but without any animosity toward the owners. Saturnino, over time, had established a solid relationship with the company's executive staff, especially with Leo, toward whom he had a great sense of devotion.

Many years had passed since their first meeting, which

Saturnino remembered as the day that forever changed his life, offering him the dignity of a job with decent pay and chances at advancement. The same opportunities were made available to Romoletto; having taken professional training courses, he soon became a floor foreman. From the very beginning, Saturnino was a member of the Socialist Party, but he always found himself torn between political ideals and the fondness for his employers. His role was above all that of mediator between the owners and the working collective, and he did his best to cool off the hotheads on the one hand and to win concessions on the other. He was especially vigilant in restraining the youthful impetuosity of Romoletto, who became the party's point man in the plant, calling assemblies and playing the part of political commissar and agitator.

The morning of the strike, Saturnino arrived in the factory at six in the morning, as was his custom. All was calm, the machinery was stopped, the workers were all gathering in the refectory for the assembly. Saturnino looked around for a young apprentice he could trust and put a sealed envelope in his hands.

"Son, I want you to take this to Signor Ducati. You have to give it to him, and no one else. This is important, now get going, run… and don't you dare to dawdle along the way, or I'll beat you like a drum."

The lad took off running and an hour later he reached the house on the Pincian Hill; he walked through the garden full of hydrangeas and, at the door, managed to convince the butler that he had to see Signor Ducati concerning an extremely urgent matter.

When Leo opened the envelope, he read:

"moust eksellent signò ducati. I want to camunicate to you that the strike is begun. our layborers are preparing for the prossession that's gonna go down into town where awl the other socialist prossessions will be assembling for the big

demonstrayshun. my son romoletto whose leading them tells
me that they're going to be marching against the war that
is taking all the lads and turning them into soljers and also
against the high prices of things and the low salleries to pay
for them. signò, the best thing would be if you stay home
because I hear that the gendarmes mean to stop the prosses-
sion outside the plant and that there's gonna be a fight. don't
ekspose yerself to danger. yours respeckfully saturnino."

It would have taken more than that to stop Leo. He immediately ordered the carriage to be readied and he arrived at
the plant just as the procession was exiting the gates, men and
women marching side by side, all of them wearing red neck-
erchiefs. Romoletto, in the front row, was carrying the party's
banner, while all the others carried signs with their demands.

Just then, a platoon of mounted gendarmes pulled up, ten
or so men led by a sergeant. They took up a position in the
street outside the front gate, creating a barricade. Leo ignored
them and headed for the gates. He found himself face to face
with Romoletto. The young man raised an arm and halted the
procession; then, he turned to Leo.

"Signò, I'm sorry to say but I can't let you in. The plant is
closed. The collective has occupied it and access is off limits."

"Romoletto, don't give me this trash. This is *my* plant and
I can enter it whenever I please. Where is Saturnino?"

"He's inside. He's standing guard while the procession
goes down into the city."

"Stand aside," Leo said in a peremptory tone.

Romoletto hesitated, swept his curly locks back from the
forehead, running a hand through his hair, and turned to look
at the comrades who were pressing in behind him. Impatient
voices were raised: "Hey, Romolé, you're not going to move,
are you?" "What are we doing here?" "Come on, show him
what's what!"

Leo took a step forward and tried to elbow Romoletto aside to make his way through the crowd. Romoletto wouldn't move. Others circled around Leo, enclosing him in a human vise. Leo flailed to break free of that encirclement. With a tremendous shove he knocked a man to the ground and emerged from the fray with his hair all askew and a torn sleeve.

The sergeant, who had just been waiting for any pretext to act, having noticed the gathering brawl, decided that the situation had become dangerous and ordered his men to open fire—in his report, he wrote that the workers had become violent and had opened hostilities by attacking the owner of the plant.

A burst of gunfire slammed into the helpless mass. Two men fell, mowed down by the bullets. Others were wounded, some in the shoulder, some in the leg, and were given aid by their comrades. One woman was hit in the eye, and she slumped to the ground, lifeless, her face transformed into a bloody mask.

Leo took a bullet to the chest, which sliced through an artery and penetrated his lung. He tumbled forward, into Romoletto's arms. Clutching the body to him as if in some final embrace, Romoletto raised a fist against the platoon and shouted, in a voice choked by emotion:

"You filthy sons of bitches! You killed him! You killed him!"

"Arrest that man!" ordered the sergeant.

Four cops got off their horses and waded into the group. Two kept their rifles leveled, the other two went over to Romoletto. Leo was laid down next to the other corpses on the jackets that the comrades had spread out on the cobblestone street. The bodies were covered by a blanket of red carnations that the men wore in their buttonholes and the women in their hair. All the voices fell still. Now there was a sacred silence. All that could be heard where the abrupt commands of the cops and the sounds of their busy activity.

Romoletto was led away in handcuffs. He passed between two flanks of comrades who stood motionless, hat in hand and faces frozen. Silent tears ran down from the women's fierce eyes. Romoletto marched between four gendarmes. It seemed as if his red neckerchief had spread over his white shirt, descending from his shoulders to cover his chest. It was Leo's blood.

After the investigation and the trial, Romoletto was given a thirty-year prison sentence for second-degree murder. The judge accepted the version of events set forth by the police, according to which Romoletto had assaulted Leo with a knife, stabbing him in the chest. The medical examiner's autopsy confirmed that the fatal wound was from a blade, not a firearm—though the weapon was never recovered. Several eyewitnesses described the events as they actually unfolded, but they were held to be unreliable because of their political beliefs and their close ties to the defendant.

Pietro never had the slightest doubt about Romoletto's innocence and he hired him one of the finest lawyers in Rome. He himself appeared before the court to testify on Romoletto's behalf; he spoke of his honesty, of his sound moral rectitude, of his devotion to the plant and his employers. But the judge found this testimony to be rather eccentric, and even unseemly, on the part of a respectable citizen whose brother had met his death at the hands of an "anarchist," and chose to have it stricken from the record. The police were determined to cover up their misdeeds and the legal institutions were determined to preserve the proper political and social equilibrium which alone could ensure the successful operation of the state. To declare a Socialist agitator innocent and the police guilty was tantamount to a subversion of the established order.

Saturnino witnessed Romoletto's arrest, because he had come running out of the plant when the burst of gunfire echoed through the air. He was devastated by what happened and he never quite recovered. He quit his job and withdrew to the mountains, where he lived alone with a flock of sheep to the end of his days. He only came down out of his alpine hut from time to time, to go visit Romoletto and bring him a basket of fresh cheese. When he died, already quite well along in years, Romoletto was still serving his sentence.

The news of Leo's death was telegraphed to America as a special, urgent dispatch. André was brokenhearted at the idea of missing his father's funeral, and mourned Leo's loss for a long time to come. During that period of introspection, he realized just how vast was the distance separating him from Italy. The physical distance, which could not be spanned by a simple day-long trip, and which had excluded him from an event of such vital importance, offered him a way to gauge the psychological distance that had come about, by now, between himself and the life that was once his.

André realized that the step he had taken was a definitive one. Now that Leo was gone, the links to his past were becoming increasingly tenuous. The reality in which he now lived absorbed him in an overwhelming, all-exclusive manner. Through his skin, he was absorbing the energy of that savage land, the force of its constituent elements, the powerful rhythm of the long ocean waves that broke against its coast, the allure of the vast spaces of the desert that freed his spirit. All these things fed his creativity and sustained the intense pace at which he was working. He'd already directed a great many films and was rising ever higher in the firmament of Hollywood. He wrote Pietro to say that he intended to become an American citizen and marry a producer's daughter. He meant to go into business with his fiancée's father, and to use part of the capital he'd inherited from Leo to do so.

Pietro liquidated his brother's assets and split up their shared property, and then he deposited Leo's share into André's account in an American bank. The plant was sold because Pietro was unable to manage it— his state of health was deteriorating from one day to the next—and he did the same with the construction business. In the process of completing this transaction, Pietro made sure that the pension fund for the older workers had been properly invested, and he also set up a lifelong annuity for Romoletto's wife and for the widows of the comrades who died during the strike.

Pietro also sold the villa in Ostia, at André's request. But he insisted on keeping in the family the house on the Pincian Hill, with its garden full of hydrangea bushes. Elisa's husband bought it and, over time, it filled up with a small army of children, because the young couple was fervent Catholics.

The house in Turin also remained in the family. After the death of the Ducati grandmother, Cecilia had taken the veil and withdrawn to the Ursuline nunnery. The house had been left vacant and so Pietro decided to buy it, purchasing both Leo's share and Nelli's. Subsequently, he gave the property to Ada as part of her dowry.

II

Life was no longer the same in Cortalba. A shadow of sorrow weighed over everyone and everything. To Ada's eyes, the foliage of the linden tree was no longer so green; the wisteria had faded, and was now verging on gray; and the crowns of the sunflowers in the farmhouse gardens had lost their golden splendor, now taking on the drab hue of polenta.

When October rolled around, Pietro decided that there was no reason for the family to return to Rome, and instead they extended their stay at the castle for the rest of the winter. Olga accepted willingly because she felt that the countryside was good for Luca. But the girls received the announcement as a grim condemnation. "They might as well have just locked us up in Bluebeard's room," said Lidia, alluding to the ancient prison cell high atop the tower that still contained chains and shackles dating from the Middle Ages.

There was nothing to be done. Like it or not, the girls were going to have to adapt. The rains came, along with the truffles and the roasted chestnuts. Then came the snow, and it transformed the gardens and the woods into an enchanted landscape. Ada painted, Lidia played the piano, and Giulia studied with Miss Langfield to complete her education. All of these activities, however, were secondary, because their chief responsibility was to care for Luca. Olga demanded their absolute devotion and availability. Luca was about ten years old and very far behind in his studies, despite the fact that Monsieur Lesavoir had applied special teaching methods. And in his everyday life, he required constant care and assiduous attention—at least, so Olga was convinced. In later years, the doctors who examined him as an adult said that it had in fact been his mother's overblown concerns that had kept him from becoming an independent and self-reliant person.

"Ada, put away your brushes and go play with Luca. Lidia, you too, stop strumming and spend some time with your brother. Giulia… where is she? Giulia's never around. You, girls, always leave that poor child all alone," Olga would lament several times a day.

"You always leave me all alone…" Luca would echo her, with a frown on his cute face.

Actually, though, his sisters were endlessly solicitous and they spent long hours with him perusing the illustrated volumes of the Imageries d'Épinal and glueing stamps into the album of his collection. They'd even invented a new game that often took up whole days at a time, "the photograph game." This game consisted of dressing Luca up in costumes from various historical eras and then photographing him in the appropriate context. They went through various phases: they had to come up with the scene, construct it, place Luca in the proper pose and the right light and, finally, take a series of shots from different angles. Luca enjoyed this game, because he was vain and he very much liked being admired. He was also flattered by the handsome costumes that Olga ordered made to measure from the tailoring shop of the Teatro Carignano, the most prominent theater in Turin; those costumes transformed him into exotic and charming characters. Here he is as a miniature Casanova, with a satin redingote, a white wig and a tricorne hat, as he gallantly bows to an imaginary damsel, somewhere outside of the frame; or else as a Renaissance page in hoses and doublet, sitting in a Savonarola chair in front of the vast fireplace in the grand hall of honor, holding a delicate lute in his lap; or, again, as a Little Lord, in a velvet suit, with his blond ringlets tumbling over a broad lace collar. Luca obediently followed all of Ada's instructions, as she had taken charge as director, and allowed himself to be positioned and poised like a mannequin—the head turned slightly more in profile, the arm a little higher, the leg less bent. Ada also tried to get him to put on the right expression, suitable to the character. Still, in spite of his sister's efforts, in all the photographs Luca is wearing the same stunned expression in his cerulean, lifeless eyes, and a faint smile seeking his audience's approval: "I'm handsome, aren't I?" he seems to be asking.

"Ah, my little darling!" Olga exclaimed as she dissolved into a puddle of delight. "I'll never get tired of saying it, you're the handsomest boy on earth. Come, come, a nice round of applause." And she clapped her hands, encouraging all those present to do the same. All of the domestic help were under orders to witness the final phase, the actual taking of the photograph, and to make a show of their approval with enthusiastic applause. Monsieur Lesavoir always made sure he was in the rearmost row so that his scanty enthusiasm might pass unnoticed.

Pietro refused to take part in those charades, to Olga's enormous disappointment. He remained shut up in his study, immersed in his thoughts. Thoughts that were anything but cheerful, because he realized that the end was nearing and that he would be unable to do anything more for Luca, to remove him from Olga's influence, to allow him to live a normal life.

Despite these distractions, life was sheer torture for the girls. They regularly received letters from Rome. Their girl-friends wrote them about receptions, the theater, art exhibits, fascinating new books, engagements and weddings, and they felt they were stranded in solitary exile. The castle was too empty without the cheerful summer company. Letizia and Riccardo spent the winter in Genoa at her home. Viola traveled with a lady in waiting and no one ever knew exactly where she was. Magda never budged from Paris. Leo and André were lost for good. That thought made the emptiness even more intolerable to Ada.

III

When a suitor stepped forward in springtime, Ada was ready to accept the offer of marriage. And in the fall she was married. The solitude and forced stay at the castle contributed to her decision. But these were not the only reasons. Ada had had a chance to evaluate her future husband, and to appreciate him, during the few short months of their courtship. Ernesto Bonardi was a gentleman, a landowner, and easy to look at, to boot—so much so that when he was a child, he had been called "*Ernestino bello*" because of his wheat-blond hair and his cornflower blue eyes. Now he wore glasses and his hair had thinned somewhat; to make up for that, he had a handsome handlebar mustache, the tips pointing rakishly upward. In short, he still struck quite a figure. Moreover, he had an artistic talent for photography, which in the years that followed offered him professional opportunities and even won him international recognition.

Ernesto lived in Colisso, a small town not far from Cortalba. Or really, we should say, his parents lived there. They were the owners of vast estates with wheat fields and vineyards. He had attended the University of Turin and had taken his degree in law; then he'd decided to stay on in the city, returning to Colisso only in the summer months. His parents were simple folk. His father, Giovanni, in his day, had taken a surveyor's diploma and had dedicated himself to running the small family farm he inherited. With time, Giovanni had managed to expand his landholdings, which now stretched as far as the eye could see, over fields and hillsides. Ernesto's mother, Almetta, took care of the home and the two children, Ernestino and Carolina, with the assistance of a pair of housekeepers, feeling perfectly satisfied with the life she led.

The only thing was that, at a certain point, she started to worry about Ernesto. It struck her that his life as a bachelor in the city wasn't quite respectable—even though, knowing her son as she did, she understood that his inclinations weren't so much for the cabaret, as for the intellectual and artistic circles. Ernesto had already turned thirty-five—he was midway upon the road of our life, as Dante famously put it, and now it was time for him to start a family and live like a Christian, as Almetta less famously put it.

And so she got busy searching for a suitable wife. She turned to Don Gerolamo, who as parish priest would know the parish priests of the neighboring towns, and instructed him to gather reports on potentially marriageable young women—from good families, attractive, with docile and God-fearing personalities. When it came to these prerequisites, Ada certainly possessed the first two; the second two traits weren't immediately apparent, but no one bothered about that. After speaking with Don Barbisio, Don Gerolamo asked Almetta to come to the rectory, where he could report to her on his findings. He told the sexton, using the local dialect, "Go call *Madama Bunàrd*. I need to speak with her."

And so Almetta learned about the Ducati daughters, the castle, and all there was to know about the family—

"They're genuine aristocrats," she thought to herself, "I'll have to tell Giovanni to put Ernestino in his will as universal heir, so that he can hold his head up in their presence. And as for Carolina... well, that's the way it is."

Don Gerolamo also showed her a photograph, borrowed from his friend the parish priest, showing the four girls and their little brother. "They look like the daughters of the Czar," Almetta commented. "There was a photograph in the news-paper. There was him, Nicholas, with the Czarina and their daughters. Identical. The same white dresses, the same hair-dos, the same poses, even the same little brother..." Luckily, they didn't meet the same fate, but that was something Al-metta couldn't know.

Almetta studied the photograph carefully, reasoning aloud about each candidate: "This one is married, so we'll discard her immediately [*scratch Elisa*]. This one's too young for Ernestino, the young ones are fuzzy-headed [*scratch Giu-lia*]. This one has a sweet little face but too frivolous, with that tip-tilted nose, and who knows if later... better not to run risks [*scratch Lidia*]. This is the one, a tranquil beauty, I can see from her gaze that she has deep thoughts, but no fire... you know what I'm talking about, Father."

"I know, I know. The things I hear in confession," said the good parish priest, rolling his eyes heavenward.

This conversation, like the one that followed between mother and son, took place in dialect, which was the language commonly spoken in Colisso. But I'll keep my readers from being subjected to the challenge of such a complicated form of spelling. Leaving aside the fact that south of the Po, Pied-montese is a foreign language.

"Which one?" asked Ernesto, gazing at the photograph once he'd been informed of the situation. Almetta laid a finger on the figure of Ada.

"You chose well. Still, you and your Don Girula[1] always stick your noses in my business."

"Don't call him that. He's a holy man."

"But that's what I've always called him. Ever since I started going to the Oratory. All the boys called him Don Girula. Not to make fun of him, but because we liked him, because we wanted to call him by a name we'd made up ourselves."

"All right, all right. But not in my presence. Now get ready to go meet her, and when you're there, take care not to act like a fool, because if she turns you down, then there's only one 'girula,' and that will be you. Now come here and give me a kiss... Go on, get away with you now."

The meeting went well and the wedding took place in September, in the chapel of the castle, which Pietro had had renovated while the main restoration work was underway.

The newlyweds patiently posed for the photographer: at the head of the procession emerging from the chapel, in smaller groups of guests skillfully choreographed, and all alone. Among the guests, who had come from Rome, Turin, and even Colisso, the men in frockcoat and top hat alternate with the ladies in light-colored dresses, forming a sort of checkerboard in black and white. The ladies wear broad fancy hats with undulating brims trimmed with ostrich plumes. The children in the foreground are all in white, the little boys in sailor suits and the little girls in organdy dresses with large bows in their hair.

The couple is photographed against a backdrop of wisteria—"That's real wisteria, you know," Almetta would always point out later when she showed the photograph to her girlfriends, disabusing them of the notion that it might be one of those painted backgrounds that were so often used in cut-rate

---

1. The nickname in dialect suggests the word 'fool', with an affectionate connotation.

photographers' studios. The photograph was probably taken after the ceremony because the bride and groom are standing close, intimately locking arms, their fingers intertwined. Ernesto has put the other hand in his trousers pocket in an effort to look nonchalant; his frockcoat is pulled back on that side and it reveals the dazzling white waistcoat, crisscrossed by an elegant gold watch chain. He seems contented. Even though his face is serious, his turned-up mustache gives him a cheerful look and his cornflower blue eyes, free of spectacles, are clearly smiling.

Ada's expression is less easy to read. We may perhaps glimpse the trace of a smile on the tranquil oval shape of her face, but it's an elusive smile, like Mona Lisa's. Who can guess what she was thinking that day beneath the white veil hanging over her forehead, held down by a small crown of orange blossoms. Her slender, lithe figure is highlighted by the cunningly cut wedding dress, medieval in style, like the dresses worn by the ethereal fairies in Art Nouveau-style illustrations. The simple silk muslin tunic is gathered by a ruffle just below the bosom, emphasized by a string of orange blossoms reminiscent of the motif of the veil. The tunic gently narrows around her ankles, and then spreads out in the back into a sinuous train.

They left that same day on their honeymoon. Descending the lane on Ernesto's arm, Ada turned for one last glance back at the old castle where she had been a little girl, and then a young woman, and to which she would return, of course, but in quite a different stage of her life, and with far different responsibilities. A phase of her life was coming to an end. With a lump in her throat, Ada raised her hand to wave goodbye to the little group that was waving back from the height of the Hello Garden. They were all there—Olga, Pietro, the aunts, the sisters, the cousins, Luca, Riccardo and Letizia, as well as Miss Langfield and Monsieur Lesavoir. They were standing close together, feeling safe, beneath the spreading umbrella of the linden tree.

* * *

The newlyweds were obliged to give up the traditional honeymoon trip abroad because Italy had entered the Great War just a few months earlier. All of Europe was a theater of war. And so they headed south and spent an enchanted month on the Bay of Naples, amidst the orange groves of Sorrento and the steep cliffs of Ravello that plunge down into the turquoise sea. The roar of the Austrian artillery as it mowed down Italian infantry along the line of the Isonzo front could not reach those mythical shores, and the harsh reality of that terrible war still hadn't touched their lives.

When they returned, they set up housekeeping in Turin, in the house on Corso Massimo d'Azeglio. This is where Gio was born. And, later, Mina.

Part II

Between Light and Shade

7

The Piave Whispered
1917-1919

I

Mina was born in a period of huge worldwide disruption. In that year, 1917, Europe was being ravaged by the Great War, the United States entered the conflict, and Russia embarked on its great revolutionary adventure.

The locomotive entered the large shed roof of the Porta Nuova station, puffing as it went. Ada was standing by the window and her eyes searched for Ernesto among the crowd packing the platform. She was tired and could detect a faint sense of nausea due to her pregnancy. It was the beginning of September. She'd had to cut short her summer holiday in Cortalba because the blessed event was drawing near and the doctor had ordered her to return to Turin in plenty of time.

She turned around to make sure that Gio and the nanny were ready to get out of the train. Gio, little more than a year old now, smiled at her and held out his arms while the nanny, tried to tie the laces of his bonnet.

"Nanny, get ready, because we're here. Now listen carefully, I want you to stay good and close to me when we get out, because the place is sheer pandemonium with all these soldiers rushing in all directions," said Ada with some apprehension.

The station was packed to the rafters on account of military transport trains. The ones that were departing for the front were taking on fresh troops, with boyish faces and brand new uniforms, just issued. The infantry marched in small units, with backpacks and rifles, doing their best to maintain their martial demeanor. But it was impossible to ignore the procession of women striding along beside them. Mothers, wives, fiancées, and sisters were calling them by name, and struggling to get closer, to give them one last embrace before they boarded the train that would carry them off.

One soldier stood on tiptoes and craned his neck:

"Maria, when I come back we'll get married!" he shouted to a young woman who was drying her tears with an oversized handkerchief.

"Mamma," shouted another, "I'll write you every day!"

And a third, "Gina, tell the children not to forget their Papà!"

When the train began to move, a sad song filled the air:

The transport train pulling out of Turin
no longer stops in Milan,
no, it goes straight to the Piave,
cemetery of our youth...

A sonorous wake of profound disheartenment trailed after the departing train. Ada opened her window to hear better, and she was struck by those words and their clear awareness of impending death.

It was the third year of war and things at the front were going poorly for Italy. The trains coming back from that part of the country pulled many Red Cross carriages. Out of those carriages soldiers would hobble on crutches, some of them hopping on a single leg; others with empty jacket sleeves, dangling inertly from their shoulders; still others with bandaged heads beneath their regulation kepi, supported by Red Cross nurses with white veils and blue capes. The stretcher bearers transported the most seriously wounded; they lay on their backs, their faces as white as the sheets that covered them.

Here, too, there were women. They awaited their men with trepidation, clearly afraid they might not see the face they loved emerge from that crowd. When they did find their man, they'd throw themselves into his arms. They greeted him, ignoring crutches and bandages, happy just to see him alive. Others would lean over the stretchers to kiss the wounded survivor, or to brush his forehead with a caress. The less fortunate ones would hide their faces in their hands, and sadly retrace their steps.

Distracted by that spectacle, Ada failed to notice that Ernesto had just approached the train. Now he was right beneath her window and was trying to attract her attention.

"Ah, here you are," said Ada when she saw him. Then, turning to look behind her, "Nanny, let's go!" She got out of the passenger car, reaching down for the supporting hand that Ernesto was extending in her direction. The porters were bustling along behind her, with suitcases and hatboxes.

Ernesto kissed her affectionately on one cheek and gave Gio's chubby cheek a playful pat. "Ciao, little one. How you've grown! It's been a month since I saw you last and already I don't even recognize you."

"Ernesto, let's not waste time. This place is a madhouse," said Ada, impatiently.

"Yes, you're right. I've hired a cab. It's waiting for us at the exit."

In the cab, Ernesto took her gloved hand. "And how are you, *chérie*? Everything all right?"

"Everything's looking normal. Professor DeBiasi spent a week in Cortalba and he had all the time he needed to observe me in various situations. He said that he foresees no complications."

"I'm sure of it. DeBiasi is a luminary in his field. You'll see, it will be just as easy for this boy as it was for Gio."

"It might be a girl," Ada retorted, with a hint of a challenge.

"I'd be only too delighted if that were the case," Ernesto replied. "Anyhow, Veglia has prepared everything."

"She's no doubt prepared everything after her fashion. There will be a great many things that need changing."

Ada didn't care much for Veglia, the maid that Almetta had sent her from Colisso immediately after the wedding. She considered her an inconvenient presence. Veglia came from one of the Bonardis' farmhouses and had entered the masters' service when she was still just a girl. She was about ten years older than Ernesto and, at the time, they had given her the job of keeping an eye on the boy and playing with him when the grownups were otherwise occupied. In Colisso it was whispered that later on, when Ernestino entered adolescence, there was also a romantic interlude between the two. That might just have been gossip; but even if it was the truth, these are the things that happen when you're young. Now Veglia was pushing fifty, and for some time there had emerged a clearly hierarchical relationship between the housekeeper and the master. She no longer called him "Ernestino," or even "Signorino Ernesto"; now she called him *Munsù Bunàrd* like all the others.

Almetta relied on Veglia's devotion and had insisted that she move to Turin and continue to look after her son. "Ada is a good girl," she said, "I'm not trying to imply anything. But these city signorinas aren't like us, and Ernestino is accustomed to being well cared for..." here her lips tightened with disapproval "...except when he lived in Turin all on his own, and I don't know how he did for himself then."

Veglia was docile and obeyed Ada's orders without ever venturing to contradict her, sighing in silence. Ada's hostility made her suffer, and there were times when she complained to Almetta. But her mistress insisted that Veglia had to accept that sacrifice for Ernesto's good, and Veglia resigned herself. Still, despite her apparent submissiveness, her sorrowful sighs revealed a latent critical attitude toward Ada. The more Veglia sighed, the more impatient Ada became. "Don't put on those airs of a wounded victim, or I'll send you packing, straight back to Colisso."

In time, they found a modus vivendi. Veglia took on the duties of the family cook, an activity at which she excelled, which limited her interactions with Ada to a single meeting each morning to decide the day's menu. But she remained an important, if unrecognized, presence in the home. During the last years, when Ada lay sick and immobilized in bed, Veglia was of immense assistance in the supervision of housekeepers and nurses, and a constant comfort to Ernesto. Despite her age, she outlived them both.

The cab proceeded slowly, due to the traffic. Trolleys, carriages, carts, and military convoys jammed the broad boulevard that ran straight down to the river Po from the train station — Corso Vittorio Emanuele, one of the main thoroughfares that intersect at right angles in the urban grid of Turin. This distinctive layout still bespeaks the origins of the ancient Augusta Taurinorum, erected on the street plan of the Roman military camp built by Caesar's legions in that northern outpost, during their challenging march into Gaul.

Along the road, Ada noticed a large poster for the Credito Italiano, a major bank. The imposing figure of an infantryman in a gray-green uniform emerged from a trench against the background of a spectacular explosion in shades of orange and yellow. His right hand firmly grasped the rifle, holding it vertically, a phallic symbol of power and daring; his left hand was pointed at the passing public, his forefinger at eye level to underscore the direct and imperious gaze from beneath the steel helmet. "All of you, do your duty!" read the slogan. Beneath that, the poster urged all Italians to underwrite the cost of the war through the National Bonds.

Ada thought of the special contribution that they too had

been obliged to make. Like all owners of urban villas, they had sacrificed the elegant wrought iron fence that enclosed the perimeter of the garden. It had been melted down to make cannons. A crew had come to rip out the metal fence and had replaced it with a wooden one, leaving—who knows why— only the front gate. And so it had remained until my times. I remember the villas along the tree-lined boulevard with their ornate front gates, and stretching out on either side, modest wooden fencing, disguised beneath dense growths of jasmine.

The cab turned down the side street, running alongside the garden and pulling to a stop in front of the door. Veglia was on the threshold to welcome them.

II

Two weeks later, a pink ribbon appeared on the front door. It remained there until the day of Mina's baptism, which took place in late November. The night of the ceremony it had snowed heavily, and the bow stood out against the unbroken whiteness of the winter landscape like an early spring bud. The few passersby smiled when they saw it, their spirits lifted.

Inside the house, there was considerable cheerfulness as well. Ada was receiving friends and relatives in the veranda overlooking the garden, where she had installed Mina's cradle. The trees and bushes covered with snow outside the plate glass contrasted pleasantly with the mild warmth of the radiators—an innovation that Pietro had insisted on installing in his day.

Almetta and Giovanni weren't up to undertaking the journey from Colisso and they settled for the photographs that Ernesto sent them. Almetta was proud of her little granddaughter and said so over and over again to anyone who would listen, "They gave her my name..." adding however with disappointment, "even if you'd never say so, because they just call her Mina, after all."

Olga came with Luca and stayed for two months. Pietro had died shortly after Ada's wedding. Olga no longer wished to go back to Rome. She sold her property in Palazzo Castellani and took up permanent residence in Cortalba with her son. She spent the coldest months of the year in Genoa, in her family house, together with Letizia and Riccardo, and she often went to visit one daughter or the other, invariably accompanied by Luca. Lidia had recently married a Roman judge, and had set up housekeeping in a six-story apartment building in the center of the city that she had been given as part of her dowry. Elisa, too, had remained in Rome and had gone to live with her numerous family in the house on the Pincian Hill. Giulia lived with Ada. She'd finished her studies with Miss Langfield and was now studying at a teacher's college. She intended to become an educator; but she had been unwilling to part ways with her eccentric governess, and Ada had gladly agreed to take Miss Langfield in, as well.

The veranda echoed with exclamations, laughter, and overlapping conversations. The presence of close relations helped to forget the war for a little while, to muffle the anxiety that the newspaper headlines infused into their souls. Missing among the guests were the young draft-age men. They were all fighting at the front.

Aunt Magda managed to send a letter from Paris, but she couldn't come in person because it was impossible to cross the border. She was all alone in her big, empty home. Francesco and Luigi had been drafted and the banker D'Ambrose had insisted on enlisting *"pour l'honneur de la France!"* in spite of the fact that he was fifty years old and had a weak heart. He died in the trenches, of a heart attack.

When Countess Zini arrived, the atmosphere grew sad. She'd lost her husband, a poet and a pilot, in a dogfight. She was dressed in mourning, with a black veil hanging from her hat and covering her entire face. Ada went to greet her, hugged her affectionately, and led her toward the cradle. At the sight of that grim figure, Mina took fright and burst into tears. Countess Zini wept as well, and then moved off with Ada into a quiet corner, where she proceeded to confide her sorrow to her friend.

"Poor Marisa," Ernesto commented. "And to think that we spent such lovely moments with her and Marino. He was a talented poet, a member of the avant-garde, a genuine innovator. Like so many of his fellow Futurists, he experienced his aesthetic moment in full. He'd even written as much in one of his poems: '*Death will fly with me / on the spread wings / of my steel Pegasus.*' "

Ernesto was speaking to Riccardo, who had come alone because by now Letizia was too fragile to take on the hardships of the journey. The two men were leaning against the far wall, taking in the overall scene.

"An enviable death," Riccardo replied. "They refused to allow me to go to the front, these days they only give me ceremonial responsibilities. I missed my chance to die young and with honor."

"Too many young men have died. Italy should never have entered this war. The Germans are slaughtering us."

"The blame belongs to General Cadorna, who had adopted the wrong strategy and let himself be caught flatfooted at Caporetto. He hadn't realized that von Bülow's troops were arriving to reinforce the Austrians. But now that the king has replaced him with Diaz, there's going to be a decisive turning of the tide. In less time than it takes to say, we'll drive the enemy back across the Isonzo line. Victory is assured. But it won't be easy, in part because of those ragged Bolsheviks, Lenin's revolutionaries, who seem to be interested in making a separate peace with the Kaiser."

"Peace wouldn't be a bad idea." Ernesto leaned down to pick up Gio. The little boy had crawled up to him, escaping his nanny's supervision, and now he was tugging on the hem of his trousers. With the baby in his arms, Ernesto continued, "This tense atmosphere, of sacrifice and uncertainty, isn't good for the children. You saw how Mina reacted. This generation will grow up with jangled nerves."

III

News arrived in early January that André was in a military hospital. The letter was in English. It came from American headquarters in France, but it was postmarked Milan. It was addressed to Olga. It informed her that Captain André Ducati had been wounded on the field of battle at Caporetto and had received multiple injuries, including a serious head wound. He'd been given first aid on the spot, and had then been transported to the American hospital in Milan. After two months in the hospital, his general state of health had improved, but it was feared that he would remain blind. Major Spencer, who had signed the letter, also wrote that Captain Ducati was not yet ready to be moved, but that when the weather improved he hoped to spend some time in Cortalba before going back to America.

Later, the family learned directly from André the circumstances that had taken him into the thick of battle. When the United States decided to join the war and sent their expeditionary force to Europe, André felt it was his duty to support Italy in the war effort. But he wanted his contribution to take the form of communication, not combat. He wanted to shoot documentaries on the fighting at the front: to record the reality of trench warfare, the conditions under which the soldiers were fighting, their daily life under enemy fire, the happenstance of their deaths, like birds in a hailstorm.

He obtained permission to join ranks as an American officer with the Italian army fighting on the Austrian front, even though the United States had not declared war on Austria, only on Germany. There were other foreign soldiers like him—Americans, British, and French—who preferred the eastern front. They considered it to be more "picturesque." But after the unexpected German attack at Caporetto, there was no longer any difference. Among the Americans, there was a young man named Hemingway, barely eighteen. He was an ambulance driver, but before enlisting he had been a journalist. He made his observations concerning the war, and described episodes and individuals in a vivid writerly language, occasionally consulting the Moleskine notebook that he kept in the breast pocket of his jacket. André had spent many evenings with him at the officer's mess, together draining many bottles of grappa. These conversations gave him ideas for his documentaries.

The day of the attack, André was shooting the scene of the infantry in retreat. In the confusion he lost his helmet, more concerned with protecting the movie camera than himself. A phosphorus shell exploded just a few yards away. The explosion destroyed the movie camera and caused serious fractures throughout his body. A blast of flame hit his face. After that, all André remembered was waking up again at the camp hospital in complete darkness.

He recounted these details when he came to Cortalba in May. He arrived by car, accompanied by Major Spencer and an attendant named Billy whose job it was to assist him, invalid that he now was. He'd completely recovered the use of his legs and he could get around without crutches, but he still wasn't entirely used to the long white cane that served to help him find his way, and he required the eyes of a sighted guide.

Major Spencer stayed on for a few days because he wanted to visit the medieval abbeys in the area. In civilian life he was a professor of art history at Georgetown University. He spoke Italian, having studied the language, along with the country's art and culture. Sitting under the linden tree at tea time, he conversed with Olga.

"I got to know Italy before the war. I'd come here for study and research. I saw magnificent frescoes, spectacular cathedrals, masterpieces of painting and sculpture; I made acquaintances with fellow professors and functionaries at the ministry. In other words, I saw the 'official' face of Italy. But in the past few months that I've spent behind the line, I saw the real Italy. Soldiers and civilians, simple, courageous people. They don't believe in this war, but they do their duty, the way they have for centuries. Without them, there would be no great works of art, because those artworks were all built on their backs."

"Yes, they're good people," said Olga. "But most of all, we're lucky to have an enlightened monarchy that will lead us to victory. And we're also grateful to the United States which has intervened as an ally of the Triple Entente."

Spencer half-smiled, but the blue eyes beneath the blond bangs remained serious. "These days, governments fight over maps, but men combat on the field of battle. If the bombs exploded on the maps, there would be no more wars."

Olga looked at him, baffled, and thought to herself that maybe the major just didn't know how to express himself clearly in Italian.

At that moment, André arrived, escorted by Billy. Their heads emerged from the steep little lane that ran up to the Hello Garden. The effect was of a sudden apparition, because people remained hidden behind the boxwood hedges until they reached the summit, and then came into view all at once.

"Andy, over here!" shouted Spencer to guide him with his voice.

They had met in Milan, where André had been transferred during the retreat of the Italian troops. The little field hospital on the banks of the river Piave, where he was taken in at death's door one rainy night, could offer no more than the most rudimentary forms of first aid. Lying on his cot in those first few days, André was unable to see the surrounding scene, the hustle and bustle of surgeons and nurses, their lab coats spattered with blood, hands and arms gruesome and red up to the elbows, dark circles of exhaustion under their eyes because of the unbroken shifts at the operating table. But even in his state of semi-consciousness, he could still perceive the horrible screams of soldiers having their arms and legs amputated, with only a glass of grappa for anesthesia.

Spencer worked at the American hospital in Milan. His job was to act as liaison between the wounded soldiers and their families. He was responsible for visiting the patients, establishing a human relationship with them, offering the comfort of a conversation, and then assisting them with their correspondence and personal contacts. He also served as a middleman between patients, doctors, and the high command when, once their hospitalization came to an end, it became necessary to decide whether to send the wounded man back home or back to the front. When he learned that André was Italian, the bedside conversations became lengthier and more frequent. They would talk about art, in particular, and the movies were included in that category. But they'd also talk about politics, making observations about how the finest films of those years, *Cabiria* and *Birth of a Nation*, formed part of a "hegemonic discourse," each in its own context. Of course, they didn't use those exact words, because such terminology was not in common use prior to Gramsci and Foucault. But they realized that art inevitably contains a political message, as an expression of the historical and social context, even when it is being presented in purely aesthetic terms.

A few at a time, everyone showed up, as was customary, for the afternoon tea. That day Uncle Candy was there too. He had come especially from Turin to see André. It had been, in fact, André who had first called him Uncle Candy, when he was still just a little boy, and the nickname stuck for generations to come. Uncle Candy was Olga's brother, and he was the co-owner of the renowned confectionery company B&M, which ran a pastry shop and tea room on Piazza Castello, displaying the refined décor of the Piedmontese Settecento. When they were still kids, André, Ada, the sisters, and especially Luca hardly knew where to begin when Uncle Candy arrived with his exquisite delights. They'd tear open sacks made of shiny paper, untie colorful ribbons, break the seals on golden boxes, and unleash cascades of candies and chocolate bonbons. The candies were all wrapped individually, with legends written in different colors according to the flavor—strawberry, lemon, mulberry, plum—and the two ends of the wrap were twisted in a way that made them look like two fish fins, or two butterfly wings. André used to say that Uncle Candy was "the sweetest uncle he had," because of the fragrance that wafted off of his packages.

Now, sitting in the family circle, André joked, "Uncle Candy, I can see you with my nose. You never lose your sweet fragrance."

"I brought you your favorite candies," the uncle replied, feigning cheerfulness.

Ada sat down next to André to help him with his teacup. She enjoyed doting on him in these small things. The passion that had once been there had died away by now, replaced by a sentiment of maternal solicitude. For her, their romantic interlude had ended years ago, giving way to the reality of a comfortable domestic life, though one that was punctuated by dissatisfactions and occasional bursts of irritation. She had even given up painting, little by little, without fully realizing it. The preoccupations of house and family prevented her from finding the required concentration. Moreover, there was already an artist in the family, namely Ernesto, and rather than competing with him, she preferred to participate in his photographic pursuits by posing for his compositions. She had the figure and the talents of an actress, as revealed by many photographs that have since become collector's items.

André frequently sought out Ada's company. As he had long ago, he found a sense of stability with her. Through her eyes he regained the world that he had abandoned, but not suppressed, and which now reemerged, insistent, overlapping on the images of his present life—the white house on the green lawn, the blue swimming pool surrounded by palm trees, the wife on the lounge chair with her long legs stretched out in the bright sun, the children on the grass with their nanny.

He liked to sit with Ada at sunset, on a bench along the "observation wall," with his face turned toward the tower. He'd question her, and Ada would answer.

"The sun behind us must already be quite low. What color is the tower?"

"It's pinkish, but in the shadow zones it's a reddish brown, and the gaps, where a brick or two is missing, are so many dark patches. There's no light there at all."

"And the ivy?"

"The ivy has grown considerably, and now it covers it all the way up to the fourth floor. It contains a thousand nuances of green, depending on the location and density of the leaves. There are tufts of a deep green, because from here you only see the backs of the leaves, where the sun doesn't shine. But at other locations, where the leaves display their surface, the effect is that of a brushstroke of silver. Where the ivy works around the windows, leaving them uncovered, the sun lights up the glass panes with a luminous reflection that takes on the same coloration as the vegetation itself."

"I can hear the swallows flying around the tower. It sounds like there are lots of them. Right? Are there lots?"

"Lots and lots. Like every year. At this time of the evening they wheel around in a frenzied rush. They form a dark ring against the sky."

"And have they already nested? Do you remember when we went hunting for the baby swallows that had fallen out of their nests, to rescue them? We never did manage to find a single one still alive. They shattered themselves when they fell from that height. And even if they did survive, cats were sure to eat them."

"You shouldn't have reminded me. It's a horrible thing. It makes me shudder."

"Sorry, I didn't want to upset you. What else do you see in the garden?"

"There's the wild grapevines, with white grapes the size of medlars, just a few, two or three in each bunch. They run along the wall, and at one point they climb over it and descend like a cascade to the piazza in front of the church. And there's the imposing looking Osage orange tree, it still bears that exotic fruit that looks just like ordinary oranges."

"We were so tempted to eat them, but they told us ten times a day that they were poisonous, and we never dared to try... What else?"

"And then there are the palm trees. African palms, short, squat, with hairy trunks..."

"I remember them, I always thought they were so out of place in this setting and this climate. There are palm trees where we live in California, but they belong in that landscape. They're tall and flexible, they twist and bend in strong storms. We have wind storms in summer, and they can be scary, but they're always a spectacular show."

Ada brusquely changed the subject. "André, we know so little about you. We didn't even know you were in Italy with the army. You never wrote us about your children, your wife, or your life. Your family must be very important to you if it replaced us all."

"Cathy and I have three children. The youngest, Leo, was born when I was at the front. I decided to name him after father. Maybe I was influenced by the fact that I was in Italy and I felt I had come back home. The eldest, Jane, is three, and Jimmy is a year and a half."

"You must miss them terribly. I couldn't live for a long time far from Mina and Gio."

"I do, I miss them very much, but especially I miss Cathy. It was hard to pull myself away from her."

"Do you love her so much?"

"I do love her, but that's not the crux of the matter. It's something more than that. Cathy has become an obsession for me. She's a beautiful woman, and she's also fickle and capricious. She was raised like a princess, and her father granted her every slightest wish. And the same was true of the swarms of men who came courting her. I don't know why she married me. Maybe because I possessed a certain exotic allure—the allure of the Latin lover. Or else it might have been because her father appreciated me as a partner and encouraged his daughter's interest. I believe that she loves me. I wouldn't have married her if I hadn't believed that. But Cathy isn't a typical wife. Even after we were married she continued to have suitors and to attend the parties of the Hollywood aristocracy, actors' mansions, restaurants, and nightclubs. I go with her when I can, but often I'm busy. She always tells me that I'm the only one who matters to her. That all the others are just family friends, companions, squires for an evening out. But still, I'm jealous. Insecure. Because Cathy is elusive. I can't seem to possess her. You see, in many couples there is discord between husband and wife, they come close to hating each other, and yet they can't do without each other either, there's a symbiotic dependency. Between the two of us, on the other hand, there's a perfect accord, especially when it comes to sex, but there's no symbiosis. Cathy is still independent. I'm not indispensable to her. She can live without me."

"You'd like to control her, maybe even subject her to your will, but circumstances make that impossible. You feel like you are her husband, but not her master, and you're incapable of resolving this dissonance. That's why you're obsessed."

"I have no interest in these psychological nuances. All I know is that I'm jealous."

"But it's all too clear that you're still thinking in terms of the Italian way. Here, the husband is always the master. Even in the best of cases, when we're talking about a good, mild-mannered husband. Like Ernesto, for instance. It's not up to him, it's a matter of convention and social norms. Certain suffragist movements insist that it's also a political matter, because women don't enjoy the same rights as men; but I'm not sufficiently well informed on these notions to delve into the subject. In any case, it's enough to take a look at the way people live. There are very few women who consider their condition to be a fair one. Most of them resign themselves to accepting the status quo, and manage to carve out their own personal niche of moderate independence, defending that territory with small acts of domestic rebellion that are promptly dismissed as capricious. But there are also women who can't adjust, and they slip into neurotic fits or even wind up committing suicide."

"Aduccia, you're blowing my head up like a balloon. What's going on? We were talking about swallows and wild grapes... how did we get to women committing suicide? Wait, I want to show you a photograph of Cathy with the kids, maybe that'll help you understand. She sent it to me after Leo was born."

Cathy is sitting in an armchair. She's holding the newborn child on her knees, and he emerges from a cloud of organdy and bows. Jane is standing beside her, her long blond hair fastened on the top of her head by an artistically knotted ribbon. She has one hand resting on the baby's lace cover and she's turning her head three-quarters to observe her new brother. Even with her head turned, it's easy to see that she's very pretty and that she resembles her mother. Jimmy is sitting astride the armrest and looks as if he's having the time of his life in that unusual and privileged position. Cathy has one arm around his waist to make sure he doesn't fall. They form a tight little group, a composition without voids, cemented by the convergence of their gazes.

Ada thought that there was no room for André in that photograph. But she said nothing. She paid him many compliments for his lovely family. Then she asked, "André, has Cathy heard about your disability?"

"Yes, they contacted her from the hospital."

"And how did she take it?"

"She thinks I'm going to recover. She's convinced that with the medical treatments we have in America, I'll recover my sight. Otherwise, she says, how will I be able to keep working in the film industry?"

"That's the point," thought Ada. And she felt a surge of pain for him. *"The trauma is permanent, all the doctors are in agreement. He won't be able to make movies anymore."*

She took his hand and said, "That's what we all hope."

IV

André left at the end of the summer, right after Mina's first birthday. A car sent by Major Spencer came to pick him up and take him to an American navy ship that was returning home with a cargo of invalids. Roughly a year went by before Ada had any news about his state of health. The news that arrived, albeit indirect and fragmentary, made it clear that André's life had completely fallen apart.

It was a letter from Billy to Olga. Ada translated it because Olga had a hard time reading English:

> *My dear lady,*
> *I'm writing to you in hopes that you can and are willing to let me have Captain Ducati's current address. When he took ship, I returned to the front and remained there until the end of the war. After I returned home, I went to his home in Hollywood to see him, because I had grown to consider him a friend during the months in which I served as his at-*

tendant. While I was there, I learned from a member of his domestic help that his wife had filed for divorce and that, with her father's assistance, she had succeeded in gaining control of the captain's entire estate. All that is left to him is his military pension and he has been committed to a rest home for invalided veterans. I wrote to Major Spencer, but he too has lost touch with the captain because he now lives in Italy, where he is a professor in an Italian university. I therefore hope that you can assist me by sending me the captain's address, which he must certainly have communicated to you. Thanks very much for your help, with my warmest regards, etc. etc.

It was a harsh blow for them all. It took years before Ada could think of André at all without a crushing sense of grief for the injustice involved in his tragic fate. Olga too was heartbroken for her nephew; what's more, she was bitterly disappointed at the loss of half of the Ducati fortune—Leo's entire share. They hired lawyers. Ernesto took charge of that aspect. They tried to reach out to André's ex wife, but they received a letter from her lawyer informing them that she did not wish to have any contact with the family and that Mr. Ducati had left no forwarding address. They did their best. They even wrote to the Veterans Bureau, but their efforts amounted to nothing. Little by little, they consoled themselves with the thought that one day André himself would get in touch with them.

Meanwhile, life went on, now in an atmosphere of optimism for the signing of the peace treaty. After the battle of Vittorio Veneto, *"victory unfurled its wings in the wind,"* the Piave campaign entered the realm of legend, and the dead became heroes. Those who survived it with their bodies and their lives torn to shreds, like André, were gradually forgotten.

8

To Arms, We're Fascists
1927

I

This photo isn't in the album. It's framed—a 12x16-inch en-largement—and it's on a wall in my living room. It's a study in chiaroscuro, an art photograph, one of the many works that Ernesto produced over the years. The large glass door to the greenhouse is letting in a shaft of sunlight. The round arch of the door fits into the larger arch that is the curve of the vaulted ceiling. This two-fold motif serves as a background to the two female figures seated in the radiant spray of light that comes from the garden. They constitute the focal point, in the middle ground, at the center of the frame. Their light, translucent dresses accentuate the interplay of light. Their pose echoes the arch motif and completes it, forming a circu-lar composition. They're both leaning slightly forward, their heads practically converging. They are observing a piece of embroidery they're holding in their hands and which joins the curved line of their arms. Their knees are almost touching, as are the pleats of their dresses and the tips of the slippers that emerge from beneath them. The two figures are contained in a luminous circle formed by their own bodies.

Mina is wearing a particularly elegant dress. She had been given it the day before for her birthday party. She'd just turned ten, and that struck her as a major milestone. Ada too is ele-gant in her filmy chiffon dress. Fashion had changed since the days when women wore "boaters" and ties; now she is wearing short sleeves, above the elbow, and her neck emerges unfettered from a comfortable neckline.

They'd taken their seats on the chairs arranged in the area with the ideal lighting and were just waiting for Ernesto to finish readying the camera.

"I'm thinking about yesterday's party," Ada said. "It really turned out well. You stood out among the other children, so lovely, my little dragonfly. I received lots of compliments for you from all the guests. Did you have a good time, sweetheart?"

"It would have been a nice party, but there was too much chocolate in the cake, and I like vanilla frosting. The cook knew it, but she always does what Gio tells her."

"Who, Pina who loves you so well?"

"No, the new one. Elvira."

"Did Gio tell her to put the chocolate in the cake?"

"Yes, yes, it must have been him, because he likes chocolate, and so does everyone else. So they just ruined my party."

"Eh, men..." said Ada, as if emphasizing the point that they're all the same. "Gio is a good boy, but he's just like his father. Men don't have our sensibility. You know what? Tomorrow let's go to Asti, and I'll take you to that pastry shop, the Pasticceria del Corso, and we'll get beignets with vanilla cream. All right?"

"I don't want beignets. All I wanted was a nice party, and instead they ruined it for me," said Mina with the demeanor of someone who's suffered an irreparable loss, a loss that no beignet can ever make up for.

"I'm ready," said Ernesto, coming over. "Take your poses." Ernesto too had changed in appearance since their wedding. He no longer had a handlebar mustache, but a short and fashionably well trimmed one—as it was called back then, "à la Menjou."

"But Ernesto, don't you see that Mina is upset? Wait a moment, couldn't you? Try to show a bit of sensitivity," Ada rebuked him, as she dried two fat tears rolling down the little girl's cheeks.

"Ah, of course, of course, *pardòn.* Just tell me when you're in the right frame of mind…" And he muttered to himself as he walked away, "It's just that then the light will have changed." Evidently, the light didn't change, because the photograph was a masterful success and was then exhibited in many art shows.

II

After the long pose, when Ernesto finally uttered the long awaited words, "I'm done. You can go," Mina jumped up from her chair and galloped off to her bedroom to change out of her party dress and into the cotton smock that was her ordinary attire.

She dressed in great haste, inserting the buttons into the wrong buttonholes, so that the dress is all tilted to one side. Mina paid no attention to these details; there was always someone who straightened things up for her—the housekeeper, Ada, and even Gio sometimes. But, despite all the attention she received, Mina always seemed to have a ribbon slipping out of her hair, a stocking that drooped, or a dress stained with fruit and gelato. After changing, she rushed down the stairs and out into the garden to catch up with Marilù who was waiting for her as was her custom in mid-afternoon. That day, Mina was running late.

Marilù was her favorite cousin and her best friend. But in the family, within her dense network of cousins, Marilù and her brother Piero occupied a position that was far from privileged. When they gathered in Cortalba during the summer, Elisa would arrive from Rome with her five children, all in progressive scale—I only remember the names of the two eldest girls, the twins Marta and Chiara. Lidia too would arrive with her children, Lucilla and Marcello. When they were there, and with Mina and Gio, the castle filled up with sounds and colors. Olga and Luca gladly welcomed that cheerful crew who broke the monotony of the bucolic tranquility.

The children in Cortalba enjoyed a great deal of freedom, provided they remained behind the castle walls. From the age of eight or ten years on, they could freely roam without supervision through the grounds and the woods. But Giulia's children didn't enjoy the same favor and they only formed part of the group to a marginal extent. They didn't stay in the castle, but in a modest little house just outside the perimeter of the walls, which belonged to their father, the fascist-appointed mayor of Cortalba, the *podestà* Aurelio Costa. One side of their garden was delimited by the castle's southern wall, which towered thirty feet overhead. From that height, Mina and Gio would lean over to call Piero and Marilù when Olga gave them permission to invite them up. The invitation, however, was always extended with a restrictive rider: "Grandma said that you can come, *but after snack time.*" The messengers relayed Olga's words with great nonchalance, unaware of the wrong they were inflicting on their cousins. If anything, they were happy that they'd been able to deliver this good news. Those feelings, for that matter, were fully shared by Piero and Marilù, because it never would have occurred to anyone to think that their world was anything less than perfect.

When she was in her declining years, Alma thought back ruefully to the exclusive snacktimes and the excluded cousins. Telling me this story for the umpteenth time, she admitted with real regret, "I lived superficially, without realizing so many things." Perhaps Marilù, too, thought back with regrets. In any case, she had a very troubled life that ended in tragedy. When she was still in her early forties, she committed suicide: she turned on the gas and caused an explosion. The firemen found her charred corpse on the kitchen floor.

To go back to that summer, Mina had wrangled permission to invite Marilù over every afternoon, and she was very pleased because she didn't get along with her other cousins.

"Marilù! Come over, it's time," called Mina, poking her head over the top of the wall.

"Coming right away."

In two minutes, Marilù was at the little gate between their two houses. Mina welcomed her in and together they headed off to the belvedere under the cedars of Lebanon. That belvedere was their favorite place to play.

"What shall we play today?" asked Mina.

"Let's play store."

"No, we played store yesterday."

"Well then, let's play seamstress shop."

"But we don't have the tape measure or the pins, we'd have to go get them. No, let's play school."

"Yes, yes. I'll be the schoolteacher."

"No, I'll be the schoolteacher."

"But you're always the schoolteacher. It's not fair."

"I'm the one who invited you over. So I get to choose."

"All right. But only if you promise that next time it's my turn."

"Yes. I promise."

They got notebooks and pencils out of a secret hiding place in the trunk of one of the cedars and Marilù sat down on the little bench. Mina found a stick and rapped the top of the railing three times sharply:

"Silence! When I'm speaking I don't want to hear a fly buzz. Yesterday, I assigned you a passage to read: 'My duties as a Young Italian Girl.'[2] You, Costa, give me a verbal summary."

"Stop!" Marilù exclaimed as she raised her hand to stop the game. "I didn't read that passage."

"Then you just make it up. Come on, let's continue."

"Young Italian Girls have many duties. But their first duty … umm… their first duty is to attend the assemblies. They al-

---

2.   In Italian: Piccole Italiane, the national fascist youth organization for girls.

ways have to make sure their uniforms are clean and pressed and deliver the salute with their arm straight in the air. They also have to know how to march without falling out of step…"

"Costa! These are details. Get to the meat of the matter."

"But these are very important things. My Papà, who is the podestà, after all, always says so." Whenever she was having difficulties, Marilù fell back on the stratagem of citing her father, who was the most important local authority.

III

When Giulia met him, nine years earlier, Aurelio wasn't podestà; he was a handsome young man with great expectations, but he "hadn't a penny to his name," as Olga wryly said.

Olga had consented to their marriage reluctantly. She'd given in to her daughter's insistent requests only because she had realized that Giulia was going to get married no matter what, with or without her permission. Perhaps Pietro would have been able to exercise his paternal authority. But Pietro was gone now, and Olga preferred not to make the situation worse by putting up any opposition. Still, her hostility toward her son-in-law remained unmistakable and, indeed, extended to include Giulia and their children.

The Costas had always owned the small house beneath the castle wall. No one could remember when and how they had arrived, but already in the years when Pietro first bought the estate, the Costa family vacationed in Cortalba every summer. Even though Aurelio was the same age as the Ducati girls, over the course of the years they had never developed any relations. The Costas were never invited to the castle, except for the day of the annual charity benefit, when the gates were opened to the public. The wall that divided the gardens separated two worlds as well. The Costas owned a stationery shop in Turin and they led a modest but dignified life. Olga tried to dissuade her daughter from that marriage with an argument that struck her as irrefutable: "They may be perfectly respectable people, I wouldn't know, but they're just shopkeepers."

"I don't care. I love him."

"You've let yourself be swept away by Miss Langfield's overactive romantic imagination. And to think that we've only ever been generous to a fault with that woman..."

"Miss Langfield has nothing to do with it. I decided all on my own."

"Giulia, think carefully. You'd be uncomfortable around us. Look at your sisters: Elisa married an ambassador, Lidia married a senior magistrate, and Ada married a large landowner. And this Aurelio, what is he?"

"He's an accountant."

"Exactly. It doesn't surprise me one bit that he sees this as a good place to hang his hat."

"Mamma, you're not being fair. Aurelio loves me."

"All right. Since you're going to be so stubborn, I won't oppose the marriage. But I'll give you a dowry befitting your new husband's condition, a very small sum in cash and nothing more. Leaving aside the fact that you deserve nothing better, I have to preserve Luca's inheritance until he reaches age twenty-one, in keeping with your father's will."

The wedding was held in the parish church, not in the castle chapel. And the reception was a small affair, with only a few guests. Aurelio's parents were able to go up to the castle with a personal invitation for the first time, but that was also the last. Giulia herself only went up there from time to time, and Aurelio in turn accompanied her even less frequently. They were happy, that way, in their untroubled family life, until adverse circumstances intervened to turn their lives upside-down.

They met by chance in the summer of 1918, when Aurelio returned from the front. He was one of the fortunate combatants who hadn't suffered any grave injuries. Despite the fact that he had experienced hunger and cold, his robust constitution had seen him through. Aurelio was an athletic young man, a member of the Rowing Club of Turin, where he trained for races on the river Po. During a stay in Cortalba a minor mishap occurred that brought Giulia into his life—an entirely routine episode that had serious consequences, the way things happen in novels.

"Lillì ran away! Lillì ran away," Luca was shouting. "Hurry! Go catch him!" Luca was weeping and increasingly upset; his doggie had run out the little gate, which someone had carelessly left open. Though he was fifteen years old, Luca had slow reflexes and moved awkwardly, so he went into a state of despair and remained glued to the spot, with no idea what to do.

Giulia came running at the sound of his cries. "Where did he go?"

"That way, out the gate," said Luca, pointing his finger.

Giulia went running out the gate and looked in both directions. The piazza in front of the church was deserted and there was no sign of Lillì. Before she could make up her mind whether to turn right or left, she heard a high-pitched, insistent barking along with a soothing male voice saying, "Good dog, good dog. Now come here and I'll take you back home."

The voice came from the garden of the house next door. A moment later, Aurelio emerged from the front door with Lillì in his arms. When he saw Giulia, he walked toward her with a broad smile.

"I imagine you're looking for your dog. It got into our back garden and I was just returning it. I knew that it came from the castle, because they don't have dogs like this in town."

"I can't thank you enough, and I apologize for the trouble Lillì has caused you."

"No trouble, no trouble at all… My dear Lillì, I'm afraid here is where we part ways, we spent far too short a time together. Come on, now, be a good girl and go back to your young mistress."

"Lillì is my brother's dog," said Giulia, taking him from Aurelio's arms. "This is his third Volpino Italiano, and he looks exactly like the other two. And they're all named Lillì, even the males, like this one."

"That's a new one on me," said Aurelio, laughing heartily.

"That was what the first dog was named, a little female. But she died young because she got into some rat poison. Luca can't live without Lillì, and if his dog dies or gets sick, we immediately replace it with another one exactly like the last."

"Giulia!" called Luca from high atop the wall. "You found him! Come back right away before he can run away again."

"I have to go now. Thanks so much." Giulia hurried away, taking her leave.

In the days that followed, the thought of Aurelio resurfaced in her mind insistently. She saw him as if in a series of flashing images. During their encounter on the piazza, they were standing in the noonday sunlight and the glare had been blinding. Giulia had had to squint her eyes; she only opened them from time to time to focus on him, after which she'd lowered her eyelids to protect herself from the glare. It was especially difficult to have to look up, since Aurelio was so much taller than she was. In those brief instants, several image fragments had impressed themselves on her visual memory, and now they reappeared to her like intermittent flashes—an open smile; a strong set of teeth; a thin mustache over a well defined mouth; honey-brown eyes, cheerful and kind; hair slicked back with brilliantine; broad shoulders and powerful biceps that swelled beneath the tight-fitting sports T-shirt.

Giulia found a pretext to see him again. She decided that Luca ought to send him a small gift in token of his gratitude, and talked her brother into sacrificing an issue of the *Gazzetta dello Sport*—he had a collection of back issues—which featured an article about the national rowing team.

With the newspaper in hand, Giulia went over to the front door of Aurelio's house and pulled on the doorbell.

Aurelio came to the door. "Oh, what a surprise!" he said, sincerely astonished. "Please, come right in."

"Just for a couple of minutes. I'm here because my brother really insisted. He sent me to give you this newspaper in gratitude for your help with Lillì."

"You're too kind. Can I offer you a glass of lemonade?"

Sitting beneath a pergola covered with grape vines, sipping lemonade, the "couple of minutes" turned into a couple of hours.

Filtering through the grape leaves, the sunshine created charming light effects. It illuminated Giulia's hair, picking out the highlights of tawny gold; but it left her face in the shadows, emphasizing even more her already strikingly intense blue eyes, lively and inquisitive—Giulia was different from her sisters, who were all dark in coloring. She had taken more from Pietro than from Olga.

"How lovely this late summer is turning out to be. It's a pity to have to go back to the city," she said, just to get the conversation started.

"Yes, it's true. Unfortunately, I'll be leaving in two days' time. I have to get back, because training is resuming." Aurelio had to make an effort to keep himself from reaching out and plunging his fingers into that mass of golden hair. "And you, signorina, are you leaving soon for Rome?"

"I don't live in Rome anymore, I live in Turin. I'm staying with my sister Ada. I've just got my degree and next month I'm going to start teaching at an elementary school."

"Really! You choose to work? There aren't many young ladies like you who decide to take that path." Aurelio seemed to be interested in what Giulia had to say, but his attention was actually focused on the girl's wet lips as she sucked lemonade through a straw, and a dimple that appeared at the corner of her mouth.

"I think everyone ought to work, everyone should contribute to society in some way or other," said Giulia, setting down her glass. Now her eyes were an even more intense blue. "And what kind of work do you do?"

"I help out my folks in the family store. I have a degree in accounting and I keep the books. But I also like working at the counter, because so many children come to the shop. It's a stationery shop, and students come in to buy pens and notebooks."

"Where is your shop?"

"On Via Madama Cristina, near the schools."

"What a coincidence! That's right where I'm going to be teaching. I chose that school because it's not far from where Ada lives. And you, where do you live?"

"We have an apartment above the store, on the fifth floor. Perhaps I'll see you from the window when you take your pupils outside."

Aurelio not only saw her from the window, he even went to meet her at the front entrance of the school. Their friendship grew, strengthened, and was transformed. Soon they confessed their love to each other. The problem was how to introduce Aurelio to the family. Yielding to Giulia's insistent requests, Ada agreed to have him over for tea, as "an acquaintance from Cortalba."

For the occasion, Veglia had baked a large batch of *brùt e bun*—hazelnut biscotti that, as the name in dialect suggested, were ugly to behold but delicious to taste—and had insisted on serving them herself so that she'd have a chance to get a good look at Giulia's new gentleman friend. She took an immediate liking to Aurelio, and in her heart she allied herself solidly with the young couple. Miss Langfield gave a demonstration of how to make tea "English style" because, according to her, there is no other country on earth that makes a palatable tea. As she handed a cup to Giulia, she whispered in her ear, in English, "Quite a handsome lad, darling." Ada and Ernesto entertained their guest with commonplace conversation: the weather, sports, the finer aspects of Piedmontese cuisine, excursions to the Monferrato region… and so on and so forth. Giulia was on pins and needles, hoping against hope that Aurelio would avoid making gaffes. Aurelio felt like a young pupil facing an exam board.

When he left, the comments about him were rather laconic.

"He's an ordinary young fellow," Ada commented.

"He's just a good-looking guy, and that's that," Ernesto agreed.

Veglia overheard them, and in turn commented on her employers' attitudes, muttering under her breath in dialect, "They gave him short shrift."

Giulia had developed a habit of spending all her afternoons away from home. She'd come home at midday for lunch, then go out again and not come back until dinnertime. That was a source of some concern for Ada, who felt responsible for her sister. Often she'd interrogate her.

"Do you have to work after school again today?"

"Oh, yes. In fact, now we're working double shifts because the classes are so much bigger and we have to break them up."

"Then you'll be home late."

"Yes, yes. Don't worry about me."

"At least try to be back in time for dinner."

"I'll be quite punctual," Giulia called over her shoulder as she hurried down the hallway.

Veglia was on the threshold, holding the door open with a conspiratorial look on her face. "Go on then, go on, sweetheart," she said under her breath. "But behave, you two…!"

Giulia often got someone to substitute for her in the after-school hours and met Aurelio at the corner of the block. The rows of plane trees, along the boulevard, were already dense with leaves. The air was warm and redolent with the scent of flowers. Down the boulevard you could glimpse the grounds opening out before the Castello del Valentino, a magnificent Baroque edifice located at the center of the park. It had once belonged to the court of the house of Savoy and it now housed the university department of architecture. In the rear, the castle was reflected in the green waters of the Po. On either side there was an extended pedestrian wharf lined with weeping willows and dotted with stone benches, little grottoes, and basins with miniature waterfalls, a favorite spot for young lovers who marked their presence with arrow-pierced hearts and intertwined names, carved into the wood, scratched into the stone, or scrawled with chalk on the metal railings.

Giulia and Aurelio often strolled along that trail, stopping at a small embarcadero where you could rent a little rowboat. Aurelio had strong arms and he could quickly take the boat to secluded bends in the river just outside of the city limits. The boat scudded across the water surface, leaving behind the smokestacks of the industrial outskirts, and pulled up on riverbanks free of urban cement. They'd land in the shade of a century-old oak that extended its roots from the riverbank into the water. Aurelio would tie up the boat and help Giulia to scramble along the intricate welter of that natural bridge. They'd stroll along the shady bank among the shafts of sunlight descending through the vault of the oak branches, falling upon them like golden drops. Or else they'd lie down beneath the foliage... —and here I'll leave them.

After all, Giulia was my great aunt, and it hardly strikes me as seemly to speculate about the intimate details of her personal life. So I'll retreat, like in a reverse zoom, until my imaginary frame expands to include the horizontal line of the river, the rounded shape of the big tree, and a thin slice of sky. The figures of the two young people are gradually lost in the mass of foliage.

Giulia told Ada about these afternoons in the countryside, many years later, and the two sisters would laugh about the naïve contrivance of the "after school." Since then, every time she came up, Ada would affectionately say, "Eh, Giulia was a rascal…"

IV

After they were married, Giulia moved to the Costa family's apartment, upstairs from the stationery shop. Aurelio's bedroom was big enough for the two of them. Giulia liked that arrangement well enough. Actually, since she wished to go on teaching, it came in handy that her mother-in-law herself kept house, with the help of Teresina, a fifteen-year-old maid, and that later she also helped look after the children. But Giulia wanted Aurelio to free himself financially from his parents and with her modest dowry she helped him to open a toy shop.

For a couple of years, Aurelio managed to remain in the black, though he wasn't making any notable profits. He devoted himself enthusiastically to his variegated, brightly colored merchandise and the faithful ranks of his youthful clientele. For Mina and Gio, too, that shop was an obligatory stopping point whenever they went out for a walk with their nanny. Alma told me more than once, "We were little, I might have been three years old, no older, and Uncle Aurelio was always very kind to us. He always gave us some little gift whenever we came to the shop."

But those were grim times for Italy, which had been bled dry by its wartime effort. Foodstuffs and consumer goods of all kinds were in short supply, and this fueled inflation which hit the less well to do with particular cruelty. Discontent spread throughout the streets of Italy. The Socialist Party had gained strength in the parliament and was turned to more radical political strategies. Many factories had been occupied. In some cities, the workers' movement had established independent administrations modelled on the Russian Soviets. In Rome, the government continuously fell and was replaced by another, like leaves from a calendar. In the end, the country turned once again to Giolitti, but his government too proved to be weak and ineffectual. Strikes were frequent and massive; the police couldn't keep the strikers under control and frequently civil disorder spilled out into the city streets. It was a widely held opinion among the bourgeoisie, both grand and petty, that only the squads of the *Fasci di Combattimento* would be capable of reining in the red menace that was threatening the nation.

The *Fasci*, recently founded, had spread rapidly, drawing into their ranks the great mass of veterans of the Great War who had been unable to find work—the unemployment rate was sky high—along with common criminals and thugs from the streets, who were always ready for a brawl. They'd sprung up almost everywhere around the country, but they had especially solid roots in the Po Valley. Here, under the leadership of local "ras,"[3] they were calling the shots, ignoring the law, and applying a single principle of justice that could be summarized in the formulation, "Either with us, or against us." They possessed no real ideology, and were driven solely by a vaguely nationalistic concept; they despised the liberal-bourgeois parties, which they considered corrupt, and they hated the socialists, whom they considered "internal enemies." At the end of 1921, the uprisings of the workers' movement that had so profoundly alarmed the populace, along with the last surviving shreds of resistance of the militant fringes of the Socialist Party, were quashed by the squads of the Black Shirts.

In those last few days of the Red Biennium, Aurelio's toyshop was attacked and set afire. The clash between the

---

3.   Term for a local leader taken from Amharic.

two factions took place right in front of the plate glass window of his shop. The Black Shirts were bludgeoning heads and shoulders in all directions; the Reds were retaliating with sticks and fists. Some of them had knives and Molotov cocktails. A Molotov cocktail was thrown at a group of fascist *squadristi* who had been pushed up against the wall of the building. The bottle missed its target, broke the shop window, and smashed against the floor. A burst of flame was released that spread with lightning speed to the shelves, and then slid up the walls, devouring plush teddy bears, rocking horses, and kites.

Aurelio ran outside, shouting, "Fire! Fire!"

The fire truck wasn't far away; as always, it was on the ready during this kind of unrest. An hour later, the fire had been put out. The brawl ended, and the militants on both sides dispersed.

Aurelio found himself all alone in the blackened grotto that had once been his shop, surrounded by the charred remains of the furnishings. A doll lay on the floor, its celluloid face crumpled, a grotesque hole in place of the mouth; only the glass eyes with blue irises had been left intact and seemed to stare in an expression of horror.

Aurelio went out onto the sidewalk to send away the small knot of rubberneckers who had gathered to comment on what had happened. A man emerged from the group and walked over to him.

"If I may," he said, extending his hand, "Vittorio Cortese. I'm so sorry for what happened here. I'd like to put myself at your service at this moment so difficult for you, sir. Of course, you must be upset, it might help to talk with someone. Let's go have a coffee here, across the street."

Aurelio noticed that the stranger was very well dressed, with a white panama hat and a bow tie. He might have been thirty or so. His manners were impeccable. Feeling weak and helpless, he was pleased to accept the offer.

Sitting at the café table, close to a large plate-glass window, they could see the devastated shop across the street.

"It's a disaster," said Aurelio, heartbroken. "I have no insurance, which means that the whole inventory is a dead loss. I'd bought it with my wife's money, and I'd hoped to be able to pay her back... And instead... And the landlord is going to want me to pay for the damages, even if it wasn't my fault... I'd already fallen behind with the rent... and now... If I can't pay, he'll sue me... Ah, what a lousy situation."

"From what I'm able to understand, you find yourself in a financial bind," Cortese said in an inquisitive tone.

"We live well enough. My parents help us and my wife works, she's a school teacher. We lack for nothing. But facing up to this disaster is simply beyond our means."

"What you need is a job, a position that can assure you of a reliable monthly paycheck, even if it's not a large one. That way, you can make an arrangement with the owner of the building to repay your debt, a little at a time."

"Why do you say such a thing? Excuse me, but... just who are you?"

"I'm a journalist. I'm a functionary in the propaganda and press office of the NFP."

"What's the NFP?"

"It's the National Fascist Party, which was just founded on the base of the *Fasci di Combattimento*. We tried to keep those red devils from burning your shop—I was there as an observer. Unfortunately, we weren't able to prevent it. But the guilty parties won't get away with this, we know who they are. Our militia will bring them to justice."

"Let's hope so. I've heard that your movement is becoming quite a considerable power."

"The movement has existed for more than two years now, and we've had thousands of new members. The ranks of our militias are swelled every day by throngs of young volunteers; we owe it to them that Italy hasn't been plunged into the chaos of socialist anarchy. Now, though, we have to think about the cadres. Between the militias and the higher ranks of the fascist hierarchy, we need a mid-level managerial apparatus, made up of people devoted to the Fascio, who share our patriotic ideals and are willing to support them. In our office, for instance, we really need young people like you, people with an education... I imagine that you have at least a high school diploma."

"Yes, yes, of course I do."

"The work I can offer you would consist of gathering news and issuing press releases—in fact, not merely gathering news, but creating news, so that public opinion can focus on a consistent, constant message. People need guidance, they need to be clearly shown the direction to move and the objective to pursue. Mussolini is an enlightened, decisive leader, and the people who know him are ready to follow him. Our task is to make sure he is known in every corner of the nation, and we can do it by spreading his word."

"And you think I could do that?"

"Don't worry, I'll teach you. In fact, let's be on a first-name basis from now on, because I already think of you as a comrade.[4] Come to headquarters tomorrow morning and we can draw up papers." Cortese placed a calling card in his hand.

So it was that Aurelio joined the ranks of the party. He did his work diligently, without asking too many questions about the veracity of things he wrote and distributed. When the NFP became a parliamentary party—and then the sole, unopposed party, once Mussolini assumed full powers—the relationship between truth and political discourse turned incestuous. The one generated the other, and vice versa. The discourse generated the truth of the regime, and the truth of the regime in turn legitimized the discourse, insinuating itself

---

4   In Italian there are two terms: *camerata*, for the fascists; *compagno*, for the communists and other leftist groups. The distinction is lost in translation with the use of the term, "comrade," for both parties.

into the popular consciousness. It was among the working people that Fascism had its most solid and enthusiastic base. But not everyone was contaminated. The anti-fascists best known for their activities were exiled, incarcerated, or assassinated. Others, who were suspected of failing to sympathize with the government, were put under surveillance and, from time to time, threatened by the squads of the militia, which had now become the MVSN—the state police. Others still, although not entirely convinced by the fascist rhetoric, conformed, receiving various benefits by doing so. This group included large-scale industry, which gained a powerful ally in the government in the person of Mussolini, as well as citizens at every level.

Aurelio was one of these. The reliable paycheck at the end of each month came in handy, especially now that they had children. What's more, he liked the work. He concentrated on the aesthetics of it, the iconography, the rituals, the slogans, and did his best to overlook those vulgar and violent aspects that the regime concealed behind the façade. He also enjoyed wearing the uniform, with the shiny boots and the leather bandolier, which made him even more attractive in the eyes of women. Giulia, however, found it ridiculous, like "a costume out of an operetta." She never approved of Aurelio's job and relations between them were tense and frequently stormy.

Aurelio grew increasingly dependent on the party. Cortese gave him other responsibilities. Because of his athletic abilities, he was made the editor of the sports section, in charge of inspiring the country's youth to lead a healthy, active life and to publicize sports competitions and events by taking part in them. He was appointed podestà of Cortalba, even though he spent very little time there. The more he believed he was building a record of achievement, the tighter the noose that subjugated him to the political apparatus wrapped around his neck. He failed to see that he'd entered a blind alley with no exit, a trap.

V

Marilù came home that evening, after playing with Mina, and she had a question she couldn't get out of her head. Once dinner was over, she followed Aurelio into his study and asked him, "Papà, what is the first duty of a Young Italian Girl?"

"The first duty is to attend the assemblies..." Aurelio stopped short because just then a series of loud knocks rang out imperiously at the front wooden gate. The arrogant tone of that knocking was unpleasantly familiar to him, and he decided to go and answer in person.

"Marilù, we'll talk about this tomorrow. Now go in the other room with Mamma, because I have some work to do," he said, stepping out into the garden.

At the gate were three figures dressed in black shirts. Aurelio recognized Romano, Codliver, and Intrepid. These were their *squadrista* names; no one even remembered their real ones.

Romano was the *ras* of the area. He'd taken part in the March on Rome and he was feared and respected. He often grinned with a superior air, flashing a gold incisor. Codliver was crosseyed and had a harelip, attributes that had made him the butt of much mockery in the past. Now he could take his revenge—with cod liver oil, naturally. It was said that Intrepid resembled the Duce, and so he shaved his head and clenched his teeth to accentuate his prominent jaw. Therefore, he never spoke, only rolled his eyes with a ferocious glare.

Romano walked into the study, pulled up a chair in front of Aurelio's desk, and arrogantly took a seat, as if to make clear who there held the power.

"Signor Podestà, rumors are circulating that we don't like one bit. It's about the family in the castle. Have you not heard anything?"

"No, not a thing. What's this about?"

"And yet, it's not as if you're exactly a stranger to those people. Your wife..."

"Explain, I'm listening."

"We've known for some time that they have no sympathy for the fascist movement. None of them are enrolled in the party. Ernesto Bonardi has even chosen to give up his profession rather than carry the party card and join the official bar association. So far, we've turned a blind eye. But failing to show respect for the Duce, no, that's something we will not tolerate."

"What has he done?"

"Done? Nothing. But he said something he never should have. In public, he takes pictures of the Balilla Fascist youth, and even has them published in the illustrated magazines, but then, in private... In short, he called the Duce *'cul cujun d' Musolini'*. "[5]

"As you rightly said, these are rumors. How can you be so sure?"

"We have our informants among the domestic help. We're quite certain that he said it."

Aurelio remembered that Elvira, the new cook, was Romano's lover. He started to sense that he was in danger. The sense of unease that he'd felt at the appearance of those three grew into fear. Romano toyed with his pistol. He kept the holster thrust into his crotch, so that only the grip emerged, and with one hand he kept moving that artificial phallus up and down, up and down... Codliver and Intrepid remained standing behind him, as if ready for action.

"What do you want from me?" asked Aurelio.

"Listen, you, don't get smart with us." Romano stood up, placed both fists heavily on the desk and leaned in toward Aurelio. Now his face was scant inches from his adversary's. "The only reason you're podestà is because we supported you, but we can kick your ass out whenever we please. We need to teach those shitheads a lesson. And it will be a lesson for you, too. You need to show us that you have guts and that you're loyal to Il Duce."

---

5. Piedmontese dialect: That asshole Mussolini.

"What do you want to do?"

Romano took his seat again, leaning back in the chair in a relaxed and provocative pose.

"A gentle operation. Just a warning, for now. We want to hang a dead animal on the front gate." He grinned, revealing his gold tooth. "The idiot's little dog." Now the pistol was completely unholstered and aimed casually at Aurelio. "And you'll have to kill it."

Aurelio felt as if he'd just been punched in the gut and his face turned pale. He remained silent and motionless.

"Hey, buddy, wake up. Did you hear what I said?"

"Yes, but... there might be some other way ..." Aurelio stammered.

"Ah, ma t' ses pròpi 'n piciu..."[6] Romano let slip in Piedmontese—a dialect that was no longer used because the fascist regime prescribed the exclusive use of pure "Italian." He promptly shifted back to the official language. "Look, we're here to help you, because our militiamen have a rather dim view of you. Don't they, boys?"

Codliver and Intrepid said, "Yes, yes," and energetically nodded their heads, so that the tassels on their fezzes swayed.

Romano went on, "They don't like your wife, who's of the same ilk as those people. People that give themselves airs. And we also know that in the city she frequents subversive intellectual circles. Who can say, maybe someday something will happen to her. But you can keep that from happening by demonstrating your loyalty to the Fascio."

Aurelio was petrified, and he stared right at Romano, as if those words somehow were failing to penetrate into his brain.

"Get ready," Romano went on. "We'll expect you tomorrow night at eleven o'clock behind the old farmhouse. And if during the day you let slip so much as a word of this, I can't be responsible for what might happen to your wife."

With those words, he stood up and a moment later he was

---

6. Piedmontese dialect: Oh, so you really are just a dickhead...

gone, followed by his henchmen. Aurelio heard the front gate slamming and their voices ringing out loudly through the nocturnal silence in a raucous litany, echoing off the tightly shuttered housefronts. Romano would sing a verse and the other two would respond:

"About the authorities . . ."

"I don't give a damn!"

"About the Podestà . . ."

"I don't give a damn!"

"Of the party I carry the card. . ."

"For the Duce, I've got it hard!"

"What did they want?" asked Giulia, walking into his study.

"Nothing, nothing," replied Aurelio absent-mindedly, trying to regain a normal demeanor.

"You're pale, you don't look well. What did they want?"

"They want me to go to a meeting of all the podestà's of the district tomorrow night. It's at Pralongo, there will be a dinner, then speeches. I'll be home late."

Giulia didn't believe him. She understood that it was something else and that Aurelio couldn't talk about it.

"They're blackmailing you," she said indignantly.

"Shut up! Don't let anyone hear you." There was fear and anger in Aurelio's voice. "You can't say these things. You can't even think them. Go to bed, I need to be alone."

The next night, at eleven, Aurelio arrived at the old farmhouse. There was a full moon casting a spectral light over the abandoned construction and all the surrounding area. The three *squadristi* were already there. With them was Cussót—Little Pumpkin—holding a sack in his arms.

Cussót was just a kid, thirteen years old, and an orphan. From the day he'd been found, abandoned as a newborn in the vegetable patch of a farmhouse, he'd lived for a while with one family, and for a while with another, adopted by everyone and by no one. They'd given him that name because he'd been found next to a pumpkin vine, but it also suited him because he had a large round head, and he'd been shaved bald. For some time now he'd been working at the castle as a helper in the kitchen. Elvira had brought him to work there because Cussót had lived at her house for a year or two, and now the family wanted to get rid of him. Romano ordered Elvira to persuade the boy to steal the dog. Lillì trusted Cussót and was happy to be with him. Luca, too, liked Cussót; they often played together, even though Luca was now twenty-five, and they taught Lillì various circus acts they'd seen in an illustrated book.

"Cussót, get the dog out of the bag," Romano ordered.

The boy seemed confused, as if he didn't understand what was happening.

"Come on, give me the dog!" Romano grabbed the sack from the boy's arms.

Cussót protested. "Why are we here? Elvira told me that Lillì was a gift for me, that I could keep him. . ."

"Shut up, you," Codliver hissed in his face, grabbing him by the arms and holding him fast.

Romano set Lillì down on the grass. The little dog looked even whiter by the light of the moon. A perfect target.

"Now it's your turn, Podestà. Get busy. Let's get this done."

Aurelio tried not to think and reached for the pistol. Cussót let out a cry, "No, it's my dog. No, Lillì . . ." Intrepid clapped a rough hand over the boy's mouth. Cussót struggled, but Codliver had him in a firm grip.

Lillì didn't move. By now he was getting along in years and he wasn't as spry as he'd been when he made his way into Aurelio's back garden on that sunny, long-ago morning. He recognized his one-time friend and weakly wagged his tail in greeting.

Aurelio fired.

Lillì let out a little yelp and the blood spurted out of his head, staining his white coat.

Cussót managed to break free and lunged for the dog. He sobbed as he hugged him.

"Now you've got to kill him, too," Romano ordered. "He can cause problems for us."

Aurelio began to tremble and felt a warm flow run down his legs, seeping over his boots.

"You've pissed your pants, Podestà. What are you going to tell you wife when you get home with pee-stained britches?" Romano flashed his gold tooth in the moonlight. Then, once again serious, "Go on, shoot."

At that very moment, Cussót looked up and understood their intentions. He leapt to his feet and ran.

"Shoot, you asshole, shoot!" Romano urged him, beside himself with rage.

Aurelio shot and missed the target, maybe because his hand was trembling, maybe because he wanted to miss.

Romano fired and hit Cussót in the back. The boy fell and lay there sprawled in the grass, twisting and moaning. Romano went over to him and finished him off with another shot.

Then he retraced his steps and addressed Aurelio. "Your balls are made of ricotta, Podestà. But we're going to forgive you because you're one of us. Whether you like it or not, you belong with the people. We are the ones who make up the Fascio, and it's the Fascio that has the power."

Overwhelmed with fear and horror, Aurelio remembered what Giulia had said during one of their frequent set-tos, playing off the meaning of *"fascio,"* a bundle of rods. *"You're a 'fascio' of imbeciles, you and those hoodlums in the militia. You're nothing, you're just little cogs in a gigantic machine. They make you think you're the masters and they turn you into slaves."*

The other two men had picked up the dog and were dropping it into the sack now.

"Dig a grave, all three of you," said Romano. "And then get out of here. We don't know anything about the boy. We never saw him."

He threw the sack over his shoulder and headed off along the path that led up to the castle.

The next day it was Luca who found Lillì hanging on the smaller gate. That was a passageway that was rarely used; everyone else either went through the main gate or the serviceman's entrance. Luca had a nervous breakdown. They found him rolling in his own vomit. The physician who came to examine him diagnosed a cerebral inflammation and ordered complete bed rest and cold-water compresses. When Luca regained consciousness, at the end of the second day, he found Lillì sitting on the floor, waiting for permission to jump onto the bed. He promptly recovered. No one could ever tell whether he realized that this was a new Lillì. Perhaps he simply forgot what he had seen. The whole episode was buried in his subconscious like a nocturnal nightmare.

That's not how it was for the others, who began to analyze the sequence of events. They suspected some connection between the killing of the dog and Cussót's disappearance. Olga wanted to question Elvira, but the cook didn't show up for work that morning. Then her brother came to the castle to explain that Elvira had quarreled with her boyfriend and had left town; she had gone to live with certain relatives of hers in the area around Cuneo. They realized that the Black Shirts were behind what had happened. Those were the only criminals left in the district because they themselves had eliminated all the others, the common criminals. But they never suspected Aurelio, whose peaceful nature and decent sentiments they appreciated, even though they deplored the fact that he was collaborating with the fascist regime. As a family, they clearly understood that they were being threatened, but they bravely reported the matter to the authorities. And that was the end of it.

After that night, Aurelio took to his bed and gave orders to tell anyone who came looking for him that he was feeling unwell and couldn't receive any visitors—much like that notorious curate who, after his encounter with the *bravos*, ordered his housekeeper *"to fasten the doors well: not to set foot outside; and if any one knocked, to answer from the window, that the curate was confined to his bed with a fever."*[7]

Giulia needed no explanations. She could easily imagine what had happened. From that day on, the last shred of respect that she'd had for her husband vanished. She also stopped loving him, or perhaps, she clearly realized that she no longer loved him. The distance separating them became an abyss, a gap that could no longer be bridged.

VI

When they returned to the city, Giulia became even more assiduous in her contacts with the group of intellectuals that met secretly in a private room at the Caffè Garibaldi. Here she met Matteo, a philosophy professor. They became lovers. Giulia did nothing to conceal the truth from her husband, and together they agreed that it would be better to maintain the appearance of a normal marriage. Preserving family decorum was important for the children; and it was essential for Aurelio, in his position.

One morning, Cortese walked into Aurelio's office and suggested they go out for a walk. He needed to speak to him in private, he said. It was raining. They strolled up Via Roma in the shelter of the porticos.

"I'm sorry to be the bearer of bad news, but we've been friends for many years now and I need to warn you," said Cortese gravely.

---

7.   From *I promessi sposi* (*The Bethroted*) by Alessandro Manzoni, 1827, a classic of Italian literature.

"I thank you. Tell me what it is." Aurelio was alarmed and was expecting the worst.

"I've learned that they're preparing a roundup of the group that meets at the Caffè Garibaldi. Your wife needs to escape, there's not a minute to lose. Here are two passports for France. It'll be easier if she has a traveling companion, that professor friend of hers."

Aurelio could only stammer in reply. "I didn't think you knew about my wife… about us. But why do you want to help us? You're running a terrible risk."

"I told you. I'm your friend. But there's also another reason: we don't want word getting out about this. It's not good publicity for us if people find out that the wife of one of our functionaries is conspiring against the government."

"But they know about it internally. What measures are they going to take against me?"

"We know that you're loyal to the Fascio and we want you to go on working for us. To justify your position with the internal hierarchy, I wrote in the report that it was you who reported on your wife and informed us of the group's activities. Publicly, you'll have to say that she's sick and that she's been sent to a clinic in the mountains."

Once again, Aurelio felt helpless in the face of the supremacy of the political apparatus. And once again, he complied. He had no other way of saving Giulia, the family, and himself.

Giulia left the next day with Matteo. In Paris they were greeted effusively and accepted into the little colony of political refugees. For a few months they lived safely. But the long hand of Fascism was capable of reaching them there as well. Matteo was murdered one night by a hitman on a dark street, as he was returning home. Giulia, sensing the danger, managed to get a safe passage to the Soviet Union with a group of leftwing comrades.

From that point forward, accounts of her whereabouts are infrequent and confused. She seems to have worked for several years as an Italian teacher for the intelligence services. Then, with the beginning of the terror, in 1936, she was declared an "enemy of the people" and deported to a camp in Stalin's gulag. Only much later, in the Sixties, when the USSR under Krushchev gave amnesty to political prisoners and rehabilitated thousands of former detainees, was the family informed that Giulia appeared to be on the list of the deceased.

9

Champagne Bubbles
1932-1933

I

The tradition of the charity benefit began when Pietro purchased the castle. It was Olga who had the idea of holding a fair on the grounds of the castle for the townfolk and the people from the surrounding area, and to donate the proceeds to the Cortalba kindergarten, operated by the nuns. The ticket only cost a few cents, but receipts by day's end were quite substantial because people came in the hundreds from the farmhouses and villages. The prominent guests, who came from neighboring villas and castles, made generous donations. Moreover, Pietro matched the sum with his own personal contribution.

The designated day was Luca's birthday. In the late morning, Luca appeared on the wall that rose above the town square to announce the official beginning of the festivities. When he was still small, it was Pietro who opened the festivities. As he gave the announcement, Pietro very generously tossed a handful of gold coins to the gathered crowd so that they, too, would receive a gift on that happy day. Only a lucky few actually managed to lay their hands on one of the coins, and it was always the same young men. The townfolk told me that when their grandfathers were children, they'd train all year long to be the fastest to grab and collect as many coins as possible.

Then they would open to the public the lower gate that gave onto the town road. It was an extraordinary event for the townfolk who had few if any opportunities to venture inside the castle walls. But they didn't get far. They'd walk thirty feet or so and then they were admitted to a vast lawn usually employed as a croquet course. The paths leading to the upper gardens remained securely closed.

Over the years, the basic amusements remained unchanged—the sack race, the tree of treats, breaking piñatas, bocce tournaments, lotteries, and a raised dance floor. But at a certain point, a new attraction was added, the *tableaux vivants*, a spectacle that left the public gaping and was the talk of the district for the days and months that followed—for years, actually, because when I went back to Cortalba recently I met people who still remembered them.

I met Vigìn at a little tavern, the Osteria della Posta, down below the castle on the town road. I had just stepped in to get a drink before leaving. Vigìn was the only other customer in the place, seated at a small table under the eaves in the backyard. He must have been eighty if he was a day. He was sitting there, leaning forward on his cane, watching a soccer match on TV. He wore the black felt hat that farmers never took off, even in the house. He had a half liter of wine on the table and a Tuscan cigar that had gone out in the corner of his mouth.

He looked at me with the expression of someone wishing to show hospitality to a visiting stranger.

"Have you come to see the castle?" he asked.

"Yes, I heard that they'd restored it and opened it to the public as a hotel and cultural center. I'm happy to see that it's operating again after so many years. It once belonged to my family."

"Oh, it did? That wouldn't be the Ducati family, by any chance?"

"Yes, that's right. Alma Bonardi is my mother."

"Signorina Mina? Well now, of all things!"

"Do you remember her?"

"Ehhh… do I remember her! We all dreamed about her. All us boys. We'd wait outside the gate to watch her go by, sometimes we'd stay there all day and she still might not come out at all. She was a fairy, she was, she was… I wouldn't know how to put it… like seeing springtime arrive."

"Did you ever speak to her?"

"Me to her? Never. But once she did say something to me, and I just stood there like a fool. I might have been thirteen and she was a year older. They'd summoned us up to the castle to assemble the stage for the charity benefit. I was the carpenter's apprentice. So there I was driving nails into the stage where they held the *tablovivàn* and she told me to move an armchair over next to a red curtain that served as a backdrop. I just stood there staring at her, speechless, rigid as a stick of wood. Whereupon she shrugged and said, "This boy must be deaf." Then she turned on her heel and left."

"Did you go to the benefit every year?"

"Yes, everyone would go. It was quite an event. I'm talking about the Thirties, when there was nothing to do in town, not like now when we've got TV. At the fair there was the band, there was a dance where the girls would find themselves a boyfriend. I was good at bocce, but Signorino Luca would play sometimes, and when he did you had to let him win, because he was like a child. He was pushing thirty, but if he lost he'd throw a tantrum. You know, he was… how to put this… he just wasn't right in the head, there, that's it. Still, he took part in the *tablovivàn* himself. I remember that the fascists told us that we weren't supposed to call them that, that we were supposed to call them *quadri plastici*, because no one was supposed to use foreign languages. They had even warned the owners up at the castle, more than once, but those paid them no mind. And so, in the end, the fascists just let it ride because they enjoyed the festivities as much as anyone else, and had just as much fun."

"And what were those *quadri plastici* like?"

"They were marvelous. Every year there was a new one. I'd never been to the theater, but the ones who knew about these things said that it was just like the actual theater, only the actors neither moved nor spoke. The curtain was pulled back and everybody went, 'Oooh!' in a single voice. Then, silence. Afterward, the schoolmaster, who had also been my schoolmaster, explained that it was a copy of a painting that was in the museum, that they copied the characters and the costumes and assumed the same poses to recreate the same identical scene."

"Do you remember any of them in particular?"

"There was one, though I can't remember the name of the painter, but it showed the family of the King of France, the ones that had their heads cut off later, in the revolution. But here they were all still safe and sound, they were in a room all full of mirrors and gilt frames and wearing satin costumes in all sorts of bright colors and white wigs with long ringlets. Signorina Viola, who was already getting along in years but still beautiful, was the queen, and Signorina Mina was her daughter. I can still remember that she wore a sky-blue dress with a plunging neckline... eh, I was a young man, and I noticed things like that. Signorino Luca played the king and they said that he resembled him very much, because he had a pudgy face and a not-very-intelligent expression. And then there were all the others, even Signora Ada, because the room was full of people."

I had finished my drink and I wanted to leave right away so I could get home before dark. I said goodbye to Vigìn and told him I'd come back to hear another slice of his memories.

"Come whenever you like, I'm always here. And tell your Mamma this: A big hello from Vigìn—even if she doesn't know me."

II

I went in search of the photographs of the *tableaux vivants* in the various albums, but I didn't find any of the court of Louis XVI. Other pictures, though, caught my attention. Luca was present in all of them, and in them all he was in the center of the shot. Clearly, for him this was an extension of his childhood games, when Ada dressed him up and applied makeup for the photographic sessions. And I couldn't rule out the possibility that those same *tableaux* developed out of those first attempts to "do theater." There are mythological scenes, Bible scenes, scenes from ancient Rome, and scenes from *The Arabian Nights*.

In one of these photographs, Ada is an odalisque, in a dance pose, her figure and her face wrapped in soft veils. She's still young; confirmation is provided by the fact that Mina and Gio are small. They're wearing harem pants and small turbans with plumes, and they're accompanying the dancer on tambourines. Luca, dressed as a pasha, is reclining languidly on a pile of cushions—the pose emphasizes his round belly. He's bringing to his mouth a bunch of grapes that dangle from his raised hand, while a slave (unidentified actor) waves a feather fan.

These aren't photographs taken by Ernesto. They're commercial products from a photographic studio that Olga hired every year for the occasion. Their main purpose was to amuse Luca, who led a rather monotonous, isolated life.

In those years, Ernesto had embarked on far more serious enterprises. Aside from his own personal artistic pursuits, he was operating internationally as a promoter of the art of photography. With two partners, who were like him lawyers and members of the Subalpine Photographic Society, he had resumed publication of *Il Corriere Fotografico*, transferring the offices from Milan to Turin. People called them the "3 B's" because the other two men's surnames also began with that letter. When Ernesto died, in 1958, *Il Corriere Fotografico* published a very nice article commemorating "the unforgettable Mastermind, Coeditor, and Friend," and it included the following passage:

> *...With his passing, we have lost one of the most eminent figures that the Italian photographic art produced in the years between the two World Wars...*
>
> *He played a great part—"magna pars"—in the transformation of this magazine, with a view to accentuating its artistic nature and making it better suited to the goals set forth [...] He also devoted fervid energy to the initiatives that sprouted in the context of the* Corriere *to encourage the development of the art of photography in Italy: among them we should mention the* Light and Shadows Annual *and the famous Piedmontese Group for Artistic Photography, which held those International Salons of the Photographic Art that took place many times in Turin between the two World Wars, which were—in spite of what many ill informed observers may claim today—by far the most intriguing, eclectic, lively, and cosmopolitan exhibitions of photography that have ever been seen in our country.*
>
> *His art cast its glow not only in the context of such exhibitions, but also in many brilliant personal expressions: shows and publications in which it was possible to glimpse the various genres that were most congenial to his creative temperament, from scenes of private life to portraits (let us recall a stupendous series of portraits of the Alpine guides of Valtournanche), to photographs of children, Alpine landscapes, and scenes of the Piedmontese hills. With a discerning selection of the work of the finest photographers of his time he assembled the handsome volume* How We Take Pictures Today, *published by Hoepli, which constitutes an excellent anthology of the world's photographic art in the first half of the twentieth century.*

For several years now, he had retired to his large and handsome family home, with a vast view over the expanse of the vineyard-covered hills of the Asti region; and there he gently passed away one spring morning.

Olga had a special fondness for Ernesto and turned to him whenever she had a problem. And so it was to him that she went when Luca was declared incompetent by a court of law, and it became necessary to appoint a trusted person to serve as his guardian. Ernesto took the position, a job that he performed conscientiously for the rest of his life. Unfortunately, this was a belated remedy that was put into effect as a consequence of a very serious mishap: Luca was swindled by a con man and robbed of his entire estate, which he had acquired as Pietro's sole heir. All that was left was the castle.

III

Luca was sitting with Olga on the terrace of the Grand Hôtel of Santa Margherita. He was wearing an elegant white linen suit and his customary gold-rimmed pince-nez. He was savoring a cherry sherbet, looking out over the expanse of the sea beyond the colorful line of changing cabins and beach umbrellas. Lillì was curled up on his lap, dozing off. Every year, mother and son went to Genoa for the winter season and, at the turn of May, they spent two weeks in Santa Margherita before heading back to Cortalba.

Luca really liked the sea. As a boy, he enjoyed building sand castles where the waves lapped at the beach. He'd fill his pail, press down hard to make sure the sand was compact, and then turn it over, lifting it to release the cylindrical shape of the contents. "This is our castle," he used to say; then he'd place a small celluloid figure atop it and add, "... and this is me." There are some funny old photographs of Luca from those days, in a one-piece knit swimsuit with horizontal stripes and a sailor's cap, on a background of waves gently lapping onto shore. Even now that he was nearly thirty, he would have liked to build sand castles, but Olga wouldn't let him.

"Luca, darling, do be careful with that sherbet. Look, you've already stained your jacket," said Olga in a tone of gentle reproof.

"Too bad I didn't think to wear my red jacket," Luca replied, laughing softly in delight at his riposte.

The terrace was on the same level as the grounds of the hotel, shaded by the pines that protected it from the glare of the late afternoon sun. It was aperitif hour. The waiters bustled from table to table, where the customers clustered in small groups before dinner. A tenor voice, coming from a gramophone, sang an aria from *La Traviata*.

Another customer at a nearby table addressed Luca, "The voice of Caruso... unmistakable! What a divine melody."

"That's not Caruso, it's Beniamino Gigli," Luca replied in his faint, nasal voice. "I know because at home I have a gramophone and a big stack of records. I have a collection."

"Oh really?"

"Yes, my son knows everything about opera and the singers. He's really quite remarkable," Olga confirmed.

"I feel so ignorant. And yet I truly love music. Perhaps your son could teach me a little something. I'm here on business, but I have a great deal of free time."

Olga was flattered by the stranger's words. It was a rare occurrence for anyone to appreciate her son's finer qualities, which was something that deeply wounded her maternal pride.

"Why of course," she replied impulsively. "Right, Luca? It would be a pleasure for you to talk about opera with this nice gentleman."

Luca nodded with a foolish smile as he scraped the bottom of his bowl, happy to be the center of attention.

"If you're all alone and have no other engagements, why don't you spend the evening with us," Olga suggested. "We usually play bridge after dinner, and this evening we're missing a fourth. You see, Luca and I play together, as a single hand. Then there's Count Ralli, a relative of ours, and a married couple that we know. But the husband just left this morning. So there'd be a place at the table for you."

Just then Riccardo showed up.

"Forgive me if I'm late. I took a spectacular walk right out to the point of Portofino, but the walk took longer than I expected. Unfortunately, I'm not as young or as fast as I used to be."

"Why no, your timing is perfect. Allow me to introduce a new acquaintance, Signor. . ."

"Gino Barone, delighted to meet you."

"Barone as a nobleman or as a cardsharp?... Ha ha ha!" Riccardo let out a hearty laugh, and then hastened to apologize, "I'm only joking, don't take it the wrong way. Laughing is good for your health."[8]

"Of course, certainly, you just have to know how to go along with the joke," said the other man with an uncertain smile.

Olga, too, put on a smile of circumstance to cover the uneasy development. She didn't approve of Riccardo's exuberant personality. Above all, she criticized him for a certain lack of tact. She had told her closest friends how, not long after Letizia's death, Riccardo had had the impudence to ask for her hand in marriage—"My dear Olga, now we're both widowed and we could keep each other pleasant company. I could ask for nothing better than to marry the daughter of my beloved Letizia." Perhaps Riccardo merely wanted to further legitimize his position in the family, because he had inherited from Letizia the residence in Genoa that ought to have been

---

8. Here Riccardo plays with the word *"barone,"* which in Italian means "baron," but it can also be twisted to mean a "big cardsharp." The pun is lost in translation.

handed down to the children, and they hadn't taken it well. He received an abrupt refusal from Olga. Still, they remained friends, and they worked out an exchange of hospitality: Olga and Luca spent their winters in Genoa and Riccardo spent lengthy summer vacations in Cortalba.

From the very first time he saw him, Riccardo felt a visceral dislike for Gino Barone. His markedly parvenu appearance annoyed him aesthetically. Gino dressed in the poorest of taste and there was something unctuous in his manners and in his person. His complexion was dark and porous; his hair was greasy, not from the barber's brilliantine but from his own overabundant natural sebum; he always had a handkerchief in one hand to mop the sweat off his brow; even his hands were sweaty and slimy to the touch. He was rather short and wore elevator shoes to gain an inch or two. He always seemed nervous, his eyes darting from place to place, except directly in the gaze of others. He must have been about forty.

In short, that is how Riccardo would have described him if anyone had asked. But there was no need, because the entire family got the same impression when Gino arrived late that summer in Cortalba.

Only Olga saw him differently. To her, Gino was first and foremost her son's friend, a steadfast and affectionate friend. After the departure of Monsieur Lesavoir, there was no longer a companion in Luca's life who might share his amusements and pursuits. Olga hadn't even inquired into Gino's social standing, merely accepting every word he'd told her about himself, "I live in Turin. I'm a financial trader and I work in the field of international transactions. I'm now in a solid economic position thanks to my years of hard work and a healthy helping of luck."

To anyone who expressed a negative opinion about him, Olga replied just as she'd replied to Ernesto when he'd tried to warn her, "I know that you speak with good intentions and I usually trust you implicitly. But in this case, you're wrong.

You and the other sons-in-law, you're all jealous of Luca because he's the only male offspring, and so he enjoys a certain privilege over his sisters. You're jealous because he inherited his father's entire estate and so you pile on, emphasizing the naivete of his personality. Whereas Luca, however innocent he may be in so many ways, has a rare and very particular intelligence, that only a few people of special sensibility, like Gino, are able to appreciate."

The friendship between Gino and Luca grew stronger. Gino frequently came to visit Luca in Cortalba and he'd stay for several days. For Luca, those were days of celebration. Gino brought new records and together they'd listen to the opera, or else they'd play bocce, or spend the afternoon in Asti, at the Caffè Centrale, where they could observe the promenade.

Young women, with their girl friends or squired by a man, strolled past the café tables in tight-fitting silk dresses that emphasized the curves of their slender bodies. Gino pointed out to Luca certain feminine attributes that he'd never consciously observed before. Perhaps he'd been attracted by a generous bosom or a rotund derriere and had experienced a tingling of desire, but he'd never put those feelings into words. Gino forced him to recognize these instincts.

"Do you like that one?"

"Yes, she's cute. She has on a cute little dress."

"Forget about the cute little dress. Don't you see the tits on her? That's a lot of delicious butter right there. Madonna… She's killing me, she is. Go on, don't tell me you wouldn't love to screw her."

Luca laughed, blushing and confused, uncertain what to say. Gino continued.

"But haven't you ever screwed a woman? You know what I'm talking about… *zin-zin*," and he accompanied the question with a lewd gesture.

Determined to keep up with his new friend, Luca lied.

"Sure, of course, lots of them. All of them real lookers, with great big tits."

"I knew it, I did. You act like the little angel, but you're a dragon, you are. I understood that you know how to act with women. If you ever come to Turin, I'll take you out one night to Madame Irene's. You should see the broads she has. We'll have fun."

And so it was decided. Luca obtained Olga's permission and set out for Turin at the end of the summer. Aunt Magda said she'd be glad to have him stay with her.

                              IV

Magda had been living in Turin for more than ten years. She had moved there with Luigi right after the war. Francesco had stayed behind in Paris to replace the recently deceased banker D'Ambrose as the head of the consortium. Magda had a large apartment on Corso Vittorio Emanuele, with tall windows above the arcades of the porticoes. She often entertained there because she frequented the high-society circles. Since she was a widow, rich and beautiful, she had plenty of suitors. But she didn't encourage them, preferring instead to carry on a discreet liaison with a "prominent individual," that she had begun many years earlier during a vacation on the Côte d'Azur, while her husband was still alive. No one ever mentioned the name of the "prominent individual," but it was known that he was close to the royal court, even though he did not live in the capital because he found Roman society rather vulgar and preferred the refined elegance of the old milieu in the former Piedmontese kingdom.

The "prominent individual" was a famous explorer of Darkest Africa and he was often gone on his many expeditions. Once he returned from one of his voyages with a leopard cub which he chose to give Luigi as a gift. The cub was adorable. It lived with Luigi in his private suite, drank milk from a baby bottle, and spent the day playing and rolling on the carpet. They called it Kili.

Luigi insisted on redecorating the rooms so that Kili would feel at home and grow up without psychological complexes and traumas. He ordered new rugs with patterns featuring tropical vegetation and hung on the walls large reproductions of the fantastic jungles of Le Douanier Rousseau, in bright colors, with ferocious creatures that seemed to leap right out of the frames. He also replaced the traditional furniture with light pieces made of bamboo, and placed potted palms and hibiscus in every corner.

Among friends and relatives, "Luigi's leopard" became the topic of the day. In the first few months, they lined up to come and play with that adorable big kitty. Then, Kili grew and turned into a magnificent animal. He was no longer a plaything, now he was a wild beast that struck fear and respect into those who saw him. The visitors grew less frequent and, eventually, stopped coming entirely. The door to the hallway that led to Luigi's rooms was equipped with a bolt. Only an especially courageous male housekeeper would venture past that door to do the cleaning. The rest of the domestic help had made it clear that they weren't about to get within reach of the leopard, even if that meant they would be fired. At the end of the first year, Magda realized that it was time to find a new home for Kili. But Luigi did everything he could think of to put off the impending moment of separation, which was sure to be painful for him.

At first, Luca hesitated to accept Aunt Magda's invitation on account of the leopard. He was especially worried about Lillì, fearing that Kili might eat him. Then, when Luigi promised that he'd keep the wild animal under lock and key the whole time, he came around. Still, out of an abundance of caution, he left Lillì in Cortalba.

He had Aunt Magda give him a room on the opposite wing from Luigi's quarters. He was afraid, no doubt about it. Still, having heard so much about Kili, he was also curious to see the animal. One day, he asked Luigi if he could just take a look at the leopard through a crack in the door. He was captivated by the sight. His approach was gradual, day by day, with Luigi's assistance. And, in the end, Luca and Kili became great friends.

Luca spent much of his time away from home. Gino frequented him as assiduously as ever. Each day he'd show up with a tempting new program of activities. They'd go to the theater, to the Ristorante del Cambio, to a soccer match, or else they'd rent a cab for an outing to the Monte dei Cappuccini, where you could fill your lungs with clear, clean air and enjoy a magnificent panoramic view of the city. All this was underwritten by Luca, while Gino acted as treasurer. Luca appreciated his friend's helpful services and happily and trustingly handed over his wallet.

One evening, Gino arranged to go to Madame Irene's. They went on foot, crossing Piazza San Giovanni and venturing into the neighborhood of Porta Palazzo along narrow, dark side streets. They stopped outside a small doorway. All the windows were shut and a dim light filtered through the slats of the shutters. The push-button doorbell was illuminated by a faint lightbulb, but there was no name on the plate.

Gino rang the doorbell and what looked like a real gorilla came to the door; he was so big that he blocked the doorway entirely.

"Who are you?" he asked.

"We're friends of Madame Irene's," Gino replied.

The man looked them up and down and then stepped aside, admtting them to a small waiting room. Just then, a door opened, letting through lights, sounds, and laughter, and Madame Irene appeared in person. She was a little over fifty, corpulent, corseted, and heavily made up, and she wore a satin dress that was as red as her hair.

"My dear Gino, what a pleasure!" she exclaimed. "I'm so pleased that from time to time you think of us. So you brought a friend? Very good, very good indeed." She went on talking as she escorted them through the drawing room, "I'm so sorry that Irma is taken this evening—she has a general... I know that she's your favorite, but you'll see, I'll find you one who's even sweeter. And for your friend—we'll need to treat him well, so he'll be sure to come back—we'll give him Catarì. She's just arrived from Naples, a tender rosebud. Come along, sit down at this table. I'll send the girls right out with the champagne."

They sat down. Luca was visibly frazzled by the surroundings.

"Gino, I don't want to stay here," he said in his thin, faint little voice, which grew increasingly nasal when he was upset.

"What, are you joking?! Don't be a fool. Come on, we're just coming to the good part."

Young women in dishabille sat on customers' knees or sprawled on the sofas in provocative poses. One had extended her legs and put her feet on the table; it was evident that she wore nothing under her half-open flowing robe. She was smoking from a long cigarette holder and between one puff and the next she was humming along to a song that came from the gramophone:

Il m'appelle sa pétite bourgeoise,
la tonqui-qui, la tonqui-qui, la tonquinoise.
Je suis vive, je suis charmante
comme un petit oiseau qui chante.

Lola and Catarì arrived with the champagne and sat down on the velvet settee next to the two friends. Gino noticed Catarì and was immediately captivated. The girl was between eighteen and twenty years of age; her generous body, spilling out of a black dressing gown dotted with red geraniums, made his head spin; she wore black stockings and a lace garter belt; her mop of hair was as shiny and sleek as a silk cloche cap, and her eyes glowed like embers from Mt. Vesuvius. Gino would have preferred to have her for himself, but he didn't dare lay claim to her.

"Hey now, here's a handsome boy!" said Catarì, rubbing up against Luca. "What's your name, then, my fine hunk of man?"

"My name is Luca."

"And you even have a lovely name." Without any further preambles, she laid a hand on his crotch. "What other lovely things have you got for me?... Do you want to show it to Catarì?" And with those words, she squeezed him and, leaning over, submerged him in her overabundant bosom.

"Signorina, I'm sorry. I have nothing to show you. I haven't even brought you a little gift."

"Aren't you a treat? But do you really not understand? Then you must just be a child." She stood up and took him by the hand, "Come along, little one, I'll take good care of you."

"Are you leaving already? What about the champagne?..." asked Gino.

"You drink it. The bubbles make my nose tingle," Luca retorted as he walked off.

"The bubbles make your nose tingle... Oh, you're a laugh riot! Ha, ha, ha. . ." Catarì laughed with gusto, pulling Luca after her up the stairs, covered with a red runner.

An hour later, Madame Irene knocked on the door: "Catarì, it's time to come downstairs. You've already gone past the time limit. Signor Gino is waiting for his friend."

"I'm coming, I'm coming," Catarì replied, putting on the robe with the geraniums and brushing her dark brown mop of hair. She turned to Luca who still hadn't stirred, "Wake up then, little one. What are you doing still in bed? Get moving."

Luca covered his head with the sheet and whined, "I don't want to go away, I want to stay here until tomorrow."

"All right then, I'll have a word with Madame Irene. But this isn't going to be cheap, you know. She's going to want a lot of money."

"It doesn't matter. I can pay."

Someone knocked at the door again.

"I'm coming, I'm coming already," said Catarì impatiently. "Jesus, what pains in the ass they all are!"

Gino had to leave all alone, after paying the extra charge
for Luca. Madame Irene was happy with the profit and Luca
was happy with not having had to give up Catarì's company.

For Luca these were all new sensations. It was as if his entire body were filled with an immense unrestrainable joy,
that suddenly resolved into a state of satiated beatitude. He'd
only perhaps ever attained such a state as a very small child
when he fell asleep on the ample breasts of his peasant wet
nurse, after slaking himself on her sweet nectar. Those long-
ago memories surfaced in his subconscious as he drowned in
Catarì's welcoming arms.

Now he spent his days waiting for nightfall, the moment
that he would once again enter the accommodating boudoir,
and find the warmth of that woman's body, the strong scent of
woman that stirred his vigor. Luca was undergoing a strange
transformation: he felt physically stronger and bolder, while
mentally he was regressing to an increasingly infantile state,
identifying the woman with the mother, and abandoning
himself to a complete dependency. More than loving Catarì,
he wanted her to love him. His emotions were childish and
self-centered.

Catarì became an indispensable part of his life, a source of
pleasure, a good thing he could not do without. He wanted
her all to himself, always present. He wanted to tell her so,
but he had no way of expressing his feelings, save in his awkward, imprecise manner.

"Now, get this damned thing from in front of your eyes," said
Catarì, taking off his pince-nez. "Your mother gave you pretty
eyes, like the sea at midday, when the water is aqua color. But

there's nothing in this sea, there are no thoughts. Why do you hide them?"

Luca lay with his head on Catarì's bosom, their bodies resting perpendicular to each other. She held him in her arms the way you'd hold a small baby.

"Do you like working here?" Luca asked.

"Do you like… don't you like… What does that even mean? The question makes no sense. It's a job, and that's that."

"Well then, you don't like me?"

"What does that have to do with anything? You're a whole different matter. You're a child, and I hold you in my heart."

"What about the other men?"

"The other men… the other men… I don't think about them a bit. I'm just used to them. I started in this life when I was a young girl. We lived in the Quarter… you know, the Spanish Quarter? There were us seven sisters, Papà and Mammà, all of us in one room, *nu vascio.*[9] Papà worked for Don Generoso; he made shoes, sitting outside the door in the alley. Every Saturday, Don Generoso would come round to pick up the shoes and drop off the money. If I was there, he'd pat me on the head and say, 'You're getting to be a big girl, Catarì.' Then, Papà got sick, they took him to the Pellegrini Hospital, and that's where he died. I was fourteen years old, and I was the oldest of us sisters, and Mammà sold me to Don Generoso. She was sobbing, she looked like the Madonna in front of her son on the cross. She kept telling me, 'I'm doing this for you, Catarì. You're going to be taken care of with Don Generoso… And I'm doing it for your sisters, because otherwise these poor creatures are going to starve to death.' Don Generoso had a big apartment on Piazza del Gesù. He treated me well, he gave me plenty of gifts, new dresses, hats with silk ribbons, and on Sundays he'd take me to the Caflisch Café to eat rum babas. He always said that I was like a daugh-

9.   Neapolitan dialect. A small, ground floor apartment, usually without windows or light.

ter to him, but when night came he'd slip into my room and into my bed. His wife was jealous and couldn't get over it. She wouldn't stop nagging him, and saying, 'Genni, I don't want that girl around. It's not right. You've gotta get rid of her.' And he'd answer, 'Nunziatì, don't make me lose my temper. She's a good girl and she stays.' And I did, I stayed with them for four years. Then one night, Don Generoso was stabbed to death by his own men in one of the alleys of Forcella, where they had their business. And the very next day, his widow took me to a brothel."

"It seems like a story by Dickens," said Luca, saddened.

"Hey, this is my own true life story. Who's this Dikki supposed to be?"

"He's a man who wrote stories about unfortunate children. But not in Naples, in London."

"And was you ever in London before?"

"In London, yes."

"And in Naples?"

"In Naples, no."

"Well, you ought to go sometime. Naples is beautiful. I think about it all the time... I get so dreary... because far from Naples you cannot live."

The more the days passed, the more Luca thought about how he could secure Catarì's love, and keep it, exclusive and permanent. Until he finally found the solution: he would marry her. He talked it over with Gino, who approved the idea enthusiastically. This fit in perfectly with the plan that he had been devising for some time.

Luca went to the most renowned jeweler in Turin and purchased a magnificent array of diamonds and rubies. The set didn't include a ring, because it was customary to give one's fiancée a family ring. He decided he would ask his mother for one later.

He showed up with the jewel case in one hand and a shy but dazzling smile on his lips.

"What on earth have you done? I can't keep these jewels. Take them away, or I'll have to give them to Madame Irene," Catarì exclaimed, surprised and upset.

"But I love you."

"And I love you too. I love you with all my heart. But this ain't right."

"I want to marry you."

"Hey, little one, let's not talk crazy. Marry *me*?"

"Gino told me that it's possible and that he'll help me to sign all the papers."

"Don't let that guy pull the wool over your eyes. He's a type that I don't like a bit. A little bit of a gangster, if you ask me."

"Gino is a friend and he'll help us."

"Dang, but you're hardheaded. Listen to me, there's no way around it."

Gino was putting his plan into effect, gradually and with masterful skill. Getting Luca to marry Catarì was nothing more than a pretext for undertaking a larger, all-encompassing design. After lulling his victim into a blissful state of relaxation over several months, he decided that the time had come to unleash the final attack.

Returning by carriage in the early hours of the morning after an evening out at Madame Irene's, Gino savored the aroma of an Egyptian cigarette and looked over at his friend, half-asleep on the seat facing him.

"Are you tired? That girl makes you work hard, doesn't she? How many times did you do it tonight?" he asked.

"Catarì is nice. I'm not tired, I'm just worried because she says that she doesn't want to marry me."

"That's what she says, but it isn't true. She told me that she's willing, but first she wants to be certain that you're serious about this. The problem isn't her, it's your mother."

"Why? I don't understand."

"Your mother will never give her consent for you to marry Catarì. What you need to do is confront her with the done deed, and at that point she will have no choice but to accept the situation because she loves you and will not want to run the risk of losing you entirely. So, not a word to her. You must keep your lips sealed. This must remain a secret between the two of us. As for the wedding, I'll see to all the details. Don't you worry about a thing."

"I don't know how to thank you. You're a real friend."

"These are things you do for your friends. Though you should also think about your finances. You have vast wealth and you need a trusted administrator. Till now it's always been your mother who's managed your assets, but once you're married, you'll no longer be able to rely on her. We don't know how she'll react to the news, and you need to have full control of your fortune. Finance is my business, you know, so I'm entirely at your disposal to manage your funds. I'll draw up a series of documents for your signature and I'll make an appointment with the lawyer."

"Sure, but hurry up, because I want to get married right away."

The day they had an appointment to go to the lawyer's office, Gino came to pick up Luca at Aunt Magda's. The butler asked him to wait in the front room. While he was strolling back and forth in the spacious hall, admiring the large canvases of neo-classical landscapes, Gino sensed a presence behind him... and then heard a guttural sound, as if of some muted rumbling. His blood ran cold. He stood motionless. Then he heard the sound of heavy paws on the marble floor—*plof, plof, plof.* He turned around with some circumspection and found himself face to face with Kili. The leopard was staring at him with his yellow predator's gaze. Gino stepped backward in sheer terror until his back was pressed against the wall. Kili's eyes locked on him, pinning him in place. Gino was sweating profusely, but he didn't dare to move a muscle or emit a sound. He just stood there with his eyes bugging out, arms and legs slightly splayed like a cockroach. Just as he was about to faint from his fright, Luca came running in, out of breath.

"Kili, my dear Kili, I was looking for you," he said, stroking the animal and taking him by the collar. "What are you doing here? Let's get you back to your rooms. Come on, come along." Kili followed him obediently.

A few minutes later, Luca returned with gloves and hat, ready to go out. Gino was mopping his brow with an oversized handkerchief.

"Gino, I'm so sorry for what befell you," he said contritely. "Luigi isn't here today and Kili was all alone. I went to visit him this morning and then forgot to shut the door. You're not scared, are you?"

"Christ! That bastard of a leopard came this close to ripping me limb from limb. And you ask if I'm not scared?"

"I'm sorry. Kili is a good cat. He only does that with people he doesn't like."

"Thanks for the compliment... that's the last thing I needed. Come on, let's forget about it. And let's get going, I don't want to make the lawyer wait."

That day, without realizing it, Luca handed over his entire fortune to the impostor—deeds to land and buildings, shares and securities, and cash—everything, except for the property in Cortalba, to which Olga held the right of usufruct.

Whereupon, Gino announced that he had to go away on business, that the date for the wedding had been set in two months' time, and that he'd be back for the preparations. Meanwhile, he advised Luca to go back to Cortalba, in order to ensure that Olga suspected nothing.

"Remember, don't let a word slip," he urged him. "I'll take care of Catarì. When everything's ready I'll come to get you."

V

It was late autumn by the time Luca returned to the castle. Giusto drove the gig to the train station to pick him up and spread a woolen blanket over his legs. There was a sparkling fizz in the air that announced a harsh winter.

"Cover up nicely and stay warm, Signorino Luca. We certainly don't want you getting sick as soon as you get home. If you only knew, Signora Olga is so worried. She was uneasy the whole time you were away. She reminded me a thousand times to make sure and cover you with the blanket. There we are, all set. Are you comfortable?"

"Yes, yes, I'm fine. And how is Lillì?"

"He was sad too. Anyone could see that he was sorry to see his master was gone."

Giusto seemed older than his sixty years. Since he'd lost his son in the war, his shoulders had grown curved and his hair had turned white. Giustino had never come home from the Carso campaign. He'd just become a nameless cross in one of those countless Alpini cemeteries high in those harsh mountains.

Giusto went on talking the whole way, recounting the little events that constituted the life of the town. The harvest had just taken place, and his nephew Vigìn had won the prize as the best grape-presser; there had been four of them in the vat, crushing the grapes with their britches rolled up above their knees, then one by one the other boys had given up, but Vigìn had gone on pressing for eight hours. Tunìn the gardener's son had gotten married but his mother Maggiorina had been unable to come to the reception because she was sick and in the hospital. The people at the Bric Rutund farmhouse had sent their youngest son to study as a priest because the curate had told them that he was a bright young man and shouldn't be sent to work the soil like his brothers. And so on.

Luca listened absent-mindedly, as the gig moved into the

valley. On the hills, the rows of grape vines had been pruned and the fields tilled, the trees were barren and the grass was dry. Everything had taken on a brownish tinge, and the sun that filtered through the light fog painted the landscape with a thousand nuances of color, from dark brown to rust red, to ochre, and pale yellow. The closer they came to the ramp leading up to Cortalba, the more Luca felt himself being sucked back into the atmosphere of his home town, as if returning to his mother's womb. The image of Turin seemed to recede in the opposite direction and become ever smaller, like when as a child he amused himself by looking the wrong way through a spyglass, putting the big end against his eye, so that everything got smaller and people looked like Snow White dwarfs.

But one image remained vivid in his mind and carved into his memory, preventing him from fully abandoning himself to the charms of his childish world: Catarì's face during their last meeting. A sorrowful, furious face.

The meeting had been stormy.

"Let me get this straight. You and your friend, what is it you want from me?" Catarì began, clearly irate.

"Don't get mad, Catarì. I beg you," Luca implored, on the verge of tears.

"Ah, I'm not supposed to get pissed off. That guy robs you blind and you don't even notice it. He came here yesterday, that cockroach. He offered me money if I'd tell you I wanted to marry you. Look out for him, this is some kind of con game. How many ways do I have to tell you?"

"Gino has prepared everything. You can trust him."

"That guy's going to get me into trouble. And you're in it with him."

"Now I'm going home to my mother's, but in two month's time I'll come back for our wedding."

"Ah, you're leaving? Then go on, get out of here. I thought you were different, but you're every bit as much of an asshole as all the others. Don't let me lay eyes on you ever again!" Catarì yanked open the door and shoved him out of the room.

"Catarì, I'm begging you, wait for me. . .," said Luca with tears rolling down from under his pince-nez.

"Get out of here!!" *Slam*, she swung the door shut behind him.

In Cortalba, Luca resumed his regular routine, slow and enveloping as a loving lullaby. Still, in spite of his apparent languor, he was in the throes of anxiety. The absence of Gino, the uncertainty about his relationship with Catarì, the secret that separated him from his mother—who was the pillar upon which his entire world rested—all put him into a state of depression. He'd frequently doze off during the day. He felt like sleeping for two months without stopping, until his wedding day.

Toward evening, Erminia would knock at the door, "Signorino Luca, dinner's on the table. So the Signora said to call you."

Since there were only two people, they would not eat in the large dining room with the carved walnut buffets, but in the green drawing room, which was more convenient and modern, furnished as it was in Art Nouveau furniture. Here, Olga, worried by the changes in her son's demeanor, had tried repeatedly to question him in a bid to learn the cause. But Luca kept silent and seemed extremely uneasy. Then one morning, everything became clear.

Olga was in her ground floor study, with the windows that looked out onto the Hello Garden. In the summer, the wisteria hung down off the outside wall covering half the windows, and creating a natural awning against the glare of the sun. Now, though, there were only barren skinny vines, and the light that came in was as milky as the fog on the hills. The room was small and cozy, with little stuffed armchairs, satin cushions, Oriental rugs on the terracotta tile floor and, on the walls, paintings and photographs of the House of Savoy, from the founder of the dynasty to the current monarchs; every time a new baby was born, prince or princess, Olga added a new framed portrait.

That morning, as usual, Olga received the domestic help to give them their instructions for the day. When Luca came in with Lillì under his arm—he carried him that way, like a package—Olga was talking to the cook.

"Pina, remember to tell the butcher that we're going to want a five pound veal roast for tomorrow, because Count Ralli will be here, too."

"Is Uncle Riccardo coming?" asked Luca.

"Yes, he's coming to get us, to go to Genoa, just like every year. I've already made arrangements for your trunk."

Luca sat down without speaking. Olga dismissed the cook and turned to him: "What is it, sweetheart, you seem worried about something."

"I'm worried that when Gino comes, he won't find us."

"You just need to let him know that we're leaving for Genoa."

"But he's not here now. He'll be back in two months, and he'll come here expecting to find me. He said that he'll need to give me a report, now that he's the administrator of my property."

Olga turned pale. "Luca, what are you talking about?"

"I just wanted to take one more responsibility off your shoulders, Mamma. This way, you won't have to add up numbers and spend all those hours at your desk. Finance is his profession, and he's just happy to be able to help us."

Olga sat white and stiff as a wax statue, eyes open wide and staring. When Erminia walked in, she took fright and raised her hand to her mouth. "My goodness!" she exclaimed.

"Erminia, my smelling salts. . ." muttered Olga.

VI

By the time Riccardo arrived, Luca had already told the whole story, included the planned wedding. Riccardo asked for all the details, names, addresses, everything that Luca could remember clearly. Then he went to Turin to lodge a formal complaint at Police Headquarters. That winter they didn't go to Genoa, but instead moved in with Aunt Magda so they could be closer to the scene of the investigation. A great many people were questioned, including Catarì who was ultimately cleared completely of any suspicion of collusion. Thanks to Riccardo's determination, as he pushed the investigators throughout each phase of the case and monitored police and magistrates, Gino Barone was arrested, tried, and sentenced to a stiff prison term for "taking advantage of a person of unsound mind."

But it proved impossible to recover the money and assets. All of the property and all of the stocks and bonds had been sold off, as had all of Olga's jewelry that had been stored in the safe deposit box. What had become of the cash remained a mystery. My information on these points remains quite vague. I heard this story from Alma, who was just fifteen years old at the time and had only a limited understanding of what happened. She remembered the comments of the adults, snatches of conversations overheard at meals or in the drawing room, and also the headlines in the newspapers that reported on the episode in the crime pages, with ironic comments—"*Naïve Millionaire Falls Victim to Outrageous Fraud*," "*Loose Women and Champagne for the Defrauded Millionaire*," and so on. Over the course of her long life, Alma told me this story many times, often in the context of a bitter lamentation about the twists of fate and the adverse circumstances that had affected the family.

"If it hadn't been for Uncle Luca we wouldn't be in these conditions," she'd start out. "Of course, I can't really blame

him because he was what he was." Then she'd shift her sights
to other targets. "The ones who were really at fault were my
grandmother and my father; she let herself be swindled by
that scoundrel, blinded as she was by her love for her son,
and father never knew how to put his foot down in time, always timid, always cautious, with no interest in anything but
photography." With the passing of time, in Alma's mind it
was Ernesto's interest in photography that became the root
cause of the family's decline, and this kept her from appreci-
ating her father's art, which she unfailingly treated with con-
descension, as if it were some unfortunate hobby, or even an
addiction. "This isn't just talk, I know whereof I speak. My
father has been totally irresponsible. First he sold all the lands
in Colisso because he didn't feel like looking after them; all he
wanted to do was stroll on his lands, and take pictures of pretty farmgirls with sheaves of wheat. Certainly, we lived well,
with plenty of resources, because the proceeds from the sale of
those lands were wisely invested and generated a substantial
return. But after the war, with the devaluation of the lira and
the collapse of the stock market, there was nothing left, just a
handful of dust. And he did the same thing with Uncle Luca's
last remaining piece of property, the castle of Cortalba. Since
he was Uncle Luca's guardian, he wanted to create a source
of income for him after grandmother's death, but he sold the
property at a pre-war price, and so Uncle Luca too remained
penniless. My father was an honest man, but he wasn't exactly a genius when it came to business. The new owners, who
were commercial people, immediately clear-cut the woods.
Centuries-old trees, a crime... Those magnificent cedars of
Lebanon, it took six men with their arms outstretched to embrace the trunk of one of those trees. That was an ecological
disaster. Just by selling the timber, they completely earned
back the price of the property. And what a piece of property... because my father left everything in the castle, to convey with it: eighteenth-century furniture, fine artwork, silver,

Sèvres porcelain. I just can't forgive him for his carelessness. My mother used to say the same thing. She often grew irritated with Papà, and when she came close to being fed up, she'd issue a threat, but taking care not to be overhead by him, 'I've had it up to here. One fine day I'm going to take back my dowry and leave.' I remember when I was little that the thought frightened me, because her dowry was our house in Turin. At night I would dream of my mother as a snail that took its house away with it, leaving us out in the open. In any case, this is where we ended up, out in the open..." And here her voice would break, and hot tears of dismay would roll down her lovely face.

Luca only partly understood what had happened. To him, money was an abstract concept with which he had no emotional relationship. Therefore, having been defrauded and robbed resulted in no real sense of loss. He was sorry that he'd lost a friend, more than anything else. In his perception of what had happened, Gino had abandoned him because Luca had betrayed their secret. And then things had gotten all tangled up. Riccardo had gotten involved and then... At this point Luca's thoughts broke off. The investigation and the trial, at which he had been obliged to testify, had been a traumatic experience that his mind had refused to record. Luca remembered very little of the whole thing.

When the trial came to an end, Olga threw a party for Riccardo in recognition of his invaluable contribution to the final victory—even if that victory was strictly moral in nature. It was the last evening of their stay in Turin, before returning to Cortalba. They invited Ada and Ernesto over, along with a small group of intimate friends. The toasts and the celebratory speeches began even before sitting down to table, when the guests gathered in the drawing room for the aperitif.

Olga shook the little silver bell that sat on the side table... *ding-ding-ding...* all conversation broke off and she began to speak. "My dear Riccardo, we are all so grateful to you for your magnificent achievement. Thanks to your warrior spirit, sustained by legitimate outrage and a firm sense of honor, justice has been done." The room broke into applause.

Riccardo struggled to his feet, hampered by the onset of gout that had been afflicting him for some time, and took the floor. "Thanks, friends. This old soldier who can no longer fight with the sword must now fight with tongue and pen. It is with a hint of pride that this evening I drink with you to the defeat of the enemy... ahem... of a fraud and a con artist who, for many years to come, will be unable to do any more harm to society."

Then it was Ernesto's turn to speak. "Riccardo, I can only join in the universal chorus of praise and congratulate you wholeheartedly for your brilliant summation in court, worthy of the golden oratory of a master lawyer. As you know, I no longer practice as a lawyer for various reasons, but chiefly because I dislike conflict and fighting of any kind. So I am grateful to you for having taken on this burden. Now, however, the time has come to give you a well deserved break. Today I have accepted a new responsibility as Luca's guardian, and I shall perform this duty with fondness and tenacity, to the best of my abilities." Everyone applauded again.

In the general thrill of excitement, no one paid the slightest attention to Luca. He sat off to one side, feeling sad and lonely. Kili too was gone, they'd donated him to the zoo. For days, Luca had been searching for the ideal moment to elude his mother's eagle eye and slip outside. He wanted to rush to see Catarì, explain to her that adverse circumstances had kept him from returning as he had promised to do, but that he'd been thinking about her the whole time, that he dreamed of her love, that he felt sad and lonely. Between one toast and another, he managed to sneak out unseen.

Once he was outside, he realized that he'd forgotten to bring his hat and scarf, and he shivered at the intense cold.

But he wasn't willing to turn back. He walked down the road he'd strolled down so many times before with a light step and a heart brimming over with joy. But that same road now seemed long and hard.

It was particularly difficult to make his way through the center of town because it was a Carnival night. From Piazza Vittorio, the enormous square on the banks of the river, where every year rides and amusement stands of all sorts were set up, a cheerful flow of masked people moved up Via Po and poured onto Piazza Castello and the surrounding streets, running and shouting.

Luca had difficulty making his way through that heaving throng, in part because he was corpulent and not sufficiently agile to go with the flow of the crowd, and in part because he was terrified by that swirling tide of masks, which struck him as grotesque and malevolent. Hooked noses, rapacious talons, werewolf fangs... it was as if all the fearsome nightmares of the fairytales were materializing before his eyes. The confetti got into his mouth and made him cough; from the market stands, the sickly sweet aroma of nougat and cotton candy saturated the air, making him feel nauseous; the paper streamers wrapped around his ankles like snakes and made him stumble and fall. He lost his sense of direction and was forced to ask the way. He addressed a mask that seemed better-natured than the others, a Gianduja[10] with a wart on his nose and a bottle of Barbera red, already empty. But the Gianduja could barely stand up, and his eyes were drooping shut. The Giacometta who accompanied him said, "He's drunk, doesn't understand a thing anymore. I need to get him home," and the two of them staggered off, weaving and wobbling.

At last, Luca managed to find the gloomy little street and the house with the darkened windows. He rang the bell. The bouncer came to the door and ushered him into the waiting room. Then Madame Irene arrived. She no longer had her

---

10.   Gianduja and Giacometta are the regional masks of Piedmont.

usual saccharine expression. Now she had a harsh, hostile look on her face.

"What do you want?" she asked in a cold voice.

Luca was stunned. He was accustomed to a far different reception. "But... it's me, Luca... don't you recognize me?" he stammered.

"Yes, I'm afraid I do recognize you, all too well. I'd have much preferred never to see you again. We've been through a great deal of trouble on your account. That friend of yours wound up in prison... that's not very good publicity for us, for people to know that some of our customers are criminals. The *carabinieri* were here, they insisted on questioning the girls, and especially that Catarì. So, afterward, I fired her. We're not looking for scandals. This is a respectable brothel, and the girls who work here are all law-abiding."

"But where has Catarì gone?"

"I have no idea. That's none of my business. But one thing is clear, from now on she only has two options: work as a scullery maid, or as a streetwalker."

Luca left with a heavy heart. He felt sad and lonely. Abandoned. They were all gone now: Catarì, Gino, and even Kili. He caught a cab because he didn't feel a bit well. By the time he got home he was feverish and he was put to bed with a serious case of bronchitis. "I always tell him to make sure he bundles up, with hat and scarf..." Olga said over and over, twisting her hands. It became necessary to put off the departure for Cortalba.

Surrounded by loving care, Luca gradually got better. He regained his good humor, as well. The image of Catarì vanished from his memory just the same way that, many years before, Monsieur Lesavoir used to remove a drawing from the blackboard with a sweep of the eraser—the image would disappear and that reality no longer existed.

10

The Enchanted Wood
1933

I

"Here, here, Gio. It's right on this leaf, catch it. Hurry!" Mina pointed to a dragonfly with iridescent wings that had just landed on an aquatic plant in the goldfishbasin.

Gio swung his net, but he missed. The dragonfly took to the air, tracing a kaleidoscopic arabesque as it went.

"You're always half asleep. You're going to have to get faster, otherwise the game is no fun," Mina scolded him. She was sitting on the edge of the basin, rippling the water with one hand and directing the action with the other.

"First of all, this is no game," Gio retorted in a didactic but indulgent tone of voice. "I'm putting together an insect collection, which is a serious matter. Next point, I'm not asleep, because I've already caught dozens of them—dragonflies, butterflies, bumblebees, stag beetles, and beetles of every description." Gio maintained and added to his collection with scientific interest. He classified every specimen and kept it impaled on a pin in special display cases.

"Beetles give me the creeps, they all look like cockroaches. You need to eliminate them," Mina commented, with a little smirk of disgust.

"Eliminate them? These are particularly tough species. They're as old as the castle... in fact, much older. They've existed for thousands and millions of years and will continue to exist long after we're extinct. When the castle is just a ruin and the outer walls are buried in vegetation, the tower tumbling down, the lanes and gardens overrun by weeds and brambles, insects will once again take over the location and will continue to prosper and multiply."

"Maybe so. But you have to get the beetles out of the collection. I don't like them. Put more dragonflies in it."

Gio said nothing, as he always did whenever he wanted to put an end to an argument with his sister. It was a tactic he had learned from an early age. He had learned that Mina always had to have the last word, whether she was right or wrong; that she was hard-headed and would dig in her heels like a young mule; and that once she'd made up her mind she rejected out of hand all arguments to the contrary—"don't preach your sermons to me, I won't even listen to them." Mina had a fanciful mind, an artistic temperament, and a rebellious personality, intolerant of rules and restrictions. Since she was very sensitive, she tended to react disproportionately to even the slightest provocation, and with the fervid imagination she had, she often invented those provocations. When she felt that some wrong had been done to her, whether real or imaginary, at first she reacted theatrically, with tears and recriminations, and then with rage and determination, committing to a personal challenge with herself and others to prove that, in spite of everything, she knew how to get by in cases of adversity. Gio realized that Mina was anxious by nature and that her aggressiveness was a form of self-defense, and so he indulged his sister. He felt protective toward her, because Mina was younger than he, and because she was a "female." And so, the two siblings grew up in perfect accord, enjoying each other's company.

Mina exerted a powerful allure over others, precisely because of the complexity of her personality, but also because of her uncommon beauty. Still, everyone admired her "at a distance," as it were, with uneasiness, because she only took a chosen few into her confidence. Toward the rest of humanity, she displayed mistrust or, in the best of cases, indifference. Now that she was sixteen years old, certain intemperate responses could no longer be attributed to childish tantrums. Mina might have been a Libra, but an unbalanced one. And rather than trying to correct her, Ada always sympathized with her.

Gio changed the subject. "I'm going with Davide to Le Gaggìe today to pick up some honey. Do you want to come with us?"

"That farmhouse is far away. How are you going to go, on foot?"

"No, by bicycle. It's only three miles."

"But doesn't the farmer bring the honey to us?"

"Yes, he usually does. But I want to go see the new beehives that Grandma had them put in last month. I hear that they're different, more modern. And that the bees that live in them are an African breed, bigger than ordinary bees."

"But why is Davide coming, too?" Mina asked, suspiciously.

Davide Della Rocca belonged to a noble family that spent their summers in the castle of Roccalta, on the hill facing Cortalba. Olga and the Della Rocca family were long-time acquaintances and they exchanged regular courtesy calls. Davide and Gio were the same age, and they were high-school classmates.

"Oh just because... for the company," Gio replied. And then, with an ironic little smirk, "Or else, maybe, because he hopes to see you. He has a crush on you. He thinks you're very beautiful, he told me so, loud and clear."

"Well, I think he's very ugly. With that white, white skin of his and his red hair, so curly and tangled... he looks like a ghost with the head on fire."

"Davide is very intelligent. You can talk about anything with him, from insects to philosophy. And then, when it comes to math he's a real genius, everyone says so. So if you want to come, we need to meet in an hour at the crossroads of the little chapel."

"I'm only coming if Piero and Marilù come too."

"We'll call them. And why not invite the other cousins as well ? We can have a nice big outing, all together."

"No no. Lucilla is a weakling and a sissy, she doesn't even know how to ride a bike, she always falls over. And Marcello is too fat—Marcello the Marshmallow."

"That's a nickname you gave him."

"Yes, and it's a good one because now everyone calls him that."

"Should we tell Marta and Chiara?"

"Oh, lord, no! They're goody-goodies—"Santa-Maria" and "Ora-Pro-Nobis." The way they always talk is as if they were saying their rosaries, one of them starts a sentence and the other one finishes it. Don't you dare even think of inviting them. In fact, we need to scamper out of here without letting them spot us, otherwise they're sure to want to tag along."

They came back toward evening. It was still light out and the sun, hanging low in the sky, lengthened the shadows of the bike riders along the road and made them drag along the banks. The fine tufa-stone dust that was kicked up by the bicycle tires whitened their tanned legs, their sweaty faces, and their unkempt hair.

"We look like floured fish, ready for the frying pan," Marilù commented, prompting a resounding burst of laughter.

"Now we all look like Davide, we're all as white as he is," added Mina. Another burst of laughter. Even Davide laughed, tickled by the joke. He was willing to accept Mina's sarcasm and her brusque manners, contented just to be able to be near her.

Their shadows glided over the humble vegetation lining the country road: the dense acacia flowers, the blackberry thorn bushes, the shrubbery of red dog rose, and the fluffy balls of chicory—ethereal globes that would carry off wishes in a puff. The plants, too, were covered with a blanket of white dust kicked up by some flock of sheep, or one of the few passing vehicles, most of them ox carts.

Piero pointed to the blackberry thorn bushes. "Look, even the blackberries are white. Never mind, we can dust them off and then they're delicious. Let's stop for a minute."

They got off their bikes and got busy picking the succulent berries, scratching their hands and arms on the thorny branches to reach the biggest and prettiest ones.

Piero picked a poppy flower from the edge of a ditch. "This poppy has lost its blood-red color. It's so pale. Perhaps it's a dead poppy." The others laughed at that strange idea, but Piero remained lost in thought.

When it was time to leave, Davide went over to Mina, picked up her bicycle, and took her hand to help her get on.

"Don't touch me," said Mina, pushing him away. "And don't touch my bicycle. I don't need any help. You'll make me lose my balance."

"Excuse me," said Davide, mortified.

"Davide, don't you know her yet?" Gio broke in. "Mina is persnickety, Signorina Don't-Touch-Me."

"Don't you try to get funny," Mina upbraided him. "You men always stick together."

They resumed pedaling at a solid clip to regain the time they'd lost. At the crossroads of the little chapel, the bell towers of Roccalta and Cortalba chimed seven o'clock, with the peals bouncing back and forth from one hilltop to the other like ping pong balls. Davide peeled to the left, the others took the switchback road on the right. At the top of the hill, on the piazza in front of the church, Piero and Marilù said goodbye. Mina and Gio made their way through the small gate and then pushed their bicycles by hand up the driveway. They left the bikes in the gardener's shed. Gio took two large jars of honey from the basket on the rear fender and headed for the kitchen to put them in the pantry. Mina ran to her bedroom to wash up before dinner.

There still wasn't an aqueduct in Cortalba. It was built later, in 1935, a gift from Mussolini, and inaugurated with great pomp and circumstance: a brass band, a parade, a benediction, speeches, and tastings of the "potable water." At the castle, though, there was a highly efficient independent plumbing system, designed by Pietro back in the day. Every bathroom was equipped with its own zinc water tank near the ceiling, in turn connected to faucets and showers. The system was also in use for the water closets. The tanks were filled every morning with well water. Moreover, from the kitchen they would carry pitchers of hot water for those who preferred a tub bath.

There was an attendant specially assigned to the water supply, called Kerplunk after the sound that the bucket made as it rose and dropped into the well, punctuating the early hours of the day—*ker-plunk, ker-plunk.* The well was in the Hello Garden, next to the big linden tree, and it was sheltered by a decorative eight-sided wooden pagoda. It was two hundred and fifty feet deep, and produced a light, cool water that no aqueduct could ever hope to equal. In fact, they continued to draw the castle's drinking water from that well. Until the well was contaminated by an ugly incident... but that took place many years later, during the German occupation.

When Mina arrived in the dining room, the soup had already been served. With downcast eyes, she hastily slipped into her chair. Her hair was still wet and it stuck to her forehead and cheeks, even though she had pulled it back with a couple of hairclips. Erminia approached with the soup tureen to fill her bowl. Olga stopped her.

"Erminia, Signorina Mina is going to skip the first course this evening. The rest of us have finished. You may change the dishes and move on to the second course."

Everyone else at the table pretended not to notice the incident. Mina said nothing, but she thought to herself that when she had a house of her own, she wouldn't impose schedules for lunch and dinner, and she'd eat at all hours, when and how she pleased.

Gio, who was sitting beside her, whispered, "What took you so long?"

"There was no more water in the bathroom. I had to call for them to bring pitchersful. What about you, how did you do it so fast?"

"I went to the extra bathroom on the ground floor. I knew that you were upstairs. Anyway, Grandma is right about punctuality. You know that Uncle Luca can't wait even a minute when it's time to sit down for a meal."

Riccardo interrupted the various conversations, demanding everyone's attention. "Friends! It is my pleasant duty to announce that the winning dish this evening is…" and he extracted a slip of paper from a small bowl, unfolded it, and read aloud, "*La bonne et l'aiguiseur*. Who has it?"

"I do, I do," exclaimed Luca. "I win!"

"Always so lucky, our dear Luca. The prize will be a second helping of crème caramel," Riccardo concluded.

Mina applauded like everyone else, but under her breath she said to Gio, "I can't believe we still play this same stupid game every night. We've done it as long as I can remember."

"True, and when we were little we loved it. It was the high point of the evening. You didn't care whether or not you won, but you always wanted to have that same dish, The Servant Girl and the Knife Sharpener. And if they ever forgot to give it to you, you'd start crying and refuse to eat."

Mina shrugged her shoulders and smirked at him, as if to say, "So what?"

The game involved a particular service of Sèvres china, with a decorative theme. Every dish was different from the others, and each depicted a naïve vignette of domestic or city life, typical of popular etchings and illustrated magazines.

The dishes were set at random, and the winner was drawn by lot. The dish in question depicted a servant girl, a *bonne*, who was having her knives sharpened on the street corner, and she paid the knife sharpener with a little kiss, delivered on tiptoe. The caption read, *"Petit service, gros gâgne."* Small service, great profit.

Whoever received this dish hastened to offer it to Mina, who at the time might have been six years old, the age at which children were first allowed to eat at the table with the grown ups. They did so with solicitous care, in order to avoid her annoying tantrums. Even Marta and Chiara and the young cousins courteously handed over the dish. Only Lucilla refused to yield. If her mother urged her to give it to Mina, she would reply, "They gave it to me, and I'm going to keep it," while giving Mina a triumphant look. Perhaps the dislike that Mina felt toward Lucilla over the course of their long lives derived from those episodes.

Unlike Mina, Lucilla was always perfectly neat and tidy, with coquettish little dresses and a light-blue ribbon in her hair, matching the color of her bright, mischievous eyes. Lucilla was quite rotund, in figure and in face. When she was small, she was an adorable doughball. But when she grew up, her rotundity gave her a somewhat unrefined appearance. Ernesto didn't like to take pictures of her, and when people asked him why he replied, "Lucilla is a lovely little Dutch girl," making reference to the chubby peasant girls on the cheese labels.

Ada was trying to calm Mina's sobbing with blandishments of all kinds. "I'll give you my dish, which is even nicer. Look, it's the one with the cat that wants to eat the canary in the cage, and the little girl is pulling its tail."

"No-o-o!!!! I want *la bonne!*"

"Don't be like that. Stop making that racket, or else Grandma will send you away."

The threat of being evicted from the table did have a certain effect, because Mina couldn't have tolerated a further humiliation. And so she tried to stifle her sobs, expressing her sorrow with big silent tears that fell into the "ugly" dish. She felt like one of those little birds in the large hunting picture above the buffet, lifeless and dangling from a string, sacrificed for the table.

For the rest of her life, Alma felt a profound sense of injustice. But only where she was concerned. It did not extend to the realization of a larger, universal injustice. At the age of eighty, she still complained that she had always been subjected to "mistreatment and abuse," and she congratulated herself for having been able to overcome these calamities with her own strength. She admitted, though, that her childhood and youth had been, by and large, happy times. Especially the summers spent at Cortalba.

Mina saw herself as a little girl again, together with Gio. They were walking along holding hands down the suite of drawing rooms, heading for the tower room, tiny in those immense spaces with their dizzyingly high walls.

Gio cracked open the door that led into Luca's room. "Uncle Luca, shall we play the button game?" he asked. He remained hidden behind the door, with only his head visible. Mina was behind him, leaning over to one side, craning her neck to show that she was there, too. They were three or four years old and they found Luca to be an excellent playmate.

The tower room, adjoining the library, had once been Pietro's study. When Luca moved into it, it became his play room. He brought the gramophone and many stacks of records. He filled the lovely circular room with crates of newspapers to which he subscribed, and which he never read, but still meticulously collected, year after year, volume after volume, from the *Corriere dei Piccoli* (*The Children's Courier*) to the *Gazzetta dello Sport* (*The Sport Gazette*). Some of the newspapers had been bound in annual editions; in particular, *Mon*

Journal, a French magazine for kids with illustrated stories and articles about people and countries, scientific discoveries, and so forth. He also had a nice series of Imageries d'Épinal, large-format books with pages in paper as thin as onionskin and illustrations embellished with gilded details. And then there was the *Enciclopedia dei Ragazzi* , a six-volume children's encyclopedia; books by Jules Verne in original editions that he liked to have Monsieur Lesavoir read to him; and many other marvels that made Mina's and Gio's jaws drop. Among them was a wooden box with a red inscription on the lid, *Jeux Nouveaux*. It contained all sorts of puzzles and brain teasers, each in its own little colorful box: *Casse-tête Chinois, Les Sept Cartes Mystérieuses, Les Dés Acrobates, L'Étoile Merveilleuse, Jeu de l'Araignée, Jeu de la Chasse au Loup, Images des Dominos*, and many others besides.

But the greatest wonder of them all were "the goggles." They were a stereoscope, a metal device with floral motifs in the Art Nouveau style, which took the form of a mask with special lenses. You placed the mask against your face and you could look at a stereoscopic postcard inserted in the appropriate slot a certain distance from the lenses. The postcards were switched out at regular intervals. Photographs of exotic scenes of nature, foreign cities, architectural complexes, snowy landscapes, and wild animals emerged from the frame in three dimensions, drawing in the viewer. It was a genuine virtual experience.

The path to all these wonders was the "button game." Luca would take a seat in a straight-backed chair as big as a throne, with a carved wooden frame and a velvet seat. On either side of the chair were two sphinxes whose heads served as armrests. Mina and Gio would climb up on the sphinxes and the friezes surrounding them until they reached Luca's level, then they'd reach out an arm and, taking turns, press their little fingers on the buttons of his jacket. Each time a button was pressed, Luca would emit a sound. Often the sound was *bong*, which meant that you lost. But every so often the sound was *bing*, and that meant you'd won. Then the winner could claim the prize that she or he desired: to leaf through an illustrated book, take on the challenge of a brainteaser, or admire the 3D images through the "goggles."

Luca was an equitable dispenser of *bings* and *bongs*, but he invariably found a way to end the game so that the last *bing* always belonged to Mina. To make her happy. And Gio willingly accepted this convenient fix in the rules.

II

The morning after the outing to the Gaggìe, Mina was awakened by the usual background noises. *Ker-plunk, ker-plunk* went the bucket in the well; *trr-rack, trr-rack* went Tunìn's rake over the gravel in the garden; *arf, arf, arf* went Lillì as he chased after the mailman. Mina loved to laze under the bedclothes until Erminia arrived with breakfast. She could hear her coming for a long way down the hallway: *ting-ta-ting, ting-ta-ting* went the silverware and dishes on the tray.

Erminia came in and set the tray down on the bed. She opened the shutters on the window that overlooked the garden, allowing the intense scent of the wisteria to enter the room; on this side, the room was on the second floor, and therefore closely linked to the activities of domestic life. Then, Erminia opened the window on the opposite side, where there was a thirty-foot drop to the Lane of Roses beneath, and then the dense underbrush of the woods, enclosing the mysterious allure of untouched nature. The woods ran down the slope to the valley below, where it stopped as it came even with the farmland and the meadows. From there, the sounds of grazing cattle rose to Mina: *ding-dong, ding-dong, ding-dong* went the cow bells. From the forest came only the calls of birds, the monotonos *coo-coo* of the owl at night, and in the morning, a frenetic cacophony of a hundred independent cries, each with its own tone and rhythm.

"Did you sleep well, Signorina Mina?" asked Erminia.

Mina nodded her head, unable to speak because she'd just sunk her teeth into a large bite of bread and honey, and her mouth was full.

"Take it easy there, chew thoroughly or it'll get stuck in your throat," Erminia said, filling a cup with *café au lait*. "Here, have a sip of this and it'll go down easier."

The country bread—*pane rustico*—was one of the delights that made life in Cortalba so very enjoyable. Mina couldn't get enough of it, as she preferred it to any delicacy. The oversized loaves arrived in the morning from the oven, hot and fragrant. Aunt Delina brought them in her basket, covered by an expanse of white canvas. She had married Erminia's uncle, Bastiàn the baker. She was younger than her husband and went around making deliveries. He always stayed in the bakery, close to his grotto of flame, sliding loaves and breadsticks into and out of the oven with a long wooden peel. Every so often, when Mina and Gio were small, Erminia obtained permission from Ada to take them to the bakery. The visit to the workshop of "Stromboli" was a thrilling adventure for the children. Uncle Bastiàn struck a certain fear into them, like an ogre from a fairytale. He was a giant with a shiny, bald head that gleamed like a bocce ball. In contrast, he had a large bushy mustache that covered his mouth and made it impossible to see if by some chance he were smiling; as a result, he always seemed to have a grim expression. But the thing that most fascinated Mina and Gio about that face was a glass eye that never shut, and which reflected the dancing flames in the furnace. Uncle Bastiàn had lost that eye in the war, when he was with the Alpini mountain brigade, and the Fatherland had given him the gift of that marvelous colorful marble. There was just one thing: the Fatherland had made a slight mistake and had sent him a marble of the wrong hue. And so, Uncle Bastiàn had one dark eye and one blue eye. Mina and Gio clung to Erminia's skirt, afraid to speak, following every movement of that fantastic individual. Uncle Bastiàn remained absorbed in his work, giving no sign that he'd even noticed their presence. But when it was time to go, he'd wrap up a package of biscotti and hand them to Erminia, saying, "For the children," and then turn with his peel back to the oven.

Erminia had finished serving breakfast. "Unless you need me, Signorina, I'll go back downstairs. There's such a lot of work to do today. We're expecting Signora Magda."

"Go right ahead, Erminia. I don't need anything," Mina replied, dismissing her.

Mina needed her space and often the presence of others annoyed her. Until just a few years earlier, she'd had to share the room with Gio. But at the age of twelve, Gio was moved into a small bedroom on the ground floor in order to give Mina her *privacy*, to use the English word—and also because at that age it just wasn't right for brother and sister to sleep together.

Before then, though, it had been comforting for Mina to have Gio in the nearby bed. Noises in the nighttime frightened her. From outside came the baying of the dogs, now unleashed, tearing around the grounds in a savage rampage. Titì and Totò, so gentle with the children who brought them a chunk of bread during the day, when they were on the chain, were transformed into ferocious guardians emitting bloodcurdling feral cries when the sun set. Indoors, the castle was full of mystery and arcane presences, and the noises of the night instilled fear. They could hear keys turn in rusty locks, the creaking of doors opening, squeaks, dull noises that echoed in the cellars, the clubfooted steps of heavy boots on the floors of the attic above, lightfooted steps in their very same room, as if of some disquieted soul, unable to find rest—they knew that this was the young Marchesina who had committed suicide. Frequently, Mina couldn't get to sleep and she'd call out to her brother. "Gio, did you hear the footsteps? There's a ghost in our bedroom."

"Yes, I heard them; but it might have been a mouse. Put the covers over your head and stop thinking about it."

Then in the morning all the nightmares would dissipate, evicted by the joyous reality of the day. Mina and Gio would stand a few minutes looking out the window thrown open onto the woods, while Erminia laid out their breakfast on the table. Their eyes were searching for *the* tree, a tree unlike all the others, with huge surface roots and low branches that allowed them to climb it easily. They'd point it out to each other—"I saw it first." "No, I saw it first." The tree was very tall and had a very particular top because of the branches that folded in upon themselves high up. It towered like the bubbling spray of a fountain over that carpet of foliage viewed from above. Even its color was strange. It looked blue instead of green. No one knew what kind of tree it was, so the children decided to name it the "sesame" tree, a word that was phonetically evocative of plants, and which also had certain magical, Arabian Nights connotations.

In the period from age eight to twelve, Mina and Gio would venture every day into the depths of the woods and climb up the "sesame" tree. They'd reach a sort of broad, flat platform at the confluence of two branches, and there Gio would swing on a rope that hung from a higher branch—"... and then Tarzan returns home swinging on a liana vine, with the treasur coffer that he found in the abandoned temple tucked under one arm, and Jane is there waiting for him..."

"No, Jane isn't there anymore. She ran away with Sandokan.[11] She was sick and tired of spending all her time up in this tree waiting for Tarzan."

"But that's not possible. Sandokan belongs in another book."

---

11   The lead character of Emilio Salgari's adventure stories for teens and pre-teens, very popular in Italy at the turn of the 20th century.

"Well, I want to put them together. While Tarzan went out to play with his monkeys, Sandokan shows up with the Tiger Cubs of Malaysia who had ventured into the depths of this unfamiliar jungle, and he stops at the foot of Jane's tree to ask for a glass of water. And when he sees how pretty she is he asks her if she wants to come away with him, and she says yes. And the Tiger Cubs shout: Hurrah!"

"This story doesn't add up. Sandokan is a warrior, and he can't take a woman everywhere with him."

"But the story isn't over. Sandokan teaches Jane how to use a sword and, once she learns, she takes a horse and travels the world on her own. And one day she dresses as Zorro, another day as Robin Hood, and another day still as the Red Corsair, and she has the time of her life because she wins all her battles."

"There's no playing with you. You don't play by the rules."

"And you don't know how to keep up with changes. You're a knucklehead."

III

After Erminia left the room, Mina took her time finishing her breakfast. She stretched and yawned and cast a glance at the woods outside the window. The expanse of trees seemed like a continent on a map, with depressions and elevations according to the subtle shades of color. Right now, the "sesame" was invisible. Grownup eyes could no longer pick it out. But the forest had maintained its ambiguous allure, the charm of a wild place full of adventure and danger.

Mina soaped up her face and ears, brushed back her heavy golden-chestnut hair, and was ready to go downstairs. She devoted no particular attention to her physical appearance. She had no need. She accepted her beauty as a given which required no care, no contrivances. When I was already a big girl, I was intrigued by the fact that my mother, unlike all the other women I'd ever met, wore neither bra nor high heels. I asked her the reason why many times, and the answer was always the same, "They're a nuisance." In those days, no one used the word feminism; for that matter, my mother had never made a political gesture, hers was quite simply a rejection of constrictive, pointless instruments.

Certainly, a brassiere would have been superfluous. Mina's breasts were firm and round as in the classical sculptures of nymphs and undines.

As for high heels, they would have been superfluous, too. Mina was tall and had long, shapely legs. In fact, I ought to emphasize that they were extraordinary legs, legs that made men fall in love and women seethe with jealousy. Lucilla confessed to me when she was already aged, speaking of those long-ago summers, that certain of Mina's attributes filled her with envy. "She walked with such negligent nonchalance, with a natural elegance, on those gleaming, tanned legs of hers. She had long legs, but not like the spider legs of these supermodels you see nowadays on television. She had genuine women's legs, like Marlene Dietrich's, but even more beautiful. A design that could only have sprung from the mind of God, directly, without the interference of DNA."

All this can also be deduced from the photographs of those years. One of them depicts Ada between her two children. It's a snapshot, not posed like most of the pictures in the collection. You can imagine that the photographer, happening along, might have said, "Why don't you stand in front of that bush. You, Mina, to your mother's right. Gio, to the left. There, that's it, hold it!… You look wonderful." Ada has the appearance of a middle-aged lady, even if she was only forty or so. Her hair is streaked with gray and pulled up on the back of her head, her dress is elegant but understated. Mina is wearing a tight-fitting blouse and a slightly flounced skirt that is just below knee-length. A bit of the shirt tail is coming untucked from her belt. Her pose is coquettish. She's wrapping one arm about Ada's waist and tilting her head toward her mother's shoulder as if in search of support and affection. For all her vaunted independence, Mina still counted implicitly on the fact that Ada was always ready to console her in her sorrows, solve her problems, and provide for her needs. Gio has a more detached pose; he isn't touching his mother, and his gaze is directed outside of the frame. He's wearing athletic attire, white flannel trousers with wide pleats that sag over the tennis shoes and an open necked shirt with a long, pointy collar. He's a handsome young man, with raven hair and dark eyes, like Ada. Mina, in contrast, is lighter in complexion and hair.

Mina's colors can't be appreciated in a black-and-white photograph and must be described separately. Her hair, dense and smooth, was a handsome chestnut hue with golden highlights, and the same highlights picked out golden straws in her hazel eyes, brightening the sweetness of her gaze with a vivid and penetrating light. Ever since she was small, Riccardo had developed the habit of commenting, "With those bewitching eyes she's going to turn a lot of men's heads." This harmonious color palette was completed by her skin tone, tea rose petals with hints of incarnadine, taut and glowing over the sculptural features of her face—a broad forehead, determined, well shaped arched eyebrows, high cheekbones, a strong nose and a broad smile that revealed all her teeth, gleaming and even.

Mina walked out into the Hello Garden. She saw Riccardo reading the newspaper under the linden tree. His gout had worsened and during the winter they had had to amputate two toes on his right foot that had become gangrenous. Now he spent most of his time sitting with his foot resting on a cushion. The minute he spotted Mina, he called to her.

"Minabella, come here, come here. Come sit with me for

a while. A pity that I'm not much of a *preux chevalier*. When your mother was your age, we battled furiously on the tennis court, but now the most I can do is take you on at bridge... Oh the pain, oh the pain... Mina, please come and adjust this cushion under my foot. Just make it a little higher. That's good, thanks."

"You're quite welcome. This morning I have nothing else to do, so I can keep you company. I was looking for Gio... You haven't seen him, by any chance?"

"An hour ago, he went by here with his insect net and cages. He said he was going down to the meadow." Riccardo picked up the newspaper that he'd laid down on the table. "Here, take a page for yourself, the crossword page. It's certainly the most interesting page in the whole paper."

"But what kind of news do they have on the front page?"

"Excellent news, naturally. Every day we read the same things. Another hydroelectric power plant has been inaugurated... A new stretch of highway is going to be completed ahead of schedule... This year the wheat harvest will outstrip even the rosiest predictions—and how could it have been otherwise after Il Duce had himself photographed bare-chested on the harvester? The truth is, my dear Mina, that all of that is just dust in our eyes. In spite of these grandiose public works, the economy is in a deplorable state and the country is getting poorer by the day. Unfortunately, it pains me to acknowledge that the king too is partly responsible for this state of affairs. I've always been loyal to the monarchy, and I still am, but the king has simply been too weak. He should never have allowed this petty plebeian, this failed socialist, to take power. If I were a young man, I'd put myself at His Majesty's service to make a clean sweep of these hooligans from the government."

"Uncle Riccardo, I need a word across that begins with COR and ends in ION, there are five empty boxes in the middle. The definition is: 'Union of workers and industrialists.'"

"The word you want is CORPORATION. You'll hear that word more and more often because it's the basis of our new economic and political structure. It's a way of exercising increasingly close control over enterprises and individuals. The idea so appealed to the new German Chancellor that he decided to restructure the German state in accordance with Mussolini's model. Another petty plebeian with imperial aspirations. Both of them are of the same ilk."

"I heard Papà saying more or less the same things."

"Mina darling, it might be best for you to forget everything you've heard. What your father said, what I said… Don't tell anyone about it. We live in dangerous times, even if the life we lead is quite privileged. But everything can change, from one day to the next. Even for us."

IV

In effect, things had already changed at the castle, and not because of the fascist regime, but because of Luca's ill-fated adventure. Olga had been forced to retrench considerably, giving up much of the lifestyle to which she had become accustomed, cutting back on her entertaining and travel. Now, when Ada, Elisa, and Lidia came to visit with their families, they contributed to the cost of food, and each of them unfailingly brought at least one maid to make up for the shortage in staff. Olga had to look after Luca with the means at her disposal; her resources had been reduced to an annuity left to her by Pietro—adequate but not abundant—and what little remained to her of her dowry. There was a moment when she believed she'd had a stroke of good fortune. The excitement lasted for about a month, then it all ended in disappointment.

It just so happened that Gio, digging near the greenhouse wall to extract the root of a plant that he was observing, had uncovered an old urn, its lid sealed by a thick layer of wax.

The urn contained a hand-drawn map, rudimentary traced. The sheet of paper was perfectly preserved, in spite of the fact that the outside of the urn was encrusted and covered with mould. From many different clues, it was possible to deduce that it had lain there buried for several centuries.

First Olga asked Riccardo for advice, then she turned to Ernesto, and finally consulted with her daughters; Luca, too, asked to see the mysterious sheet of paper; then it was the grandchildren's turn. Mina and her cousins gave it a curious but superficial glance; Gio studied the map minutely, bringing all his scientific rigor to bear. It was agreed, with general consensus, that it was a treasure map. The point marked with a red cross was identified after measurement and investigations. It was located in the *infernotti*.

"*Infernotti*" is a common term in the Piedmont region. It denotes the cellars of old buildings, consisting of several interconnected rooms, or else rooms linked by galleries and tunnels. *Infernotti* can be more or less complex. The ones in Cortalba were a veritable labyrinth that snaked from the castle out under the woods and then extended downhill. There were various exits, concealed behind the vegetation and situated in strategic locations to facilitate the escape of the inhabitants during sieges. But ever since sieges had fallen out of fashion, the *infernotti* of Cortalba had for the most part been shut down and forgotten. Only the part underneath the kitchens had remained functional, since it was used as a wine cellar. There were the large wine cellars, the *cróte*, where barrels and kegs of wine were stored; and then there were the smaller cellars, the *crutìn*, where bottles for everyday use were kept; then there were the special *crutìn* that were kept under lock and key, where prized bottles of special vintages were squirreled away.

A team of laborers was assembled—diggers, masons, and even a couple of dowsers with their forked branches. Tunìn was appointed foreman of the project, because he knew all the secrets of the castle. He had scampered through it as a child, exploring all its innermost recesses, ignoring Olga's prohibitions and regularly risking a beating from his father.

According to their calculations, the point of access closest to the location of the treasure was an exit giving onto the woods, well concealed behind dense shrubbery. The aperture had been carved into the tufa stone and the arch that led into the tunnel was supported by large surface roots that constituted a load-bearing structure. As work was about to begin, the family assembled at that point to witness the opening of the small door, which was extremely heavy and barred shut by a huge iron bar. Olga was in the front row, along with Luca—they were the chief stakeholders.

"Gio, this is the 'sesame,' " Mina whispered, elbowing her brother in the ribs.

"I see it," Gio replied. "It's surprising that back then, when we spent days at a time here, we never realized that there was this door."

"I thought that the roots were sleeping pythons that might awaken at any moment and crush us to death. So when I walked over them I kept a very light step, and in two leaps I reached the highest branches. I always did my best to avoid looking at them closely."

In a capophony of hammer blows and the squeaks of hinges and bolts, the door swung open. The flashlights illuminated a short stretch of the tunnel. The rest remained shrouded in darkness. It was no more than a yard wide and the ceiling was so low that a person of average height had to walk with bowed head and hunched shoulders. Dank air wafted out, smelling vaguely of mushrooms.

There was a moment of hesitation. Then Tunìn grabbed the end of a long rope and took command of the situation: "Let's go guys. I'll go in first and you all come behind me. Hold on tight to the rope and don't stop. We need to walk for 300 yards and then we'll arrive in an open space where we can regroup and decide which way to go. We'll use only my flashlight to illuminate the path. The rest of you, don't waste your batteries."

"I'll come with you," said Gio. "I want to see what's down there."

"Then I'll come too," said Mina.

"You'd better not, Mina," Gio tried to dissuade her. "We don't know what we'll find. It could be dangerous."

"If you're going, I'm going. Don't you think I'm capable of taking care of myself?"

"No, no, of course I don't think that. I was just saying that to make sure you're on your guard. You might run into real trouble."

"I didn't ask for your advice. You're always trying to get in my way, force me to do what you want... But I'll do as I please."

"All right, then. Well, you go first and I'll follow you."

Mina and Gio grabbed the rope after the last laborer and went into the tunnel.

"Be careful, children. Don't do anything reckless," Ada urged them as she watched them vanish. But her voice was drowned out in the rest of the chatter, as the company headed up along the paths leading out of the shadows of the woods, toward the lanes and higher terraces awash in sunlight.

As they ventured deeper into the tunnel, what little light had been filtering in from outdoors disappeared entirely.

"Gio, I can't see a thing. Turn on the flashlight," said Mina.

"I don't have one. Tunìn has it. All that matters is that the one who's at the head of the line can see."

After a few minutes: "Gio, it's cold in here."

"All I'm wearing is this shirt, I can't help you."

The boy who was ahead of Mina turned around, as much as he was able, and said, "Are you cold, Signorina? As soon as we stop, I can give you my jacket, after all I don't need it."

"I'd accept it gladly. You see, Gio, I don't need your help."

Gio spoke to the boy, "Thanks, Dino, you're very kind."

They went on walking.

"When are we going to get there?" asked Mina. "This tunnel just goes on and on."

At that moment they heard Tunìn's voice: "We've arrived. Over there, to the left, there's a hole in the wall. You need to bend low and get through it. I'll stay here with the flashlight and let you get through one by one, then I'll come through last. In the meantime, Rico, since you'll be going through first, when you get over onto the other side, in the big room, you switch on your flashlight. And remember to stay together in a group." Tunìn slapped Rico's back and said, "Come on, get moving." Rico squirmed thorugh the hole, followed by all the others.

Then it was Mina's turn.

"Hold my hand, Signorina," said Dino, who was already on the other side.

"No, I don't need any help," Mina replied, and she scampered through the opening with great agility. But she scraped a knee on a jagged spur, and then complained that Tunìn hadn't properly illuminated that hazard.

Two or three men on the team had now switched on their flashlights and the beams of light moved over the walls, revealing a number of different galleries ending up into that place. Tunìn unfolded the map, turned it to match the orientation of the room, and pointed a finger toward one of the galleries.

"There, that's the one. We need to go in that direction. This is a larger gallery, which means we'll be able to walk more comfortably. But be careful to stay in single file and not to take a wrong turning, because there are plenty of forks and turnoffs into other galleries that lead in various directions. Follow me. At the end, we'll come to another room just like this one, and that's where we can start digging."

They all renewed their grip on the rope and the line moved forward. It was easier to walk now. They could stand erect and no longer clustered one against the next. Dino had turned on his flashlight and was illuminating the end of the line.

"Gio, are there bats in these tunnels?" asked Mina.

"No, usually you find bats only in natural caverns."

"That's good. I wouldn't want to run into one. But is there anything at all here?"

"It doesn't look like."

"Then it's not interesting. There are no colors, only smooth yellowish clay walls. And there are no stalactites and stalagmites like there are in Tom Sawyer's cave."

"We're not in America. And then, like I told you, this isn't a natural cavern."

"I'm almost ready to go back."

"Come on, buck up. We're almost there. It will be more interesting once they start to dig."

They walked for a good half hour. At last, the tunnel ended in a fairly large space, which had clearly been designed as a halting place or a refuge. There were seats carved into the tufa stone, a projecting board that served as a table, and a niche with various shelves.

Tunìn once again checked the map. "I think that the treasure is underneath the niche. Where are the dowsers? Come on, boys, search here."

The dowsers walked over to the location indicated. Both their forked sticks bent forcefully.

"For Christ's sake, it's really tugging!" exclaimed one.

"There's a lot of traction," confirmed the other.

"It's here, then. Come on, let's get busy," Tunìn ordered. The men pitched in with picks and shovels.

Time passed and Mina grew increasingly impatient. She was huddled on a seat, wrapped in Dino's jacket. The dampness was intense and bone-chilling.

"Gio, what time is it?" she asked.

"I don't know, my watch has stopped. But don't worry, Tunìn knows when it's time to go back."

"But I don't feel like staying here anymore. I'm cold, my knee hurts, and I'm also starting to get hungry."

"Then you can go back all by yourself," Gio said with a laugh.

Mina took that phrase, uttered in jest, as a direct challenge. She took advantage of a moment when Gio was intently observing a family of strange chalice-shaped fungi, took a flashlight from the pile of tools and headed off, unobserved, down the gallery through which they had first come.

She was angry with Gio, who had taken her words lightly and had shown no consideration for her state of misery. She might catch pneumonia, or develop an infection in her knee and lose a leg, but Gio didn't care. "I can't count on anyone. I'm going to have to rely upon my own resources," she thought, and her eyes filled with tears, mixed with pride and self-pity.

She walked and walked, and weariness began to creep over her. The jacket weighed down upon her shoulders. She decided to empty the pockets and get rid of all those heavy objects: a clasp knife, a bunch of keys, a screwdriver, a corkscrew... Out with them, one after the other.

While she was focused on this task, she failed to notice that she had turned off the main gallery and into a secondary tunnel. She was walking along, aiming the beam of her flashlight into the depths, hoping to see the large opening appear where she knew she'd find the small aperture that led into the exit tunnel. But the gallery seemed to go on forever, leading deeper and deeper into the belly of the hill. Mina realized that she had made a mistake, that she had lost her way. She turned around and looked behind her. In that direction, too, the gallery vanished into the darkness. It was impossible to think of turning back. All the more so because there was the danger of making yet another wrong turn.

For a moment, Mina was at a loss. But only for a moment, which was immediately followed by a surge of defiance. Now she was no longer crying. She felt a great anger at the circumstances that had pushed her into that situation. And that anger gave her the strength to act. "I have to do it," she told herself. "Whatever the cost."

She resumed walking with greater determination. She noticed that the gallery now began to run slightly uphill and deduced that she was getting closer to the foundations of the castle. And in fact, after another long stretch, she saw a flight of steps that led up to a small iron gate.

Mina struggled to climb, holding on to the irregularities projecting from the wall because the steps were narrow and slippery and she knew it would be easy to fall. When she reached the top, she clutched the bars tight and turned her flashlight toward the interior on the other side of the gate. It was a *crutìn*. The *crutìn* of the fine wines, to which only Olga had the key. On special occasions, Olga would pull the key off the bunch and give it to a trusted person so they could go and fetch the precious bottles. The key opened a door from the interior; no one knew of the existence of this little exterior gate, which stood concealed behind a set of shelves full of bottles and kegs.

The gate was fastened shut by a sliding bolt that drove into a hole in the wall. There was no padlock on it. Mina pulled on the handle and… the bolt shifted by a fraction of an inch. Her hopes of salvation gave her redoubled strength. She planted both feet firmly on the top two steps, one up and one down, to better distribute her weight … she took a deep breath… and then hauled with all her strength. The gate swung open.

With extreme care, Mina slipped into the space between the gate and the shelves and moved forward, little by little, creeping against the wall until she found a gap between two uprights and was able to get into the room. She allowed herself to drop onto a stool, exhausted. For a few minutes, she thought of nothing, as if, having finally reached the end of her troubled journey, her body and her mind sought only rest.

Then, suddenly, the flashlight went out. The batteries were dead. Mina was plunged into absolute pitch darkness. The shock roused her from her torpor. Fear, rage, instinct of self-preservation—everything reactivated. She'd noticed that there was a lantern next to the stool. She felt for it in the dark. Next to the lantern, she also found a box of sulphur matches; of course, they were there for the use of whoever came to fetch the bottles. Mina had to use three sulphur matches before she was able to light the wick. In the process, she burned a finger.

"Damned matches!" she swore, and sucked on the finger where a white blister now appeared. "Damned *infernotti*, damned treasure, damned everything!!!" she shouted in a hysterical crescendo. "I want to get out, out of here! Come and get me!"

She grabbed the stool and slammed it against the interior door... *Bang!* The echo resonated through the empty grottoes.

"Where are you?" she asked, addressing an imaginary audience that was indifferent to her shouts. "Answer me!!"

She took a bottle from the shelf, grabbed it by the neck with both hands like a baseball bat, and smashed it furiously against the corner of the upright... *Swish... Crash!* The bottle exploded into fragments. A very fine vintage Freisa spurted foaming all around her and drenched her from head to foot. A shard of glass hit her in the shoulder and the blood that oozed out of the wound mingled with the wine stains on her dress.

Then, it was the turn of a very fine Moscato... *Swish... Crash!*

Then, a superb Barbaresco... *Swish... Crash!*

"I want to get out! I want to get out!" she shouted in her ravaging fury."Doesn't anyone hear me?!"

"Mina!..."

"Signorina Mina!..."

The voices of Gio and Dino reached her from a distance.

The two of them were in the gallery, at the base of the little staircase that led up to the *crutìn*.

"I'm here!" Mina shouted, latching onto those voices with some trepidation, like a shipwrecked sailor grabbing a life-saver. Then, imperiously, "Hurry!"

A few minutes later, Gio and Dino emerged from the narrow passageway behind the shelves.

"Mina, are you all right? You gave us quite a scare," said Gio, running toward her with open arms.

"We were very worried, Signorina," Dino agreed.

Mina didn't move. Standing in the midst of puddles of wine and shattered glass she did her best to put on a dignified demeanor. Her gaze had hardened and the golden filaments in her darkened irises jabbed like needles. In one hand, she still held the jagged neck of the last bottle. Gio stopped, not daring to embrace her.

"Finally! You two took forever to find me," she said aggressively.

"We came looking right away, the minute we realized you had left," Gio justified himself.

Mina felt she was safe now and out of danger. The tension relaxed and her nerves gave way. She was shaken by racking sobs and collapsed onto a bench.

Gio went on, "The important thing is that nothing's happened to you and it's all ended well. Come on, take my handkerchief."

"Nothing's happened to me?! That's easy for you to say," said Mina, blowing her nose and wiping away her tears. "But you don't know the things I've been through. The horrible situations I've been through. I don't know how I managed to survive... with the sheer force of desperation, I suppose. You could have easily found me dead. And you say that nothing's happened to me... look at the state I'm in," Mina spread her arms to show off her filthy dress. Then she pointed to her shoulder and her knee, "Look, just look. And look at this finger..."

"I'm really sorry, Mina," said Gio, contritely. "But soon we'll be out of here and you can receive all necessary medical care."

"And how are we going to get out?" asked Mina. That thought brought her back to practical reality. She stopped crying. She took a defensive position. "I'm not going back out into that gallery. Let that be clear."

"No, certainly not. Tunìn will come to open the door from inside. Dino, you explain."

"I'd better start from the beginning," said Dino. "When it was time to stop work for the day and head home, we searched for you, Signorina. But you were nowhere to be found. That's when I said to myself: Darn it, who knows where she's gotten to? We decided to all go in search of you together. And while we were walking through the gallery, Tunìn stopped the line and called me. He says, 'Dino, take a look, isn't that yours?' I look, and I see that my knife is there, and then a little further along in a gallery that cut to the right, my keys, and then all the other stuff I had in my pockets. And then we understood that you had come through there and that you'd taken a wrong turn. Well, Tunìn, who is definitely cut out to be a leader, immediately had a plan ready and waiting. He says, 'I know this gallery because I often took it when I was a boy. It leads to the *crutìn* of the good bottles,' and then he explained it all to us—the steps, the little gate... Then he tells us what we need to do, 'Dino and Signorino Gio, you go that way, and when you find Signorina Mina wait in the *crutìn* and don't move from there. I'll take the men out the woods exit and then I'll go get the keys from Signora Olga. Wait until I get there.' Now, it's been a fairly long while since then, which means he ought to be here any minute."

And in fact, just a few minutes later, the key turned in the lock and Tunìn opened the door.

* * *

This unfortunate episode took place at the beginning of summer, roughly two months prior to the day we're describing here. Mina was succored, consoled, and coddled for the abuse she had suffered, and Ada even held her up as an example for the fortitude and courage she had displayed. Olga commented, "Too bad about the bottles, those were irreplaceable vintages. But, of course, we can hardly blame Mina, given the circumstance. Poor girl. *Quel cauchemar!*" And Ada weighed in, "Mina can be proud of the way she behaved in that situation. Gio didn't do it on purpose, but men simply lack sensitivity. They don't understand that an ill-chosen word can wound a feminine soul. And Mina is, indeed, so very sensitive. Poor little thing. She's bound to suffer a great deal in life." Gio made the required act of contrition for having been such a dolt and provoking the incident. Mina accepted his apologies with some hauteur, and in the end they made peace and life went on as before.

As for the treasure, the team worked for another couple of days until their picks struck against a metal surface. Then, Tunìn told them that he no longer needed them. Many years later, one of the laborers spoke of how surprised they had been that they were sent away right then, but they'd kept silent and pocketed their pay. At the end of the project, Tunìn went to see Olga and delivered his report with a great show of chagrin. "Just to think that we did all that work, Signora Olga, and it wound up like this... We didn't find a thing," Tunìn concluded, shaking his head and throwing both arms wide as if to attribute that failure to the adversity of fate.

It was a great disappointment for Olga who had hoped to rebuild the family fortune. But for better or worse, she accepted that version of the facts and resigned herself to the straitened circumstances of her new condition.

A few months later, she also lost her gardener. Tunìn announced that he wanted to change his profession and move to Turin with his wife. It was later learned that he went into business and opened a wholesale warehouse for sales of fruit and vegetables, and he became one of the largest suppliers in the area.

V

The bell tower chimed eleven.

"Magda ought to be here soon," said Riccardo. "Mina, if you let me lean on you, we can slowly make our way down to the 'observation wall' to see when the car arrives."

Magda was the first member of the family to use an automobile. Recently Ernesto had purchased Fiat's latest model, but since the turn of the century, Magda had been traveling in a luxurious Bugatti cabriolet. It was the "prominent individual's" car. She often went on romantic outings with him along the *corniche* when they first met on the Côte d'Azur. He had driven the car himself on those dangerous switchbacks, since he was a car aficionado. Later, he put the car at her disposal, along with a chauffeur and a personal squire. The squire was General Camilletti, unfailingly loyal for all those years; he'd recently retired as an officer, but he still filled the squire position very effectively. Magda was a legend in Cortalba and surrounding areas because of the impression she made as she roared through the streets of towns and villages in her open car, with an oversized hat adorned with ribbons and plumes, and a light veil that covered her face and fluttered in the wind, in an ethereal, floating wake behind her.

Now she had a different car. It was a black limousine, setting a more restrained tone. And her hats were different, too, in keeping with fashion. They were smaller and without frills.

Magda arrived on Camilletti's arm, and there were the usual polite exchanges of pleasure.

"Dearest Olga!" "Magda dearest!"—the most delicate of kisses, taking care not to disturb fine hats and hairdos.

"My dear Count..."—a half bow and a click of the heels from Camilletti. "General..."—a nod of the head from Riccardo.

"Donna Olga..."—clicked heels and a kissed hand. "Delighted to see you, General"—erect back, a faint smile.

"Riccardo, you look fit." "Magda, you're magnficent as always,"—Riccardo kissed her hand, no click of the heels, because one of his feet was bandaged.

And so on with all the rest, one after the other.

Magda came to Cortalba every summer for a short stay. Here she could see all the members of the family, older and younger, at least once a year. Usually, she stayed no longer than a day. She'd get back in her car and leave before sunset.

"Luca, come give me a kiss. The countryside is doing you good, you look hale and healthy. Luigi sends his regards... Elisa, Lidia, what news from Rome? I'm so happy to see you with your children," Magda caressed each of them, from the older to the small ones; Marta and Chiara sketched out a curtsey. "Lucilla, you're growing more adorable by the day. And you, Marcello, you're turning into a big boy; but you need to do some sports... Ah, Piero and Marilù, so you're here, too! How nice, how nice... Darling Mina, I heard all about your unfortunate adventure. I'm so glad to see you've recovered."

"Aunt Magda, it was horrible. My nerves are still shot."

"You'll get over it, you'll get over it, you're young... Viola, I really do need to come to Cortalba to see you. You're a world traveler!" For years Viola had been living in London where she devoted herself to poetry and was a regular in literary circles. She lived with an inseparable female companion, a poetess as well, but she would come to Cortalba for a short time every summer, even though she'd given up horse riding—by now she was getting along in years. What's more, the stables were empty. The only horse left was Arrow, who was as old as Giusto and could barely pull the gig.

"And where is Gio?" Magda went on, glancing around.

"In the fields... Ah, here he comes now, the dauntless entomologist ..." said Mina.

Gio came running with all his instruments, apologizing for his lateness.

"Our young scientist... What did you catch today?" asked Magda.

"A few rare specimens I was still missing." Gio displayed a net full of brightly colored winged creatures.

Then everyone took a seat. Erminia served lunch on a large table set under the linden tree, hurrying back and forth because of the shortage of staff. Aunt Delina from the bakery had come to lend a hand, but Olga ordered her to stay in the kitchen because she didn't have the fine manners of a genuine tablemaid.

Aside from the members of the family, Miriam Della Rocca was there, a friend to Ada because they both had boys enrolled at the same high school. Miriam, née Lehrmann, had moved to Italy from her native Berlin when she married one of her father's business partners. Herr Lehrmann was the owner of steel mills and Count Della Rocca was in charge of the Italian market, which chiefly consisted of major government orders for the arms industry.

"My dear Miriam," said Magda, "what a pleasure to see you again after all these years. The last time we met here in Cortalba, Davide was still a little boy. I remember him well. How is he? Gio told me that he's just a phenomenon at school, far ahead of all the other students. Especially in maths."

"Yes, it's an advantage and a problem at the same time," said Miriam. "He'd like to skip the last year of high school and go straight to the university. But there are signs of bureaucratic resistance. The principal recommended we avoid attracting too much attention to him. He says it's better to follow the normal course of study to keep from arousing envy and stirring resentment. We'd even thought of enrolling him at Heidelberg, but my father talked us out of that. In his opinion, the new government is fomenting a hostile atmosphere toward the Jews, which would have repercussions in the universities as well. So, for now, we're just going to wait to make a decision on the matter."

"That would be the best idea. The situation here in Italy is very unclear. It's not evident where this political regime is heading," Ernesto commented.

"We need a new broom to sweep clean with this government, they all must go. Am I right, General?" Riccardo tossed out.

Camilletti choked on his food. He started coughing and was forced to step away from the table for a moment.

The conversation continued to fluctuate among the people around the table, on a wave of questions, answers, reports, observations, comments, witticisms, accompanying the various dishes: *gnocchetti* with Castelmagno cheese, roast rabbit with rosemary potatoes, and ladyfingers with *zabaglione*, all of it washed down with a cool white Roero d'Arneis.

They'd reached the coffee at the end of the meal and the young people were anxious to be excused so they could go back to their activities. But they had to cool their enthusiasm because Magda insisted on having a group photograph taken and asked Camilletti to click the shutter.

There they are now, caught between light and shade, beneath the foliage that filters the rays of sunlight creating dark patches on the faces, gleaming reflections on the hair. The strong chiaroscuro confers a surreal tone to the image. The figures are white silhouettes against a black background, ethereal phantoms. It's an enclosed picture that contains the space. No detail escapes the boundaries of the frame to indicate any potential spatial extension. Moreover, they're all perfectly static. There is nothing to connote the slightest dynamism—nothing like an interrupted gesture, an involuntary expression, an incomplete movement. It's an image frozen in time. It suggests a terminal point, far more than it does any future proceedings. It is an image that heralds the end of the story.

Part III

Out of the Shade

11

Enter the Pirate
1937-1939

I

It was St. Lawrence's Eve, the night of the falling stars. Mina had climbed up to the crenellated terrace high atop the tower. Now she enjoyed the glittering spectacle of the shooting stars with a field of view covering three hundred sixty degrees. Spreading her arms, she turned around as if to embrace those luminous comets and gather them into a bunch. A bunch of wishes. A cyclorama of dreams.

She was so close to the sky, and the sky belonged entirely to her. No one else dared venture into that place. It was absolutely forbidden to climb the spiral staircase that led up to the terrace, considered highly dangerous because of the many crumbling steps. And in fact, the access door was locked and bolted shut. But Mina had found the hiding place where the key was kept, in a chink between two bricks, and every year, in utter secrecy, she crept up there on that magical night.

For her, this was a special year. In two months, she'd turn twenty and leave for Rome. After completing her teaching degree, Mina had refused to go on studying in the field of education. She wasn't drawn to it. Above all, she was uninterested in children and had no intention of spending her days with a classroom full of little snot-noses, she said. Mina had a clear idea of what she didn't want, but she hadn't a clue of what she really did want. She took a year off and allowed Ada to take care of finding what was right for her. Ada evaluated the situation and in the end decided to enroll her in the Academy of Dramatic Arts, a university-level institute that was very recently founded—it had just opened the previous year, in 1936.

Like all totalitarian regimes, Fascism encouraged the arts and the cultural institutions in general, provided they conformed to the ideology and remained in obeisance and service to the state. The Fascio thought, correctly, that the Italians were "a nation of artists," as well as "saints, navigators, scientists," and other fine professions, and so it took interest in all the aspects of artistic pursuits. Among the many initiatives, the government underwrote scholarships for the students at the Academy and procured funds for theaters and traveling dramatic companies.

Like most people, Ada paid little attention to politics. She thought that this would be an excellent chance for Mina to develop her dramatic talent, her stage presence, and her warm, melodious voice. This attitude was a clear reflection, deep down, of her own frustrations: her abandoned love of painting, the amateurish performances of the "quadri plastici," and her secondary role as a model in her husband's photographic compositions. Ernesto raised no objections, in part because of his pacifistic inclinations, which always led him to avoid arguments, and partly because he appreciated the arts no matter what form they took. Mina had learned of her mother's decision with great enthusiasm. Perhaps not because this was truly her calling, but because she saw it as an exciting and out-of-the-ordinary adventure. In preparation, she took private lessons from an elderly former actress of the Moscow Art Theatre, who had arrived in Turin in the period of the earliest emigration. Irina Nikolaevna applied the Stanislavski method and went into paroxysms of delight at Mina's progress. She never tired of telling her, over and over again, "*Minotchka, dorogaya, vy prosto voskhititelna.*" And then, since Mina didn't understand Russian, she'd translate, "Minotchka, sweetheart, you're simply enchanting." On the strength of her natural talent, and her teacher's encouragement, Mina passed the admission exam with flying colors.

Mina came back down a half hour later to make sure no one had noticed her absence, and joined the family group watching the falling stars in the Tower Garden, where there were no trees to block the view.

"This reminds me of troop maneuvers when I was a lieutenant in the artillery division," Riccardo commented. "Except that the pyrotechnical spectacle of the cannons also involved loud explosions; here there are only cold lights, the flashes of flames dying out; in fact, flames that died out millions of years ago." He was speaking to Gio who stood behind him, pushing his wheelchair. In recent years, Riccardo had lost his legs. Because of his gout, gangrene had spread to his right foot and had quickly climbed up to his knee. They were forced to amputate the limb. But that was not all. The following year, the gangrene moved over to his left leg and they had to amputate that limb as well.

Gio stopped the wheelchair near Ernesto who was leaning against the thick wall, evaluating the aesthetic potential of the star-spangled sky. "It's a pity that such a spectacle as this can't be captured on film," he mused. "But the day will come when we can. Technology is making giant strides."

Ada was sitting on a bench with her sisters. Mina walked over to her, sat down beside her, and put an arm around her shoulders, "What did you wish for, Mamma?"

"I can't tell you, or else it won't come true."

"I made lots and lots of wishes, that way at least one will come true. It's like playing the lottery. The more tickets you have, the better your chances."

"Good girl. I'm sure you have the winning ticket. But the important thing is to advance your career and create your own economic independence. And never depend on a man.

In any case, we'll always be here to support you and help you when you need us. I was just now talking with Aunt Elisa about getting you situated in Rome."

"Mina, I'm sure that you'll be comfortable at our house," said Elisa. "I've arranged to give you the bedroom on the garden side, with the windows overlooking the hydrangea bushes. It's the one that's farthest from the children's rooms. For that matter, they're getting older, too. The youngest is ten years old, and they won't bother you. Marta and Chiara have a bedroom near yours, but they're a pair of angels and they'll be good company."

"Aunt Elisa, I thank you. But I don't think you'll be seeing much of me. I'll be extremely busy all day long with my classes and I won't get home until it's dark, and I'll be so exhausted I won't want to do anything but go to bed. Certainly, I'd appreciate it if no one made any noise because I'm a light sleeper, and if something wakes me up I just can't get back to sleep at all. And the next day I have a terrible headache."

The twin girls, who were sitting not far away, overheard the conversation.

"Dear Mina," said Marta, "we're so happy that..."

"...you're coming to stay with us," Chiara concluded.

Mina shot them a polite smile. Ada replied for her, "You're both so kind. Thanks to you, Mina won't miss us as much. Isn't that right, Mina?—*Say something nice!*," Ada whispered in her ear.

"Ah, yes, of course..." Mina mumbled.

"Mina, I hope that every so often you'll come to see us, for lunch, or for dinner, whenever you can," Lidia broke in. "What's more, Lucilla knows the city so well, and could give you a guided tour."

Lucilla wasn't there and had no opportunity to weigh in on that offer. But Mina was preemptive in her reply. "Aunt Lidia, Lucilla won't be continuing her studies and so she'll have all the time she needs for archeological excursions, but I'll be far too busy. As I told you before."

Erminia arrived with the refreshments—petits-fours and *gianduiotti*[12] chocolates, accompanied by a shot of straw wine. Luca, who was sitting next to Olga on a wicker settee, was the first to help himself to a substantial portion: "My wish has come true," he said, cramming his mouth full. "I was just thinking of Uncle Candy's *gianduiotti*." The lenses of his pince-nez glittered with joy in the bright starlight.

Olga ate nothing, and a short while later got up to retire for the night. Ada hastened to offer her arm. These days, Olga walked with a cane and often complained about sharp gastric pains. She would have liked a cup of tea, but since the League of Nations had imposed sanctions against Italy in the aftermath of the invasion of Abyssinia, tea had become impossible to find. There were only bland mushes that came from the colonies, like *carcadè*, as hibiscus tea was known. Everyone stood up to wish her goodnight. Despite her precarious state of health, Olga still oversaw the administration of the castle and the conduct of life in the household. As she passed Mina, she stopped and said, "I made a wish tonight myself. Could you come to my study tomorrow morning? I want to talk to you."

"Yes, Grandma. Sleep tight," said Mina.

Late the next morning, Mina walked into Olga's study. The white muslin curtains at the windows were barely fluttering in the scant breeze that came in along with the scent of wisteria and the humming of bees. Olga was seated at her desk. Despite the heat of the muggy day, she was holding a hot water bottle on her stomach to alleviate the pain.

"Come in, Mina. Have a seat," she said, pointing to a chair across the desk. "These days there's an electric atmosphere around you. Nobody's talking about anything but your departure. But have you really given it adequate thought?"

"No. What do I need to give adequate thought?"

12. Typical Turin chocolates, made of a paste of cocoa and hazelnuts.

"You need to think about what an important step this is, and how it could determine the course of your life."

"I'm certain that I'll like that life. And if I don't like it, I'll just come back here and live with you."

"The future is unpredictable and choices entail consequences for which we become responsible. I'd like you to understand that there are other possible choices. For instance, the young Count Della Rocca came to see me recently. He knows that his chances are slim at best, but he wanted my opinion about a matter of the heart. In brief, he's in love with you and would like to ask your hand in marriage."

"My hand? You tell him that he won't have even a nail of my pinky finger."

"A pity. Davide is a good match and he's a nice young man. He'd be able to provide you with a comfortable, safe life…"

"… don't forget boring. No, no, not even a fingernail."

"I know it's impossible to change your mind once you get an idea into your head. In this case, moreover, your mother's encouraging you, your father consents, and I have no say in the matter. Still, I wanted to present you with an alternative and ask you to give the matter some thought. If you're determined to plunge into this adventure, I can only wish you the best of luck. You'll need it."

Mina left in early October. Ada and Ernesto accompanied her, saw to her accommodations in Elisa's house, and made certain that everything at the Academy was in order and convenient for her. Ada hired a gig and gave her an orientation tour of the city, pointing out the places she had loved best in her youth. They even went by the Trevi Fountain. Ada looked up at the windows of Palazzo Castellani, returning in her thoughts to the days when she'd been Mina's age and had a head full of dreams—painting… André… She wondered what had ever become of him…

"Mamma, throw a coin into the fountain, that way you can be sure you'll come back here to visit me," said Mina, taking her mother's mind off her thoughts.

Ernesto photographed his daughter in front of the Colosseum, on the Spanish Steps, and beneath the pine trees of Villa Borghese. "We want to take you home with us, along with a slice of Rome, to shorten the distance and to feel that you're closer," he told her.

After a week's stay, Ada and Ernesto went back to Turin and Mina began her new life.

II

Mina went back to Cortalba the following summer. During the winter she'd never once left Rome. At first, she'd been afraid she might miss her mother, but she was quickly distracted by a thousand new experiences. She promised to reply to the long letters that Ada sent her. Instead, she did no more than to send a few postcards.

Mina was forced to travel with Aunt Elisa, who had reserved two train compartments to accommodate the throngs of her children and her housekeeper. She would have preferred to do without all that intrusive company, but it simply wasn't done for young ladies from good families to travel without a chaperon. It was a matter of etiquette, but also a measure of protection because men showed no respect for unaccompanied women, and behaved as if they had every right to importune them just as they pleased.

Mina had learned that fact at her own personal cost. On the crowded trolleys of the city, touching and rubbing were everyday occurrences. She had quickly developed her own methods of self-defense and now she was quite adept at delivering an elbow to the gut or a knee to the crotch with well-aimed precision, all without ever losing her ladylike discretion. Not only was Mina beautiful, she also gave the impression of being sweet and vulnerable, which only heightened the interest of the men around her. She looked like easy prey, a helpless young fawn. No one ever expected a violent reaction. But Mina never held back, even with the most arrogant bullies.

One day, as she was walking down an empty street, she was accosted by two militiamen, bold and proud of their slick uniforms.

"Hey, pretty, wanna give me a kiss?" said one of the two, grabbing her ass.

Mina, with a lightning move, whipped her purse on its long strap through the air and hit him in the head. The fez flew off and rolled across the sidewalk, landing in the gutter in a puddle of water.

"Ah, look at this slut! Who you think you are? I'll have you arrested! You yokel!" the militiaman cursed as he picked up his now filthy piece of headgear.

The other one intervened. "Just forget about her. Your luck wasn't running. Come on, let's get out of here." Then, gallantly, "Signorina, I hope you'll forgive him, your beauty made his head spin."

"This time, it just made his hat spin. But he'd better not dare try and touch me again," Mina admonished the bully with the tone of a swashbuckling swordsman putting his weapon back in its scabbard in the presence of a chastened enemy. Then she turned her back on them and continued on down the street, erect and with her shoulders thrown back.

Mina had a simple relationship with men. In her estimation, they were different creatures that you couldn't trust, and should therefore be kept at arm's length. In practical terms, this philosophy translated into violent reactions of self-defense against the more daring males, and a superior and patronizing attitude toward the more courtly suitors. And, of the latter, she had dozens. Her favorite that first year was a certain Claudio, a student in the upper classes, who was specializing in directing. She allowed him to sit next to her at the trattoria when they went out for dinner in a group, or to carry her bookbag when it became too heavy, or to lock arms with her during a visit to this or that museum. She even indulged him with the occasional quick kiss in a doorway. Claudio, who happened to be a very bright young man, allowed himself to be treated like a performing circus dog, executing the various routines upon command. "Claudio, bring me an espresso... Claudio, find me a more comfortable chair, this one is too hard... Claudio, close that door, there's a draft... Claudio, walk a little faster, you're slow as a snail." The more he obeyed her, the more she crushed him underfoot. Until she finally came to consider him to be "an intolerable fool." And at that point she dumped him.

One of the reasons that contributed to the breakup was the fact that she'd met Dardo. You couldn't exactly say that they had met, because Dardo was a classmate and they'd known each other since the beginning of the schoolyear. But since he'd paid her no particular attention, Mina had barely even noticed his existence. She'd been too busy handling her own court of suitors and wooers to take any interest in other men. She lacked the instincts of a huntress, she'd never have lifted her little finger to win a man's heart. It was safe to say, rather, that she had the instincts of a damsel to whom adulation was due and expected, and whose role consisted of reviewing the various admirers and then issuing her verdict, thumbs up or thumbs down.

It was chance that one fine day threw Dardo in her direction. And that day, he entered her life like a cyclone.

For her final examination, Mina had been assigned to perform a scene with Dardo. The curriculum called for the students to prepare various scenes with different partners over the course of the year, and then the roles for the final exam would be assigned at the last moment.

The list of roles was posted on a bulletin board in the hallway. There was a throng of students in front of the board discussing excitedly the array of roles assigned. Mina pushed through the students and read: "*The Taming of the Shrew.* Petruchio: Edoardo Celti. Katharina: Alma Bonardi."

Someone behind her placed a hand on her shoulder and said, "Apparently, you're going to be my sweet Kate."

Mina turned around and found herself face to face with Dardo. At that distance she was struck by his eyes, an unusual shade of turquoise in color, which smiled at her, bold and provocative.

"Apparently. But only on the stage," Mina conceded, shaking that hand off her shoulder. And then she added, "Excuse me, but I have to go."

"No. Wait a minute. We should at least rehearse the scene a few times. We've never done it together before," said Dardo, tossing his blond, wavy hair back with a movement of his head.

Mina noticed that the hair hung down over his ears and appreciated that touch of eccentricity. But she didn't want to take him into her confidence. "We can do it tomorrow at the general rehearsal. That should be more than sufficient. Ciao."

The performance was a great success. Mina and Dardo received repeated ovations from the audience and compliments from their teachers. After the performance they all went out for dinner at a trattoria, and dined on *porchetta*[13] and wine from the Castelli Romani. It was a cheerful, fun event. Everyone was thrilled with their achievements, their successes, for the schoolyear that was ending and the summer that was beginning. For that special evening out, Mina obtained Aunt Elisa's permission to come home at midnight, provided she take a taxi and come straight home from the trattoria.

"Oh lord! It's a quarter to twelve," Mina exclaimed all of a sudden as she glanced at her watch. "I have to run," she added, getting up hastily.

13. Suckling pig roast. A typical dish of Roman cuisine.

"I'll call you a taxi," said Claudio considerately, leaping to his feet.

"There's no need. I'll be glad to accompany her myself." Dardo was already at her side and had locked arms with her, with the confident demeanor of someone who's accustomed to taking whatever he likes. Claudio stood aside. Mina didn't object. Dardo guided her toward the exit.

They took a shortcut through narrow, deserted lanes. The Academy was on Piazza della Croce Rossa, not far from Porta Pia, and they had a good long walk before they reached the Pincian Hill. Moonlight illuminated the roofs, but it couldn't penetrate down into the winding, narrow alleys and lanes. They walked in partial darkness, doing their best to avoid the stray cats that came out at night to lay claim to their territory.

"You were fantastic. A perfect Kate. Still, you didn't have to slap me quite so hard. I'm all for realism, but… The audience had quite a reaction when you hit me, you know," said Dardo.

"It just came spontaneously. I really was furious with that Petruchio, arrogant imbecile that he is. And you played him perfectly."

"Petruchio isn't an imbecile. He wins out, at the end."

"Wait, you're not telling me you take Kate's monologue seriously, are you? '*Thy husband is thy lord, thy life, thy keeper, Thy head, thy sovereign…*'" Mina declaimed in a mocking tone. "Kate is making fun of him. If you don't understand the irony of the finale, then you're every bit as much of an imbecile as Petruchio."

They had just emerged into Piazza Barberini. Dardo barred her way, standing in front of her, facing her. Their eyes met along a horizontal line of high-tension current. Dardo was no taller than Mina, but he had a powerful physique, nicely balanced on his solid legs, the legs of a mariner firmly planted on the deck in a raging tempest.

"Stop attacking me. What are you so scared of?" he said.

Mina raised both hands to push him away and he grabbed her wrists.

"Let go of me! You're hurting me," Mina said angrily.

Dardo gripped even harder. His turquoise blue eyes had turned murky and dark. In them Mina could detect violence and passion and could hardly resist their magnetic charge. Their faces were so close that their mouths were practically touching. Mina could feel his hot breath on her face.

"Let go of me!" she said again.

"You won't be able to get away from me. No matter how hard you try."

A solitary taxi appeared.

"Taxi, taxi!" Mina shouted.

The taxi pulled over and stopped right in front of them.

Dardo released his grip.

Mina climbed into the cab and slammed the door.

"You won't be able to!" Dardo shouted after her as the cab drove away.

III

Time passed very slowly in Cortalba. The hours struck by the bell tower seemed endless. It had only been a single day since her arrival and Mina was having trouble readapting to those bucolic rhythms. She missed the action, the discoveries, the unexpected, the tension, the stimulus, the challenge, and also the danger, the fear, the struggle, the disappointments, the failures, the recoveries, and the successes—everything that engaged and honed her senses.

She was strolling in the Lemon Garden waiting for Marilù. The small trees with their golden fruit were drooping in the earthenware vases; it was clear that no one had watered them anytime recently. The garden looked ill cared for. Tufts of weeds sprouted up here and there on the gravel and at certain points had begun to spread like oil stains. The goldfish pond was full of slimy green water; the fish were all dead and frogs had taken their place. The other gardens, too, looked neglected. The boxwood hedges along the lanes, long since left unpruned, had swollen and now actually obstructed free passage. The woods seemed even wilder, and nettles had grown in the tennis court. Olga no longer had enough money to hire new staff. Kerplunk was still there, because he had no place else to live. He continued to draw water from the well—just a few buckets for meals—and he tended to the Hello Garden as best he could, what little sufficed to keep it from wrack and ruin. Erminia, too, had stayed on, in a sign of her devotion to Olga, but now, with her rheumatic back pain, she could hardly move. The summer guests would bring their own housekeepers with them. For the past several years, Ada brought Veglia down from Turin to ensure that there would be at least one decent cook. Veglia would have preferred to go home to Colisso, as she used to, but she had to obey because Ada was quite strict and Ernesto always listened to his wife. "The lady is mean…" Veglia would say when she confided in a friend, "and he … he's just a good fellow." With this attribute she did not mean to describe him as a good man, but rather to imply that he was weak-willed.

Mina leaned over the railing and let her gaze range over the surrounding hills. When her eyes reached the peak of Roccalta, she stopped, pensively. The castle had been left shuttered that summer. Gio had told her about the ugly news that was circulating. No one knew anything for certain, but people said that recently Davide and Miriam had been arrested and deported to Germany. As far as anyone knew, there were no specific charges against them. The action had been taken as part of more general security measures that concerned the Jews, with a view to a new law about to enter into effect. Count Della Rocca, in spite of his close contacts with the highest reaches of the government, had been unable to prevent it. In fact, he too was on thin ice because of his past business dealings with his father-in-law. Herr Lehrmann's steel mills had been confiscated, along with all the rest of his property. He had been forced to leave his large apartment in Berlin and move to the ghetto with nothing but a single small valise. Perhaps Davide and Miriam had joined him there. Or perhaps, something worse… It was whispered—but these might be mere fantasies—that in Germany they had built vast concentration camps for the Jews, in order to isolate that supposedly contaminating race from the rest of the Aryan populace.

Gio was the one most deeply affected by that episode because his bond with Davide was one of truly sincere friendship. But everyone in the family was struck by the absurdity of what had happened. Olga commented, "And to think that I encouraged Mina to consider that marriage. It seemed like such a solid family." And Riccardo, "With that gang running the government, there's nothing that would surprise. Wait and see, this is only the start." And Ernesto, "That asshole of the Duce has signed up for the Axis and now he has to try extra hard to keep in with his new Friend Fritz." And Ada, "Miriam never expected it. We were supposed to meet for our weekly tea at the Arts and Culture Society, but she didn't show up. She just vanished like that, before I even had a chance to say goodbye to her." Riccardo was right, this was only the beginning: the Italian racial laws were issued that very same autumn of 1938, and from that day forward the persecution of the Jews was official policy.

Mina looked toward the summit of Roccalta and it seemed to her that a large black cloud had gathered around the turrets of the castle, as in some child's drawing. But in reality the sun was shining on the unchanging landscape of hillsides and vineyards, and the black cloud was merely a reflection of her thoughts.

Marilù came in through the little gate, striding up the drive with a quick, agile step. There were no more prohibitions at this point, no special permissions or concessions; not because Olga had abandoned her age-old resentments, but because she now lacked the mental energy and physical stamina to maintain control over specific situations and individuals. Her health problems had grown worse and kept her confined to an armchair most of the time.

Mina saw her emerge from the hedges and ran to meet her. The two cousins embraced and jumped up and down, exchanging giggles and shrieks. They hadn't seen each other in almost a year and they had many things to talk about. Mina especially, because Marilù's life hadn't been all that exciting. After accounting school, she'd taken a job with a company as a bookkeeper. Moreover, she was expected to look after her father and her brother, with the assistance of loyal Teresina who had been with them for all those years. Piero was attending the university and he had a fairly independent life, but Aurelio depended on Marilù in all ways and for everything; he saw her as a surrogate for the wife who was no longer there, and he selfishly placed an enormous physical and moral burden on his daughter's shoulders.

Mina and Marilù locked arms and started along the Lane of Roses—by now nothing but thorns—heading slowly down toward the terrace below. The arrived at the belvedere and sat down under the cedars of Lebanon.

"Do you remember all the games we played in this place?" asked Mina.

"Yes, and I remember that you were pretty bossy, and you could always get away with it because I was two years younger than you, and smaller, too."

"And now you're bigger," said Mina with an amiable smile, as if to make up for those childish faults of hers.

Marilù was a few inches taller than Mina—"She's a beanstalk," Ernesto liked to say, and he considered that trait to be anything but attractive. She had her father's athletic physique and she cultivated that inheritance, playing on a basketball team when her other obligations didn't keep her from it. She had Giulia's features, with high cheekbones and big blue eyes; but her hair was black, and this created an interesting contrast. In other words, she was a good-looking girl and had nothing to be ashamed of in comparison with Mina.

"I heard from Grandma that you have a suitor," said Mina ironically.

"Who?" asked Marilù, feigning astonishment.

"Why... Uncle Luca. Or am I wrong?"

"They're driving me crazy with this idea. Can you imagine anything so absurd? Uncle Luca has taken a fancy to me, and he's gone to confide in Grandma. Grandma summoned me to her study and gave me the news, informing me that such a marriage would be an honor for me, an opportunity to elevate myself from my petty bourgeois condition, because even if Uncle Luca has lost his fortune, he's still a gentleman of high birth... and other nonsense of the sort."

"And what did you say to her?"

"I was astonished by such arrogance. And deeply offended. I knew that's how Grandma has always thought of us, but she'd never said it so openly. I was literally speechless, my jaw dropped..."

"And what did she say?"

"She told me not to answer right away. To think it over for a while, and then we could talk about it again later. In the meantime, there's Uncle Luca making googoo eyes at me, and every so often he takes my hand as if there was already an understanding between us. Aside from everything else, do you realize just how old Uncle Luca is? He's almost forty."

"Then you tell him loud and clear to get that idea out of his mind right away."

"You're right, and that's just what I'll do the minute the right opportunity presents itself. Papà gave me the same advice. But he has his own reasons. He doesn't want me to get married to anyone, because he needs me there to run his household."

"That's a selfish attitude, too, just like Grandma's. And you, poor thing, you're stuck in the middle."

"What can I do? I could never abandon Papà. One day Piero will go his way and Papà would be left all alone."

"That's what you say because you still haven't found true love. But when it happens, you'll change your mind."

"I hope I'll never have to face that dilemma... What about you? Have you found true love?"

"No. A few inconsequential flirtations, though lots of boys have fallen in love with me and have suffered because I rejected them."

"Oh, really? And how did they suffer?"

"They couldn't eat, they couldn't sleep at night, then they'd show up all pale and emaciated and said that they were going to die, and it would all be my fault."

"What did they mean, all your fault? What did they want from you?"

"They wanted to make love."

"And you didn't want to?"

"No. I didn't like them."

"Why? Were they ugly?"

"No, they were handsome. But they lacked *sex appeal.*" Mina liked to toss out certain shock phrases that she'd learned recently. "You know, there has to be that magnetic field that is generated between two poles, when you can feel the current running through, attracting you inexorably, a current that you can only interrupt by flipping an imaginary switch, but even if that switch existed you wouldn't want to turn it off. Do you follow me?"

"No. I don't understand. I don't know what you're talking about."

Mina realized that she was talking about Dardo.

IV

Dardo arrived at Cortalba entirely unexpectedly. He hadn't been invited, but to him that was an unimportant detail.

Mina was immersed in a book, stretched out in a lounge chair at the far end of the "observation wall." She would take refuge in that peaceful corner whenever she wanted to concentrate without being disturbed. As a little girl, she used to come here with Gio to "make the cucumbers explode." These were strange little plants, no taller than your hand, with fleshy, velvety leaves. They grew thick along the base of the wall. Gio had even tracked down their scientific name, *Ecballium elaterium*. The fruit of these plants, which resembled cucumbers, would explode at the slightest touch of a finger and fly into the air. Even now the little plants were heavy with flying cucumbers and, from time to time, you could hear them blowing up when a cat walked by or a bird landed.

Mina heard a sputtering sound, but it wasn't the cucumbers. The sound of Don Giordano's motorcycle on the municipal road down in the valley distracted her from her book and made her look up. Marilù had told her about this new parish priest, so young and dynamic, interested in the needs of the parishioners and sympathetic to their problems. He was very different from Don Barbisio, who'd only recently retired. The older priest never did anything more than dispense benedictions and penitences that did nobody any good. Don Giordano, on the other hand, often went to visit the parishioners who needed a word of comfort or some material assistance. He got around on an old motorcycle he'd found in some junkyard and rebuilt with his own hands, piece by piece. He'd even attached a sidecar so he could transport those who lacked resources or strong legs. People said that the authorities, both ecclesiastic and civil, disapproved of this populist attitude of his, and that he had been transferred to Cortalba from a much more important urban diocese as an unmistakable warning.

Mina peered over the wall. Despite the large cloud of dust, she could glimpse a passenger in the sidecar. After a few minutes the motorcycle pulled up on the piazza in front of the church, beneath the castle walls. Mina thought to herself that even when it came to the way he dressed, Don Giordano was an eccentric character: he kept the hems of his tunic tucked into his belted trousers so that they couldn't interfere with his movements, and as a headcovering, instead of the usual priest's hat, he wore a black beret crushed over to one side. The passenger was an odd duck, as well; definitely not a local. He wore a red bandana on his forehead, folded into a strip, and had a rucksack on his back.

"Thanks for the ride, Father," he said as he got out.

"Don't mention it, absolutely. I'm happy to have met you, otherwise you would have had to walk that whole way. It's six miles from Asti, and at this time of day there are no buses."

They exchanged a few more words. Don Giordano pointed the stranger to the gate and walked away, waving goodbye.

That was when Mina recognized Dardo.

She couldn't tell whether she was pleased or annoyed by this unexpected appearance, euphoric or furious at that intrusion into her private life. In this state of upset and uncertainty, she rushed down the drive to stop him before anyone else should see him. She was embarrassed by what a vagabond he looked like.

They met under the arch of the drawbridge.

"Hey, not bad…" said Dardo without any preamble, looking around. "You found yourself a cozy little place to live."

"I didn't find it, my grandfather found it. I was born here, practically," Mina retorted dryly.

"Good job, Grandpa," Dardo drove home his point as he set his backpack down on the ground.

"So what are you doing here in the first place? How did you track me down?"

"I called your aunt's home and they told me that the family had left for Cortalba. They also told me how to get here."

"Why did you come?"

"I couldn't live without you," and the corner of his mouth twisted in a smile of caddish amiability, making the statement and denying it at the same time.

"That's what they all tell me," panted Mina, trying to calm her emotions. "Try coming up with something new."

"All right then, let's try this…" Dardo grabbed her hand and jerked her close to him, wrapped his arms around her till she was helpless, and gave her a good long kiss.

At first Mina felt flabbergasted and outraged, then subjugated and conquered, then just confused. When they separated, Dardo said: "Now, if you want me to leave, you need only say the word."

"No… yes… that is, I mean to say…" Mina didn't know whether to slap him in the face or ask him to kiss her again. Just then, Gio emerged from the greenhouse.

"And who would this be?" asked Dardo, clearly annoyed.

"This is my brother… Gio! Come here, I want to introduce you to a classmate of mine from the Academy, Dardo Celti."

Gio walked over. "My pleasure," he said, shaking Dardo's hand. "I don't know any of Mina's new friends. You're the first."

"The pleasure is all mine," Dardo replied. "For a moment I thought you might be her fiancé."

"Gio, Dardo is on his way… to the mountains… Gran Paradiso, to go hiking," said Mina, pointing at his backpack. "Since he was passing this way, he decided to drop by for a brief visit." She emphasized the word "brief," shooting Dardo an eloquent glance.

"Ah, yah…I can't wait being up there with the steinbocks."

"Well, you will at least spend the night here. Come right this way, let's go find Erminia and get you a room," said Gio with solicitous hospitality.

Mina watched them go as they moved off, conversing animatedly. Since there was nothing she could do about it, she'd have to accept this *fait accompli*. The Gran Paradiso story struck her as plausible. And in fact, everyone believed it, or at least pretended to.

"I've heard you're quite the mountaineer," said Ada when they sat down to eat dinner. Good manners required that she start the conversation on a topic designed to put their guest at ease.

But Dardo didn't seem to appreciate the courtesy. "Actually, I've never been to the mountains before. I'm of maritime descent," he replied.

Mina gave him a kick under the table to make him realize that he needed to cooperate. Then she said, good and loud so that everyone could hear, "Dardo's family is from Naples, and that's where he lived before moving to Rome. Now he wants to see new places."

"Is this the first time you've been up north?" asked Ernesto, just to keep the conversation going.

Dardo detected a hint of superiority in that question, an expression of a deep-rooted prejudice toward the people of the south. He replied with a defiant tone, "My family *comes* from the north—a north that's even further north than Turin. One of my ancestors, Sir Edward Walton, was a *privateer* under Queen Elizabeth."

"What does *privateer* mean?" asked Olga, who was studying her guest closely. She pronounced the foreign, English word carefully.

"It means 'merchant,' Mamma," Ada explained. "A *privateer* is a private shipowner who places his merchant vessel at the service of the state."

"Actually, it means 'pirate'," Dardo specified in the tone of voice of someone eager to shock his audience. Another one of Mina's sharp kicks under the table had no discernible effect. Dardo went on, "Sir Edward had a ship armed with ranks of cannons. He crossed the Atlantic Ocean many times, shuttling back and forth between England and the new American colony of Virginia, and along the way he attacked hundreds of Spanish galleons and confiscated their precious cargo in the queen's name."

The other diners around the table had stopped eating and were now observing Dardo with a blend of curiosity and skepticism.

"And how did this Sir Edward arrive in Italy?" asked Riccardo.

"One day, as he was sailing a north-by-northeast course homeward, his ship was dragged by a strong current into the Strait of Gibraltar..." Dardo continued, increasingly animated, "... and landed on the island of Malta. There lived a small colony of Englishmen, known throughout the island as the Celts. Sir Edward liked the place and decided to put an end to his maritime raids and instead to take up residence on terra firma. With all his wealth, he built a great mansion for himself and began a thriving trade with Africa and Italy. He was also a patron of the arts. He met Caravaggio and became a friend of his, commissioning several paintings from him. Then, because of an incident whose details escape me now, but which had to do with a question of love and honor, Sir Edward was arrested by order of the supreme local authority, the Knights of Jerusalem—later known as the Knights of Malta—and shut up in a fetid prison. He managed to escape by bribing a jailor, and took ship aboard a brigantine owned by a Neapolitan merchant, his business partner. So it was that he arrived in Naples, where he was forced to start over from scratch, because he had lost his entire fortune. He also changed his name, to ward off the danger of assassination by Maltese killers for hire, and also to fit in better in his new home. He became Don Eduardo Celti." Dardo stopped to catch his breath.

There was a moment of silence. Then Luca clapped his hands and exclaimed, "Bravo!"

The others joined in with a polite round of applause and a chorus of benevolent observations:

"What a fine story!"

"It hardly even seems real!"

"He really told it well, like the true actor that he is!"

After which, no one made any further inquiries into Dardo's cultural and family background.

Only Mina brought the subject back up when they went out into the garden after dinner. "You were a complete boor. Why did you tell them all that rubbish?"

"I wanted to amuse them."

"No. You wanted to provoke them. But you couldn't do it. My family is very open-minded and they understood what game you're playing."

"But, basically, it was a true story. I embellished the details here and there, but the substance of the story isn't far off. Even today, in our neighborhood, my grandfather is known as 'the Maltese.' "

"Why?"

"It's a tradition. Or maybe because he did a lot of traveling. But between one trip and the next, he still found time to have twelve children, including Papà: Zi' Guglielmo, Zi' Enrico, Zi' Carluccio, Zi' Gaetano, Zi' Tittina, Zi' Annarella…"[14]

"That's enough! Don't give me a birth registry. I get it, you come from a big family."

"Those are the *zietti*—the uncles and aunts. I only have two brothers and three sisters: one is called Giacomo, like Papà, and the other one…"

"Don't start with the lists again. Your father must be well to do in order to maintain all these children."

"We aren't rich, quite the contrary. But Papà has a good job and we never wanted for anything."

---

14. In Neapolitan, zi' is diminutive for uncle and aunt.

"What kind of work does he do?"

"He's a musician in the Teatro San Carlo symphony. He's a bassoonist."

"He's what?"

"You don't know the bassoon? It has a heartfelt tone, with a human intonation. You must have heard that aria from *L'elisir d'amore*, "*Una furtiva lacrima / negli occhi suoi spuntò...*" It's a part for the bassoon." Dardo began to sing in a fine tenor voice. Before attending the Academy, he'd studied bel canto at the conservatory.

They'd reached the belvedere. Under the cedars of Lebanon, the glow of the moonlight was unable to penetrate. The darkness was almost complete. They leaned against the balustrade and observed the distant lights of towns and villages—configurations of various sizes, each with its own particular shape, like constellations.

"Here's a game we've often played," said Mina. "We had to come up with the best name for each of the shapes. You see?... that one on the right is a dinosaur, but it could also be a teapot. The one who persuades the others of his or her vision is the winner."

Dardo put an arm around her shoulders and plunged his face into her hair, inhaling the fragrance. He pressed his lips against her ear and murmured, "What I like is *your* shape, Alma."

Alma felt an unfamiliar sensation. The sound of that voice was transformed into a warm, sweet substance that penetrated her brain, making it fluctuate, and then oozed down her spinal cord, spilling into the network of her nerve endings until it had saturated every cell in her body. Then it pooled in her pelvis, creating there a sensation of turgid relaxation.

She turned toward him. Dardo kissed her with the brutality of a passion no longer restrained. His turquoise eyes were dark as the raging stormy sea. And opaque, like the rolling waves that sweep you away without even meaning to. Pressing his body against hers, he caressed her breasts, and moving down followed the curve of her waist and hips. Then he slipped his hand under her skirt. Alma stiffened and seemed to awaken from the languor that had invaded her.

"It's late, I need to go back in. Maybe they're already looking for me," she said in an uncertain voice.

"They won't find you," Dardo breathed into her mouth, "because, right now, I'm going to kidnap you." He picked her up like a stalk of straw and started striding back up the lane with long steps, holding her in his arms.

A lightning bolt clawed across the black slab of the sky, illuminating the battlements on the tower. The ensuing thunder split the silence. The first scattered drops began to patter against the branches of the cedars as they creaked and moaned under the thrusting violence of the wind.

"Where are you taking me?" asked Alma without putting up any resistance. The wind puffed up the light material of her skirt, like a sail on the mainmast.

"To the pirate's lair," Dardo replied.

At dawn, even before the woods began its concert of song, Alma scampered out of Dardo's bedroom and went running toward her own room, taking care at every turning of the hallway that there was no one in sight. She felt the way she had when she was small and had committed some minor infraction—euphoric, but afraid of being caught.

She hadn't slept a wink. When Dardo had finally fallen asleep toward dawn, she'd remained awake to observe him. He was immersed in oblivion—his fair hair spread out on the pillow, his powerful limbs inert and abandoned, his nude body surrendered, vulnerable. Alma thought that he seemed like a beaten warrior in some scene out of classical mythology.

She went into her room and threw the windows wide open. The thunderstorm had lasted for most of the night, with various crescendos, but now all was calm. She filled her lungs with the scents that emanated from the forest—the smell of steeped dirt that emits subterranean vapors, arcane and potent; of roots that absorb the humors of the earth and push them upward along the trunks and through the networks of branches; of leaves that take in the sap and transform it, scattering into the air their light and purifying respiration.

Alma remembered other thunderstorms from when she was a little girl. It was a threatening moment that could strike fear into your heart. But instead what prevailed was a sense of comfort and a feeling of safety, protected by the castle's thick walls, surrounded by grownups with warm, soft hands who knew how to reassure with a loving caress. The impacts against the lightning rod high atop the tower were deafening, the wind howled, surging in whipping eddies, and made the windows rattle and shake. A horde of housemaids ran through the castle fastening the shutters. The hail was hammering the pagoda over the well. Everyone waited for the storm to move on, looking out on that mayhem through the slats of the blinds. Then, all of a sudden, the weather turned fine again. The children put on their galoshes and walked out into the garden to splash in the puddles. A few mischievous cousins waited until the girls were walking close to tall hedges to shake the branches and drench them. The girls ran off shrieking, pretending to be indignant, while instead it was all just part of the game—a game that, as they grew older, they mistook for reality.

Alma threw herself onto her bed. Her body felt heavy but relaxed, while her mind floated free, like after a ski competition or a swimming race, when the dopamine in the brain reaches high levels and creates a faint sense of intoxication, an internal exultation that the mind classifies as "happiness." She lay there for a long time, contemplating the ceiling, summoning up the sensations of that night as they surged back to her in waves, filling her with an intense sense of well being. Then she slid softly into sleep.

V

For Alma that had been a decidedly pleasurable experience, an exciting game, the realization of many fantasies fed by films and novels. Moreover, the underlying erotic component was reinforced by the sense of transgression which, to her eyes, gave that adventure an audacious and rebellious coloring.

Physically, there was no trauma, none of what so many newlywed brides described as a regrettable but necessary sacrifice. The fact was that Alma was no longer a virgin, as a result of an accident that had befallen her when she was about eight. Climbing a tree, she had slipped and fallen, landing with her full weight straddling a rough branch. Her flesh was torn and she lost a great deal of blood. She was confined to bed rest for several days. When the wound healed, the doctor said that she had lost her hymen. "Too bad," Ernesto commented. "So much the better," Ada countered, "that only makes matters easier." Still, they told their daughter nothing, in order to keep from creating psychological issues at that tender age. When Mina turned eighteen, Ada would have liked to be able to give her a scientific treatise on sexuality, but *The Kinsey Report* still lay in the future and so was not an option. She therefore limited herself to providing Mina with a few rudimentary notions about sex. She also told her about the accident that had befallen her when she was a little girl and emphasized that that was a private matter that concerned her and her alone, that she was not answerable to anyone else, much less some man, whether he be a fiancé, or a husband. "It's none of his business," she concluded. Concerning the morality of sex, she had nothing to say, but she did tell Mina that it was better to wait until she was married to begin having sexual relations with a man, to avoid the consequences of a possible pregnancy.

* * *

The morality of sex was something that Mina had learned at middle school, taught by the nuns of the Santo Spirito. It was a very peculiar sexual education, because those pious women firmly believed that the ways of the devil passed through there—just look what happened to Eve...—and they therefore labored tirelessly to instill in the girls a distaste toward the filthy reptile who might lead them into temptation.

One of the most active propagandists in favor of the Sixth Commandment was Mother Palmyra. "I assumed this name when I took my vows with a thought to the palm of martyrdom," the good mother announced to the new class of twelve-year-old girls that included Mina. "I wear it as a banner, this name, to remind all of you how important it is to struggle against sin. After the Confirmation that fortified you, you became 'soldiers of Christ.' And so, you must be ready to sacrifice yourself for Him, willing even to die rather than to yield to the devil."

In order to reiterate this concept, she told them bloody tales of martyred female saints during the sewing and embroidery hour while the young girls stitched; or else she'd read aloud, with plenty of dramatic coloratura, from those exemplary lives in affordable mass-market paperbacks from the Vatican press. In those stories there was always plenty of mention of the preservation of purity, virtue, and virginity, as well as severed heads, dismembered bodies, and chests run through with swords and daggers. The martyred female saints were subjected to all manner of violence, but the one form of violence they never seemed to suffer was carnal violence. It's hard to believe that their tormentors never resorted to rape in order to obtain what they wanted, before executing their victims. But this variant was strictly ruled out, because the narrative convention demanded that the maidens die inviolate.

The martyred female saints accepted the most savage tortures out of love of Jesus, as could be seen in the color pictures that Mother Palmyra handed out to the class before beginning the reading. They were small-format pictures, like baseball trade cards; and in fact, they were occasionally used for that purpose. The girls collected the images and enlarged their collections with complicated forms of barter. The images had a certain point value. For instance, if you wished to acquire an image of St. Agatha, it would take two of St. Agnes—though no one seemed to know why. Perhaps having your breasts ripped off of your chest was a greater martyrdom than simply having your head lopped off; in the latter case, all it took was an axe blow, and you're done. Another highly quoted saint was St. Lucy, who held her own eyes on a tray as if she were serving a couple of fried eggs for breakfast. Sometimes, images entered the market from outside the school, pictures of ordinary saints who had died natural deaths. These saints had a very low rating. One day, a girl brought an image of St. Rita because she was shown with a crown of thorns and this seemed like a great torture. But when Mother Palmyra saw it, she said, "No, the crown of thorns isn't martyrdom, it's just a penance. It's a stigma, a gift of the Lord that one accepts with joy and wears like a hair shirt. And another thing, St. Rita, though she is a wonderful saint, isn't for girls. She's for married women. When she became a nun, she'd already had a husband and three children. I have no idea why they accepted her. Clearly, there must have been some special dispensation from the Holy Father." Whereupon St. Rita's quotation collapsed to zero.

When the day came for confession—generally, it was a Friday, which is already itself a day of penitence—Mother Palmyra would assemble the girls in the chapel and deliver a little preparatory sermon. Each time, it was more or less the same: "Approach this sacrament with the greatest possible humility. Remember, girls, that you are all born sinners and therefore, undertake a profound examination of your conscience so that you can bring to light all those dark stains that you carry on your soul. Your soul must return to a pure and gleaming state, like those of the blessed maiden martyrs, and if you were to find so much as a shadow that dulls its purity, then you must open your heart to Don Martino and ask him to grant you absolution."

At that point, Mina would shoot a sidelong glance toward the confession booth. Don Martino was seated with the door still open in that oversized cupboard, which very much resembled Grandma Olga's armoire, all made out of shiny carved walnut, missing only the mirror for the resemblance to be complete. She tried to concentrate and come up with a full list of the sins committed that week, but sometimes she couldn't seem to think of even one. When that happened, she'd just invent them, because she didn't want Don Martino to think that she was lying. According to the instructions of Mother Palmyra, the two sins you should never leave out of any proper confession were: "I've had impure thoughts" and "I've talked about dirty things with my girlfriends" (nowadays we might say they should be included by default). To these, Mina would either add two venial sins, or one mortal sin—such as having missed Mass on Sunday, for instance. This, she thought, carried a certain weight because, being a mortal sin, it was equivalent to murder.

For Mina, topics and practices of the sort remained sequestered behind the walls of the Catholic school. When she left in the afternoon with the noisy horde of her classmates, the heavy door that shut behind her back served as a barrier between the real world and the world of the nuns—"nuns," not real people, but a biological species, like "moles," "termites," or "moths," who lived in their own particular habitat. Theirs was a world of muffled footsteps, rustling skirts, dim lights, hallways scented with bleach and sawdust, spiritual exercises with whiffs of incense and tapers, and tragic visions of massacred virgins.

* * *

The real world, in contrast, was cheerful, sunny, and very pragmatic, both in her family and among her friends. Ada and Ernesto were good bourgeois Catholics, who went to church when duty required it, but who remained immune to all forms of mysticism. Whenever they had any doubts about moral matters, they relied more on common sense than on religious doctrine. They believed in God and the whole heavenly court, as if those were some sort of benevolent Lares and Penates, rather than abstruse divinities. There were no crucifixes at home; they both had too refined an aesthetic sense to allow certain grotesqueries. Instead, there were reproductions of works by the Renaissance masters depicting Nativity scenes and the Holy Family and, on their night stands, the occasional small pictures of celebrated pious persons for whom they had a certain fondness, as if they were late and lamented family members. There was also the Guardian Angel in the children's bedrooms. Mina felt reassured when, at night, as she fell asleep, she turned her gaze to the friendly figure who had no other task in the universe than to protect her. The angel was handsome and elegant. Beneath his long silk vestments, Mina imagined him as strong and athletic, well suited to combat and rescue. All the same, unlike warrior angels that wore knee-high legionary's sandals and carried flaming swords, this one didn't look especially manly; his hermaphroditic face, crowned by ringleted hair, had an expression of affectionate concern as he covered an errant little girl with one wing to keep her from the brink of a precipice. That maternal attitude inspired great faith in Mina toward her otherworldly friend.

As for her earthly friends, Mina frequented a healthy group of young people. They were also friends of Gio's, a number of girls and boys like them, with whom they went skiing in the winter and played tennis in the summer. When they reached adulthood—at the ages of seventeen or eighteen, let us say—they'd set out on these excursions without chaperones. Mina was placed in Gio's care. Sometimes, they'd spend two or three nights in alpine huts high on the snowy peaks, where in those years there were no cable cars, no ski lifts. You had to climb up the back of the mountain, skis splayed in the "fishbone" step, and it took the whole day. Then you'd rest at night, and ski down the next morning, tracing broad slaloms through the powdery snow; at every curve your skis would kick up crystalline wings, glittering in the early morning sunlight.

There wasn't much sleeping done at night. There was too much fun to be had. In a crackling fireplace, they'd heat up the provisions they'd hauled up the mountainside in their backpacks, and they'd accompany that crude but delicious food with the inevitable bottle of red Barbera wine. They'd talk, they'd laugh, and they'd joke until the wee hours, perhaps stepping outside in the cold for a few minutes to admire that blanket of stars so dense that it looked like a solid cloak of diamonds. Then they'd tuck into their sleeping bags, the girls on one side, the boys on the other. And they'd sleep until sunrise.

It's not as if there weren't fraternization among them. There was. There were flirtations, they'd fall in and out of love, of first this one then that, and more or less stable couples would form—people would say, "A is B's boyfriend," and "X is Y's girlfriend," and so on. But those were, as far as could be told, platonic relationships. For certain, when they were together as a group. As for the rest of the time, no one could say.

For a long time, Mina seemed unable to reconcile the idea of romantic love—the gifts, the kisses, the thoughtful signs of attention, the whispered sweet nothings—with the notion of sex. Even though she rejected the concept of the devil—stuff for the nuns—she still perceived something dark and violent in that unexplored territory, something that made her uneasy and yet, at the same time, tickled her curiosity. The more she learned about the subject, the more confused she became. In the library at Cortalba, she had chanced upon a slender volume of poetry by Aunt Viola, *The Exultation of the Satyr*, which someone had concealed behind a double row of weighty tomes. Mina had heard it said, ever since she was a small girl, that Aunt Viola's poetry was "Dannunzian," beautiful but quite *osée*, and that, therefore, it was strictly for adults. Considering herself by now to be adult—rightly so, for she was almost twenty—she took the book to her bedroom and read it from the first page to the last. She found no clear answers to her questions, but she did fall under the spell of the goat god who aroused orgiastic pleasures in bacchantes and nymphs.

On the occasion of a visit from Aunt Viola, Mina decided to question her, under the guise of a conversation about poetry. Aunt Viola was well along in years by now; younger than Olga, she was still well over sixty. But she had kept a youthful, subversive spirit, and so she decided that it was time to talk openly to Mina and tell her the way things stood. They were walking along the Chestnut Lane, on the carpet of dead leaves that was beginning to form toward the end of summer, and she locked arms with her niece (great-niece, to be exact) and said:

"Poetry is a metaphor that reveals the essence of things. In my verse, I treat the topic of erotic pleasure, as you've clearly understood. And that is why my work is considered so 'daring.' There is strong misgiving, I'd even say aversion, when it comes to sex in the dominant conversation of the better sort of society. Why? Because people are afraid of it. Sex frees us from our inhibitions and takes us back to the animal state, to the nude, crude substance of biological life. It gives us the intoxicating sensation of discovering the living body. Our bourgeois society wishes to camouflage sex by calling it love, surrounding it with little hearts, Cupids, red roses, and other such sentimental frills to soften it. That's a trick, though, because love is tenderness and understanding, while sex is something primitive and brutal. And that is its chief attraction. It is a glorious moment of Dionysian exaltation, a great power that unleashes our senses and annihilates our reason. And that is why people are so afraid of it. Because it is a subversive force that threatens the status quo. In fact, the phallus, in the literary and iconographic tradition, is a symbol of power and violence. Sexual pleasure is difficult to understand without experiencing it. You see, people say that sex is dirty. And they're right, in the sense that it brings us closer to the animal kingdom. The more we manage to degrade ourselves, the more we are able to enjoy sex. But at the same time, paradoxically, we arrive at this degradation through an aesthetic process. In sex, you have to go all the way. You have to recognize this terrible force. You have to accept the abandonment to your senses, the spiritual *néant*. Otherwise, you reduce it to an athletic exercise that may be more or less pleasurable, a repetitive game of no particular consequence. Or, even worse, to a bland and often unpleasant duty imposed by society as a condition of matrimony.

"I want to tell you about an adventure that befell me, to give you a concrete picture of what I'm talking about. When I was young, during a stay in Baden-Baden, I made the acquaintance of Prince Dimitri Lvovsky, captain of the Imperial Guard of His Majesty the Czar of All the Russias. That spa city in the Black Forest was one of the Russian aristocracy's favorite gathering places. We met at the stables. He was a splendid horseman, in a white uniform with gold braid and a visored cap that was scarcely able to contain the tawny curls of his leonine head of hair; a leather belt marked his slender waist, and his tight-fitting trousers revealed the massive musculature of the thighs that clamped down upon the flanks of the mare, in a masterly grip. Mitya (that was his nickname to friends and family) had just completed the obstacle course with a dangerous and spectacular jump, and as he reached the exit he was still at full gallop, trying to rein in his fiery little filly, stretching and taut in the excitement of the challenge met and bested. I was just entering the track. My horse, a stallion, caught a whiff of the presence of the filly and began to kick. Then he reared up and almost threw me. By this point, Mitya was quite close. He dismounted with an agile pirouette and grabbed my horse's reins, on which I had quite lost my grip. He made my horse feel his firm hand, all the while caressing his velvety muzzle and speaking tenderly to him. "*Chto ty, mily? Uspakóysia, nye buntùy. Tikho, tikho…*" he kept saying to him. I didn't understand Russian, but I thought to myself that the very sound of those words, the melody of his intonation, had a calming, seductive effect. And in fact the horse calmed down. Whereupon Mitya handed me the reins, clicked the heels of his boots and, with a bow, introduced himself. Thus began our friendship, which lasted the entire duration of that vacation, two weeks. After which, we never saw each other again. But those weeks were intense, and counted more than certain insipid relationships that drag on for a lifetime.

"We were both staying at the Grand Hôtel of the Source. I was there with Olga and Pietro. Pietro's doctor had ordered him to take a sulphur water cure. The year was 1896, I still remember because it was the year of Nicholas II's coronation; in fact, Mitya had come to Baden-Baden to rest from the interminable and exhausting ceremonies that accompanied that event. Also with us was our brother, your Uncle Candy, and a married couple, friends from Rome.

"That same evening, we invited Mitya to our table. Pietro had given in to my repeated requests and had sent him a note under the pretext of wishing to thank him for his intervention, which had prevented a terrible accident. The hotel restaurant was a vast room with spaces cordoned off by tall green plants and floral arrangements in large Chinese vases. The skylighted, domed ceiling allowed sunlight to stream in by day, creating the effect of a greenhouse. At night, discreet opaline lamps spread a soft light over the tables and diners. Mitya usually sat at the 'Russian table.' That's what the guests and hotel staff called it because it was unlike any of the others. There was always a very numerous and noisy contingent seated there. In spite of the fact that the maître d' had placed them in a secluded corner, bursts of laughter, toasts followed by the crash of shattering glasses, poetry declaimed with great pathos, rounds of applause and choruses of song spilled out from that table to the rest of the dining room. There was also a trio of gypsies that played and danced just for them—Mitya later told me that a high dignitary had brought them from St. Petersburg with his entourage.

"Mitya was sitting across from me. His gaze, fixed and insistent, forced me to look into his eyes. And when, obeying its bidding, I allowed it to penetrate me, we stayed that way for a long time, isolated from the surroundings, connected by invisible but concrete waves that annihilated all the distance between us. In our gazes, there were neither words nor thoughts. Only instinct.

"Because of our fellow diners, we often had to break off our mute connection and take part in the general dinner chat. The language used was French, which with the Russians was the lingua franca. Mitya ordered vodka and caviar for everyone. The hotel had plentiful stocks of vodka, which it imported directly from Moscow to satisfy the demand of its special clientele. But there was never enough caviar, since it was only imported in small quantities to ensure it remained fresh. To bypass the shortcomings of the hotel's supply chain, Mitya had ordered an enormous load of caviar from one of his landholdings on the Caspian Sea, and every night he treated the 'Russian table' with generous servings of the expensive beluga roe.

"That night, a faceted crystal bowl the size of a washtub was brought to our table, full to the brim of that black delicacy. The presentation was a work of art: the crystal bowl was set on a silver tray covered with chipped ice, and on either side towered two life-sized swans made of butter. We were captivated by that wonderous creation. Pietro spoke for all of us when he said, '*Prince, nous sommes rôvis.* Your munificence is a delight for our eyes.' 'And for your palates,' added Mitya, stroking his mustache. And, as the waiters bustled in to serve the guests, he preferred to serve himself, scooping out a ladleful of caviar so generous that it resembled a billiard ball. Then he picked up his knife and carved a curl of butter from one of the swans, spread it onto a piece of toasted bread, loaded the toast with a thick layer of caviar, and lifted it to his lips.

"Mitya chewed slowly, savoring the caviar with every tastebud in his mouth. Our gazes were once against locked into each other. A magnetic wave transmitted to me the flavor of that chunk of bread with its black spread and the voluptuous sensation that he felt as he chewed it, and I felt surging up inside me an impelling desire to tear off a piece with my teeth, and mix my lust with his.

"Mitya served himself two or three more times. Then the other courses arrived—boiled trout with mayonnaise followed by *salmi de lièvre*—and he ate abundant amounts of those as well. He had opened the top buttons of his tunic to feel more comfortable. The open collar revealed a neck that was shapely but as solid as the trunk of a beech tree. I could smell the pungent woodland aroma from sheer visual suggestiveness. I noticed, on one side of his neck, a vein that pulsated when he laughed, and I tracked it right up to the back of his ear, where it was lost in his dense curls.

"Mitya freely mixed wine and vodka. He drank wine as an accompaniment to the various dishes, and he drank vodka to fill the time between one dish and the next. He continuously raised his glass in one toast after another, all of them in tribute to the ladies: 'To our fascinating guest' (Olga); 'To the most extraordinary horsewoman' (me); 'To the most spectacular Latin lovely' (the third woman at the table).

"When we got up from the table, the company headed toward the terrace where coffee was being served. Mitya came over to me and managed to slip his arm around my waist without being observed by anyone else. There was no need for any explanation. He whispered in my ear, 'When?' and he slipped a note with his room number into my hand. I replied, 'Tonight.'

He was the first to leave. As he kissed Olga's hand, he did not limit himself to a ritual, symbolic gesture. Instead he pressed his lips powerfully against her little hand, and kept them there for longer than seemed quite decent. And in fact, Olga blushed. Pietro pretended not to have noticed that indiscretion, but after Mitya moved off, he commented, 'The prince has had quite a bit to drink this evening.' 'He's a charming gentleman, but just a bit too *nature*,' said Olga, leaning on Pietro's arm as if to regain her balance after that shock.

"It was past midnight. The few guests still on their feet had gathered in the roulette room. On the upper floors the hallways were dark and silent. I rapped lightly on his door, and it swung instantly open. Mitya grabbed my hand, which was still lifted, and yanked me roughly inside. 'I was waiting for you,' he said, clutching me to him with such force that it took my breath away.

"We kissed passionately, at first our mouths; then, greedily, the face, the ears, the neck... Mitya freed me of my clothing as he went on kissing me, sliding his lips down my body, my breasts, my thighs, my feet. Then he stood up, took a step back, and looked at me. 'You're beautiful,' he said. He was wearing a long black velvet robe over his naked body. He opened it slowly, deliberately, like an eagle spreading its wings. He unveiled his proud manliness and offered it to me. 'This is for you,' he said. It was magnificent.

"We fell, embracing, onto the deep carpet. We took our pleasure one from another in a whirlwind of intertwining limbs, wrapped in a natural dance, an amalgamation of bodies that no longer distinguished between interior and exterior, instead forming a single volume, a spatial dimension of sheer delight.

"When we separated, Mitya lifted me up and set me down on the bed. Then he walked over to a table decked with an array of bottles. Also on the table was the spectacular bowl of caviar, still half full, that one of his valets had brought home from the restaurant. Mitya filled two glasses with vodka and came back to sit beside me. He lifted one of the glasses to my lips and insisted that I drink it 'down to the last drop'—'*do dna, do dna, milaya,*' he encouraged me. Vodka, he later explained to me, isn't something you sip, you have to put it back in a single gulp. I couldn't do it, and copious rivulets of that nectar dripped down my chin and my throat. Mitya lapped at them, working upstream, and from my mouth he sucked the excess liquor I had been unable to swallow.

"But that was the drop that literally made the pitcher overflow. Suddenly Mitya stopped, and a strange expression appeared on his face, a mixture of surprise and disappointment. He raised one hand to his belly. 'Forgive me, dear, I don't feel at all well,' he said. Then, repressing a queasy urge to throw up, he lurched to his feet and grabbed the first receptacle within reach. He vomited into the caviar bowl.

"After which he took a gulp of champagne directly from the bottle and rinsed his mouth, ran a linen napkin over his mustache, and was once again at my side. We resumed our erotic play with renewed ardor. That incident had by no means quenched my lust. If anything, it had kindled it."

Mina found the conclusion to that story absolutely repugnant, and decided that it was true what people said about Aunt Viola, that she was quite the bohemian. For her, Signorina Don't-You-Touch-Me, sex never rose above the level of mere "athletic exercise."

VI

When Alma reawakened, it was already late morning. She went downstairs to the garden floating on a pink cloud. She found herself in a sort of excitement that put her in an excellent mood. She saw Dardo pacing back and forth, smoking a cigarette, and approached him with a dancing step.

"*Buongiorno*! I hope you slept well," she said, throwing her arms around his neck.

Dardo gave her a rapid peck. "Yes, I'm fine. I was just waiting for you, to say goodbye. I'm taking the noon bus."

"What!? You're leaving!? You're not even going to stay for a day or two?" Alma exclaimed in disbelief, taking a step backward.

"I'm not comfortable in this environment. Everyone's very polite, but this Turinese politeness annoys me, so contrived and superficial. You'd be well advised to get out of here yourself."

"Don't tell me what I ought to do."

"All right then, I'll see you back in Rome."

"No, I never want to see you again." Alma burst into tears and ran back down the drive, venturing further into the woods.

Dardo put on his backpack and headed off in the opposite direction.

Of course, they did see each other again. Alma returned to Rome at the end of the summer. Over the course of that winter, the winter of 1938-1939, Alma and Dardo were married. It was a marriage that caught everyone by surprise.

This event was not, so to speak, "recorded" in the family history. There are no photographs, there are no stories, there are no memories. No one, down the entire hierarchical scale running from Ada to Veglia, ever made the slightest reference to the event. Alma never spoke of the ceremony, the reception, the gifts—probably, there were never any such things. It's not even known in which church they were married, or whether it was merely a civil wedding ceremony.

Only now do I realize just how strange that situation was. When I was small, and even later, I never asked any questions, because since it was a non-event, I felt no interest in it. I was influenced by Alma's attitude: the matter was of no interest to her and therefore, indifferent to me as well. My relationship with Alma was exclusive and obsessive. All I cared about was that she existed, nothing else mattered. When I was a child I had practically no relationship with Dardo, for various reasons that I'll explain further on. Nevertheless, he interfered negatively in my life, because he had a certain amount of power over Alma—the power, it seemed to me, to make her unhappy.

VII

During the summer, Dardo gave into his father's nagging and agreed to bring Alma to Naples so she could be introduced to the family. He hadn't returned home in almost two years since he'd started attending the Academy, because, having made great efforts to lose his Neapolitan accent and achieve an uninflected, neutral diction, he didn't want to run the risk of reacquiring his regional cadences. The previous summer, when he was unable to rely on the funds from his scholarship, which were only disbursed during the academic year, he had served temporarily in the Fire Department—"Anything rather than come home. That fool goes off to fight fires!" his father had commented, bitterly. But once they were married, the situation had changed. Ernesto had rented a small apartment for the newlyweds, and had sent them an additional check during the summer months. And so, one June afternoon, Dardo and Alma arrived at the Naples Central Train Station on Piazza Garibaldi.

The piazza was full of movement: carriages, taxi cabs, porters with luggage carts, trolleys, automobiles, bicycles, the ice cream vendor with a three-wheeled cart, *tarallucci*[15] vendors, the water vendor with his keg… Alma felt her head start to spin.

"Dardo, let's get a taxi," she said. "Let's get out of all this confusion."

They stopped for a moment on the sidewalk. Dardo set the suitcase down. A *scugnizzo*[16] slipped up, unobserved, grabbed the suitcase, and took off running.

"Come along, *signurì*," he shouted over his shoulder. "I have a lovely carriage just for you."

"I don't want to ride in a carriage," said Alma. "Dardo, go get the suitcase back."

"You have no idea what a Neapolitan *scugnizzo* is like. He's never going to let go of that suitcase. We have no choice but to follow him."

"Come on, come on, *signurì*," the boy kept calling to them, pointing to a carriage with a plumed horse and a driver with a bowler hat. "Look what a magnificent carriage old Peppino is driving. Tell him where you want to go. But first, pay me for the service."

Dardo slipped him a coin and helped Alma into the carriage.

"What buffoonery. I feel like I'm at the circus," said Alma in annoyance.

Dardo paid her no mind and spoke to Peppino, "Quartiere Materdei. How much is the fare?"

"At your pleasure, *signurì*, at your pleasure."

"I'll give you one lira."

"Eh… one lira is too little."

"But you said, at my pleasure."

"Then just double your pleasure, *signurì*."

---

15. Sort of bagels.
16. In Neapolitan: urchin.

Peppino pulled up and let them out in front of a five-story apartment building that dated back to the era of Bourbon rule. He could have driven through the carriageway, which had been built especially for coaches, and rose all the way to the floor of the third story, but instead he stopped next to the sidewalk. Dardo had given him only one lira.

Dardo picked up the suitcase and, with Alma, walked through the atrium. They found themselves in a large courtyard with a flowerbed in the center, where a little bit of yellowish grass grew around a sickly looking palm tree. There was also a fountain in the shape of a seashell, with a child triton sitting on the upper edge as if he were driving a coach. The triton was blowing into a sort of horn from which a stream of water had once gushed. But now the fountain was dry. Two vast stone staircases ran up to the floors above, one on the left and the other on the right.

There was great expectation in the Celti home for the arrival of the bride. The father insisted on giving the young couple the master bedroom. He no longer slept there. After the death of his wife Rosella, two years ago, the room had begun to seem too empty. He had set himself up in the boys' room, now used only by Giggino, who was still in high school. Giacomino, the eldest boy, had married and now lived in Nettuno, where he worked as an engineer at the military Arsenal.

The sister Manon, had taken a degree in English and was a teacher in the province of Salerno. Still, she came one Sunday because she too wanted to meet her sister-in-law. The other two, Norma and Lucia, were still living at home. Both of them were about to graduate from the conservatory, after which they intended to pursue a career as concert pianists. They practiced every day, taking turns on the concert grand that enjoyed pride of place in the best drawing room, and so their playing resounded all day long without interruption.

The neighbors had complained more than once. This circumstance had unleashed a full-fledged war that had been going on for years now. The families had stopped speaking, and they limited themselves to an exchange of shouted insults from the balconies: "Don Giacomo, you're determined to make us lose our minds. Those thoughtless rude daughters of yours won't give us a moment's peace. Do re mi... si la sol... From morning to nightfall, from morning to nightfall..."

"Donna Concè, my daughters are artists with great musical talent. So shut up and take it. There!" And with that Giacomo flashed a pair of finger-horns at her, a grave insult.

Norma and Lucia were of average height and were slightly heavyset, like their brothers. They had handsome faces, with powerful jaws and straight, narrow noses. They resembled Dardo, in the color of their eyes and hair, as well. They were fascinated by Alma, who struck them as the living incarnation of the ideal of feminine elegance and refinement represented by the models in their fashion magazines. In that period, Alma was already five months pregnant, but she betrayed no signs of her pregnancy.

"Have you seen how pretty she is, Papà?" asked Norma.

"She's pretty, she's certainly pretty. But she looks drawn. She's so skinny, like stick people..."

"What are you talking about, skinny, Papà," Lucia broke in. "She's slender, long-limbed, like the women from the North. What did you expect, a nice fat doughball?"

Giacomo thought of Rosella's abundant, rotund shape, which brightened his bed and his heart for thirty years. He still couldn't resign himself to her sudden death of a heart attack. He'd never suspected that his wife had a weak heart, otherwise he would have hired her another household helper. Instead, she had only Michelina, a young housemaid they kept out of charity, and who was little more than a child and therefore didn't do a great deal of work. Rosella wore herself out raising six children. She spent her days cleaning, cooking, and doing laundry, never uttering a word of complaint or giving the slightest hint that she was exhausted. And then one day she just toppled over while she was sitting on the balcony, cleaning the broccoli for dinner.

Now the family was much smaller. Michelina had gotten married, and Norma and Lucia had taken on the domestic chores that had been somewhat lightened. Norma cleaned house and Lucia tended to the cooking. There remained one task, however, that was exclusively Giacomo's domain: the ritual of the coffee.

It had always been like that, even when Rosella was still alive. His first act of the day was always that of going into the kitchen, filling the coffee grinder with the dark, glistening, aromatic beans, squeezing it between his knees, and turning the handle with a precise, regular movement in order to obtain a fine, uniform grind. After which, he'd measure out the exact quantities of water and coffee into the invaluable *Napoletana* coffee maker and, the moment he heard the first sounds of boiling water, he'd turn it upside down with the dexterity of a prestidigitator. During the years of fascist autarky, when coffee was only available on the black market, Giacomo subjected his family to a regime of austerity just so they could afford it at least on Sundays.

But on the occasion of Alma's and Dardo's visit, he decided to go for broke, and pawned Rosella's gold earrings in order to buy enough coffee to drink it every day of the week. In the morning, at eight o'clock, he knocked at the door of the newlyweds' bedroom, "Eduardo, open up. I brought you *'na tazzulella 'e caffè.*[17] Just smell the aroma ..." he said, luxuriating in the perfume that rose from the tray. "Don't open the door," Alma said, "coffee on an empty stomach makes me sick. And I want to get some more sleep. Tell him not to bother us." "Papà," Dardo answered, "just put the tray on the floor, and I'll come get it. And don't worry about us if we get a little more sleep." "All right. Go ahead and sleep... But this coffee isn't going to stay hot forever, after all, and you know as well as anyone that a good cup of coffee needs to be as hot as

---

17. A sweet cup of coffee.

hell and as sweet as heaven," Giacomo retorted as he walked away. Passing by the room again half an hour later, he sadly saw that the demitasses were still on the floor outside the door. You can't reheat coffee, that's a mortal sin. He'd have to throw it away. All that money, down the drain.

Alma gave him other reasons for sadness. She never seemed happy and she never returned the affection and the kindnesses that she received. At meals, she ate little and without appetite. She'd eat a couple of forkfuls of spaghetti and then leave the rest in her bowl. "Eat, eat, sweetheart, it'll do you good," Giacomo would encourage her. "You've given me too much food. I can't possibly finish," Alma would retort. "Put a little more *pummarola* on top, it'll go down easier," he'd say, spooning more tomato sauce over the pasta. "Otherwise, Lucia might get offended. She might think you don't like her cooking," Giacomo would go on, resorting to that little trick of moral extortion. "Well, Alma, it's alright. If you don't like it..." Lucia would say mildly, with the attitude of someone accepting an insult with resignation.

"Don't insist," Dardo would break in. "Alma never beats around the bush, if she says 'no,' she never means 'yes.' In Piedmont they don't engage in these elaborate pantomimes—'if you please, take some'; 'no, no, thanks all the same'; 'I insist, have some, please, just try it'; 'oh, all right, if you insist...'—Up there, they pass the serving dish and if you say, 'no, thanks,' just to be polite, the dish zips past you as fast as lightning. When I first ate at Alma's house, I didn't even have a chance to say 'no, thanks' and the serving dish was already vanishing into the distance, and there I sat, like a fool, with my stomach grumbling. I'd look at the maid continuing her way around the table and I'd think, 'And now what're you doing, are you leaving? Darn it!' Then I learned their ways."

"So you see?" Giacomo said, turning the argument on his head to prove himself right. "You learned your lesson. You have to do the way a family does. Alma needs to learn to do the way we do."

Alma didn't reply. She checked out of the conversation with a faint smile of resignation that meant to convey the idea, "Speak all you like, I'm not listening to a word you say. I'll do as I please."

The *zietti*—the uncles and aunts—also wanted to meet the bride, but to keep from overwhelming Alma with too many visits, they decided to throw a get-together for everyone at the home of Zi' Guglielmo and Zi' Zazà. They had a very large apartment, in the same part of town but in another building. Guglielmo had been born in that apartment, and he'd grown up there with his six brothers and five sisters. Then, little by little, the brothers got married and set up housekeeping elsewhere, while the sisters found husbands and left the family. Only a few remained at home: the father, Eduardo "the Maltese," who lived a very long life and died well into his nineties; Tittina, who remained an old maid; Gaetano with his wife Carmela, because he was an employee of the Royal Post Office and received too small a salary to be able to afford decent accommodations; and of course, Guglielmo and Zazà. As the firstborn, Guglielmo was considered to be the owner of the apartment, and none of his siblings would have dreamed of contesting his right to the inheritance when their father died.

That night they were all there with their respective families. The living room was full. The early arrivals got comfortable on the sofas and armchairs; then, as the other guests arrived, it became necessary to bring in chairs and stools from every room, and even to borrow some from the neighbors—which meant they had to invite the neighbors in as well.

After the refreshments, which consisted of beignets and flake pastries with a limoncello liqueur, Zazà prepared to entertain her guests with her *bel canto*. Norma and Lucia would take turns accompanying her on the piano. Until that moment, Alma had been the center of attention, kissed, embraced, observed, scrutinized, evaluated, and criticized… But once Zazà floated across the room with her sashaying, still provocative gait, which impressed an undulating motion upon her generous, abundant figure, all eyes turned to her. She wore a very tight-fitting purple silk dress—too tight fitting when it came to the cushions of fat that had accumulated around her waist and hips in recent years. Her bosom projected like a small balcony from a plunging neckline. Thick black tresses, pinned up like a crown around her head, were garnished with a white flower.

Standing next to the piano, one hand lightly resting on the instrument, her head tilted to one side and her eyes turned upward with an air of inspiration, she looked exactly like the photograph of her that enjoyed pride of place on the console table with the mirror above it. She began her repertoire with the heartbreaking notes of *Core 'ngrato*. Alma had always heard that song performed by a male voice and she very much liked that violation of the traditional role. There followed *I' te vurrìa vasà*, *Dicitencèllo*, and *Reginella*… Zazà interpreted those impassioned songs with a robust contralto voice, with great tonal range and a strong and incisive timbre. Alma thought about what Dardo had told her:

"Zi' Zazà says that all the best Neapolitan songs were written by men and for men. There's not even one for a woman's voice. 'The man sings,' she says, 'and he depicts the woman—*'a femmena*—the way he wants to see her. For the most part, they're *malafemmene*—bad women. One of them *s'è pijata 'a vita sua*—has taken his life from him—and now *nun ce pienz' chiù*—she doesn't give him another thought; another woman *je mise int 'e vene nu veleno ch'è doce*—injected a sweet poison into his veins; and yet another, *ca nun chiagne, chiagnere lo fa*—who never weeps, makes him weep; and then there's the one who *je turmienta l'annema e nun lo fa campà*—torments his soul so he can't go on living.' And so Zi' Zazà decided to ignore the assigned roles and appropriate the male parts, partly to take her revenge on the opposite sex, but primarily out of artistic necessity. For the simple satisfaction of singing beautiful songs.

"And she does the same thing with opera. All tenor arias. You should hear her sing the part of Mario in *Tosca,* when he 'dies in despair.' And her big number is an aria from *Turandot,* 'Vinceròoo… Vincéeerò…' She's really great. But she can only do it in private. At the opera house, everything goes by the rules. Zi' Zazà is a member of the chorus at the Teatro San Carlo, where you stick to the score note by note. Papà helped her to get in, he gave her a special recommendation because, with her past, they didn't want to take her. They had learned that, in her youth, she'd been a *chanteuse* at the Caffè Parisien here in Naples. In those day, Zi' Guglielmo was an habitué of the house—''*A mossa, Zazà, 'a mossa!'* he would shout along with all the other dandies sitting at their tables, urging her to make her famous move… Drum roll, cymbal crash… *Brrrr-oom…* Zazà's chest, belly, and buttocks were shot through with an electric shock… followed by a burst of applause. First he had a crush on her, then he fell in love with her, and finally he understood that he couldn't go on living without her and decided to marry her. And he made the right choice, because they're still in love. They had no children and devoted themselves to each other. Zi' Guglielmo cultivated his wife's artistic talent and helped her to study with first-rate teachers who elevated her to a high professional level. And grandfather encouraged him to do so, because he too likes Zi' Zazà ."

Alma wanted to know more about Dardo's grandfather, who struck her as an interesting sort. That evening, he remained seated in his easy chair, listening to Zazà's singing with a sort of whimpering sound from under his white handlebar mustache, a whimpering that seemed to have been meant as a musical accompaniment. "Papà, please!" Guglielmo scolded him. The old man would fall silent, and a short while later, resume.

Dardo continued:

"When grandfather retired, Zi' Guglielmo took his place as the manager of a jewelry company, a major corporation with many retail outlets and local branch offices. Grandfather traveled a lot in his day. He'd even go to Africa to acquire precious stones. There's a photograph of him on a camel, with a pith helmet and a safari jacket, in a silver frame on his night stand. When I was a little boy, every time I came to see him, I wanted to look at that photograph and I'd ask him, 'Grandpa, is that really you?' 'How can you ask, don't you see me?' he'd say. And I'd ask, 'Will you take me for a ride on the camel, too?' And he'd reply, 'Of course I will. I already told the camel you were coming. I said to him: Stay right there, because I'm going to bring you a fine young man named Eduardo, just like me, and he's going to take my place.' I knew he was saying it just for fun. And we'd laugh about it together. The two of us always had a special understanding. Grandfather had had dozens of grandchildren, but I'm still his favorite. When he wants to pay me a compliment, he says, 'You, Eduardo, you've got imagination.' "

The day of their departure arrived and Giacomo sent Giggino to find a taxi and accompany the newlyweds to the station; and to carry their suitcase to the train for them. Once they were comfortably settled in their compartment, Dardo leaned out the corridor window to say farewell to his brother. Giggino was standing on the platform in a tweed suit with knickerbockers and a belted jacket that Giacomo had given him for his fifteenth birthday. Now he was almost eighteen, but he hadn't been given any new clothing. Prices had risen on everything, and Giacomo had to economize. Dardo thought that he looked like a little boy in that outfit, even if he had a powerful physique, like his own. A lock of hair hung over Giggino's eyes and made him look like an urchin. Giggino was the only one in the family to have smooth black hair, like

Rosella. His eyes, though, were the same as his brother's, an intense turquoise blue.

Dardo felt a surge of tenderness. He said, "Giggì, now you're here all alone, taking care of Papà and our sisters."

"Don't think twice about it, Dardo. I'm a big boy now. I know how to take care of my responsibilities."

"In any case, you can always call on me. Just let me know if you all ever need anything."

At that very moment, the train began to move, "*Statte buono, Giggì!* Take care!" Dardo called from the window.

Then he turned around to join Alma in the compartment and ran smack into a pair of German soldiers, who had hastily boarded the train at the last minute before the whistle of departure. They were mid-ranked officers, majors, as far as Dardo could tell, though when it came to military ranks he didn't know much.

The officers entered the compartment and set their luggage on the rack.

"Ist free here?" one asked. Alma barely deigned to give him an arrogant glance and nodded imperceptibly. She meant to say that the seat across from her was free, but that kraut just went ahead and plopped down beside her.

Dardo, who had been out in the corridor, now came in. "*Bitte*, if you don't mind, I'd like to sit next to my wife," he said.

"Ah, *bella signorina* is your wife? Unfortunate me." Lothar, for this was his name, laughed to show he was joking. Then he stood up and moved over to sit next to his fellow officer. The other German clearly didn't understand Italian, but he seemed to be able to get just enough to follow the conversation, and he supported anything his companion said with broad smiles, a stream of "*ja ja ja,*" and slaps on the back.

Alma looked out the window, focusing on the landscape and ignoring those present in the compartment. Dardo scanned the paper and every so often raised his eyes to respond with a distracted nod to Lothar's attempt at conversation.

Lothar lit a cigarette and offered one to Dardo.

"Thanks, I prefer 'Nazionali'," said Dardo, reaching for his own pack.

Lothar tried to catch Alma's attention, "Does *bella signorina* smoke?"

Alma shook her head vigorously and said, "Absolutely not. No." She had tried it once, but the acrid taste of the smoke had burned her throat and made her eyes water. After that one attempt, she never touched another cigarette as long as she lived.

Lothar spoke once again to Dardo in broken Italian. "You on honey month in Naples?" he asked.

"No, family matters," Dardo replied. Then, in a sort of provocative echo, "What about you?"

Lothar failed to pick up on the irony. "We are on leave," he replied. Then he explained as best he was able, that they had accompanied the General... (he said the name, but it wasn't a particularly well known one, and later Dardo couldn't remember it), they'd accompanied him on an official visit to Rome for important meetings with the Chiefs of Staff, with a view to certain operations that would be undertaken that very same autumn. Here, he put on a grave expression, in order to impress upon ordinary mortals like Dardo his privileged position as the depositary of vastly momentous state secrets. But, because Dardo failed to react to this revelation, he resumed the cheerful and festive demeanor of a few minutes earlier.

"We have took a week's leave before returning to Germany. Naples, Amalfi, Capri... *bellissimo! Signorine, bellissimo!* And the *vino*, also very *bellissimo!*"

"*Bellissimo!*" the other man confirmed, and pulled a bottle of Capri wine out of a valise, showing it to his fellow passengers and kissing the tips of his fingers the way he'd seen the tavernkeeper do when he'd sold him that bottle.

Lothar took the bottle out of his companion's hands, pulled the cork with a corkscrew that folded out of his admirably efficient multipurpose pocket knife, which contained numerous tools, all folding out and back, and took a long swig from the neck. Then he offered it to Dardo.

"No, thanks," he said. He had no wish to fraternize with those two. Still, to keep from seeming discourteous, he added, "I don't drink in the morning."

"We do, at all hours," Lothar boasted. Then he turned to his companion and spoke in German, whereupon the two of them exchanged a series of comments, evidently highly comical, because the two of them laughed loud and long, handing the bottle back and forth. Once they'd drained it, they fell asleep.

The two heads rested against each other, side by side. Both of them were ruddy-cheeked from the effect of the wine and were breathing with their lips just parted, so that they seemed to be smiling. They had an expression on their faces of languid beatitude, like what you see only on the faces of infants still in a state of preconsciousness, or, on the other hand, in individuals who have an absolute consciousness of their special state, superior and invulnerable.

Dardo turned to Alma who was reading a book, "*Bella signorina*, you've won the heart of a German." Alma shrugged her shoulders without taking her eyes off the page. Dardo continued to tease her, "Too bad that I'm here, otherwise maybe he'd invite you to dinner tonight."

"One man is already too many for me. So just imagine two…" she replied.

"Ah, so I'm too much for you!" Dardo exclaimed, offended.

"*Shhh*, don't raise your voice. Let them sleep, that way they won't bother us. I can't stand the way they talk, the way they act. If I hear him say just one more time, '*Bella signorina*,' I'm going to reply, 'Ugly mug.' "

Dardo couldn't help but laugh, even though he was angry at her for her stinging riposte. He asked himself for the umpteenth time why he'd fallen in love with her, and for the umpteenth time he answered his own question the same way, "She's different from all the others."

The train was arriving at their destination. Lothar opened his eyes, ran a hand through his hair, and jabbed his companion in the ribs. Both of them yawned and stretched.

Lothar consulted his high-precision steel chronometer, and said to Dardo: "In twelve minutes and twenty-five seconds we're going to arrive in Rome. Your Duce makes the trains march perfectly according to schedule."

"Eh, sure, sure," said Dardo as if he were talking to himself, "he makes everything and everybody march."

"Bravo!" Lothar chimed in. "Our peoples will march together for a great shared enterprise."

Dardo and Alma interpreted those words as one of the many propaganda slogans, and gave them no notice.

Three months later, Germany invaded Poland, which marked the beginning to the Second World War. Shortly thereafter, Italy too would join hostilities.

12

The Ape's Island
1939-1944

I

I came into the world easily, I am told, quickly and without outside help. Alma told me so every time my birthday rolled around. "You've been independent since the day you were born. You did everything on your own. I never even noticed. At a certain point, they just told me, 'It's a girl,' and there you were." She seemed very appreciative of my consideration on that occasion, and I was happy that I didn't cause her any major discomfort. Our love story began in that first instant.

When the time came to give me a name, Dardo proposed Rosellina, in memory of his mother. But Alma found that it was an insipid name, "like saying Margherituccia, or Ranuncoletta,"[18] and chose Antigone instead. Since she studied the classics, she took a liking to that character with a rebellious nature—years later, she would perform it on stage in Anouilh's version, not because she was interested in the political underpinning of the play, but because the categorical intransigence of *"la petite Antigone"* suited her—and so she stuck me with that name in defiance of general opinion. She did accept, however, that I was commonly called Nina.

Dardo ignored the registry and continued to call me by the name he preferred, especially when he sang me my lullaby. On those occasions, he joined his hands to form a sort of cra-

---

18. Margherituccia and Ranuncoletta are diminutives of flower names.

dle that held my whole body, like a hammock, and he'd rock me back and forth, singing, "*Ninna oh oh oh / Rosellina s'addormentò.*" And sure enough, suiting action to his words, I'd fall asleep. These, though, were rare moments. Most of the time, Dardo was absent from my life, whether due to circumstances beyond his will, or because his work interests kept him away. And, eventually, that name vanished entirely.

In October of 1939, Ada and Ernesto came to Rome for the blessed event. Ernesto documented the first few months of his granddaughter's life with a series of splendid photographs, many of which wound up reproduced on the cover of the magazine *Mamme e bimbi*. The publication had a full-color cover, and Ernesto was therefore obliged to hand-color his photographs, because the only film available on the Italian market under autarky was black and white. Even outside of Italy, for that matter, color film was the exception to the rule. In fact, it was only in that year that Technicolor had made its great debut in America in *Gone with the Wind*.

Those photographs are now in the family's private collection. In one, Nina's sleeping in her cradle; Alma is standing, in a sky-blue silk robe de chambre, her hair hanging loose around her shoulders, leaning slightly over her, as if she had just come over, summoned by a noise or some presentiment, to make sure that everything was alright. In another picture, Alma is seated and is holding Nina upright on her little legs with her hands under the baby's arms; the two figures are gazing into each other's eyes, smiling in mute dialogue; the camera has caught them at an angle, in a three-quarter view, through a gap in a gauzy curtain protecting their intimacy. In a third photograph, Nina and Alma are asleep, the two heads in the foreground on a single pillow; Nina is holding her right hand balled up in a tiny fist close to her face; Alma is repeating the same gesture, creating a rhythm of similar, adjoining shapes; the hem of the sheet marks the base of the frame with a diagonal line.

There are dozens of pictures like that. But what is missing are the ordinary snapshots that document everyday life: an unassuming family vignette, or a moment of silly spontaneity between mother and daughter. Dardo never appears. Evidently, Ernesto found him uninteresting as a subject. Or, perhaps, he himself was unwilling to pose with *"mamme e bimbi."* The fact remains that as Nina grew up, leafing frequently through those handsome pictures, she ended up confusing the enchantment of aesthetic representation with actual reality. That world of utmost beauty and happiness became, for her, a sphere of exclusive existence, hers and Alma's.

When Ada and Ernesto went back to Turin, in January 1940, they took Nina with them. Alma was rarely at home. Both she and Dardo were cast members of the Academy's Company, which hired the best students for theatrical tours, and that meant they spent a lot of time on the road. It was she who had asked her parents to take care of Nina. Alma loved her little daughter and found her adorable, with her turquoise eyes just like Dardo's and a vaporous blond fuzz of hair on her little round head. She hated to be apart from the baby. But she also loved her profession, and she believed that Nina ought to grow up in a stable and protected setting, for her own well being.

Ada and Ernesto were no longer young, and they weren't entirely enthusiastic about taking on that responsibility. Moreover, Ada was starting to display the first symptoms of the disease that was later diagnosed as multiple sclerosis affecting the spinal cord. Her step, which had normally been so brisk and energetic, had since become halting and unsteady. She often stumbled over even a slightly uneven sidewalk. Alma, unaware of the gravity of the situation, would scold her. "Mamma, what kind of way to walk is that?" she'd say disapprovingly, as if Ada were violating some basic tenet of social etiquette, let's say, like sneezing right in the middle of a concert.

At first Alma's request struck them as inopportune. But after talking it over at considerable length and sizing up the situation, they came to the decision that Alma needed their help to be able to pursue her career, and they agreed. Dardo, too, believed that this was the best solution.

Only Nina was opposed. If she had been able to speak she would have told everyone that the last thing she wanted was to be separated from Alma, that in those three months their bond had grown strong and that to be taken from her would have inflicted a laceration so profound that it would never, never heal. A love wound forever bleeding.

She set out on her journey in the arms of the nanny, wailing and objecting as best she knew how, while Alma hurried away from the train, still standing in the station, drying her eyes with a lace handkerchief, to keep from aggravating Nina's grief with her presence.

In the house in Turin, Nina and her nanny occupied a bedroom on the second floor, next door to Ada and Ernesto's room. The windows overlooked the garden and, when spring came, Nina was enchanted by the spectacle of the flowering magnolia and its branches, which brushed against the windowsill. The nanny would hold her upright on a small table placed near the window and had to struggle considerably to keep Nina from falling out, as she reached out her little hands to grab those white chalices. When she went downstairs and out into the garden, Nina discovered other surprising flowers—roses, which filled an entire flowerbed, sumptuous and fragrant, yellow and red, and jasmine which, though it might not be much to look at, still awakened the senses with its intense perfume. The nanny would carry her around from the flowerbed to the hedge, from the hedge to the lawn, from the lawn to the magnolia tree, pointing out a blossom here, a birdie there, and here still an ant or a ladybug. Nina filled her eyes with everything she saw, and she added to that array her own personal discoveries, such as the nanny's coral necklace—

ah, the satisfaction of being able to grab it!—and the colorful flounce skirt that she made sway as she walked. Nina had to twist downward in order to be able to watch those colors in movement, struggling against the nanny's solicitous hand as she tried to keep the baby upright.

After the trauma of separation, Nina had adapted to life without Alma. Cheerful by nature, she could easily appreciate the fine things that she found around her, and learned how to compensate with new experiences and sensations for the emotional void that no one had filled. The nanny was kind and goodhearted, but there never developed a deep and lasting relationship between them. Ernesto was busy with his activites and only took interest in her when he wanted to portray her in some photographs. And Ada—Nina sensed this clearly—didn't love her. She had chiefly taken her in to do Alma a favor, more than any feelings she might have had toward the child. Nina lived with her grandparents for six years and, as an adult, when she thought back on that period of her childhood, she couldn't bring to mind a single instance in which Ada had cuddled with her, embraced her, or showered kisses on her the way you do with children.

All the same, her days passed pleasantly, because the image of Alma had little by little withdrawn to that zone of her subconscious that houses the mythical reality of a lost blessing for which you perpetually yearn, but which remains removed from the sphere of daily life. It was therefore a shock to her when, one fine day, Alma reappeared. It happened in the summer, during her first vacation at Cortalba.

II

Italy had just declared war alongside Germany, but ordinary people weren't yet feeling the impact of that tragic adventure in their everyday lives. If anything, there was an air of great optimism, kindled by the fascist propaganda—newspapers, radio, posters, assemblies, military parades, speeches, fanfares—which was predicting a quick, easy victory and a future of glory for the victors. Italy's declaration of hostilities had come late. Half of Europe had already been occupied and the armed forces of the Reich were about to enter Paris when Mussolini made his fatal decision. In view of the success enjoyed by his German ally, he was keen to seize the opportunity and divvy up the likely spoils of conquest.

On June 10th, the Duce harangued a jubilant crowd that had gathered on Piazza Venezia with words of fire that drew waves of applause with every dramatic pause, "...An hour appointed by destiny has struck in the skies of our fatherland... The declaration of war has already been delivered to the ambassadors of Great Britain and France... The single order of the day is categorical and obligatory for all: Victory! And we will win!"

At first, the Duce kept out of the European theater of war and commited the valorous Italian troops to a new front in northern Africa. In every corner of Italy, the local authorities delivered puffed-up speeches on the nation's military exploits and inflamed their listeners' hearts with patriotic pride.

Even in a small town like Cortalba the atmosphere was electrified by the departure of the new recruits. The day of the farewell ceremony, the newly enlisted youths gathered in the piazza. They were still dressed in civilian attire, with a tricolor neckerchief. Like all troops heading for the front, there was a certain degree of apprehension in their hearts, though it was well concealed beneath a somewhat swaggering, smart-aleck attitude. They were well aware of the sacred mission they were undertaking and excited at the thought of setting out for exotic lands with hard-to-pronounce names, like Cyrenaica and Marmarica.

Aurelio Costa, still podestà after all those years, climbed onto the stage and delivered an impressive speech. He praised the heroic militiamen who were about to bring Roman civilization to lands across the sea, just as the legionaries of the Caesars had done in their day, to lands whose savage populations were yearning to be annexed to the Empire. Then the Fascist Party chief from Asti took the stage. He'd come to Cortalba especially for the occasion. After him came other junior officers and officials, who reiterated that message with magniloquent turns of phrase.

Last of all, it was Don Giordano's turn. From the stage, he looked out at that crowd of young men, their faces all turned upward toward him. He knew them all by name, having played soccer with them at the parish oratory every Sunday for more than three years. He felt a stab of sorrow in his heart. He began: "Dear boys, there are difficult moments in our lives that we must face with courage and honesty. This is one of those moments. We will think of you when you are far away, and we shall pray for you, that you have the strength to overcome adversities, helping each other, and also that you will show compassion toward the people that you meet down there..."

Here, the authorities in the grandstand began to feel uneasy and exchange alarmed glances. Don Giordano went on: "The thought of your families will help you go on. Think of your parents who are getting older and need your strong arms to till the earth, and your girlfriends who are waiting for you, so that they can become brides and mothers. Remember, too, that the men you are fighting will have these same thoughts, and the desire to return home to their loved ones..."

At this point, Aurelio leapt out of his seat and waved to the bandleader. "Music, Maestro!" he ordered. And turning to Don Giordano, he summarily dismissed him, "Thank you, Father."

Don Giordano stood on the stage in silence for a few moments, then he bowed his head and resumed his seat in the grandstand.

The band struck up the melody of *Vincere* (*Win*) and Aurelio began to sing the song, encouraging the young men to follow along. A proud, martial chorus filled the air.

> *Win! Win! Win!*
> *And we shall win by sky, land and sea!*
> *This is the military order of a supreme will.*
> *Win! Win! Win!*
> *At any cost! Nothing can stop us!*
> *Our hearts exult*
> *in our desire to obey!*
> *Our lips swear,*
> *either we'll win or die!*

At the edges of the piazza, among the throng of people who had accompanied the new recruits, mothers and girlfriends wiped away the occasional tear, but deep down they were proud of their boys—or, at least, that's how they consoled themselves. Young boys in Balilla[19] outfits shouldered tin rifles and sang at the top of their lungs, all the while envying their older brothers who were setting out on that wonderful adventure. But among the middle-aged men who'd fought in the Great War, there was a degree of skepticism; they knew the reality that lurked behind the romantic façade, they'd seen their fellow soldiers die by the hundreds, and therefore they took part in the general enthusiasm sparingly, and only out of a sense of solidarity with the young troops.

On one side of the piazza stood a rather small obelisk that commemorated the fallen soldiers of that other war. It was a slender column standing about ten feet tall that stood at the center of an enclosure constituted by four short pillars linked by chains. The monument had been neglected for years, the marble was blackened, and dense growths of weeds had

---

19. Members of the Opera Nazionale Balilla (ONB), a scouting-paramilitary youth organization.

sprung up around the foot of the column. No one paid any attention to it any more, except for the occasional passing dog that took advantage of the opportunity to raise its hind leg against one of the pillars.

Marilù was there in the grandstand, as she always was when Aurelio was performing his official functions. She didn't enjoy taking part in those ceremonies, but she did it out of a sense of duty toward her father. Piero, on the other hand, kept his distance as a matter of principle. He considered himself a Communist, and he often clashed with Aurelio on ideological and practical matters. But in public he behaved cautiously, never openly declaring his political position, and impatiently awaiting the moment when the revolution would finally break out, a time that could not be long in coming.

Once the speeches were over and the song had been sung, the young men boarded the waiting army trucks and the convoy set off toward the Asti train station with a great show of fluttering banners.

On the provincial road they encountered the long-distance bus that was coming from the opposite direction. The passengers leaned out of the windows to wave to the recruits and wish them good luck. Also riding on that bus was Alma.

III

At the conclusion of a series of performances in Turin, Dardo had returned immediately to Rome, while Alma chose to stay on a little longer to pay a visit to Cortalba. The family members had all been alerted and they were impatiently expecting her. She was all the more eagerly awaited because there weren't many left that year at the castle, and any visitor was a pleasant distraction. Olga had passed away that winter; she'd contracted liver cancer several years earlier, which gradually became more virulent, and eventually completed its lethal cycle. Riccardo, after his second amputation, had remained confined to his home in Genoa and no longer traveled. Elisa and Lidia, and all the other cousins, now preferred to vacation elsewhere. Therefore, the company had been reduced to Ada, Ernesto, and Luca, who now lived with them, and Nina. Even counting Veglia, the nanny, and the few domestics who still stayed on, the great manor stood practically empty.

The afternoon that Alma arrived, Nina was under the linden tree with her nanny. For a while now, the tree had been showing signs of deterioration. A few branches were withered and, here and there, you could see tufts of prematurely yellowed leaves. Once, in springtime, the linden tree had been covered with flowers, dense and soft, to such an extent that you'd think it had snowed. The flowers emanated a dense fragrance, and when they fell people gathered them in large sacks to make herbal teas in the winter. But already last spring, the linden tree had failed to blossom.

Ada consulted with Berto, a peasant who came from time to time to rake the gravel. The man examined the roots, then placed an ear against the bark and tapped his knuckles lightly on the trunk. Then he reached under his felt hat and scratched his head, saying, "This tree is sick. There's nothing we can do for it. Not even with verdigris, which does so much good for the vines." Ada knew that Berto was never wrong when it came to the vegetable kingdom, and she resolved to contact a specialist at her earliest opportunity.

For the moment, the foliage was still dense and verdant, and Nina spent the hottest hours of the day in the coolth of the tree's great leafy crown. That afternoon, she had just awakened from a lovely nap. Her nanny had lifted her out of the baby carriage and was holding her in her arms, strolling to and fro to amuse her.

Alma walked out into the Hello Garden and headed toward them with a light, dancing step, her hair tossing in the breeze, her silk dress merging with the color of the wisteria in the background, a dazzling smile on her face and her arms outstretched, ready to embrace.

When Nina saw her she turned pale. Not just pale: white as a sheet. Then beet red. She almost suffocated. She opened her mouth wide and tried to inhale a gulp of air, but she just couldn't breathe. At last, her blocked respiration gave way to a piercing shriek accompanied by copious tears. Nina turned and hid her face in the nanny's shoulder, refusing to respond to Alma's cooing call. She wanted to ignore her, cancel her from her sight. This visit pried open a wound that was just too painful.

At last she yielded, and allowed Alma to take her in her arms. When she came into contact with Alma's body, she clung to her neck just as hard as she could. For two days, there was no way to get her to let go. On the third day, Alma left again in the early morning, while Nina was still asleep. When Nina woke up, she went looking for her everywhere, and called her name over and over, "Mi-mi... Mi-mi..." Failing to find her, Nina's call gradually dwindled to a monotonous, disconsolate lament. But she didn't cry. That episode had taught her that the break would not last forever, that Alma would return. And, from that moment forward, she began waiting for her.

In the first two years of war, Ada and Ernesto maintained their regular pace of life, spending their winters in the city and the summers in the countryside. But when, in the summer of '42, the RAF started its carpet bombing of the major cities, they decided to move to Cortalba and stay there for the duration of the conflict.

For practical reasons, they only occupied a few rooms in the east wing, and they shut up the drawing rooms suite and the bedchambers on the second floor. The apartment where they set up housekeeping was situated on the first floor, and it consisted of four bedrooms—one for Ada and Ernesto, one for Nina and her nanny, one for Luca and Lillì, and one for any guests they might chance to have—a living room, and a small dining room. The kitchen was on a lower floor, and could be reached via a staircase squeezed between two walls, or else by an outside door that led out into the lower court-yard. Near the kitchen was a small bedroom for Veglia. There was no one left of the domestic staff of bygone times: Erminia had retired to her nephews' farmhouse, Kerplunk was dead, and Giusto had had an accident with the gig and had never come back from the hospital. Other household help came for the day, but they didn't live in the castle. Among them was a certain Mariuccia, the daughter of one of Erminia's nieces, an eighteen-year-old girl who helped Veglia in the kitchen and who served at the dinner table, and Celestina, a large mid-dle-aged woman who cleaned house and did the laundry.

This was Nina's world, the world of which she preserved a direct memory. If her first two years of life had been marked by impressions, emotional flashes, fragments of phrases over-heard, the years that followed were recorded in her conscious-ness in full detail.

Nina was quite precocious. From the very first months of her life, she possessed an ability to express herself that far out-stripped her tender age. She wasn't yet a year old and already she had began figuring out how to get around on her own, taking her first steps on her unsteady little legs, or traveling long distances on all four, like a little rabbit. It was necessary to keep close track of her, lest she get into some kind of trou-ble. And in fact, several incidents had occurred that had left everyone worried to death.

During her first summer in Cortalba, it only took an in-stant's distraction on the part of the nanny for her to fall off the "observation wall." She was saved by pure chance, caught by a projecting spur of loose bricks covered over by the foliage of the wild grapes. It took the fire department with their hook and ladder to rescue her from the piazza below. This episode, as it was told to her when she was a little older, reminded her of the ex-votos of the recipients of miracles that she had seen in the sanctuary dedicated to a Madonna who was particularly efficient at rescue operations of all sorts. She had very much liked those naïve little paintings, with their lively and straightforward emotions, and she resolved one day to create a dramatic image of her personal story.

Episodes of this nature continued to occur for the whole time she lived with her grandparents. Without being aware of it, Nina was expressing with this behavior her frustration with a situation that had been imposed upon her against her will. They were acts of rebellion, as it were, all the more clamorous given the fact that in everyday life she was a very disciplined and obedient child. Ada knew how to command obedience, without ever raising her voice or flying into a temper. All it required was her tone and her gestures, authoritarian and beyond appeal. Nina understood that with Ada, there was no way around it. Begging, tears, blandishments, alternative suggestions—none of it would do. Ada was inflexible. Every one of her decisions was a final verdict.

Tantrums were forbidden. Looking back, Nina didn't remember having acted out or thrown a tantrum even once in all those years. Instead she remembered a phrase that Ada had taught her, and had her repeat frequently. "How is Nina?" Ada would ask. And she'd promptly reply, "Nina is lovely, good, and never *fwows tantums*." This ritual was applied, for instance, every day before lunch, when Ada would stick a large soup spoon full of cod liver oil into her mouth. No one else could do it, not the nanny, not the housekeepers, and not even Veglia, because at the mere sight of that disgusting substance Nina would take to her heels and hide behind an armoire. But all Ada needed to do was recite the ritual formula and she would obtain the desired result.

Thinking back on that period with the maturity of a grown up, Nina realized that Ada had given her everything she had to offer, if not with great affection, then certainly with an admirable sense of responsibility. A little girl like Nina, with her fervid imagination and lively temperament, who "never gets tired of coming up with new pranks," as people said of her, wasn't easy to control. What's more, Ada's disease was progressing, and she was having more and more difficulty walking. At first she used one cane to help herself walk. Then, two canes. Then she found herself having to stick to routes carefully planned to stay close to tables, armoires, and cupboards strategically located along the path for her to lean upon. She stopped going out entirely. After five years, Ada reached the stage of complete paralysis. She spent the last years of her life flat on her back in bed; her sole pastime consisted of studying the ceiling, which was frescoed with birds of paradise with sumptuous plumage against the background of a deep-blue sky. Whenever anyone asked her how she was doing, she replied, "I'm almost getting used to it."

Still, however stern and demanding she might have been, Ada devoted herself to her granddaughter's welfare and, as long as she was capable of doing so, she took great care to ensure that her practical needs were seen to. Nina remembered how every morning Ada would step in, dismiss the nanny, and comb Nina's hair herself, piling the hair up in a roll in the middle of the head and fastening it with long hairpins, and then brushing back the light, fair hair on either side in gentle waves; how she would fill her wardrobe with lovely dresses, shorts, overcoats, bonnets, and undergarments with lace and embroideries, made to order by the town seamstress named Nardina; how she made sure Nina said her prayers at night and how she stayed at her bedside until Nina had fallen asleep; how, during the nighttime air raid alarms, when everyone would descend in single file down the narrow staircase into the underground shelters—Veglia leading the way with a candle, Luca bringing up the rear with Lillì, Nina in her nanny's arms—Ada would grab hold of the railing with both hands, and make her way downstairs laboriously, one step at a time, frequently turning around to make sure that Nina wasn't cold, "Nanny, did you bring the wool blanket? Wrap the child up snug, because it's very damp down here," she'd say, and then concentrate once again on the descent, helped along by Ernesto. Those excursions into the cellars, when the Allied airplanes flew over the hills, heading for Turin with their explosive cargo, were fascinating adventures for Nina. The candle would cast strangely shaped shadows onto the walls and ceiling. Things and people looked different. Luca and Ernesto were funny with their overcoats over their pajamas and Ada, with her hair wrapped up for the night in a long gray braid that hung over her heavy cloth dressing gown, didn't seem quite so formidable. In fact, Veglia and the nanny were less fearful in her presence, more free and easy during those brief periods spent down there. And Nina was happy to feel that she was part of a group, in an atmosphere that brought them all together, instead of dividing them.

IV

Nina had no real company. At home, there were only old people, with the exception of Mariuccia. In the fall of 1943, the nanny decided to go home to her village in Ciociaria, near Rome, to be close to her daughter, now that that region had been occupied by the Germans. They tried to talk her out of it, but she refused to listen. They learned at the end of the war that she had been killed at one of the many checkpoints along the way.

Mariuccia took over the job of caring for the child. But she had her head in the clouds, like all young people, and Nina kept slipping out of her sight. "Mariuccia is a birdbrain," Ada liked to say with disapproval from her armchair, whenever she heard of yet another sign of carelessness that might well have unpleasant results.

It often happened that Nina would walk out the main gate, all by herself, and enter the courtyard of the house next door. That farmhouse had once been the home of Tunìn the gardener, as far back as when Ada used to paint him in her canvases, a small baby in his mother's arms. The house still belonged to the castle, and now it had been rented out. Two families of evacuees lived there with their children, occupying the upper floor. And on the ground floor lived Nardina, the seamstress, who couldn't do her work on her husband's farm in a distant village, and so she had rented that lodging in town. Nardina had a daughter named Carletta who lived with her, and who was only slightly older than Nina.

To Nina that courtyard was a magnet, not only because she got along so well with Carletta, but also because the whole place teemed with interesting activities. You could play hide and seek with that gang of children, behind bales of hay and sheaves of wheat; climb the fig and pear trees and pick ripe fruit that they'd eat until they were sick; and feed the rabbits, sticking handfuls of grass through the wires of the cage and then observing that odd way they had of chewing, and laughing till they died. But Nina wasn't always allowed to play with them. For instance, when they'd dig tracks for marbles in the clayey soil, with switchback curves, uphill and downhill stretches, and then launch the colorful marbles with expert flicks of the thumb, Nina, like all the other girls, was forbidden to take part. She was only allowed to watch the boys compete, with a mixture of admiration and a hint of envy.

This exclusion from the world of boys struck her as unfair, all the more so given that she could keep pace with even the fastest boys her age, and she could scramble up trees with even greater agility. One day, putting on a brash face, she decided to take a pee up against a tree the way little boys did, noticing that when they did so, it was an act of great self-importance. But the outcome was disastrous. She had to run home, covered with shame, her ankle socks dripping and her feet slopping loudly—*shlipp shlopp*—in her sopping shoes.

Everyone laughed at her, and for a number of days Nina was the butt of every joke. In effect, that unfortunate episode offered a pretext to humiliate her. Not just the boys, but also the little girls, with the exception of Carletta, felt an ill-concealed resentment toward her. They found her to be "different" and they considered her a stranger in their midst. Whenever someone chanced to come to the courtyard and saw Nina for the first time, they asked, *"Chi a l'è sta bela matòta?"* And Nardina would reply with a certain deference, *"A l'è la nvuda d' Munsù Bunàrd"*[20]. The lawyer's granddaughter... That alone was enough to give her an air of superiority in the eyes of the other children, something however that Nina had never thought of cultivating. Quite the opposite: she wanted to be accepted and she made an effort to be part of the group. She didn't realize that no effort would ever change the fact that she came from that inaccessible world beyond the castle's walls, a world that to them meant privilege and, to her, nothing but confinement and isolation.

Nina understood none of that, but she did suffer from the sense of alienation and loneliness that she felt. She couldn't say anything to Ada, since her grandmother had forbidden her from spending time in that place. Ada considered the children in the courtyard to be "a gang of urchins," and she'd even had less than flattering things to say about Carletta, "the seamstress's daughter, and therefore not a suitable friendship for her."

It's a good thing, thought Nina, that Ada couldn't walk like other people, because that meant she wasn't capable of checking on where she was and what she did. Still, she had to keep an eye out for spies. Mariuccia never said a thing, because she didn't want to get in trouble herself, and also because she had a boyfriend named Beppe and she liked to spend time with him while Nina played in the courtyard. Veglia and Celestina

---

20. Piedmontese dialect: "Who's this lovely girl?" "She's Mister Bonardi's granddaughter."

had it in for the mistress because they felt underappreciated, and so they too kept their mouths shut. Luca never ventured off the castle grounds. That left Ernesto, fearsome because he represented Ada's eyes and ears, and if he ever saw Nina in the courtyard there was always the risk that he might tell on her. But Ernesto rarely passed that way, generally preferring to use the little gate that led onto the piazza. And if he did happen to see her, he chose to say nothing rather than get Ada angry and risk the possibility that her health might suffer as a result.

But an incident occurred that even Ernesto couldn't hush up. One day, when he happened to pass by the side over-looking the courtyard, Ernesto was shocked to see the lovely historical costumes that had been used in the past for the *tableaux vivants,* and which had been mothballed lovingly for so many years, scattered here and there in the barnyard, in the mud and the dust. The vivid amaranthine reds, the greens, the blues, and the delicate pastel hues all created a pictorial effect that was truly lovely, like patches of flowers on the bare ground. But Ernesto paid no attention to the aesthetics of the scene. Instead, he stopped to glare at the "gang of urchins" in tailcoats and satin breeches that were too big for them, as they chased each other shouting and brandishing harmless swords; and the young ladies who promenaded under the awning of the rabbit cages in exquisitely embroidered dress-es, while the hems, far too long for them, dragged in the filth. Nina, in a little blue velvet cape with gilt hems, was running around the courtyard, collecting here a musketeer's hat and there a plumed tricorne, and offering them freely to this little boy or that, saying, "Try this one on too." But, since the boys were all too caught up in that exciting game, they dismissed her with a shove. "Go over there and play with the girls, here you're just in the way," they would reply in annoyance.

There was an investigation. Mariuccia confessed that it had been she who'd opened the armoire with the costumes, using a key that she had purloined from Veglia. She had only wanted to take an outfit to show herself off to Beppe in that princess costume. But when Nina saw the costumes, she insisted on grabbing an armful to let all the other children play with them. Nina apologized and said that she'd had no idea that they could be so easily ruined. She had meant to put them all back before nightfall.

Ada presided over the hearing from her armchair. Ernesto, standing, with an elbow resting on a chest of drawers, had put on a relaxed pose as if he were a witness at a trial. Nina and Mariuccia sat stiffly in two chairs facing Ada—Nina was nervously dangling her little legs.

Ada spoke, "You're both guilty. You especially, Mariuccia, because you're a grown up and you ought to have a smidgeon of judgment. Instead you just showed once again that you're nothing but a fool. I can no longer trust you, and from this moment forward you can consider yourself fired. You, Nina, leaving aside the way you ravaged those wonderful costumes, you've committed a very serious infraction: You disobeyed me. I've told you a thousand times that you mustn't go in that courtyard. They aren't people you ought to frequent. Those children are jealous of you. Don't believe for a second that by giving them nice presents you're going to win their affections. You need to stay in your own home, between the walls of this castle, the way we've always done, surrounded only by friends and cousins."

"But I don't have any cousins," said Nina, in desolation.

Ada refused to take this mitigating circumstance into consideration and delivered her sentence, "You can't leave this house for the rest of the week."

Mariuccia blew her nose loudly and Ada noticed that she was crying. "What do you have to cry about?" she asked.

"Signora, my Papà will beat me if he finds out that you fired me." And she blew her nose again loudly.

"I don't want to hear another word. You can both go," said Ada with a tone of great finality.

The two of them withdrew to Nina's bedroom, in silence and with downcast eyes.

It required Don Giordano's intercession to persuade Ada not to fire Mariuccia outright. Don Giordano told her that Mariuccia's father was a wino and that when he was in his cups he turned violent, beating both wife and daughters. He knew of previous occasions when Mariuccia's mother had wound up at the hospital with broken bones after attempting to defend her girls. Moreover, when the father was in the throes of these episodes, he could no longer tend his farm, and the few pennies that Mariuccia was able to take home were spent on the survival of the whole family.

In the end, Ada decided that girls like Mariuccia are all the same anyway, and even if she had hired another one, she wouldn't have obtained any significantly different results. And so, Mariuccia stayed on. But her careless, dreamy character didn't change. After Lina's birth and the end of the war, Mariuccia went to work for Alma in Turin where she looked after the girls, and her incompetence only made worse a domestic situation that Alma already found intolerable as it was.

For Nina, the cruelest punishment was being grounded. While the prohibition was in effect, she was not allowed to set foot outdoors, not even to go into the garden. Ada demanded that Nina make her presence inside the house known every hour on the hour. The chimes of the big grandfather clock, soft and deep, spread in concentric waves through the rooms and the hallways until they reached Ada's armchair. As soon as she heard them, Nina suspended whatever activities she was engaged in and ran to her side. "Grandma, I'm here," she would say. And Ada would ask her, "Where have you been?" Nina would reply, "I've been playing with Uncle Ducati." "All right. Be back here in an hour's time," Ada would order.

Uncle Ducati, not Uncle Luca. That's what Ada wanted Nina to call him. He wasn't a young uncle like Uncle Gio; there were two generations of difference between him and Nina, and that fact had to be emphasized by a title denoting greater respect, she said. Uncle Ducati often came looking for Nina, because without the numerous throng of guests and relatives who used to stay at the castle, he had no one with whom to pass the time of day. Nina was all he had for company. He had brought down with him from the tower room a vast array of games and many crates of books and periodicals—such as his useless collection of the *Gazzetta dello Sport*—which now cluttered most of his new room.

Sitting at a table covered by a damasked cotton tablecloth with fringes—Nina had to put two or three cushions on the chair in order to be able to reach the table—they'd play long tournaments of "Mercante in fiera," "Omino nero," and "Tombola."[21] Or else they'd go for a virtual field trip with the "goggles." Or they'd leaf through illustrated books. Lillì, in Luca's arms, would place his paws on the table and carefully track all their movements, swinging his little head from side to side, his tiny pinkish tongue dangling.

Nina had her favorite books. She especially loved the old volumes of the Imageries d'Épinal, because, even though she didn't know how to read, she could tell those stories based on the sequence of the illustrated panels. The books were as big as a page from a newspaper, or nearly—each page was a story, each story had 16 panels, 4 panels per row. In these deluxe editions, the paper was thin as onionskin, and you had to turn the pages with great care in order to avoid tearing a corner by accident. The colors ranged over a rich spectrum, the vivid hues embellished by strokes in gold—for instance, the princesses had golden hair, and the stars in the sky and the doubloons in the pirates' treasure chests were also printed in gold. The captions were in French, and therefore not accessible to everyone, but Uncle Ducati had learned them by heart when he was small and was studying with Monsieur Lesavoir

---

21. Card games, and board games.

and, one way or another, he had recited them to Nina in Italian. Now Nina knew all those stories herself, and she would compete with Uncle Ducati to see who could tell them better. Nina always won by a convincing victory, but Uncle Ducati never wanted to admit it. When they told the story of *"Jean qui pleure et Jean qui rit,"*[22] Nina portrayed the tragic mask and the comic mask with the proper tonal inflections and the appropriate mimicry, while Luca flattened the story with his monotonously thin and nasal voice. Then, when he was done, he'd look at her complacently and announce, "I told the story faster than you. So I finished first and I win."

There were many amusing little stories like that: *"Jeannot et son veau," "Le monde à l'envers"*; and then fairytales set in the Middle Ages or the Middle East, *"Le sifflet enchanté," "Le prince Charmant," "Le lorgnette magique"*; stories with morals, *"Pierre l'incorrigible," "Louis le maladroit"*; and adventuresome journeys in exotic lands, *"Ahmed, le fanfaron," "Le capitain Bonenfant," "Comment M. Hucocotte fit le tour du monde malgré lui."* And in this last category there was also the story that so greatly upset Nina's sensibilities.

Whenever she leafed through the book and came to the story before it, Nina would make sure she turned the next two pages at once so she wouldn't have to see those illustrations. The story in question was called *"Coco, le bon singe,"*[23] and it was about a teenage boy who fetches up on a desert island after a shipwreck, where he is rescued, nourished, and cared for by a good ape. Since he is the only living creature on the island, the ape suffers from loneliness and is therefore

---

22. "John who cries and John who laughs." A few lines below, "Johnny and his calf," "The world upside down," "The magic whistle," "Prince Charming," "The magic glasses," "Peter the incorrigible," "Louis the clumsy," "Ahmed the swaggerer," "Captain Bonenfant," "How Mr. Hucocotte went around the world unwittingly."

23. "Coco, the good ape."

overjoyed to have found a companion. The ape and the boy become fast friends, and life passes pleasantly as they play games and enjoy adventures on that island abounding in wonders of all kinds, where along the mountain stream they can gather diamonds the size of hen's eggs. When the ape sees that his friend likes those glittering rocks, he helps the boy to gather a fine bagful. But the day finally comes when the boy spots a ship and decides, though with considerable misgivings, to return home with his new fortune. After one last heartfelt embrace, the youth boards the ship and sails away. In the final panel the ape is all alone; sitting on a rock by the water, he stares out to sea and big teardrops run down his cheeks and land in his lap like drops of gold.

Looking for some fun, sometimes Uncle Ducati would open the book at that exact page and, with a glint of malice in his bovine eyes, enlarged by the lenses of his pince-nez, he'd say, "Let's tell this one."

"No, not that one! It's too painful. I feel so sorry for the ape," Nina would forcefully protest, her emotions choking her. Then she'd scurry off to sob in her room.

Nina had an ambivalent attitude toward animals. If in the barnyard a cat or a dog died, she'd feel sort of sad. Then she'd join the other children to hold a funeral for them, with a grave and a cross made of sticks, and the reality of death was transformed into a ceremony. That ritual conferred a certain dignity upon the animal, making it possible to remember it with fondness. But if a chicken or a rabbit was slaughtered for the dinner table, the kitchen help would simply toss the carcass onto the trash heap after the meal, the same as they did for potato peels and other waste. That was the law of the barnyard, and Nina accepted it, the same as everyone. But there was one special case that shocked her and made her pause to reflect on the brutality of that treatment.

A young capon had been set to fatten in a cage apart from

all the others. Nina loved its colorful plumage and went to visit it frequently. There was always plenty of food around the cage—wheat mush and kernels of corn—and Nina befriended the capon by giving it plenty of those tasty treats. Over the course of two months' time, they had become great friends. From the early morning, Nina pondered each day what stratagem to employ to go see her friend the capon, because it was winter time and it was no easy matter to elude Mariuccia's supervision.

Then the holidays came, they built a manger scene, they put up decorations in all the windows, and many days went by before Nina was able to slip out of the house once again. On Christmas Day, after a plentiful and delicious meal, upon which Veglia had lavished her finest culinary arts, the grownups withdrew to their bedrooms for an afternoon siesta. Mariuccia wasn't there, she had been given the day off, and so Nina took advantage of the opportunity to sneak out into the barnyard and ensure that her friend the capon enjoyed a special lunch. She happily put on her brand-new sky-blue overcoat, just completed by the seamstress Nardina; the coat had a collar made of groundhog fur, as soft and warm as a kitten, taken from a fur coat that Ada never wore anymore.

When she reached the cage, she found it empty. She was very upset. She scolded herself: maybe last time she'd left the cage door open and the capon had escaped. She asked Carletta if she knew anything about it. "Veglia came two days ago and twisted the capon's neck. She needed to roast it for the Christmas dinner," Carletta replied with the utmost nonchalance.

Nina was stunned. She suddenly glimpsed the images of that groaning banquet table: the gleaming crystal, the delicate colors of the porcelain dishes, the holly branches, and at the center of the table, a nice big roasted chicken on a bed of soft potatoes. A violent wave of nausea surged over her and she vomited there where she stood, right next to the capon's cage, onto her elegant sky-blue overcoat.

Carletta had to run and fetch Veglia. When Ada was informed of what had happened, she assumed it must be a simple case of indigestion and gave instructions to let Nina spend the rest of the day in her bedroom with a hot water bottle on her stomach. Toward evening, dragging herself laboriously down the hallway to Nina's room, Ada went to visit her. Nina was sad and it was clear that she had been crying. Ada attributed this sadness to the fact that Alma was away. In fact, Nina was sitting in her little chair with her arms wrapped around Jocko, the plush monkey that Alma had given her on a recent visit, while the gifts that Santa Claus had brought her the night before, and which she had received with such wonder and excitement when she awakened early that morning, lay abandoned in a dark corner of the room.

Nina grieved deeply for the capon, and felt a great sense of guilt. But she also felt a burning sense of outrage for the betrayal of people she trusted, such as Veglia, who had kept her in the dark and had thus made her an accomplice in the sacrifice of her best friend. She kept her sorrow to herself. She spoke of it with no one, if not with Alma in an imaginary message. She knew that Alma was the only person on earth she could count on, the only one capable of comforting her with cuddles and caresses.

V

Alma's visits were irregular and infrequent. She always came alone, whenever she happened to be passing through the area. Once was upon her return from a tour in Bulgaria, before the war began to rage. In those days it was still relatively easy to visit the allied countries of the Balkans. The Academy's theatrical company was sent out on missions to spread Italian culture abroad and to reinforce the bonds of friendship with those nations. And to tell the truth, they were more successful on the artistic front than the Italian army ever was on the military front.

On her return from that tour, Alma brought Nina a strange and enchanting object. It was a small wooden case shaped like a minaret, containing a vial of rose oil. Nina found that fragrance inebriating, and she continued to sniff its perfume until her head span. After that, convinced she was acting for Nina's own good, Ada confiscated the wooden case and told the girl that she'd keep it for her. Nina didn't dare to contradict her grandmother, but she interpreted those good intentions as an affront. She flew into Alma's arms in search of comfort and consolation. Alma calmed her down with the sweet words that only she knew. Subsequently, she recovered the precious ampule and put it in Nina's little clothes cupboard. "Here it'll be safe," she whispered to her conspiratorially, carefully shutting the twin doors of the armoire as if it were a secret hiding place. Nina, in a burst of gratitude, threw her arms around Alma's knees—which were exactly at the height that Nina's small person could reach—and clutched them tight. From that moment on, not only was Alma the object of her love, she also became an ally.

The one who really needed an ally, though, was Alma herself. Her childish insecurities still persisted—her rages, her mistrustfulness, her agressivity, her pigheadedness. But her mercurial enthusiasms, her eccentric personality, her artistic flair and her inborn elegance camouflaged her immaturity and gave her a charm and allure that captivated family members and strangers, and in short anyone who met her. Alma lived in intentional isolation. She established ties with no one, not even her husband. But she did need some emotional support, a best friend, a person to whom she could confide her sorrows, to whom she could pour out her frustrations, in short, an ally against the whole world. Nina was her faithful ally for an unbroken run of six full decades.

When the day of departure arrived, Nina waved *ciao ciao*

from the "observation wall" as Alma boarded the bus and, as the vehicle vanished around the last curve, hurried to get the ampule from its hiding place in order to preserve the illusion of Alma's essence through that scent. Later on, in her moments of greatest melancholy, all she needed was that rose oil fragrance to summon up Alma's presence. Alma's image materialized in the room as if she had emerged from Aladdin's lamp.

Visits from her mother marked the passage of time in Nina's life. When Alma was there, past and future were nonexistent. The only real time was the present, which Nina perceived through her senses as a tangible dimension. The present was the sound of Alma's voice, the features of her face, the scent of her skin, the touch of her hands. Nina lived on her, as if she had never left her womb, inside that magic circle of time that enveloped them whenever they were together.

But Alma was subject to lightning-quick mood swings that constantly threatened to undermine that state of bliss. Nina didn't know how to explain those changes, except by rationalizing the situation to her own damage: I must have made her mad and now I have to find a way to get her to forgive me so it can all go back to the way it was before. Nina did everything she could think of to keep from provoking her. She wanted to keep Alma happy any way she knew how. But she often grew distracted and made mistakes.

Alma was always engaged in fascinating pursuits. Fascinating to Nina, who had never seen soap bubbles. On some days, Alma would sit in a sunny spot in the Lemon Garden—by now, overrun with weeds, where swarms of insects darted feverishly in the summer heat among the untended grass and the wild flowers—dip a straw into a glass of soapy water, and then blow through the other end, tipping the straw slightly upward. In the golden light, she was suffused with a luminous halo that rendered her image mythical, conferring upon her the appearance of a field nymph playing a reed flute. Out of that instrument emerged translucent spheres with all the colors of the rainbow. They would break gently free and float gracefully like ethereal dragonflies, only to vanish in the glare of the sunshine. When Nina tried, her bubbles came out misshapen and popped before they could even float free.

"You have to be more delicate, sweetie mouse," Alma would say. Nina understood that Alma expected more from her, and she'd resolve to do better next time.

In the winter, Alma would sit in a sofa looking out a window at the expanse of snow-covered hills. A white light reflected off the snow and filtered through the glass, accentuating the hundreds of colors of the balls of yarn that she kept in a basket. Knitting was one of her favorite pursuits, when she wasn't reading or doing voice exercises. From her knitting needles came cascades of colorful strips of various stitches: braid cables, honeycomb, jacquard motifs, rice stitch, torchon lace. But when the time came to assemble a sweater or a pullover, Alma lost interest and hurriedly joined all the sections together roughshod, with bumps, gaps, and overlaps. Then she'd throw it all into a bag and say, "I can't stand sewing, it's just too demanding, everything has to be so precise."

Nina, curled up on the carpet at her feet, watched the wonderful creations that came from her hands and played with the balls of yarn. She would roll them all around the room, and then go to retrieve them and start over again from scratch. Sometimes she'd make a mistake and roll the ball of yarn that was attached to Alma's knitting.

"What are you doing!" exclaimed Alma, losing her temper. "Look, you've made me drop a stitch. You've ruined all the work I've done."

Nina, mortified, would run to recover the ball of yarn. Then she'd climb up onto the sofa and throw her arms around Alma's neck to earn her forgiveness.

"You treat me without the slightest consideration," huffed Alma, still resentful.

With no idea how to react, Nina would speak from the heart, "Miminna, I love you."

"So you say, but you don't show it," Alma would retort.

At that point, in her confusion, Nina would start to cry. Then Alma would feel sorry and they'd cry together. The light gradually turned gray and the balls of yarn would lose their colors.

After a few minutes, Alma would pull a delicate little handkerchief out of the cuff of her sleeve and dab at Nina's face. She'd say, "We're a couple of dopes. We do this just because we're too sensitive. Come on, blow that little nose. Now I'll make you a lovely angora scarf. And when you're older, I'll teach you how to knit, and we can work together, side by side."

Once again the light would gleam, and the balls of yarn would shine with a hundred colors.

There was one memorable day that Nina cherished in her memory as the happiest day of her life.

It was Easter Monday in 1944, a year before the end of the war. Alma was at the castle for a short visit and she wanted to go out for a picnic, the way they had always done when she was a girl. Back in those years, on the day after Easter, the horde of cousins would exit the walls of the castle and head off down the woodland trails that led to the Spring. This was a natural water source, and the water that bubbled up, pristine and cold, poured out into the middle of a field, in a patch of mulberry trees, and then formed a stream that wended its way between grassy banks. The company would sit around the Spring, open their bags and eat their snacks, and spend the afternoon in that bucolic setting, breaking its peace and quiet with the shrill chatter of cheerful voices, high-pitched and penetrating, laughter, jests, shouts, quarrels, and tantrums.

"That's sheer madness," said Ada. "Don't you realize that

times have changed? We're at war. Are you willing to risk your daughter's life? Those places are teeming with desperados: Germans, fascist troops, partisans... You could run into some ugly characters out in the countryside."

"Mamma, you're overdoing it! Nothing's going to happen," Alma replied with an edge of annoyance. And deep down she thought, "After all, I'll do as I please." She told Veglia to prepare a picnic sack, then she and Nina walked out the main gate and headed off to the Spring.

As they went past the courtyard of the "urchins," Nina slowed her pace so they could all see what a sensational lady her mother was. No other child had a Mamma like hers, and Nina walked past them all with a look of defiance that meant, "I'm not coming to play with you. I'm staying with my Mamma."

"Are these the children that Grandma told me about?" asked Alma.

"Yes."

"And they tease you?"

"Yes."

"Poor sweetie mouse of mine. You'll have to get used to it. You're going to find this kind of hostility everywhere you go. Mediocre people will never forgive you for being better than them—prettier, or smarter, or better born, or all three things together." She sighed and added, "It's our fate." Then she straightened her shoulders and gripped Nina's little hand tighter. "But we know how to defend ourselves, don't we? The two of us against them all."

"Yes."

They reached the bottom of the hill and ventured out into the fields. The air was sweetsmelling with sunshine, the meadows dotted with flowers, the food was delicious, and the water from the Spring, gathered in the midst of the grass with a little cup, was clear and refreshing.

They lingered for a long time under the mulberry trees.

Alma made chains of meadow flowers that they had picked along the way, and Nina put them around her neck and arms. Since there were a great many necklaces, more than she could wear herself, Nina placed one on Alma's head, as a garlanded crown.

Alma brushed it away. "I don't want it," she said.

Nina, excited by the game, burst into laughter and tried again.

"Stop it! I told you that I don't want it!" Alma raised her voice and it came out strident and cutting. Then, a little calmer, "It gives me a headache. You really have made up your mind to ruin my day."

Recognizing the warning signs of a fit, Nina stopped immediately and, worried lest she provoke her further, she hurried off to chase a butterfly. When she came back, Alma was again as cheerful and tender as before.

"Are you all sweaty, sweetie mouse? You ran and ran," she said.

"No, no. I'm fine."

"Come here, come and rest." Alma took Nina in her arms and pressed her cool cheek against the girl's, which was damp and overheated. That's how it always was with Alma. It took practically nothing to provoke a tantrum and transform a state of extreme bliss into the lowest circle of hell. But, once the storm had passed, Alma forgave her and continued to love her.

"Do you want the delicious cherries that Veglia put in the bag for us?" asked Alma.

"No, I want a peach," she said, pronouncing the word *pésca.*

"There aren't any, it's not the season yet. Also, you need to pronounce it *pèsca* with an open 'è.' Otherwise, you're just saying *péscare,* meaning you're going fishing. Do you understand?"

"*Pèsca… pèsca… pèsca…,*" Nina said again and again to fix that sound in her memory.

"Very good. It's important to have proper diction."

This issue triggered quite a few storms. Every time that Nina pronounced a word wrong, Alma took it personally—"I already told you once that that's not how you say it." "I forgot," Nina apologized. "No, you're doing it on purpose to get my goat." "No no, I'm not doing it on purpose. It's a mistake," Nina would protest. Often the two of them would wind up in tears over the simple pronunciation of a word, Alma to heighten the situation's drama, and Nina because she was afraid that Alma no longer loved her. But in short order, Nina acquired perfect diction—*vénti* (twenty) as opposed to *vènti* (winds), *"vénti nanetti andavano in carrozza,"* (twenty midgets rode in a carriage) and *"la rosa dei vènti"* (the Rose of the Winds); *cólto* (learned) and *còlto* (picked), *"un uomo cólto"* (a learned man), and *"ho còlto un fiore"* (I picked a flower). Even though she went on living in Cortalba, her Italian lost all dialectal inflection. In fact, when she started school, the schoolmistress asked her where she was from, because she didn't have a Piedmontese accent, and Nina replied, "I live in Turin, but I have 'proper addiction,' just like my Mamma."

On the way back, Nina was so happy for having spent that whole day alone with Alma that she tried to prolong it in her mind. Hanging on Alma's hand she said: "Miminna, shall we come here again tomorrow?"

"No, tomorrow I'm leaving."

"Oooh." Nina wasn't expecting that cruel blow. "Take me with you," she begged her.

"That's not possible, sweetie mouse. There's an ugly war going on. But as soon as the war ends, I'll come and get you and we'll be together forever."

"Forever?"

"Forever."

"And when does the war end?"

"Soon, you'll see. Soon."

They went on walking, hand in hand. Nina lulled herself

with that wonderful thought—soon... forever... together... She tossed it in her mind like a light bouncing ball, golden and shining—together... soon... forever...

"Miminna, look, there are soldiers." Nina stopped and pointed straight ahead.

There, where the path met the municipal road, a platoon of fascist troops had set up a road block. Maybe they were on the lookout for someone.

"Ignore them," said Alma. "We'll just pass by as if we hadn't even seen them. Tell me a story, any story you can think of."

Now Alma and Nina were close to the barricade and they could see the men on the alert with their rifles leveled.

"... and so d'Artagnan pulled out his sword and launched himself into the fray to help his friends..." Nina said, fixing her eyes on Alma to keep from looking at those ugly mugs.

"Just where does this lovely lady think she's going all alone?" asked the lieutenant in command of the platoon.

"She's not alone. She's with me," Nina broke in, staring him right in the eye now.

He paid her no attention.

Alma replied with an amiable smile and her suavest voice—after all, she was a first-rate actress— "We've just been out for a picnic in the countryside. We're going home."

They all burst out laughing.

"Lovely lady, this is no time for picnics," said the lieutenant. "There are bands of rebels on these hills, live grenades... Trust me, you should take your little girl straight home." And then he added, gallantly, "And if you ever wanted to go out one evening, I'd more than delighted to escort you..."

"How very kind. Thanks for the advice." Alma and Nina had already passed the barricade and were continuing on their way.

"Wait, what, are you already leaving?!" the lieutenant yelled afer her. But he got no reply.

Once they were at a safe distance, Alma gripped Nina's hand and said, "You were wonderful, sweetie mouse."

"So were you," Nina replied. And they exchanged a conspiratorial glance. Like in the story: "One for all, all for one."

At the entrance to the town, they saw Ernesto walking to meet them. Ada had been uneasy and had sent him ahead to scout out the situation, just in case "those two hotheads" had got themselves into trouble and needed help. Ernesto took advantage of the opportunity to snap a few photographs of them, in the still strong light of late afternoon.

That series of photographs is in the album. But there's one in particular, which is neither the best one nor the most artistic, that Alma placed in a silver frame and kept on the nightstand in her bedroom for many years. The photograph shows Alma sitting in a meadow with her legs folded beneath her, angled to the right. She's supporting herself with her left arm, and she's holding out her right arm toward Nina to take something that the child is handing her. It's impossible to say from the photograph what that object is, because Ernesto took the picture from a considerable distance. What is clear, though, is that the two of them are examining the object with interest and that they're lost in conversation.

We now know that it was a four-leaf shamrock. Nina recognized that lucky leaf, because there was a picture of it in her alphabet book under the letter "S," and she knew that it was a symbol of good fortune. Perhaps, she thought, that means the war will end soon—soon… forever… together…

Nina kept that souvenir and, later, she slipped it under the glass of the frame, where it still can be found today.

13

Bella Ciao
1943-1945

I

One morning, the inhabitants of Cortalba woke up and found themselves in another country. Nothing had changed as far as the eye could detect, except that that territory no longer belonged to the Kingdom of Italy. Now it belonged to the Republic of Salò.

After the fateful day of September 8, 1943, Italy was split in two. The Allies had moved up from Sicily to Naples, but north of the city their advance had been halted. The rest of the peninsula remained under occupation, and the Germans were terrorizing the populace with roundups, arrests, mass executions, and deportations.

In Naples, this brutal treatment had caused a mass insurrection that lasted four days. The wrath of the populace was sufficient to defeat and put to flight the enemy army, and when the Allied liberators arrived, on October first, they didn't find a single German soldier. The city had liberated itself. Those were bloody days for the Neapolitans, and they left deep scars in the citizens, and in Dardo's family in particular. He knew nothing directly of those events at the time, and was only informed two years later when, with the end of the war, communications were restored. He received a letter from Manon:

My dear brother,

I write you with a heavy heart. For months and months I've written this letter in my mind, and now the time has come to put it down on paper. My dear Dardo, Giggino is no longer among us, and neither is Papà. I don't have the words to tell you what happened, but I'll try.

In the days prior to the insurrection, the Germans had become increasingly savage and cruel. They'd level entire quarters of the city with gunshot and flame, stripping the populace of all their possessions, rounding up men of all ages and sending them off to forced labor in Germany. Those vandals even burned down the University, where resistance groups had formed, and destroyed the library with thousands of books. The students were outraged at such barbarity and joined the insurrection along with the rest of the populace. On the second day, Giggino was in a group on the sidewalk beneath the University steps. Three armored cars came down the Rettifilo firing wildly at anyone they saw on the street or at the windows. Giggino was unarmed. Only a few of the students had actually managed to get their hands on weapons. But the minute it saw them, one armored car swerved and slammed right into the group. Giggino and two other students were crushed beneath the wheels. This was a greater grief than poor Papà could bear. He grew melancholy and bitter, and before long he contracted a case of pneumonia that carried him off.

What can I tell you, my dear Dardo, I've managed to transfer back to Naples and now I teach at the Liceo Sannazzaro. I'm married and I live with my husband in our old apartment in Materdei. The apartment building is miraculously still intact. But everything else has changed. The life we once knew is gone now.

Our beautiful Naples has had the worst of it. Bombs fell on the Monastery of Santa Chiara. Since the war began, the city has been bombed more than a hundred times. Historical monuments destroyed, entire quarters of the city pulverized, thousands of homeless people forced to live in caves, mother-less children abandoned in the streets, the populace reduced to starvation. The Allies brought food and money, and the Neapolitan people, so heroic, so noble during the insurrec-tion, prostituted itself for the new power. Poverty, my dear Dardo, poverty is a degrading thing, cruel to the moral fi-ber. But even those who remained honest were in some way or other involved in that whirlpool of opportunities. Norma and Lucia were hired for a series of concerts at the head-quarters of the Allied high command, and there they met two British officers and married them shortly thereafter. They later wrote me from England to say that they aren't happy in the fogs of that northern land, and that they miss the blue skies of Naples. Giacomino's family has survived as best they can; now they have four children, four lovely little creatures, and he continues to work as an engineer at the naval arse-nal in Nettuno. They had some grim experiences themselves during the Allied landings on those beaches.

I've joined the Italian Communist Party. We expect the party will play a majority role in the new government, given the immense contribution that it made to the Committee of National Liberation with the Garibaldi partisan units. Mo-rale is high, and our expectations are bright. Let's hope it doesn't all fizzle out like last time, with both sides pulling their punches."

A big hug. Your sister, Manon.

II

Naples was the only city to rise up in such a spectacular fash-ion, but it wasn't the only one to suffer. After the occupation, Rome was declared an "open city," and placed under strict SS control. In effect, it was really a closed city, and no one could enter it or leave without special permits.

Alma and Dardo had been fortunate. They'd already taken their degree at the Academy when in the spring of 1943 they had been cast in the renowned traveling theatrical troupe of Ernesto Sabbatini. The company had set out for a tour in the north, stopping first in Florence and later, in Milan and Turin. They traveled by train where that was still possible, but many stretches of the line had been devastated by bombing. The cities had been ravaged by the raids of the Flying Fortresses, and the performances were staged during the day, because of the curfews. Sometimes the performance would be interrupted by the air raid siren. The audience and the actors would all hurriedly leave. They'd cram into the theater cellars, or else, if these were hard to get to, they'd run out the door to reach the closest air raid shelter—the actors in their stage costumes, grabbing onto their wigs with one hand to keep them from flying away.

Still, Alma remembered that period as one of the most fascinating times of her life, precisely because they lived precariously, day by day, outside of the conventional schemes of behavior, lightened of the burden of rules and responsibilities. When she described those days, she said, "I wasn't afraid. I felt free and happy. I thought of nothing but art."

A further reason to feel "free and happy" was that, for several months, Dardo had been away. I have always had the impression, and Alma confirmed that impression several times, that she had a hard time putting up with the condition of being married. She found it too restrictive, too confining. What's more, Dardo was possessive and violent. He made jealous scenes, jealousy that was, moreover, completely unjustified, because Alma, even though she remained an object of desire to many men, had absolutely no interest in them. She considered them to be "a pain in the neck." When confronted with Dardo's tantrums, she rebelled with tears and insults, but in the end she always gave in because he was stronger.

"If someone bought me an espresso," she would tell me when I was already grownup, "he was capable of grabbing me by the arm and dragging me out of the café, insulting the unfortunate gentleman as he did so. But not because he loved me. It was just to assert his supremacy. He considered me his property."

Then she'd recreate the scene, playing the various roles:

Dardo: "So here you are. You're shameless. Now even in public you rub up against this miserable asshole."

Alma: "Calm down. Everyone's looking. Don't embarrass me like this."

The Other Man: "But Dardo, there must be some misunderstanding. We were just having an espresso."

Dardo: "You shut up, you motherfucker."

Dardo had left the theater company at the beginning of the summer, because he'd been drafted. He'd managed to avoid being called up until then, with one excuse or another, but now that the army had been thoroughly decimated, the mobilization became a general one, and Dardo had no choice but to enlist. He was deployed to Croatia, where Axis troops were being forced back by the fury of Tito's partisans, and reinforcements were needed. He muddled through for three months. Whether and how he saw combat remains unknown. The entire expeditionary corps was demoralized, lacking in supplies and provisions, virtually forgotten by the military authorities who found themselves, unprepared, on the brink of a massive defeat.

Good Neapolitan that he was, Dardo found a way of getting by even in the midst of all that chaos. He found a position as a mailman. He distributed to the luckier soldiers what little mail still got through, and for the others he composed letters and telegrams that, he claimed, had been lost under the bombs but that he had read and memorized, and he'd recite them with much dramatic emphasis:

"My faraway darling, every night as I go to sleep I clutch your photograph to my heart, and I fall asleep with you," writes Marietta.

Or, *"When the day dawns that I'll see you appear at the end of the lane, under the burden of your heavy backpack, my heart will leap with joy in my chest and I'll come running toward you in a whirlwind of happiness,"* writes Loredana.

Or else, *"I hope that you receive the ardent kisses that I'm enclosing in this letter. They will fly on the wings of my love and cross seas and mountains to land gently upon your lips,"* writes Ersilia.

The soldiers themselves supplied the names of the girlfriends. They were grateful to Dardo who gave them a reason to hope, however illusory, and they insisted on sharing their miserable rations with him. But Dardo only accepted those offers when he was truly hungry, since he didn't want to take advantage of those poor devils, who were no better off than he was.

After September 8th, the Italian army disintegrated. The officers fled in their army-issued cars; the soldiers, in military trucks or with chanced upon vehicles. Trucks were in short supply and precedence was given to the wounded, so the few seats remaining were up for grabs. Dardo was left behind to walk. He discarded his uniform and donned civilian clothing that he'd been given by Croatian peasants who, for some reason, sympathized with the Italians. Thus attired he walked the many miles that separated him from the border. He crossed the border at night, climbing over the lower uplands of the Carso mountain range with a small group of fellow soldiers. Once they arrived back in Italy, the survivors were considered deserters, subject to summary execution if arrested by the forces of the Fascist Social Republic. They split up to pass unobserved, and Dardo continued alone, without money, without food, hopping a freight train, grabbing onto the back of a truck, and even stealing a bicycle that he later dumped in a ditch. He covered the last stretch of road on foot, sticking to forests and riverbanks, in the cold autumn rains, and he arrived in Cortalba one morning in late October, starving, drenched, and ragtag.

III

He entered stealthily, without being seen by anyone, and appeared suddenly in the door to the dining room, where the family was having breakfast. Alma was there too, as she was visiting. At the sight of him, they all froze. Dardo looked like a ghost of his former self. He'd lost half his weight, his skin was glued to his bones, his hair was unkempt and encrusted with mud, and his turquoise eyes were dilated and expressionless.

Alma exclaimed, "Oh God!," and hid her face in her hands. When Nina saw her turn pale, she embraced her and burst into tears. Ernesto and Luca remained nonplussed, uncertain what to do next. It was Ada who took the situation in hand, though she had difficulties getting around. She invited him to take a seat, not at the table, but over by the door. Then she summoned Celestina and had her prepare him a nice hot bath and a mug of milk. At last, refreshed, cleaned up, and dressed in Ernesto's clothing, Dardo was in some condition to join the rest of the group for the midday meal.

Veglia wrung the necks of two free-range chickens and roasted them in a stewpot with bay leaves and rosemary. Then she rolled out a sheet of dough made with genuine wheat flour, flattening it carefully with a rolling pin. Then, after rolling it out, she sliced it good and thin with a large carving knife to make *tagliatelle*.

The table rocked with jollity. Ernesto went to the *crutìn* to retrieve two bottles of the special Barbera, and that only added to the general good mood. Alma and Dardo held hands and smiled at each other. Seeing that Alma was happy, Nina went over to Dardo to simper at him. Dardo bounced her on his knee, playing "this is the way the lady rides," accompa-

nying the bouncy ride with a sing-song. The greatest fun oc-
cured toward the end of the rigamarole, when Dardo came to
the last words, *"away away away...,"* and loosened the reins,
that is, his two arms, letting Nina tip backwards off his knee
until her head gently touched the floor.

In all that cheerful confusion, no one noticed that Luca,
without a word to anyone, had eaten an entire chicken, stealthily passing a few choice morsels to Lillì on the side. When Ada
realized what he'd done, she scolded him in a fairly brusque
tone, quite different from Olga's goodnatured admonitions:

"Luca, I've already told you more than once that times
have changed. You can no longer think only about yourself.
You also need to have a care for other people's needs. We ar-
en't starving, but we're not rolling in plenty either. We have
to use our ration card just like everyone else. And that means,
you have to take it easy with the food."

Veglia, sticking her head in the door to keep an eye on
Mariuccia as she served dinner, observed in dismay, "Good
Lord! He didn't leave so much as a crumb."

"But I only ate *one* chicken," Luca retorted, as if justifying
himself against an unfair accusation.

That response, uttered in all seriousness, unleashed a general wave of hilarity, and even Ada had to smile and forgive
her brother.

Ernesto was fooling around with the dials of the radio,
and he raised a finger to his lips to hush the company.

"Shhh. Silence. Let's listen," he said in a low voice and
with a conspiratorial tone.

"Dah dah dah DAH. This is London," echoed through the
room.

Nina ran toward the radio, deeply interested as always in
how Ernesto managed to maneuver the knobs so as to make
voices and music pour out of that big black box. Ernesto would
turn the dial, and the little bar would move imperceptibly
back and forth across the range of numbers; it took the precision of a violinist to tune the device on short wave broadcasts.

The voice that emerged sounded rather crackly, and was often interrupted by static. When the crackly bursts of electric current became prolonged, Ernesto gave two or three smacks to the box with the flat of his hand, on one side, then on the other, and then on the top, and the voice would return. But he kept the volume very low, and anyone who wanted to listen had to get close to the set and turn their ear, so that there was a small crowd of heads. Ada signaled to Mariuccia to make sure that doors and windows were all shut.

Toward evening Gio arrived, completely unexpectedly. He didn't come to Cortalba often, because traveling was dangerous for a young man like him. He had to make sure he attracted no attention of any kind. So far he'd managed to avoid military service by relying upon various loopholes available to university professors and researchers. In those war years, he'd remained holed up in laboratories and libraries, whose thick walls had protected him from both bombs and round-ups. He'd recently taken his degree in biology with a dissertation on the sexual behavior of beetles, under the mentorship of Professor Bizzarri, for whom he worked as an assistant. And that's not all: from spending so much time in the professor's home, Gio got to know his daughter, Isabella, a brunette with lively eyes and a quick way with words. Before long, the two of them had fallen in love and, with the approval of their families, they were engaged. Now, they were waiting for the end of the war before fulfilling their promise with a proper wedding.

Gio's visit was a result of the fact that he needed several specimens from his old insect collection for a research project he was working on. That night he slept on the couch in Luca's room, because the guest bedroom was occupied by Alma and Dardo. He spent the next morning rummaging through old things in the "steamer trunk room," which was in the uninhabited wing of the castle, near the tower. Veglia had to open a series of double-locked doors to allow him to get all the way down there.

It was like a journey back through time. Veglia opened a door and Gio would walk down a long hallway, a sequence of memories and images. Then, the next door, another hallway, and more memories flowing past him. In the last hallway was the entrance to Olga's study. Gio insisted on taking a look: grandmother's armchair, straightback chairs, and sofas, everything covered in white slipcovers; a film of dust had formed over the objects still in their places atop the desk, as well as on the pictures of the Savoy royalty on the wall; likewise on the window panes, now completely darkened by the wisteria that hadn't been pruned in a long time. Gio withdrew, almost on tiptoes, careful not to disturb that sepulchral silence.

Next to Olga's study was the "clothes cupboard room." This room was long and narrow, with two rows of clothes cupboards that stood ten feet tall along the walls. When Gio and Mina were small, they'd come here whenever they managed to elude adult supervision. For the most part, the clothes cupboards contained bed linens, tablecloths, and napkins, and then towels and washcloths, blankets, quilts, damask or velvet curtains, lace, rugs, and tapestries. But there was one particular armoire that they loved to explore. It was hard to open. Gio managed to turn the key by standing on his tiptoes and craning his arm till it practically hurt. This cupboard contained men's and women's clothing that was no longer used, some articles dating back to the end of the nineteenth century, along with shoes, boots, spats, top hats, bowler hats, cunning little women's hats adorned with flowers and ribbons, handbags, parasols and walking sticks with ivory pommels. Gio and Mina would pull a couple of tall stools over to the armoire, and climb onto them so they could reach the articles on clothes hangers. In a short while, half of the armoire's contents was scattered across the floor. Then the masquerade began. It was quite a party… Only, they were always interrupted just when the fun was getting going by Erminia, or some other housekeeper, who would hastily put all the articles of clothing away, turn the key, and hustle them out of the room in silence to spare them their rightful punishment. Driven by nostalgia, Gio opened one of the cupboard doors. Everything was still there, neat and tidy, with a whiff of mothballs and old wood. No one ever bothered those relics of the past anymore.

Last of all, Gio came to the "trunk room," so called because that was where they put the empty steamer trunks between one trip and the next, or else the trunks of the guests spending time at the castle. But there were also trunks full of things in that room; and not just trunks, but crates, cartons, boxes, and baskets, too… The room housed an agglomeration of old objects, abandoned and forgotten: mirrors, picture frames, dressing screens, rocking chairs, side tables, ewers, basins, birdcages, croquet sets, baby carriages and cradles, an accordion, lampshades, oil lamps, tennis rackets, and dolls. Gio picked up a puppet made of horse-chestnuts impaled on toothpicks. They used to make these dolls by the dozen with Mina, every fall, when the spiky nuts fell off the trees; the Chestnut Lane would come adrift with a carpet of dry leaves, so deep they came up to their knees and forced them to walk as if they were wading a rushing stream; and in the midst of the leaves they'd find the spiky shells, still green, which they'd have to crush with a rock to get out the chestnut itself, shiny and smooth; and little did it matter if, in the process, they squirted their clothing with a sticky greenish liquid that left horrible stains, after all someone else would see to cleaning them. But the day came when Mina got tired of making little puppets and came up with a new game. She ran the end of a piece of twine through a hole in the center of a chestnut, then left another foot and a half of twine, and tied the ends together. Afterwards she'd whirl it over her head, faster and faster as it built up centrifugal force, and then let it fly like a projectile straight at her chosen target. The target in question were these very same puppets, now lined up as if in a shooting gallery. Very few of them survived, and Gio remembered how, at a certain point, one of the sling shots went wrong and hit him in the forehead, raising a sizable bump. "Ouch! Look out. You hurt me," Gio complained. "Don't blame me," Mina upbraided him, "you're the one who needs to be more careful. Don't wander into my line of fire. Knucklehead!" Gio smiled at that memory... so typical of Mina always to be on the defensive.

And here were the display cases with the insects. Gio took what he had been looking for and left. As he passed in front of the door at the end of the hallway, which led to the tower and to the room that had once been Luca's, he thought he could hear the high-pitched chirping of children's voices playing the "button game," and the funny sounds of *bing* and *bong* as an acconpaniement.

He hurried away from that place, where he was beginning to feel uneasy, closing the heavy doors behind him one by one.

When he returned from his expedition around noon, Gio found the family in a state of uproar. Dino, Celestina's son, who had been a laborer at the castle in the days of the treasure hunt in the *infernotti*, had brought alarming news. He had slipped into the kitchen, in the utmost secrecy, and had first talked to his mother and Veglia. They in turn had immediately informed Ernesto, who had then summoned everyone to the living room to decide what to do about it.

Dino was a member of a partisan brigade. They called him Blast, because he knew how to plant mines and make them blow up. He'd learned while working for a demolition company before the war. The news he brought, in fact, concerned a number of mines he had planted along the road to Chivasso, where a convoy of German trucks was expected to pass. The operation had gone off at six that morning. Four well-placed mines had exploded, blowing up two trucks and their drivers, and also killing an officer in an automobile nearby. The partisans had been able to get away, but the Germans, in reprisal, were conducting roundups in neighboring towns and threatening to execute by firing squad ten civilians for every soldier killed.

Dardo and Gio were particularly at risk, since one of them was a deserter, and the other a draft evader. Dino said that they had to run away immediately, passing through the *infernotti* by way of the route that he and Gio knew so well. Veglia prepared a package of provision in great haste: a loaf of white bread, a salami, an aged wheel of *toma* cheese, walnuts, and a bottle of good wine. She put it all into a backpack that Dardo slung over his shoulders. Gio just had time enough to pack his precious collection into a second backpack and, after hasty kisses, embraces, and best wishes, the two fugitives, following Dino, vanished down the stairs that led to the *crutìn*.

In less than an hour, they emerged from the door of the "sesame" tree in the thick of the woods. There, Celestina awaited them with two bicycles. They shook hands and wished each other good luck. Dardo and Gio headed downhill, wheeling their bicycles, Dino took to the hillside trails that led up to the camp, and Celestina returned to the castle.

The two young men reached Turin by night. They had stuck to relatively little frequented country roads, cutting overland when necessary. At sundown they had stopped near Moncalieri and had waited for full darkness before entering the city. Here they had abandoned their bicycles.

They crossed the Po over the Lingotto bridge, squeezing close to the parapet because a strict curfew was in effect. They covered the last stretch along the tree-lined boulevard that skirted the Valentino park by flattening themselves against hedges to avoid the patrols on their rounds—everywhere, the

Action Squads that worked side by side with the SS had been reconstituted, and they operated with pitiless ferocity. They reached the house without incident, and two days later Alma joined them.

Alma told them what had happened at Cortalba. Shortly after their escape, the Germans had entered the town and started rounding people up, breaking into the houses and dragging all the men they found outside. There were no young men, because they had all gone to join either the partisans or the fascist army. So they rounded up a small group of old men and took them to the market square that also served as an athletic playing field. The Germans came to the castle, too. Ernesto's stratagem was of no use; he had gone to bed, pretending to be sick. The Germans ordered him up and took him away, along with Luca, who was only marginally aware of what was going on. What most upset him was the fact that the Germans tore Lillì out of his arms and threw him into a corner, giving him a kick that made the poor dog yelp in pain. Ada wanted to follow them, but she could not move. Alma went down after them.

On the square, a patrol was shouting orders in German that no one understood, shoving the men with the barrels of their rifles like a herd of cattle, lining them up against the weighing station. The oldest men walked with bowed backs, leaning on their canes, and had to be helped along by their neighbors. Luca was clinging to Ernesto's arm to bolster his courage. But Ernesto might very well have been even more scared than Luca.

An official military car pulled up, and the officer who was in command of operations in the zone got out. He looked around and his gaze fell on the little group of women off to one side who were fearfully watching the scene. Alma was in the front row, and she stood out in that cluster of villagers. The officer looked at her for a few seconds, as if hers were a familiar face, then he turned to speak to the local authorities.

Alma couldn't say with any certainty whether that was the officer she had met on the train years before, on their way back from Naples. Certainly, he resembled him. For that matter, though, in those fern-green uniforms they all looked pretty much alike. She knew that the Germans had burned whole towns to the ground, murdering women, children, and old men. She too had read the poster with the announcement by Field Marshal Kesselring that had been posted on the walls of every city and village, declaring publicly that his troops had been given the order to *"execute hostages... burn homes... hang the leaders of armed bands"* and to carry out other savage reprisals against saboteurs, whether real or merely presumed.

The officer spoke to Aurelio, who had hurried to the site with other functionaries. The two men spoke for about ten minutes. It was evident that Aurelio was interceding on the prisoners' behalf, pointing now to one, now to another. The officer once again looked toward Alma and inquired about her. Aurelio began to speak even more animatedly, connecting her with sweeping gestures to the two pathetic figures of Ernesto and Luca who had been lined up against the wall.

At the end of the conversation, the officer exchanged a few words with the sergeant in charge of the platoon, then got back into his car and drove away. The sergeant gave the order to release the prisoners. A moment later, the truck with its load of soldiers left the town.

The danger had been averted. But that episode was merely the prelude to far bloodier events that later struck the little town of Cortalba.

IV

In the last few months of 1943, Alma and Dardo continued their tours through the largest cities of northern Italy. But at the start of 1944, because of the intensified bombing campaigns, it became impossible to hold any more performances. Many theaters had been destroyed, others had been closed by decree of the military command. Moreover, the Germans were imposing increasingly strict restrictions on movements and had issued special safe-conduct passes. The touring company was dissolved. Alma and Dardo set up housekeeping in Turin and were cast by EIAR, the national radio station, as members of the Drama Company, to broadcast dramas, comedies, and operettas, very popular fare with a vast and affectionate audience.

They stayed in their jobs with the radio broadcaster, which later became RAI, until 1950, when Dardo, sick of being a mere "employee," quit so that he could launch into a risky undertaking, which ultimately proved to be financially disastrous. This was in his nature, but to many it seemed like a stark contradiction because in those years he had been an active representative of the actor's guild and, as the spokesman in the negotiations, he had won substantial victories on behalf of his colleagues. Until then, actors were hired on a flat-fee basis, as freelancers, with terms and payment determined case by case. Dardo succeeded in arranging for the members of the Drama Company at Radio Turin to be hired on a permanent, full-time basis with an open-ended contract, and full employee benefits. However, soon after winning that victory, he left, forcing Alma to follow him, with an assortment of flattery and threats. The company consisted of a dozen or so actors. In a short while, several of them opted to transfer to Rome, where the first television studios were being built, even if this meant a new, less attractive freelance contract. Other, older actors, now that they had a guaranteed pension, chose to retire instead. The actors who left were simply not replaced, and the Drama Company died a natural death, freeing RAI from a union commitment that it had never taken on willingly and which was never repeated.

* * *

In the summer of 1944, Alma took time off for her impending maternity, because Lina was due in October. Alma arrived in Cortalba around the middle of August, accompanied by Dardo who felt obliged to escort her. And that escort proved providential, because on that trip Alma really did wind up needing help.

It's a story that I've heard many times. Alma liked to tell it, perhaps because of the dramatic action, or because she felt she was lucky to have emerged unharmed from a situation that had proved tragic for so many, or else because it formed part of those years of her youth that, in her memory, were reckless, adventuresome, and romantic.

Alma told the story and Nina listened. The first time, Nina was too small to be able to understand clearly just what had happened. Nonetheless, she perceived that Alma had found herself in a dangerous situation and that, in spite of the danger, her first thoughts had been for her. She found that tremendously stirring. Later, when she was seven or eight, she too contributed to the story-telling, underscoring the action with words and gestures.

Alma started the story. "The train was about halfway between Turin and Asti, in the open countryside. I was falling asleep because we had left early in the morning, and you know how much I like to sleep in. Suddenly, we heard a deafening roar of engines."

"*Brrrrr, brrrr,*" said Nina, imitating the sound of an airplane, whirling around Alma with both arms held out stiffly like wings cutting through the air.

"The planes were already overhead. We hadn't heard them arrive, maybe because of the noise of the train. They were two American fighter-bombers. They didn't look particularly threatening. People leaned out of the windows waving their handkerchiefs in a sign of friendship.

"The first bomb fell on the locomotive. The train jerked,

then derailed. A second bomb hit a car and it caught fire. More cars were knocked onto their sides and were strewn along the gravel ballast, like so many pachyderms laid low by the poacher's rifle. The passengers jumped out of doors and windows, or struggled out of the twisted wreckage, making their way as best they could, some limping, others tending to their wounds. Then they scattered, running across the countryside in search of shelter, women with children in their arms, old men walking unsteadily, little kids lost and sobbing.

"We were lucky. Our car wasn't hit and we were able to get out without difficulty. We found ourselves in a vast field; at the far end of it was a stand of trees and beyond that, further still, we could just glimpse a farmhouse. I couldn't run like the others because of the heavy belly that weighed me down, and in a short time we were alone and isolated. The airplanes had flown away. A certain calm had been restored. A plume of black smoke rose from the train and you could hear the crackling of the flames, but no voices. The only ones left were the dead.

"We started walking along a path that ran around the field and led to the farmhouse, along the edge of a ditch with stagnant water at the bottom. We'd lost our suitcase and bags in the confusion, but I was still holding tight to the present I'd bought for you..."

"I know, I know," Nina broke in, "now let me tell. It was a paintbox with a section for pastels and a section for watercolors, and erasers and brushes. I'll keep that paintbox forever, even if now it's empty. Anyway, now you go on."

"One of the fighter planes came back around, perhaps to complete a post-operation inspection, and the pilot spotted us. Seen from all that way in the air, we must have looked like two moving, colorful puppets on that vast expanse of green, perfect for an amusing game of target shooting. And the game began. The airplane plummeted into a power dive and flow just above us at low altitude, unleashing a burst of machine gun fire straight at us, only to rocket straight back up into the sky, as if it were on the rails of a roller coaster. We hastened to reach the stand of trees, but we weren't fast enough. The airplane veered back around and came in for a second attack. We dove into the ditch. I was on the bottom; Papà was on top of me, covering me with his body. While the bullets were digging into the dirt on all sides, kicking up clods of clays and sprays of water, we managed to glimpse the faces of the pilot and his second in command. They were laughing..."

"Why were they laughing? Were the Americans the bad guys?"

"No, they were the good guys."

"But they bombed the train, and then they were shooting at you."

"Maybe those two were just drunk. They flew around again a couple of times. Then they must have gotten tired, they waved their arms as if to say, 'To hell with them!,' and flew away once and for all. We got out of the ditch, wet and covered with dirt, but unhurt. I was still clutching the paint box to my chest, and since it was wood, the inside remained dry..."

"What about Lina?"

"Lina was in her nest, nice and warm. She wasn't affected by that incident in the slightest."

They arrived in Cortalba late that evening, on a hay wagon that had picked them up on the last stretch of road, well past Castelnuovo. They'd traveled that far on a three-wheeled pickup truck, the kind with a little cabin for the driver and a square cargo deck in the back. A peasant from the farmhouse at the far end of the field had agreed to take them that first part of the distance. The cargo deck was hard and it bounced and jerked every time it hit a stone. The hay, on the other hand, was soft and sweet smelling. After the excitement and hardships of that day, Alma sprawled exhausted on that comfortable pallet.

In the already dark sky, the first stars were twinkling around a large full moon that seemed to dangle like a pendulum because of the movement of the cart. Dardo was smoking, even though that was forbidden by the blackout rules. He was sitting on the side of the wagon, one leg dangling. The other leg was bent, and the hand with the cigarette would rest on the raised knee between one drag and the next. With every puff, that tiny incandescent dot was lost among the stars. Alma fell asleep.

V

Lina was born one October evening, the same evening that three partisans were executed by firing squad beneath the castle walls. In her labor, Alma was able to hear the shouts of those three and the reports of the rifles. One of them was Blast.

The incident was the unfortunate conclusion of a plan that had been cooked up two months earlier and that had seemed to offer great chances of success. This, at least, was the opinion of Redstar, the acknowledged and respected commander. His comrades had elected him unanimously when the band was formed. Redstar was a little older than the others, thirty or so, and he was a more experienced and tested fighter. He'd been in Africa, where he'd seen combat in the desert, eating sand and drinking putrid water. After El Alamein, he'd been taken prisoner by the British with a handful of other lucky soldiers who were thus saved from that hecatomb and, during the trip back to Europe, he managed to escape and get back home. On his cap he wore a star of the Red Army that had been given to him by another veteran who'd returned from Russia. That guy was one of the very few to emerge alive from the defeat of the Italians on the Don. Nearly all the others had left their lives on the frozen steppe; he had left a hand, frostbitten inside his glove during the long retreat on foot.

That insignia on the commander's cap helped to mark the band as one of the leftist Garibaldi Brigades, and thus distinguish it from the centrist Badoglians who had a camp not far away. There was bad blood between the two factions. The Badoglians were uncomfortable allies, not true comrades but an extension of the bourgeois power and the monarchy. Still, Redstar used to say, for the moment they were all fighting for liberty and they could sort out their differences after they'd achieved victory. Nonetheless, he did try to avoid joint operations unless it was absolutely necessary.

Redstar's band consisted of only a few members, no more than twenty in all. There was Gram, who was the intellectual of the group. He'd read all the sacred texts of Marxism, risking prison or worse by doing so because they were materials forbidden by the fascist regime. He was a reserved, taciturn fellow and he had a reputation as a hardass. Ideology was his religion, and he practiced it without compromise—both in relation to the enemy and to the comrades when they deviated from the party line. In Piedmontese Gram means Bad, but he'd chosen that name because it was also short for Gramsci, the founder of the Italian Communist Party—without taking into consideration, though, that it had been Gramsci himself who first called "ideology" into question. Gram looked like a Bolshevik kommissar, with a black leather jacket that he even wore in summer, maybe just tossed over his shoulders, and wire-rimmed glasses. His face was always perfectly shaven, and to make sure that it was, he always carried a barber's straight razor in his pocket, long and sharp.

Then there was Cartridge, so called because he was the finest sniper, not just in the band, but in the entire zone. He could hit a German between the eyes at a distance of a hundred yards, even if his target were riding in a moving vehicle. He'd been a good hunter ever since he was small, and he'd gradually perfected that art, which he'd first learned from his father. There wasn't a fox or a hare that could escape his sure aim. Cartridge hadn't turned twenty yet, he was short and skinny, agile as a weasel as he scrambled through thickets and up trees to find the best vantage point from which to aim and shoot. He often worked with Blast, as a pair. After the explosion of the mines, Cartridge would slaughter the rescuers as they arrived on the site to administer first aid, *bang bang bang,* one after the other.

And Octobrine. There weren't many female partisans, and Octobrine was the only woman in the band. In theory, she was Gram's woman because he had brought her with him to the camp, but in practical terms, she was the regiment's woman. She had a generous heart and willingly welcomed into her pallet whichever partisan happened to have come down with the blues. Gram had no objections, since he was in favor of "free love." Octobrine was a pretty girl, with long, dark, ringleted hair, which she wore tucked up into her visored cap. She always wore that cap, even while she slept. She only took it off to make love; then she'd let her hair tumble free over her shoulders and bosom.

Last of all, there was Brutus, legal name Piero Costa, son of the podestà of Cortalba. After September 8th he'd left his father's house with a backpack and rifle and had climbed up into the hills. It had been a difficult decision, because Piero realized that he was putting his father and sister in serious danger. The reprisals against them would be terrible if the fascists ever learned of his activity. He had to force himself to get up and leave at night, without saying goodbye, convinced that the revolution would be victorious, and that he would soon return home to embrace them.

These were the five who in that autumn of 1944 played a primary role in Redstar's plan.

"Listen to me carefully," said Redstar, running his gaze over the faces of the partisans sitting in a circle facing him. They were all seated on the meadow outside of the cabin, because in those late August days the heat indoors was simply mur-derous. Even at night, they slept outdoors, under the trees; but never far away, so they could be ready in case the sentinel should give the alarm.

"The 23rd of September is the first anniversary of the found-ing of the Italian Social Republic," Redstar went on. "That's what they like to call it, because it makes it sound more offi-cial and legitimate... but I prefer Republic of Salò,[24] because in French it means 'Republic of Swine.' You get it? *Salauds.*"

A general burst of laughter. "What a great name!" "Swine!" "Bastards!"

Redstar brought the group back to order and went on. "In the towns, committees are being formed now to plan the festivities. They've decided to hold a special meeting for the podestàs of the area along with the officers of the Republican National Guard in order to coordinate the events. This meet-ing will take place a week before the holiday and will be held at Pralongo, in the Trattoria del Mulino Vecchio which has a dining room large enough to hold them all. After the meeting, they'll be served dinner, as well. Do you all follow me? Have I been clear thus far?"

They all agreed. "Perfectly clear." "Go on." "So what's the plan?"

"Well, that dining room is going to have to become a lethal trap. Four strategically placed bombs and...*booom!*... we'll kill them all at a single blow." Redstar accompanied the *booom* by raising his hands in a dramatic gesture that prompted great enthusiasm from his audience. Then he turned serious and reflective, smoothed his tawny beard, and went on. "We have roughly two weeks to lay the groundwork for this attack, down to the smallest details. We can't fail, or it will spell the end of our unit."

"We ought to coordinate the attack with the Badoglians. If

24. An alternative common name for the Italian Social Republic. Salò was the capital city of the new state.

we work together, we'll be stronger," suggested one man who had a cousin in the Badoglian camp.

"No. We're going to work alone," Redstar insisted in a peremptory tone. "It's going to be a surprise attack, and the fewer there are of us, the better. In fact, don't forget, secrecy is of the essence, don't breathe a word of this to anyone. Blast, you place the explosives in the restaurant and set them off. Cartridge, you finish the job if there are any survivors. Not a single one is to be left alive. Gram and I will stand watch to cover Blast's and Cartridge's escape, the Republican National Guard is certainly going to be guarding the place. Octobrine, you're going to have a very special job. At the Mulino Vecchio they always hire extra staff when they have a big crowd. You show up and ask for a job as a waitress, and once you're in, you need to find a way to get Blast in at night to place the explosives. The day of the attack, you leave and you join me and Gram outside to reinforce our field of fire; we'll bring you the weapons. All you others, you're to be standing by in the vicinity. Intervene only when necessary, and only at my command. The only one who's not required to participate in the attack is Brutus. His father is going to be one of the guests."

All eyes turned to Brutus, who clenched his jaw, furrowed his brow, and said nothing.

"Are there any objections?" asked Redstar, letting his eyes range over the group. All those present shook their heads: no no. Only Gram raised his hand to ask to speak.

"Redstar, comrades, I approve the plan and I'm ready to do my part. We have a duty to fulfil, *all of us*," he underscored the point, turning his head toward Brutus. "We must be united in the struggle because we believe in the cause. Ours is not only a struggle for liberty, it is also and especially a class struggle against the hated bourgeoisie. We cannot allow for exceptions. Any retreat, however small, can undermine the integrity of the idea. When someone enlists in our group, he renounces everything else—he no longer has a family, a father, a mother, brothers. We are now the only brothers he has. This is a pact to which we must adhere to the bitter end, if we are to have any hope of ultimate victory." He leveled his finger against Brutus. "Redstar made a mistake when he exempted him. Brutus has to make up his mind whether he wants to remain with us or leave the field. He has to decide now. All who are with me, raise your hands."

There was a moment's hesitation. The men were uncertain in the face of that decision and awaited an indication of some sort from Redstar. It was Brutus who resolved that impasse.

"There's no need to vote. I'm with you and I'll take part in the attack," he said.

Redstar stood up and gave him a slap on the back and a handshake. Others came over to him to express their fellow feeling. Even Gram insisted on shaking hands with him. "You've made the right choice," he said, but it was obvious from the look in his eyes that Gram didn't much believe in Brutus's conviction.

That night Brutus was unable to sleep. Octobrine offered him what comfort she could, but he preferred to remain alone. Stretched out on a blanket, he scrutinized the starry sky in search of an answer to his dilemma, peering into those mysterious configurations that, it is said, rule our destinies.

At the first light of dawn, his thoughts became clearer. He came to a decision. He would not betray his comrades, that was out of the question, but he would warn his father not to go to the meeting because he could be in danger. He counted on the fact that Aurelio, by his very nature, would simply say he was sick and miss the meeting, without breathing a word to anyone else.

He waited for a moonless night and left the camp, unobserved. When he reached the town, he crept along, brushing against the walls. The streets were deserted because of the curfew. The patrol made its rounds at lengthy intervals.

He went to the podestà's small house. The shutters were

fastened tight and didn't let so much as a sliver of light out. There were terrible penalties for anyone who violated the blackout. Brutus went over to one of the ground-floor windows. He knew that Aurelio was accustomed to working late in his study. He tapped lightly on the wooden shutter.

Inside, Aurelio heard that suspicious tapping and turned off his desk lamp. Then, he went over to the window and opened it just a crack. He recognized him immediately, even before Piero could say, "Papà!". Aurelio raised his finger to his lips to urge him to silence, and with his other hand waved him around to the door.

When they were together in the study, they embraced emotionally. They hadn't seen each other since that long-ago night when Piero had taken to the hills. Then Aurelio pulled back and, grabbing his son by the shoulders, shook him angrily: "You wretch, do you have any idea of the danger you've put me and your sister in? In public, I've had to lie, I've told everyone that you volunteered and were shipped to the front. So far, no one has bothered to check out the story. But we live in constant fear of something very bad happening, to you and to us."

"Papà, forgive me. I wish I wasn't in this situation. I wish there were no divisions and no struggle. Instead I'm in it, and I have to act in accordance with my conscience. But I still love you both, tell Marilù I said so, too. That's why I'm here. I've come to tell you that you can't go to the meeting in Pralongo. I'm trying to save your life."

"What are you saying? Speak clearly."

"I can't tell you anything more. But no one who attends is going to escape alive."

When Brutus returned to the camp, it was the middle of the night. He managed to get around the sentinel and make his way to his pallet. The camp was fast asleep, and no one had noticed he'd been gone. But Gram was awake. He was reading by the light of a candle, which he shaded behind his heavy leather jacket.

"Where were you?" he whispered.

"I had to take a piss," Brutus replied.

"That was quite a long piss," Gram replied, staring at him with an inquisitorial gaze.

Brutus ignored him and fell into a deep slumber.

Aurelio, after his conversation with his son, became deeply upset. For several days, he didn't have a moment's peace. What could he do? What could he do? His first inclination was to call in sick and ignore the facts entirely. But there was Piero to worry about. If he pulled some boneheaded move with those hotblooded comrades of his, he might be killed, or captured. And in that case, they would find out the truth about the podestà's son. He'd wind up being dragged into the middle of it himself. He resolved to ensure that the meeting of the chiefs was moved to another day and another place. That would sabotage the plan those bandits had concocted, whatever the plan might be, because Aurelio wasn't acquainted with it.

He went to the headquarters of the Republican National Guard and was granted an audience by the former decurion of the MVSN, or state police, Ercole Battaglia, now a captain in the RNG and the commanding officer of that detachment. Battaglia was a strapping big man who inspired fear in others. His shoulders were broader than the desk he was leaning on, putting on ostentatious display a pair of hands that were gnarlier than rough wooden clubs.

Aurelio came straight to the point. "You need to change the date and location of the meeting for security reasons. That's all I can tell you."

"Is there some danger?" asked Battaglia, clenching and unclenching his fists so that his knuckles cracked.

"Apparently so."

"And how do you know that?"

"I can't tell you anything else. Orders from high places," and here Aurelio put on an important attitude, as if he were in direct contact with senior levels.

"Well, for now I'm not going to insist. I thank you, comrade. You did right to bring me this information. Your job here is done. From here in, we'll take care of it."

The following day, all those who had been scheduled to take part in the meeting received a dispatch concerning the change of day and location, marked SECRET. Aurelio was pleased and, believing that his stratagem had worked, he relaxed.

But Battaglia, with his policeman's instincts, decided to get to the bottom of it. He picked two of his toughest militiamen, Cesare Aquiletti and Italo Scòpola, and put them on a stakeout at the Mulino Vecchio trattoria, with the order to stay at their observation post day and night, never to leave it, and to report back personally to him.

And so it was that, when Blast entered in the darkness to place the explosives, Aquiletti saw him and shook Scòpola's shoulder, awakening him from his catnap.

Through a window that had been carelessly left open, the two of them observed the action inside. When Blast emerged from the building, Aquiletti tailed him, making a mental map of the way to the partisan camp. Then he hurried to Battaglia's house and demanded his commanding officer be awakened so that he could immediately report to him on that lucky chance discovery.

Scòpola, alone now, knocked at the trattoria's front door. Octobrine, assuming that Blast must have forgotten something, opened the door. Scòpola punched her hard in the jaw and, when Octobrine fell to the floor, handcuffed and gagged her. Then, with a pistol aimed at the back of her head, he marched her to a nearby hayloft, where he tied her tight to a pole. He came back a few hours later with a van, and took her to the garrison in Asti for her interrogation.

Shortly before dawn, the partisan camp was awakened by a hail of bullets. A small unit of the Black Brigades, which had emerged without warning from the darkness of the forest, was riddling the cabin with gunfire. The partisans were on their feet in an instant, rifles leveled, but they weren't able to regroup in time. The Black Brigades commander realized that the cabin was empty and gave the order to turn their fire on the partisans scattered outside it. There was a pitched battle. A chaotic melee. Some attacked, others took to their heels, others still defended themselves, while some lay wounded. The meadow was covered with dead bodies.

The brigadiers enjoyed the advantage of numbers. Redstar realized that it would be pointless to sacrifice more of his men. He started shouting to make sure his voice carried. "Men, time to scatter. I'll stay here to defend the camp. Get going, go! That's an order!"

Whereupon he went into the cabin and barricaded the door behind him. He took the banner that stood propped against the wall in a corner and climbed onto the terrace roof. From up there he could see his men, the few that had survived, running off in various directions. He unfurled the red banner and launched a defiant challenge to the enemy.

"We die free men. You live on in chains, slaves to the Germans and the bourgeoisie. Long live liberty! Long live the revolution!"

A brigadier who had him in his sights was momentarily confused. "But wait, aren't *we* the revolution?" he asked his comrade beside him.

"Come on, don't think about it. Just shoot," the other man replied.

They both fired.

Redstar fell onto the banner.

* * *

In the chaotic retreat that followed the attack of the Black Brigades, four partisans found themselves together: Blast, Cartridge, Gram, and Brutus. After the breakneck gallop down the steep wooded slope, they stopped to catch their breath.

"Christ, what a mess!" Blast swore, wiping the sweat off his face. "And to think that it had all gone smooth as silk. I'd laid a nice trap for them at the Mulino Vecchio. How do you think they found us?"

"Someone betrayed us," said Gram, staring straight ahead of him.

"How can you be sure of that?" asked Cartridge. "Do you have any proof?"

"I don't need proof. It's the only logical explanation," Gram replied, still staring into the empty air.

"If someone did it, they're a filthy bastard. But I don't believe it," Blast commented.

"I don't believe it either," said Brutus, keeping his eyes downcast.

"We'll see about that. But for now, there's no time to waste. We have to get moving," said Gram, taking command of the situation. "We'll split up, which'll make it easier to scatter: Blast and Cartridge go that way, me and Brutus this way. We'll take different routes to get to a safe place, where we can hide for a while, and where we can find food and a bed."

Brutus had an idea. "Let's go to Don Giordano in Cortalba. He's helped other partisans before. I'm sure he'll take us in."

And so it was decided.

Gram and Brutus walked in silence. One unasked question weighed in the air between them. They made their way across a vineyard, ducking low between the rows of grapevines. They skirted around a wheat field, where there still stood a few poppy plants along the edges, left after the harvest. They ventured into a dense stand of acacia shrubs that separated the field from the road that ran alongside.

"Let's stop for a minute," said Gram. "I didn't ask you in front of the others, but I want to know who you talked to."

"You think I betrayed the band, but it isn't true. I only told my father not to go to the meeting. I didn't tell him anything about the plan. I revealed nothing." Brutus was starting to be afraid.

"Who else did you talk to?" asked Gram, circling around behind Brutus and twisting his arm.

"No one."

"You betrayed us. In the name of the revolution, I sentence you to death."

With those words, Gram pulled the sharp straight razor out of his pocket and grabbed Brutus by the hair, forcing his head back.

"I didn't betray you! I didn't betray you!" Brutus shouted.

Gram slit his throat.

Then he rolled the corpse into the ditch running along the road. The acacia flowers bending over the bank covered the partisan and stood watch over his final rest.

When Gram reached the rectory, the other two were already there. Don Giordano showed the three of them down to the cellar. One wall of the cellar projected just above ground level, and there a small window overlooked a meadow that rolled downhill.

Don Giordano got them food and blankets and asked them to tell what had happened.

"And where is Brutus?" he asked when the story was done.

"Yeah, where's Brutus?" asked Blast.

"Did you split up?" Cartridge inquired.

Gram looked at them gravely, one by one, and said: "Brutus confessed. He was the one who betrayed us. I executed him."

"What?!" cried Blast and Cartridge, in horrified disbelief.

"It's revolutionary justice," Gram decreed.

Don Giordano made the sign of the cross in the air, uttering a benediction. Then, turning to Gram, he said:

"You've sinned against your brother. I'll pray for you and for him."

The next day passed without incident. But when darkness fell an RNG squad knocked at the street door—they always waited for darkness before carrying out this sort of operation.

Signora Maria, Don Giordano's mother who kept house for him, went to the door. She took such fright at the sight of the squad that she was speechless and collapsed onto a chair, placing her hand on her heart as if to quiet a spasm within.

The men entered the house without asking.

Don Giordano hurried in, hearing the uproar.

"Where are the rebels?" asked the squad leader.

"There are no rebels in the House of God," Don Giordano replied.

"But here we're in *your* house, Father. Search the place!" the leader ordered.

Don Giordano wondered who'd given them the tip. No one knew about the situation, except for him and his mother. What he didn't know was that the schoolteacher Amalia Bacchettoni, whose windows were directly across from the rectory, suffered from insomnia, and the night before she had gone to the window to get a breath of fresh air. She heard low voices in the street and then saw several shadows slipping through the front door. Right then and there, she didn't give it a second thought, but the morning after, just to be sure, she reported what she'd seen and heard to Ercole Battaglia's detachment.

The *squadristi* found Gram and Blast in the cellar. A few minutes before that, Cartridge had managed to get away by wriggling through the bars of the tiny window. He was the only one who'd managed to get out, because of his tiny, agile physique.

They were all handcuffed and hauled off. Don Giordano and his mother were taken to jail; Gram and Blast, to the "slaughterhouse."

The place used for interrogations was the town slaughterhouse, and it had been requisitioned by the Black Brigades for that purpose. This task fell to them, the Italian fascist branch of the SS, established to do the dirty work, especially in the fight against the partisans. The interrogation took place in the shopfront, now supplied with chairs and desks. The room in the back, where animals had once been slaughtered, was now fitted out as a torture chamber. The long sharp meat hooks, in rows along the walls, were no longer used to hang up sides of beef, but the bodies of prisoners ravaged by the torturer's tools. Sometimes they would hang up people by their throat when they were still alive. After every session, they'd use a hose to wash off the floor; the spray of water pushed the puddles of blood into a drain runnel that skirted the walls.

Gram and Blast were interrogated individually. Neither of the two said a thing. Even under torture, they revealed neither names, nor places, nor anything else. They left the two of them dangling by their bound wrists from meat hooks.

Toward nightfall, they brought Octobrine from Asti to arrange a confrontation. She too showed marks of a beating on her puffy, bruised face. Streams of blood that had oozed out of her eyebrow had caked over the purplish bruise that covered her eye. She had lost her cap, her long hair had been shaven down to the scalp, and here and there burn marks could be seen where cigarettes had been pressed to her head. The three comrades showed no signs of ever having met.

They were taken out into the square in front of the church and lined up against the wall for a summary execution.

Before the burst of rifle fire, Gram shouted:

"Victory will be ours!"

Octobrine: "Murderers!"

And Blast: "I die with honor. I die a partisan!"

In Alma's bedroom, their muffled shouts mingled with Lina's first wails.

* * *

Cartridge told this story to Blast's mother, Celestina, who, in tears, told it to a trusted cousin of hers. The cousin, in turn, told it to one of her god-daughters, who then told it to her boyfriend, the pharmacist's son, who recounted it to the friends with whom he played bocce and, little by little, the whole town knew about it. As it was relayed and handed down orally, people gradually added the details that Cartridge couldn't have known. After the Liberation, the story became a part of the local saga and, perhaps, a few heroic grace notes were tacked on here and there. I've set it down here as it was told to me.

VI

Celestina grew quarrelsome and taciturn. For many months she spoke to no one, except to say, "He was my only son." After Dino's birth, she'd had some health problems and had been unable to have more children. Then her husband was killed in an accident at work. He cut his hand while he was sharpening a scythe for the harvest and caught a tetanus infection that killed him in the course of a single day. Now that Dino was dead too, she was not only afflicted by sorrow for the loss of her son, but also fear for her old age, who would take care of her then?

Celestina mulled over these thoughts and her feelings crystallized with increasing clarity into a repressed rage, fed by a growing hatred toward those who had deprived her of her son. To her closest girlfriends she confided, "If I get my hands on one of them, I'll kill him like the pig that he is."

The opportunity presented itself the following spring, when, with the general insurrection of April 25 decreed by the CLNAI (the Committee of National Liberation for Northern Italy), the German army was forced into a precipitous retreat and the forces of the Fascist Republic of Salò disintegrated, seeking shelter as best they were able, in order to avoid imprisonment in the Allied camps and the reprisals of the partisans. The biggest cities in the north were liberated thanks to the fury with which the civilian populace rose up alongside the partisan bands, and a few days later the Americans arrived.

It was noon to judge from the sun, which stood straight overhead. Franz had run through the fields for more than two hours. That morning, his company had been attacked by a partisan brigade as it was withdrawing toward the border. Those who hadn't been killed had taken to the countryside. The partisans took no prisoners.

It was only late April, but the sun was burning in the clear sky and its rays struck like flaming swords. Franz stopped in a farmhouse, driven by thirst. The welcome he received was hostile. A woman with an angry glare unleashed her dog that lunged at him as if possessed by the devil and sank its teeth into his calf. Franz got free of the dog by hitting him in the head with the butt of his rifle, and then took to his heels.

Under the weight of his backpack, Franz was sweating. He took off the helmet that was baking his brain like a copper pot and wiped his forehead, shoving back the locks of hair that were plastered to his scalp. If he only had a little water. He ran his gaze over the surrounding countryside, squinting his eyes against the blinding glare, so that there was only a pair of horizontal light-blue slits between the blond eyelashes. Nothing. Not a rivulet, not a stream, not even a dribble of water. Nothing but fields. Vast. Flat. Wide open. Here and there in the shimmering heat there appeared quavering cool visions of his beloved Bavaria, the pine forests, the chalet where he spent his summer vacations, the trout stream, the little cascades burbling over the mossy rocks, his mother standing in the doorway with a pitcher of spring water. Franz had just turned eighteen and he kept in the breast pocket of his field jacket the letter that his mother had sent to him, with her fond wishes that he might be home in time for his next birthday... Baking heat... The wound to his calf ached, and it might be starting to get infected, maybe that dog had rabies. He had to keep walking, get down there, all the way into the distance, beyind the mirage, where he glimpsed a green patch and the beginnings of a hill. High above there was a castle. Up there, there was bound to be a fountain, a well...

Alma saw him emerge suddenly from the tangled bushes that surrounded the Hello Garden. Franz looked terrifying, with his deranged face and his furtive step. Alma started in surprise. Franz was no less frightened than she was, he hadn't expected to encounter anyone in that place which, from below, had looked abandoned. He came to a sudden halt and leveled his rifle. They stared at each other, stunned, for a long moment.

Alma was sitting at a small table with Nina, under the withered linden tree that by now no longer offered any shade. They were cutting figures of dolls out of a sheet of thin cardboard, along with a lavish assortment of clothing and accessories that could then be applied to the figure by means of special hooks on the shoulders. Lina was asleep in her baby carriage to one side. They'd brought her to the castle on the occasion of Alma's visit. Otherwise, she normally stayed with the wet-nurse in the farmhouse of Mariuccia's sister. Full-service, in-house nannies weren't available around there. What's more, Ada was too sick by now to take on the responsibilities of a second baby granddaughter.

Nina was so focused on turning and pressing the scissors without making mistakes that she didn't even register Franz's apparition until Alma, cautiously, called it to her attention. On that occasion, Alma displayed cool, level-headed courage. In spite of the fact that she was prompt to shed tears over the most trivial things, when things got serious she was decisive and pragmatic. She reached out and grabbed Nina by the arm and pulled her close, smiling reassuringly all the while. She said, "Well, we have a visitor. Be good and stay close to me, and don't breathe a word." Then, without losing sight of the intruder, and with slow and circumspect movements, as if she were face to face with a wild beast and were taking care not to provoke a reaction, she took Lina in her arms and headed toward the front door, with Nina clinging to the hem of her skirt.

Franz, encouraged by Alma's attitude, followed her, trying to catch her attention, "*Bitte... Trinken, trinken...*" he repeated several times.

Alma stopped and turned around. Now the intruder was right in front of her. From that short distance, Alma could see that he was only a boy: he looked wrecked, his uniform was dusty and torn, his hair was plastered to his forehead. What struck her most was the look of profound desperation in his light blue eyes, clear and transparent as mountain lakes. Still clutching her two girls tight, Alma pointed out the well to him, under the octagonal shed roof.

The young man's face lit up, the small mountain lakes turned an even lighter blue, while despair gave way to hope. He uttered a few phrases that Alma failed to understand, perhaps they were words of thanks, and he headed for the well at a dead run.

Entering the little pagoda that stood over the well, Franz had the impression he was looking at his mother. It was no mirage. A tall, matronly woman, with gray-blond hair pulled back on her head, was standing by the well with a pitcher in one hand. Franz walked toward her with a broad smile, "*Trinken, bitte... wasser,*" he begged her, making the gesture of lifting a glass to his mouth.

At the sight of him, Celestina let out a scream. The pitcher fell out of her hand and smashed on the ground. She gave him a hard glare.

Franz remained disoriented and hesitant, *"Wasser,"* he said again. Celestina looked at him for a few seconds with a deep aversion, an alternating surge of hatred and disgust in her eyes. Then she walked away without another word.

Franz got busy with the bucket. *Ker-plunk, ker-plunk…*the bucket lurched down into the narrow depths. It took forever to reach the bottom. Finally, it filled with water. Franz started turning the handle in the opposite direction with renewed vigor. The chain was winding and the bucket was rising toward him. Franz leaned over the edge of the well to savor with eager anticipation the glittering fluid coming closer and closer.

That was when a hard object hit him in the back of the head with all the rude force of a boulder. Franz sprawled to the ground, releasing the handle. The bucket plunged heavily down and hit the bottom with a resounding *splash!*

Before dying, Franz had a last vision of the tall woman above him, with the mattock raised, ready to hit him a second time. *"Mutter…"* he murmured, incredulous. And then, he saw nothing ever again.

Alma arrived, after taking the girls into the house. She wanted to make sure the young man left the castle as soon as possible, after slaking his thirst.

The sight that greeted her eyes filled her with horror. The young man lay on his back in a pool of blood, his eyes open and empty. Celestina stood motionless, still brandishing the bloody mattock.

"Celestina, what have you done?" Alma cried.

Celestina started, threw away the mattock, and ran the back of her hand over her sweaty forehead.

"He's dead," she said. "We have to hide him."

"Where?" asked Alma.

Celestina reflected a moment. "We have to throw him down there."

"Down the well?"

"Yes. That's the easiest thing."

Alma found herself dragged into the deed without wanting to. She didn't stop to think of possible alternatives. They needed to get rid of the corpse. It was an emergency. They needed to act, and that was that.

Celestina grabbed the body under the arms and hoisted it partially onto the parapet, so that head and shoulders now projected over the void.

"Signora, help me. He's too heavy."

"What do you want me to do?" asked Alma.

"Grab his feet and lift them up."

Alma obeyed.

Celestina shoved the body over the edge.

A couple of seconds later they heard a heavy splash.

That same day, Mussolini's corpse was strung up by the feet from the cantilever roof of a gas station on Piazzale Loreto in Milan. The war was over.

14

Once Upon a Time
1945-

I

E la vita ora a Cortalba
è una vita un poco scialba.
È la vita dei perfetti,
degli eterni, degli insetti.
—GiBi, "A mia sorella," 1998.[25]

In the aftermath of the great saga of the Italian Resistance, the "red spring" faded to a pale pink and the "bright sun of the future" set too early, leaving the field open to the crossed blue shield of the Christian Democrats, under whose auspices the Catholic bourgeoisie took power.

There were many changes in Cortalba. Like everywhere in Italy, there too a series of reprisals began against those who had supported the fascists. Aurelio came close to being arrested and forced to stand trial, but once again his luck held. Under the special protection of the American high command, he moved to Rome with Marilù, and there, in the turmoil of the rapidly transforming capital, he became an anonymous citizen. This happened thanks to Leo's intervention.

---

25. *And now life in Cortalba/ is a somewhat dull life./ It's the life of the perfect,/ of the eternal, of the insects.*
   —GiBi, from the poem "To My Sister," 1998.

* * *

Leo Ducati arrived in Cortalba one morning in May of '45 and stopped his jeep at the foot of the hill after rounding the last curve in the road. He took off his dust-caked sunglasses and got out of the car to fully drink in the sight. It was just as he'd seen it in the photographs his father had shown him when he was a child. The silhouette of the castle with the crenelated tower rose up, massive, against the bright sky. The sun, still in the east, lit it from behind, surrounding it with a luminous halo.

Just like André twenty years earlier, Leo too had volunteered when the United States went to war. He had arrived with the first contingent that landed on the coasts of Sicily, and he had followed the tortuous climb up the peninsula, step by agonizing step. He spoke Italian because André had greatly insisted on that point, and this had allowed him to serve as an interpreter for the high command.

Leo got back behind the wheel, started the engine, and shifted into gear. Who knows if there are still any people left up at the castle... any of the people his father had told him about... Aunt Ada, in particular.

For Ada it was like glimpsing a ghost. Leo strongly resembled André, though his hair was lighter, a honey blond like Cathy's. He had the same ladykiller smile and the same irreverent, rowdy attitude.

He immediately conquered every female heart, including Veglia's and Celestina's—and in fact the two women vied to see who could serve him more lavishly—as well as Mariuccia's of course. She stood open-mouthed at the mere sight of him, as if a movie star from her favorite films had deigned to come down among us common mortals.

To properly fête their guest, Ada invited Aurelio and Marilù to dinner. They didn't normally socialize. They only saw each other on rare occasions on account of Aurelio's deplorable position. But, since there was no other company available, Ada had to settle.

Now that the blackouts were no longer required, it was possible to keep the windows open. The evening breeze carried into the room the aromas of the land as it reawakened. Leo, leaning with his back against the windowsill, was the center of attention. While they were waiting to sit down to dinner, Mariuccia served the aperitif, running the risk of stumbling and dropping the tray because she couldn't take her eyes off that stunning guy.

Nina had waited all day to ask him a question. She walked up to him.

"Are you an American?" she asked, trying to make herself heard by that blond head up there, at an astronomical altitude.

"Yes, but only half American," Leo replied, squatting down to be at her level.

"Are you one of those that shoot at trains?"

"What?" Leo smiled, puzzled, unfamiliar with the context.

Ada broke in, "Don't pay any attention, Leo. Nina is confused."

"And that's more than understandable. Who can figure out a thing in this situation? The cemeteries of Europe are filled with our boys, thousands of white crosses. And your cities are full of rubble. It's a nasty mess," Leo replied. Then he spoke to Nina in English, "*Come here, sweetie pie, look what I've got for you.*" And then, switching back into Italian, "I've got something for you that you've never seen before." He reached into his pocket and pulled out a thin strip wrapped in shiny paper, and said, again in English, "*It's chewing gum,*" winking an eye and speaking in a confidential tone of voice.

"*Ciuingam!*" Nina chirped as if it were the refrain to a song. She had an excellent ear for sounds, thanks to Alma's diction lessons.

"Excellent! What a smart kid. You'll see, you'll like it. But be careful, don't swallow it."

Nina gave it back to him. "If I can't swallow it, that must mean it's bad."

Ada broke in again, "Nina, stop bothering Uncle Leo with such nonsense. If you want to sit at the table with us, you need be quiet and let the grownups talk."

They sat down. They hadn't even finished the first course when Ada steered the conversation to André. That night she learned what she hadn't been able to find out in all those years.

Leo told the story slowly, in proper Italian. "Papà died when I was fifteen. He no longer lived with us. He was in a home for invalided war veterans. He never did let relatives or friends know his address, and especially not you. He didn't want to be seen in that condition. He preferred to be forgotten. But we went to see him often. We children. Our nanny would take us. I became very fond of Papà. Jane and Jim never did. They went because they had to, and they spent most of their time playing with the dogs in the rest home's courtyard. But I enjoyed every minute I spent with him. And that affection was reciprocated. It was he who taught me Italian. Talking to me, he only spoke in that language. He even gave me a few books that were among the few things that he had taken with him to the home, and it was with those books that I learned to read and write. I especially liked *Le confessioni di un ottua-genario*[26] and I worked hard to make my way through all of those tomes. But what especially fascinated me were the photographs that Papà liked to show me—of the family, of the place where he spent his childhood, and of the castle. Behind those dark glasses, he was certainly seeing those images again through my eyes. And both of us were captivated by their enchantment, we were transported into another dimension as if by magic. He never had hard words for my mother. He knew that she wasn't at fault for what happened—the divorce, the loss of all his wealth. She had always lived under her father's

---

26. *Confessions of an Italian*, by Ippolito Nievo,1867.

thumb, and on that occasion she hadn't known how to oppose him. My grandfather is still alive. He is a tycoon, wealthy and powerful. He decided Papà's fate, and Mother suffered terribly as a result. She only managed to stand up to him when it came to visitation. She promised to have no more contact with her husband, but she was able to arrange for the children to visit him. From then on, Mother took to drinking and she eventually died an alcoholic, two years after Papà."

A soggy cloak of sadness weighed over the table. Ada broke the silence, "We're so grateful to you for finally letting us know the facts of your father's life, after all these years. But especially for having comforted him with your presence in such a difficult time. Now, please tell us about yourself. What do you do? How do you make a living?"

"I live in New York. I'm the only one of us three siblings to create an independent life for myself. Jim chose to work with grandfather, and he's a major producer himself. Someday he'll inherit the studio. Jane has established herself as an actress. She's achieved a certain success, though it's brought more heartache than satisfaction. From outside, it may look like a golden world, but the truth is that in Hollywood actresses are brutally exploited by the producers. Jane was even forced to marry a colleague chosen by the studio to satisfy the expectations of her fans. It was a clause in her contract. I never much cared for that world and when I turned eighteen, I picked up and left. I took a degree in English at Columbia University, and then with the money Mother left me, I founded a publishing house. Books are my one great love, as well as proving to be an excellent business. Sales are booming."

"Are you married?" asked Ada.

"No. I haven't fallen in love yet."

Leo turned his eyes to Marilù, who had been listening to him, drinking in every word he uttered and memorizing every move he made. It was impossible to escape the allure of handsome Leo. And Marilù was swept away.

* * *

This passion marked the rest of her life. For Leo too, it was love at first sight. The short period that he spent in Cortalba was tumultuous and intense. Leo and Marilù showed no restraint in their bliss, and their behavior met with universal disapproval. It was a scandal. Marilù, always so judicious and modest, lost all self-control, and blossomed like a rose in May, acquiring a brand-new beauty that lit up her cat-like eyes and brought a patch of pink to her cheeks. Even her hair looked thicker and more lustrous, worn loose over the shoulders without ribbons or clips. Her elongated figure lost a certain unripe angularity and took on the smooth softness of a rush plant. Leo decided to marry her and take her back with him to America, and Marilù was overjoyed. They made a plan: Leo would go back to New York and there he'd start the bureaucratic process for their wedding and her visa, and in the meantime Marilù would persuade her father to accept the situation. Until that moment, Aurelio had made no objections to his daughter's liaison because he badly needed American protection so he could arrange to move to Rome. Their trip to the capital was organized in the space of a week—documents, safe-conduct passes, new identity cards. Aurelio and Marilù left Cortalba and Leo escorted them to their destination. Then, he had to leave. It was a separation full of promises, hopes, plans, and dreams...

But those dreams never came to fruition. Aurelio managed to leverage his daughter's devotion, playing on her sense of duty, and convinced her that it was her mission in life to take care of him. He told her that her sense of guilt for having abandoned him would pursue her for the rest of her life like a curse. Marilù gave in and Leo received a tear-stained letter that put an end to his dream of love. Marilù never recovered... She took a job as a secretary in her uncle's law office—that was Aunt Lidia's husband—and spent the rest of her life between home and work, maintaining her father with her own modest salary. When Aurelio died, twenty years later, Marilù finally felt free to achieve her destiny. By committing suicide.

II

In the autumn after Leo's visit, Ada and Ernesto left Cortalba and moved to Colisso. There, Ernesto still owned his father's house, with a fine garden and a magnificent view of the lands and vineyards that had once belonged to him. As Luca's guardian, Ernesto had decided to sell the castle to provide his brother-in-law an annuity on which he could live with some dignity until the end of his days. It might even have been a good idea, but given the circumstances, Ernesto made a big mistake that Ada and Alma would subsequently throw in his face for the rest of their life on this earth, and perhaps even in the afterlife.

In those war years, nobody could figure out anything anymore in terms of finance. Who was governing the country? Who was printing and coining the national currency? What was the real value of the lira? What were the Am-Lire, those little square bills, yellow with black borders, which had recently come into circulation? To say nothing of the stock exchange. Ernesto's stock holdings had gone up in smoke, his assets had been decimated. When a buyer for the castle showed up one day, Ernesto found the offer reasonable, at least, if not exactly stunning. And he took it. He had not realized that the value of the lira was still in free fall. The sum of money that was supposed to ensure a comfortable old age for Luca evaporated over the course of a few years and, after Ernesto's death, Luca ended his days at the Hospice for Old Paupers. What's more—and this only intensified Ada and Alma's bitter resentment—by an ironic twist of fate, the purchaser of the castle was non other than the former gardener Tunìn, who had made a fortune in the fruit and vegetable wholesale market and was well on his way to becoming the "king of preserves" in Italy's manufacturing boom years.

The night before they left, a furious thunderstorm lashed down. There was no longer a crew of housekeepers who would scatter throughout the castle at the first flash of lightning to fasten shut doors and windows. Now the shutters were slamming in a sinister fashion with every gust of wind and the rain was finding a way in through broken glass panes.

Ada, Ernesto, Luca, and Veglia gathered in the living room because the raging elements frightened them all. Veglia wouldn't have slept that night in any case, she was too excited to be returning to her home town, where she still had family. Nina had already left. Keeping faith with her promise, Alma had come to get her in mid-September and had taken her to Turin. Lina had remained with her wet nurse at Mariuccia's sister's, but it was already decided that in the course of the coming year, she'd come to live with the family, too.

The lightning bolts crashed down on the tower, unleashing horrendous noises. As a rule, they caused no damage, as they were neutralized by the magnetic cable that conveyed them into the ground below. But that night, as if hurled by the angry hand of Jupiter, a lightning bolt deviated from its customary path and hit the linden tree. The poor tree, already in precarious health, collapsed to the earth, spreading its mass to cover the entire Hello Garden. The heavy trunk crushed the pagoda over the well, shattering it into bits.

Tunìn, then, took care of clearing that up—the price of wood was sky-high in that period—and while he was at it, he also had the cedars of Lebanon chopped down and clear-cut the rest of the hill.

One of the great beauties of Cortalba was lost forever. That centuries-old forest never grew back. The inhabitants of the village would look up at the now bald hill, shake their heads, and say of their townfellow who'd been capable of an act of such gross foolishness, "That guy there is way behind the pig's tail," meaning, he's a moron.

III

When Alma and Nina arrived in Turin, Dardo went to meet them at the station. He was cheerful and beaming. In one hand, he held a brown cardboard bookbag with a folding handle and a metal snap. He waved it in front of Nina's eyes as if it were a toy. "You see what your Papà bought you? In just a week, school starts," he said.

Nina thanked him and gave him a hug, but she hadn't actually understood the meaning of that gesture—an offer of friendship on Dardo's part. She was too wrapped up in her own happiness. Her dream had finally come true. Alma had come to get her and had taken her away. In the excitement of her departure, she'd practically forgotten to say goodbye to her grandparents, and she'd had to retrace her steps and give them a hasty peck on the cheek. She thought that she'd glimpsed a tear of emotion on their faces, but she paid it no mind… Alma was waiting for her at the door.

Aboard the train, they sat side by the side, talking amongst themselves the whole way, ignoring the multitude of passengers crammed into the car. Nina focused solely on Alma's face in that throng of strangers. She wasn't even distracted by the landscape that streamed past outside the window, even though it was a completely new spectacle to her.

When they got home, Nina was beside herself with joy. But that moment of ecstasy didn't last long. Alma's mood changed the very instant they crossed the threshold. The cheerfulness and silvery laughter that had accompanied her throughout the journey suddenly gave way to a grim melancholy.

They entered the house, not through the front door, but by a small secondary entrance that gave onto a tradesman's staircase. It led directly upstairs where Alma and Dardo were renting an apartment. The lovely residence where Alma was born and raised, with the large drawing rooms on the ground floor, the veranda, the garden, and the library... now belonged to a new owner.

What had happened was this: at the end of the war, Ada and Ernesto got ready to return to their house in the city. But Dardo, who had taken refuge there with Alma and Gio in those turbulent years, simply and brashly declared that he had no intention of leaving. Ada and Ernesto were indignant at this abuse of their property. The conflict grew bitter. Dardo maintained his position as if he were defending some basic right, because, he said, he had no other home. There was nothing to be done. Ada and Ernesto were forced to retrench and move to Colisso. They broke off all relations with Dardo and refused to speak to him for more than ten years. What's more, they sold off the house and emptied it of all their furnishings. All things considered, it was a necessary step because the money they received, even if it was quickly devalued by the galloping inflation, ensured that they enjoyed some small income in the last decade of their lives. They died in the 1950s, one soon after the other.

Gio had left the house before the crisis point was reached. He had married Isabella and had gone to live in the spacious residence of Professor Bizzarri. He too became a professor of biology and took over his father-in-law's research chair when he died. What's more, in order to break the monotony of a long and uneventful career, he began to write verse and produced a great many books of poetry, which revealed a sensitive soul and a certain talent for literary work.

Alma took a rather ambiguous position in the dispute over the house. She stayed with Dardo out of sheer inertia, but still admitted that her parents had a point. Ada and Ernesto maintained good relations with her. What really weighed on them was the knowledge that they could no longer help her as they'd once been able to. They were especially worried about Dardo's personality, and considered him to be an unscrupulous bully. Ada, in particular, never tired of telling her daughter that she needed to stand up to him, because that husband of hers would eventually prove to be her undoing. But they never saw much of each other. Alma went to Colisso only rarely, and these words of advice came to her in the form of letters, more often than not.

The new owners, who were a childless couple, agreed to Dardo's request that they rent him an apartment on the second floor. The apartment was spacious, the bedrooms were large, and the windows overlooked the garden, where the magnolia still caressed the windowsills with its candelabra branches. Beyond the garden, they could see the green line of the Valentino Park, and then the arc of the hillside, a darker green that closed off the horizon. But if you wanted to enjoy the view, you had to open the windows, because the panes had been shattered in the bombing raids and they'd been temporarily replaced by sheets of plywood. Inside, the apartment was dark and half empty. Ada and Ernesto's elegant furniture had been removed, except for a few overlooked items that clashed incongruously in those deserted rooms—a slender marble column with a Greek urn standing on top of it, a gilt Louis XV side table, a silk privacy screen with embroidered irises... For more practical needs, there were just a couple of metal spring bed frames with mattresses, a kitchen table with a hot plate and four chairs. Still, there was also a nice bathroom that once served the master bedroom.

Alma looked around in desolation, tears streaking her face. "I'm a tenant in my own home," she kept repeating in a sorrowful refrain.

In that sort of encampment, they did occasionally have fun. Nina slept with her parents on the two metal spring bed frames, now placed side by side, and before falling asleep she always asked Dardo to "make the theater." If he was in a good mood, Dardo would tell her a story, say for instance, *Little Red Riding Hood*, playing all the different parts with appropriate voices—a thin, piping voice for Little Red Riding Hood, a booming big voice for the wolf, and a raucous little voice for the grandmother. He would also add some action, moving around the room, and at the culminating dramatic moment, he'd leap onto the bed to gobble up the grandmother, while Nina cowered under the blankets. In the end, though, Little Red Riding Hood would always win, because Alma invariably intervened to change the moral of the fairytale. In Alma's version, the little girl outfoxed the wolf: she would lay a trap and capture him, saving herself and her grandmother in the process. At that point, Nina and Alma would lunge at Dardo, annihilating him with multiple pillow blows, and everything ended in loud peals of laughter.

But most of the time, the atmosphere was tense and the house crackling with electricity, heightened by the angry glares that Alma and Dardo exhanged. Nina waited with bated breath for the inevitable spark that would set off the explosion. And in fact, the explosions took place on a daily basis, and always for the most trivial of causes. The pretext might be something as banal as a button to be sewn on. But deep down, there was a fundamental incompatibility. Dardo expected Alma to be not only a fellow artist, but also a traditional wife. In that period, when they lacked a full-time maid, he expected her to be in charge of running the household. "Am I supposed to believe that you don't even know how to sew on a button?" he scolded her.

The apartment turned into a battle field. She would sob, he would curse, and they'd compete to see who could shout the loudest. "You're a raving lunatic," Alma would attack him, "I'm not a housewife, so you can just get that idea out of your head. I'm an actress, you know. If the button needs sewing, then sew it on yourself!" Dardo threatened to beat her. "I'll smash your face in!", but then he'd limit himself to smashing a chair against the wall. Once the victim was the Louis XV side table, which flew across the room in a gilt trajectory, like a comet, and shattered against the facing wall into smithereens.

Nina would stand by, a witness to these scenes who was only too anxious to intervene, but uncertain about exactly what she should do. She was afraid that Dardo actually intended to "smash Alma's face in" and this threw her into a state of abject terror. And so she'd throw her arms around his leg to stop him, and beg him through her tears, "No, Papà, don't touch her!" He'd push her away with a bitter smile and stormy turquoise eyes. "You're always on her side," he'd say to her. Then, to Alma, "You've managed to turn my own daughter against me." She would stand up to him with phrases shouted in a professionally tragic tone of voice, things that had nothing at all to do with the current matter of debate, but which rather reiterated a state of mind betokening extreme animosity. "The child has eyes and ears and can perfectly well recognize just what sort of scoundrel you really are. I curse the day I ever met you. You want me dead, that's what you really want. But I'd rather die ten times over than go on living with you. You monster! You're just a monster! One fine day I'll up and leave and you'll never see me again."

And in fact, one fine day Alma did leave. She had her few suitcases and belongings loaded onto a two-handled cart, pulled by a man in place of the donkey, and walked along behind it with her girl. Alma and Nina, hand in hand.

They crossed a Turin that had been half destroyed, a city in ruins. The war had ended a year ago. They walked through heaps of rubble piled up carelessly, over potholes and broken, uneven asphalt. Skeletons of buildings standing askew lined the streets, and the part that remained standing looked like a cross section, like in a doll house. But here there was an immense disorder: on every floor, furniture overturned, broken mirrors, a bathtub hanging from its drainpipe, now that the floor beneath it had collapsed, ramshackle steps, doors askew on their hinges, upholstery charred and blackened by smoke.

The first time that Nina saw Turin, she wasn't surprised at these conditions. Since she had no terms of comparison, she thought that this was the customary appearance of the "city," as opposed to the "country." And so, on that spring afternoon, she walked along beside Alma feeling lighthearted, just happy that the two of them had managed to escape the "monster." Alma, though, seemed sad, and Nina felt a great pain for her. From that moment on, she resolved to make her happy.

Alma rented a small furnished two-room apartment. There they lived for four years, with Lina and Mariuccia, who joined them in the autumn. They were forced to adapt to life together in that tiny, shared space: Alma and the girls in the bedroom and Mariuccia on a cot in the kitchen. The other little room served as a joint dining room and living room. In that room, Nina did her homework, Lina played, and Mariuccia read through an issue of *Grand Hotel* and listened to pop music on the radio. With her salary, Alma couldn't afford anything better.

Alma asked and obtained a legal separation, but she was never able to cut off her relationship with Dardo once and for all. Every night, he would show up for dinner and would impose his presence at the table. If Alma refused to open the door to him, he would linger under the window, smoking one cigarette after another, until she finally gave in and allowed him to enter. Then they'd often go out together, and Alma would come home at dawn.

Nina slept uneasily those nights. She woke up every half hour and looked over toward Alma's side of the fullsized bed, but that side was still empty. Lina was sleeping peacefully in her trundle bed, blissfully unaware of the drama. When Alma finally arrived and slipped under the covers, Nina pulled her close and whispered to her, "Miminna, why do you go with him?" "Sleep, sweetie mouse. You can't understand." "Don't go with him anymore, he just makes you cry. Stay here with me." "I'm here now, sweetie mouse. I'm here with you. Go to sleep, now. Sleep." And Nina would fall asleep, contentedly, in her mother's warmth.

But sometimes Alma would come home irritated and ready for a fight and refused to listen to Nina's complaints. She'd retort, "I'll go out when I please and with whomever I like. It's none of your business. Leave me alone. Don't you start tormenting me too." At this point, she'd become emotional, torn by self-pity, and dissolve into tears: "You all just want to see me dead. But when that day comes, you'll regret it and you'll come weep over my grave." When Nina heard these words, she felt her blood run cold. The horrible vision of Alma, dressed in white, neatly laid out in a coffin, would appear before her against the dark background of the bedroom. She felt as if she were the unhappiest creature on this earth. At that point, she'd lay a hand on Alma's shoulder and whisper, "Forgive me." But Alma would ignore the request, "Leave me alone. I've got a headache now." And they would both lie there in the dark, eyes wide open, each closed up in their own individual unhappiness, until Mariuccia showed up with the coffee.

Dardo tried everything he could think of to convince Alma to come back to him. He employed seduction and extortion. In the end, he even threatened a full-blown scandal. Their separation had been kept secret because in those days a conjugal breakup was considered a moral and social stain, especially for the woman. Dardo announced that he would shame her publicly: "I'll unleash a smashup!" he said. And Alma gave in and went back to him.

There were also work-related reasons that accelerated that

decision. Dardo had founded the first civic theater in Turin, with a troupe that included a few classmates from the Academy and many students from the Dramatic Art Studio that he himself had established several years earlier. They both left their jobs at RAI and set off on that new adventure. Dardo was a brilliant company leader and stage director, and Alma was a splendid leading lady. The theater was extremely popular and met with critical acclaim. It seemed to have a brilliant future ahead of it. Instead, it only lasted a single season. Dardo failed to obtain the necessary government financing that would have allowed the theater to meet its expenses. His own personal funds, from which he'd financed the undertaking, soon ran out. The theater went bankrupt and was forced out of business. He found other outlets for his energy: shortly thereafter he won the national competition for the chair in dramatic art at the conservatory and he devoted himself to teaching and directing at the opera house. But for Alma, that episode marked the end of her career.

Many years later, I questioned her about that point. I wanted to know why a woman with her artistic gifts and her combative spirit should have renounced from one day to the next a professional life that she had conquered for herself with many years of hard work.

"Your father kept me from continuing without him," said Alma. "Renowned impresarios and theatrical producers had sought me out, they'd even offered me prominent positions. But he swore that if I dreamed of accepting, he'd hunt me down, he'd yank me off the stage, and he'd drag me home by my hair. What's more, I had two daughters, and I could no longer turn to my parents to keep them. You were just little girls, you were only about twelve years old, while Lina had barely started school... What could I do? I gave up. But I shouldn't have. I was a coward."

This sense of frustration only sharpened her mechanisms of self-defense. In her periods of depression, Alma felt a profound disgust for herself because of the way she had given in, and she projected those feelings onto others, imagining that everyone judged her to be an abject creature. And so she vented her rage by attacking Mariuccia, Dardo, the girls, the plumber, the inspector from the gas company, and everyone else, both present and absent, who populated the universe of her tormenters. Among them, prominent in the foreground, there was Signora Lalla, who was married to Mr. Gribaudo, new owner of the house.

He was tall and distinguished and always wore a gray overcoat and a Borsalino hat, and every morning he climbed into the chauffeur-driven Lancia that came to pick him up and take him to the office. Alma had practically nothing to criticize when it came to him. Instead, she saved her darts for his wife, "That Lalla, the way she gives herself airs. Who does she think she is? Everyone knows that Mr. Gribaudo married his housekeeper. She wants to treat me like a tenant, look down on me… But when I meet her I give her the cold shoulder. I don't even say hello, I look the other way." Then she'd fall into a dark state of melancholy and cry for days at a time.

Nina kept her spirits up. Faithful to the promise she had made herself that she would "make her happy," she did her best to draw Alma out of her despondency with soft words, affectionate gestures, and comical jester poses. And sometimes she was successful. Alma turned cheerful again, recovering her love of discovery and adventure. The two of them would go out together and board a trolley heading up into the hills, where they'd sit in a trattoria al fresco and eat bread and salami and laugh about nothing. Or else, they'd go to the movies, Alma liked westerns, and they'd see the same film twice in a row, munching on the *brùt e bon* they'd purchased in a little pastry shop at the corner and rooting for the cowboys—in those movies, the Indians were always the bad guys.

Alma had considerable tenacity and a remarkable capacity for recovery. Every time she hit bottom, she'd brace her shoulders and make up her mind that the time had come to start a new life. And so she'd devote herself to planning and scheming some new way to get out of the current situation, and for a while she'd be active, efficient, and self-confident. But, lacking resources as she did, her plans never went anywhere, remaining naïve fantasies in which, all the same, she continued to believe fervently. For instance, while out window shopping, Alma laid out her latest idea to Nina. "I've decided to claw my way out of this dead end. I'm going to open a boutique and I'll sell accessories: handbags, scarves, umbrellas. That'll make me independent. All I need to raise the initial capital is to win the Totocalcio.[27] I've already bought a ticket for this week. Wait and see, sweetie mouse, we'll succeed if you help me." Alma's enthusiasm was contagious and Nina could already see her in the elegant boutique, happy and surrounded by beautiful objects. But Alma's dream didn't last long, and it always culminated in another fit of depression. Still, it would soon repeat itself in other forms because, Alma insisted, "the important thing is never to give up."

Dardo often stayed away from that grim domestic setting, sometimes for weeks at a time. He'd seek distraction in the company of pretty, accommodating young women who constituted his entourage and who considered themselves fortunate to be the object of the maestro's attentions. Alma knew all about it. Whenever she heard whispers about her husband's liaisons, she'd commented, "If they want him, they can be my guests. That way, he'll leave me alone." But Dardo wouldn't leave her. He'd return as regular as clockwork, with a piece of jewelry and a ribald smile, whereupon Alma would dress to the nines and the two of them would set out for an extended stay in Monte Carlo. When she returned home, Alma would say, "That was sort of fun, but I got tired of it. A whole week with your father is hard to take." Dardo was never willing to

---

27. The soccer lottery.

acknowledge that he'd lost the war with Alma from the very outset. And so he went on battling, but all that he obtained for his efforts were brief truces due to the magnanimous indulgence of the victorious woman warrior. "She's different from all the other women," he'd often tell himself, to make sense of his undying attachment.

The girls had no familiarity with Dardo. Lina closed up into her own self, seeing that her parents showed no interest in her, and even as a very small child she sought affection and friendship outside of the family. It wasn't hard for her to find them. Everyone took a liking to her and told her that she was quite an "Angelina,"[28] with a cherubic face and a sweet personality. The first one to point out this connection was Veglia, because it had been she who came up with that name in a harsh year of war. Alma had approved of it, lacking any better ideas at the moment. This label also served to define Nina, in the opposite, negative sense, "not like Angelina," that is, as a rebellious, impertinent, and over-excitable soul. But Nina didn't pay much attention to the things people said, because Alma was tireless in defending her, and often told her, "People talk because they have tongues in their mouths, and what they say is mostly nonsense. It's true that you're lively and a bit of a rascal, but you have good intentions."

Nina remained a mamma's girl, always defending Alma when the occasion arose. She was somewhat intimidated by Dardo. She admired his wit and his flair, and his spirit of a showman that engaged the people, made them laugh, or made them dream, and stirred their souls when he declaimed lines from tragedies and classical poetry. But she never managed to overcome the barrier of mistrust that had sprung up between them from her earliest years. And Alma's hostile attitude toward her husband only reinforced that sense of estrangement. Dardo, in his turn, never knew how to win Nina's affection.

---

28. Angelina means Little Angel. The short for Angelina is Lina.

He was generous when it came to clothing and jewelry, but he was sparing with words and attentions. They never had serious conversations. They spoke glancingly, the way people living in the same home might, but never as father and daughter.

And then, frequently, Dardo would embarrass her in front of her girlfriends with his eccentric behavior. When the first snow of the season fell, he'd put on his "Uncle Vanya" boots and heavy jacket, costumes from the play by Chekov which had been part of his repertory. He'd walk out into the city streets, which had been promptly swept and plowed, as if he were venturing onto the snowy steppe, attracting ironic glances from respectable and disapproving citizens, and even ill-concealed mockery in that conformist Italian society of the 1950s, where even the slightest deviation from the straight and narrow was cause for scandal. On those occasions, Nina did her best to avoid being seen with him. Generally speaking, though, Dardo was a stickler for being well dressed and he selected his attire with great care: tweed blazers, camel-hair coats, cashmere pullovers, and suede shoes. He had cut his wavy hair short and now he wore it combed back, and a faint fragrance of cologne emanated from his perfectly shaven cheek whenever Nina leaned in to give him a kiss. Dardo was meticulous in his personal grooming, in contrast with Alma who did have considerable taste in her choice of clothing but who was also liable to exhibit a certain slovenliness. If she had a frayed hem, she wouldn't notice it, and if Nina pointed it out, she'd just tuck it up with a pin.

Dardo died young, cut down by a heart attack. Alma was struck by that sudden end, by the inexorability of death, against which there is no appeal, no recourse, all rebellion being vain. She also felt a sense of sorrow for the man with whom she'd spent twenty-five years of her life, and who had basically remained a stranger to her. But at the same time, a thought made its way through her mind and soon eradicated all the others, "Now I'm free. I can do what I want." Alma left behind that unhappy period of her life and retired to the furthest flung, most godforsaken place she could imagine, an island in the middle of the sea.

The island of Ischia was hardly a distant outpost of civilization. But for Alma it represented a break with the customs and conventions of a society that she found "mediocre, ordinary, vulgar, philistine, and blinkered." She chose that place because she'd been there once when she was a girl, and she remembered a secluded little bay at the edge of a village with just a few houses that had caught her imagination. She tracked it down and set up housekeeping there in a small whitewashed cottage surrounded by broom shrubs, halfway up the hill, between the sea and the sky. She spent the next forty years in that voluntary exile, spending her time as the impulse struck her: she'd spend days at a time on the beach, immersed in a book, often forgetting to eat; or else walking for hours along sheer trails to reach panoramic points of extraordinary beauty; or she'd paint *en plein air*, getting down on canvas the intense blue-green of the water beneath her, the fulgent yellow of the broom plants and the pure sunlight that brought colors to life, rendering them manifest.

She had a few acquaintances, other eccentrics more or less like her who lived in the surrounding areas or arrived in the bay aboard their cruising sailboats, but she rarely enjoyed their company. To say nothing of her suitors. Alma was forty-five years old when she arrived on the island, and her beauty, at its most spectacular, attracted specimens of all social classes and all ages. Gio, who worried about her, recommended she consider a good match because Dardo's pension, her sole source of revenue, wasn't much. Alma replied, "You know that I don't like being frugal. I grew up surrounded by comfort, and I wish I had more money. But men are a ball and chain. I'd rather just live alone and do as I please."

The good women in the village had taken her under their wing, and knowing that Alma didn't cook much and when she did, cooked badly, they'd often bring her a treat, samples of some special dish. But Alma found even this annoying. "When Francesca comes to bring me basil mini-pizzas, she sits down, she starts talking, and she just won't go away. Maddalena, on the other hand, is discreet, she stays outside the door, she hands me the dish, and she doesn't even ask to come in. She has the good sense not to bother people." Those gifts left her indifferent, and she frequently made no effort to conceal her annoyance with the giver.

What cheered her up, though, were visits from her daughters, who came to see her when they had some free time. Lina came every summer with her little girls, when school let out, and spent a couple of weeks. She had created a traditional family, a domestic setting that she had sorely missed during her own childhood. Lina had grown up rather lonely, without any maternal care, and now her relations with Alma were cordial but distant. When Lina's girls grew up, Lina continued those visits on her own, but more out of a sense of duty than any emotional attachment.

Nina would usually come twice a year, when she could get free of her work obligations. Now she lived in America where she ran Leo's publishing house. Her handsome cousin had never married, choosing to devote his time to his books and to the numerous girlfriends who followed one after the other in close succession in his agreeable bachelor's life. Leo thought of her as a daughter, as well as his invaluable assistant, and he was happy to have her living with him in his vast Manhattan penthouse.

All the same, even though Nina was leading an interesting and highly satisfying life, the thought of Alma was always on her mind. Their relationship hadn't changed, and every time they saw each other Nina realized that they still possessed that same great intimacy, the desire to spend time together, to tell each other stories about anything and everything, to live each day as if every morning they were about to set off on an adventuresome journey. Unfortunately, she also realized that Alma hadn't found serenity on the island. She continued to be tormented by the anxieties, uneasiness, and frustrations that only Nina knew how to sympathize with and soothe. Nina couldn't manage to suppress a faint sense of guilt at having left her all alone, even if it was Alma who had encouraged her to leave and insisted on the importance of building an independent life for herself in a more open society than that of *"Italietta borghese"* —small-minded, middle-class Italy. It was clear that Alma missed her, because she often reminded her, "Pull the string, don't forget," referring to an imaginary string connecting them: she only had to tug on it and they would be closer. They shed lots of emotional tears, tugging on that string from both sides of the ocean. But Alma would never give up the complete freedom she enjoyed in order to join her daughter in New York, nor was Nina about to sacrifice her brilliant life and the professional success of which Alma was so proud.

Four decades passed. The day that Nina turned sixty, Leo died in a car crash. Nina sold the publishing house and went back to Italy. She bought back the house in Turin and persuaded Alma to come live with her. Nina had remained single and was childless.

IV

I told Alma about my excursion to Cortalba, my encounter with Vigìn, and how the castle had been restored and opened to the public. She insisted on going to see it for herself. Lina, who had recently grown somewhat closer to Mother, came along.

We arrived in the deserted, sun-drenched town one summer afternoon. The castle, too, was empty, it only filled up on the weekend. We entered through the little gate and walked up the lane that once led to the Hello Garden.

"I always went up this hill at a dead run," Alma said as she struggled along, putting her weight on my arm and helping herself with her cane. Alma had always been healthy as a horse and she still enjoyed excellent health, but she was becoming frail as a result of her advanced age. However, she hadn't lost her indomitable personality. She pounded the tip of her cane against the pavement, saying, "This was a narrow gravel lane, which made it look natural and elegant, and it was lined by boxwood hedges and flowerbeds full of passionflower, not these brick curbsides." She extended her cane to give a number of annoyed little whacks to the brickwork lining the path.

"Mamma, don't get upset. Just walk straight and stay calm, otherwise you'll never make it," I scolded her gently.

"Don't treat me as if I were an old woman," Alma retorted resentfully. Lina followed behind her, ready to catch her if by any chance she tripped and fell.

We reached the top and Alma came to a halt in astonishment, as if she had suddenly fetched up in some unfamiliar place. That area had been transformed into a broad paved courtyard, suitable for ceremonies, conferences, and shows. There were no longer any plants, flowers, or flowerbeds. Even the wisteria had vanished from the old wall, which was now perfectly smooth and enlivened by a fresh coat of paint. Around the stump of the linden tree they'd installed a circular kiosk to welcome the public and to post the publicity for the various sponsors.

We leaned on the side wall of the well, which still stood at the center of the courtyard. The air was blazing, since there was no longer any protection against the sunrays which beat down vertically, flooding the entire space with flat light. I made sure that Alma's straw hat was adjusted so that it shaded her face—it always slid back on her head without her noticing it.

The well was closed beneath a heavy iron lid, padlocked shut. I asked the guardian who had allowed us in, "Don't you drink the well water anymore?"

"No, it's gone bad."

"What do you mean, it's gone bad?" Lina inquired.

"People say that they put a dead body in there," and he told us the story of Celestina that I had already heard before in various versions.

Once he had moved on, Alma lifted an eyebrow with a skeptical expression, "You mustn't believe everything he says. It's a nicely devised story that adds a pinch of gothic horror to the castle's aura, but..."

"I remember the day we were sitting here and a soldier came and asked us for something to drink..."

Alma interrupted me, "The water started to go bad when the linden tree got sick, or the other way around. The exams showed that poisonous fungi had developed under the soil. My father had this lid put on before he sold the property. I remember that on that occasion he said that the castle wouldn't ever be the same without that source of pure water. 'It was like sap that gave it life,' he said at the time. In fact, we know the way things went. First there was the plundering of the woods by Tunìn, then when he resold the property, the castle passed from one owner to another, continuing to deteriorate for roughly half a century. It was even occupied by a community for the rehabilitation of drug addicts for a while, and a fire broke out. When Uncle Gio came to visit the castle, ten years ago, it was reduced to a ruin, an abandoned pile of rubble, invaded by beetles and flying ants."

"And now look at it... it's practically brand new. They did miracles with this restoration," I said.

Alma looked around and the images of the old days flashed before her eyes, like on a piece of faded film projected upon the new, impersonal, and unadorned layout: the espalier of the wisteria with its mass of flowering clusters and the dense swarm of bees drunk on their fragrance; the linden tree attired in white, a blizzard of bright petals on the gravel beneath; the graceful pagoda over the well; Olga and little Luca are sitting side-by-side on the bench; Letizia is leaning on Riccardo's arm; Ada and her sisters are strolling in filmy, bright dresses that highlight their lithe figures; Pietro sits in his wicker chair, reading the paper; André waves his hat in a cheerful hello; Leo drinks tea with Magda and Viola; Ernesto is looking for the right framing in his Leica's viewfinder; Piero and Marilù on their bicycles shade their eyes with one hand and gaze off at some distant point; Mina and Gio whip the horse chestnuts around in the air… But which time is this? The ages don't match up. Ada is still a girl, and Mina and Gio are already teenagers. There must be some confusion… and yet, it's all too real.

Alma refocused on the present dimension, and commented dismissively, "Sure, it's all new, but it's not the same anymore."

"All right then, tell us the way it was…" I asked her.

Acknowledgments

To my mother, first of all, thanks for the captivating stories you told me, for the dreams you made mine, and for always having believed in me.

Thanks to my father for the creative genes of Neapolitan origin that he handed down to me. To my grandfather for having developed, along with his film, my love of beautiful pictures. And to all the others who've inhabited my life and enriched my baggage of emotions and knowledge.

I had many traveling companions during the writing of this novel, all of whom encouraged, advised, and assisted me in various ways. Among those who read the manuscript and offered critical comments, I want to thank first of all my sister Mara Maltese, and then Camilla Baresani, Simona Brancati, Paul Buckmaster, Ugo Cardinale, Ira Fabri, Cinzia Furlanetto, Ben Lawton, Maria MacKay, Riccardo Riccardi, Roberto Severino, and Domenico Starnone. Moreover, I owe a debt of gratitude to Giusi Marrano who transcribed, with loving care, some of my mother's notebooks, from which I drew further details.

A grateful acknowledgment to my friends in Cortanze who provided me with accurate and thorough information on the castle and the village, first and foremost among them former mayor Mario Magnone.

I also want to thank Edizioni dell'Orso, and in particular the editorial director Sara Massobrio, for having published the Italian edition of the novel.

Finally, a big thank to my translator, Antony Shugaar, who successfully faced the challenge of giving an English voice to this narration.

www.ingramcontent.com/pod-product-compliance
Lightning Source LLC
Chambersburg PA
CBHW031144050726
47495CB00018B/516